CISCO SERIES BOOK ONE

THE BURDEN OF TRUTH

SUZAN DENONCOURT

THE BURDEN OF TRUTH

For Coco, Shoosh and Philou

CHAPTER ONE

— 2023 —

Secrets are like bubble gum stuck to the underside of a classroom desk. That was my eldest daughter's creative analogy in response to her sister's seventh grade English assignment. It's also the reason I never chew gum in front of my girls. Not since they introduced their private code wherein chewing implies hiding something from each other.

It was over a decade ago when Grace's rationale had earned her sister an A, and it still has some merit. From how I recall it: humans are desks and gum is their secrets. Everyone knows gum might be there, but it's only an issue if someone rubs up against a fresh piece; otherwise it's no big deal. As it applies to secrets, everyone has them, and hiding them is their business. Exposing someone else's, however, is what can get messy.

At the time, it was tempting to highlight at least two ways in which Grace's example fell short, but I had to remind myself that this was an English assignment not a science project. The fact that gum could outlive the desk, and that the donor's DNA was literally preserved within it, was neither here nor there in their adolescent world. So notwithstanding the blatant disregard for school property, I chose to assume that my daughters' carefully guarded secrets were, in fact, no big deal.

Over-sharers that they are, their private thoughts would eventually be revealed in later years, and barely amounted to anything more earth-shattering than declaring cola as their favorite Hubba Bubba flavor. Which is, of course, in very stark contrast to what I have been withholding. In a category far more consequential than a teenage crush or guilty pleasure, mine is a secret borne of the secrets of others, from decades long ago. And just like those before me, I've chosen to keep it safely tucked away.

How and when it all began I really can't say, but I'm well past trying to figure that part out. What matters to me started in 1972. Not because of the horrible tragedy, but because it was my favorite summer ever, despite the horrible tragedy. That alone is a detail I've never admitted to anyone. Certainly not to Nick and the girls. To intimate that any prior vacation could rival those we had shared as a family would be scandalous. For their sake, that was better left unsaid. But Dad on the other hand, did deserve to know. And yet, I never felt compelled to tell him either.

Every time I think of the moment he swooped in like a superhero to pluck us out of our misery, I can't help but smile. It's the image I remember most vividly. Fourth grade was coming to an end, and like every other afternoon, I should have been visiting with Mom after class. But Dad had said it was okay not to see her that day, that I deserved a break. As I swayed back and forth on the swing below our apartment building, I stared down at my bare feet as they caressed the blades of grass. I was alone other than with our neighbor, Mrs. Jane or Mrs. Joan or maybe it was Mrs. Jones. Whatever her name, she babysat me from a bench, while knitting something warm on that hot sunny day. By then, my friends were keeping their distance. They didn't seem to know what to say to me anymore. That, and I probably wasn't much fun to be around. Assuming I was even allowed to have fun. Under the circumstances, their parents might have thought otherwise. But that was fine. I kept myself entertained. Trying to see how long I could withstand the tickling of the grass against my bare soles. A game of endurance. Me versus the strands. And with enough practise, I had learned that if I could make it past the peak point, the feeling would eventually subside into a tolerable, rug-like sensation.

On that specific day, the challenge was made even easier. A thunderstorm had just blown through, and though the heat was quickly drying the ground, residual moisture had rendered the grass comfortably limp. I was smiling with satisfaction at yet another victory when, out of nowhere, came Dad. Not walking slowly, glumly, as he did every other day since the incident. He was marching with determination, then stopped to face me and announced, *Jenny, we're going on an adventure. Pack your bags. We leave tomorrow.*

I suppose I should have been at least a little suspicious since we never ever went on adventures. Or even spoke about them for that matter. Nowhere near safe enough for my ultra-prudent parents. Ours was a life of guarded caution. As for packing, Mom had always taken care of the overnight bag when we visited my grandparents for the weekend. That Dad had thought I could handle it on my own hadn't even struck me as odd. Nor did leaving without her. I guess, like him, I didn't question much; I just went with the flow. And the flow at that time was a steady stream of mundane repetition. So a change in direction, no matter where, felt more than welcome.

My packing had left a lot to be desired by the time he pulled up the next morning in what he called, *Adventuremobile*. Lame name aside, my jaw dropped when I discovered we would be traveling in style. Opening the side door of what seemed like the most ginormous motorhome I had ever seen, he invited me in. All I could think as I walked through our compact kitchen/dining/living/sleeping section toward an actual bathroom at the back was, *Can we stay in here forever, Dad? Please, please, please.* I remember his response was a reassuring, *We'll be here for a good long while.*

That adventure lasted two whole months and, barring inevitable nuisances, had been an absolute blast. In only a matter of days, we mastered living without a schedule or reliable hot water. We cooked with limited utensils, ingredients and rarely electrical power. On occasion, we even ingested balanced nutrients. All this, while roaming aimlessly toward new destination after new destination. But perhaps the most surprising development was how we unearthed an ability to converse the way chatty people do. And not just to help us weather traffic jams and endless stretches of highway. We had become two introverts breaking our silence, venturing away from familiarity, finding our footing in a change of pace, in unpredictability.

But for as wonderful as our vacation had been, tragic circumstances summoned us back home; leaving us to navigate a harsh new reality upon our return. Then, as though perfectly natural, we embraced the different flow. Because that's what we did. We existed in the present without inclination to reminisce about the past. Surprisingly, given how much of our time was spent alone at home, just the two of us. And yet, not once had the subject of our journey ever come up again. Once it was over, we simply moved on.

It took decades for me to realize how much more to that adventure there had actually been. Had we not gone, my summer would have consisted of daily hospital visits with Mom, who lay in a coma with no hope of waking. By then, I was used to it. Her accident had occurred four months prior. I was told to hold her hand and to talk to her because she could hear me. It was awkward, but not as much as one might expect. Mom was a distracted listener at the best of times, so no response from her was typical. But not squeezing my hand back, not twitching her finger, ever, had become unbearable. Her sole sign of life was the warmth of her skin to my touch. After a while, that just wasn't enough. It was only after telling Dad I was running out of things to say to her that he finally admitted she was never going to recover. Soon after, we took to the road for the remainder of the summer.

It seemed so spontaneous at the time. So reckless. So fun. I was filled with joy, anticipation and excitement. And I was utterly oblivious to the need for urgency or that the distance we traveled was keeping me from possible harm.

Over the course of our journey, the daily toils of nomadic life became a crash course in resourcefulness. That skill doesn't evolve much, if at all, in an otherwise over-protective environment. Then there was the magic – and sometimes trauma – of watching wildlife in its natural habitat. I recall how we would sit for hours marvelling at nature in action as Dad whispered how much we could learn about animal instincts through careful observation.

For a long while – years in fact – I secretly hoped each time Dad knocked on my bedroom door, it was to announce we would be going on another adventure, maybe even try retracing the random steps of our last one. No such luck. He reverted back to quiet kindness. Always present. Always supportive. But not spontaneous, and certainly not adventurous. The extent of our travel thereafter amounted to repeated house moves following wherever his next contract would lead. Another new home, another new school, another new everything, rendered familiar by the same old quiet routine.

With time, my fantasy of reliving that journey slowly disappeared, as did more and more of the details I was able to recall. As they faded, the adventure itself joined my bank of forgotten childhood memories. In many ways, it seemed more like a dream or a fairy tale I had once been fully engrossed in.

Of course, had Mom been with us, she would have retained every single detail. That said, had she been there, the trip would have never occurred. Far too dangerous for someone so paranoid. A risk not worth taking. Her motto was caution above all else. And yet, our very departure is what kept me safe. From drama, from scandal, from truths best left untold.

For decades, I was clueless about all of it. Until the oddest of circumstances would require me to search the recesses of my mind. By then, I was a grown woman whose daughters were in grade-school, and I was totally reliant on Dad's failing memory for any of the details. The best I could hope for was to steer him on topic long enough to sift through his jumbled thoughts and try to make some sense of them. Our conversations occurred weekly at that time, but were extremely limited. Not just because he was a man of few words; his mind had begun to deteriorate years prior. Slowly, he had become more difficult to recognize, recounting events that never occurred or drawing a blank at those that did. Just like Mom, his memory would fail him. Yet unlike hers, his brain was still alive when that process had begun.

I'm now retired and pleased to report that both my mind and my safety have remained intact. This, despite the profound sense of loss following my husband's battle with cancer, which has sadly come to an end. Our home seems much too quiet now that our daughters are living on their own. Only the dog is left, but he's well past his prime and unlikely to be around for much longer.

At times, I admit to feeling alone as I once did when swaying on that swing all those years ago. The difference is that this solitude is more peaceful; the by-product of a life well lived. Also, I'm able to chew gum freely without fear of prompting an inquiry. So there's that.

Today, however, my gut feels ill at ease. This funeral is causing me grief, but not the kind that involves sadness. It's my own fault. I should never have accepted the meeting invitation from the lawyer last night. But his call caught me off-guard; I reacted impulsively instead of thinking it through. Now, I'm not only saddled with unfair next-of-kin duties, I'm uneasy about what's coming my way. There had better not be another letter. I have no need for an excuse as to why our relationship never was. Or worse, answers about my mother. Too much time has passed for me to care anymore. Whatever the truth, I've decided it doesn't concern me in any way.

In that spirit, I'll put my best foot forward, get this obligation over with, and trust that the past will stay where it belongs; undisturbed. Besides, like dried-up gum, old secrets can't possibly be a big deal. So really, what's the worst that can happen?

CHAPTER TWO

— 1960 —

"Wow, Con. Seriously?" mocked George, while rolling his eyes. Sporting his brightly colored Hawaiian shirt and white linen shorts, he teased, "How will the chicks ever resist you?"

Connor looked down at his white t-shirt, his favorite one. He thought the collar, three buttons and blue rim around the edge of the sleeves looked just fine. "What's wrong with a tennis shirt?"

"We're at a beach party, not the US Open!" exclaimed George in despair, while stripping Connor's headband off. "And there's no way I'm letting you wear that stupid thing around your forehead."

"Okay fine," conceded Connor, while tapping his bangs back down. He wasn't one to argue, certainly not about fashion. Though he wondered if what either of them wore ever made a difference. The ladies gave George adoring nods of approval regardless of his attire. Connor meanwhile, found it very easy to go completely unnoticed. He was far too plain looking by comparison, unworthy of a second glance.

The sun had set over the lake, giving way to the light of a bonfire blazing on the beach. A battery-operated transistor radio was tuned, full volume, to a station playing The Ventures', Walk Don't Run. The air was heavy, the threat of storms looming in the distance. But the atmosphere was light. It was a night of celebration after four weeks of daily endurance, sprints, recovery and rescue drills for this group in advanced lifeguard training. Thirty young teens under the not-so-watchful eyes of a handful of adults, eager to relieve themselves of chaperon duties, confident their absence would not be missed. Tomorrow morning, all would be heading their separate ways.

"You get that she's completely outta your league, right?" George reminded Connor as they both watched Heather sway to the music, her babydoll dress flowing as she twirled, her long straight brown hair crowned in a wreath of fresh daisies. "Plus, I heard she's changing her name to Chastity. Doesn't sound too promising for you."

Connor hadn't been able to keep his eyes off of her from the moment she stepped out of her Cadillac on the day everyone arrived at the lakeside retreat one month ago. His knees nearly buckled at the very first sight of her. Never had he seen anyone more beautiful in his life. Day after day, all he looked forward to was yet another glance. Standing at a distance, from wherever he could admire her beauty, unseen. Unlike him, she just seemed so carefree, so relaxed, so together. And tonight in particular, there was something about the way she danced, the look of pleasure on her face, the calm confidence of her solo performance that mesmerized him. And yes, he knew he didn't stand a chance, but he was far too captivated to even care.

"She can change her name to Grizelda for all I care," replied

Connor, almost in a trance as he followed her movements in and out of the light cast from the flames.

"You look like you're under hypnosis," criticized George, unamused by his best friend's fixation. "Have you done weed?" They had agreed their first try would be together.

"Nah. No need. She just has this effect on me." Connor could feel himself blushing, and was grateful George couldn't tell in the darkness.

"Well, since you're not gonna be any fun tonight, I'm gonna go work this crowd." George danced away, moving to the rhythm of the music, his stunning smile ready to charm.

It took a few seconds before Connor noticed. "Hey wait!"

George stopped and turned toward him.

"You're not gonna go after her right? I mean…give me a bit of a chance. Okay?" Connor pleaded. His thin frame, messy auburn hair and freckles were no match for George's chiseled physique and stunning good looks.

"You're in luck," George winked. "She's not my type."

For the next hour, Connor maneuvered his way from one small huddle to the next, always in synch with Heather, as though drawn by her magnetic force. He stopped when she did, then snuck himself into whichever group gave him the best vantage point from which to observe without her noticing. Quiet as he was, no one questioned that he never said a word, but instead nodded and smiled. George, meanwhile, kept escaping each time faint lightning sparked way out in the distance, leaving it to appear as though it was Connor who was the one working the crowd.

A moment of opportunity finally emerged when Heather walked over to grab a bottle from the cooler. Connor's eyes lit up. At last, she was alone.

Reappearing out of nowhere, George surprised Connor from behind and whispered in his ear, "If you don't go talk to her now, you're an idiot." He gave him a slight nudge behind the shoulders to urge him forward.

"Okay. Okay. I'm going." Sweat was dripping from Connor's forehead. *Could've avoided this if I was wearing my headband*, he thought, annoyed, hoping Heather wouldn't notice. He walked slowly, trying to decide on the appropriate pace. His attempt at swagger was awkward at best, but Heather was none the wiser with her back towards him. "Hey," he said arriving behind her.

Startled, she turned around. "Oh hi. It's…Conway, right?"

Wow. She knows who I am. He tried not to appear overly elated. *Keep it casual, Con.* "Close. It's Connor." He then blurted, "I like your dress."

"I made it myself," she beamed as she twirled to show it off.

"Really? Wow." He was genuinely impressed.

"I'm practising for when I become a fashion designer," she added, her brown eyes locked onto his.

"I could use a fashion designer," he mumbled to himself looking down at his t-shirt with embarrassment.

It was loud enough for her to hear, which made her giggle. "You're kinda cute," she said as though just as surprised as he was to hear it. "Conway," she added with a coquettish smile.

At that he froze. Social interactions were not his forte, especially not with girls. Plus none had ever found him cute, which only made it more nerve-wracking. For the master of awkward silence, his fear of babbling something geeky took hold. No matter how fast his mind was racing, he couldn't find his words. If only his body language could make up for his silence, but he just kept fidgeting. He lifted his gaze up to her, then lowered it down to the ground, then back at her, then back down again, repeatedly.

The pause lasted uncomfortably long.

"Okay…well then…I guess I'll just mosey on over to the bushes over there." She smiled and began to slowly walk backwards while facing him.

The moment she turned her back to him, Connor let his head fall forward in discouragement. He blew it. She thought he was cute, then realized he was useless. He felt like a fool.

"Hey, hey, hey, Romeo, why the pouty face?" asked George, who rushed over to toast Connor's first official female encounter.

Connor recounted their exchange and its abysmal conclusion.

"Are you kidding?" exclaimed George with surprise. "She just invited you to join her behind the bushes. Get over there right now!"

"Nah, man. That was no invitation. Not after a two second conversation. Besides, you said so yourself. She's outta my league." Connor slouched, defeated.

"Well I was wrong," insisted George. "And trust me. I know an invite when I see one."

"Oh, so you're an expert now?"

"Just get your ass over there. What's the worst that can happen? And you better go quick before this storm hits."

Connor tried to work up the nerve, advanced a few steps, stopped, changed his mind then walked back. He talked himself in and out of going, over and over again. As the sound and frequency of thunder intensified, his time to act became more pressing. He would have to muster that final bout of courage all on his own; George had exhausted his pep talk and was once again nowhere to be seen. *Don't be such a coward. If I don't do this now, I'll never see her again.* He finally began to march forward, emboldened by the pounding clouds.

The bushes were fifty feet away. Fifty awkward steps across sand that began to blow against his shins. Fifty steps across people darting past him in the opposite direction to seek cover, grabbing whatever belongings they could carry. He barely noticed as they shouted for him to head back. He was in forward motion, determined, unwilling to slow his stride. If Heather was still there, he could at least escort her to shelter. A moment of chivalry to make up for his earlier lack of charm.

He paused before making the final turn around the backside of the bushes, and inhaled a deep breath of courage. A few more steps to see if she was waiting for him. *Please be there, please be there.* He advanced and lifted his gaze.

Shock. There she was. Standing in the deep embrace of another man. Someone he had never seen at the lake. Someone far too old to even be on staff.

He gagged. His spirit crushed, he dropped his head and turned back to avoid being noticed. The last thing he needed was more embarrassment.

After only one step, he heard her shout, "Stop!"

He turned to look back, eager, encouraged, only to realize that she was addressing the other man. Her palms pushing against his chest as he pulled her close around the waist, his mouth devouring the crook of her neck.

"You know you want this," he mused as he held her tight, grinding his torso against hers. "You're such a tease."

"No! Stop!" she pleaded, now clenching her fists and pounding his chest.

He grabbed her chin forcefully and glared into her eyes with contempt. "You want rough. I can do rough." He then moved that hand behind her neck pulling her mouth close to lunge his tongue deep down her throat.

Connor could tell she was in distress, trying to scream, trying to make him stop. Anger and panic were burning inside him. At this aggressor, and at his own immobility as he stood watching not knowing what to do. *Take your hands off of her!*

Heather struggled to turn her face, letting out short screams when her mouth was free.

Does she know I'm here? Is she trying to signal to me? Connor's anger was evolving into rage. He needed to act.

"You wanna scream? I'll give you something to scream about." The aggressor ripped one strap from her dress leaving the top to fall, exposing one of her breasts.

Connor turned away instinctively, then forced himself to look, trying to build enough courage to interrupt this attack.

The man cupped Heather's breast aggressively, using his other hand to pull down her panties before unzipping his shorts.

"No stop. Stop. Stop! I'm begging you, please," she sobbed

loudly, her arms slapping, flailing in defeat. Drops of rain began to fall, her face already awash with tears.

Connor could see this monster was poised to violate her within seconds. Enraged, he let out a tribal-like scream that propelled him forward with force. Noticing Connor from the corner of his eye, the aggressor turned his gaze just as he was about to be stricken down. An explosion of blood splattered across his face as it smacked against Connor's forehead. It caused him to trip backwards over the shorts that had fallen to his ankles, landing squarely on his bare butt, grasping at his broken nose. Connor stood above him, hands on his knees, panting in momentary shock and relief.

"You're gonna pay for this, you little prick," the man threatened, as blood seeped between his fingers. He pulled himself up, tugged at his wet shorts, raising them so he could get into fighting stance. The rain was pounding even harder, quickly washing the blood down onto his shirt, giving him an even more menacing appearance. Then, just as he was about to take a swing, a bolt of lightning cracked loudly. It startled him, interrupting his advance. He lowered his fists, turned to Heather who had fallen to the ground, her face buried in her palms as she rested her elbows on her raised knees. "You could've had the night of your life, sweetheart." And just like that, he ran off in the direction of a boat pulled up onto shore.

Relieved to have averted a fight he was unfit for, Connor released the tension in his posture while holding back the urge to vomit. He watched as the aggressor reached the vessel, pushed it offshore then stepped into it. *What kind of an idiot rows in the middle of a storm? I hope he gets struck by lightning.* Immediately turning to Heather, he saw that what was left of her dress clung to her skin, darkness providing greater cover. He peeled off his soaked t-shirt and extended it to her as the rain pelted down loudly. "Here," he shouted above the heavy downpour. "It's ugly, I know, but at least no one but me will see it."

She took it, put it on over her ripped dress and raised one arm for him to pull her up. He obliged. Their first physical contact. He was flattered by her trust.

"Are you okay? I mean, I know, that's a stupid question. I mean, are you, like, okay now?" He really had no idea what to say.

"I'll be fine," she shouted, her face expressionless as they walked slowly, too slowly for two people who should be seeking shelter. "Thanks to you," she added, turning to look at him, but unable to smile.

He felt mildly heroic, but was still worried. "Who was that jerk?"

"Some creep from across the lake. I've seen him fish nearby while we train. Always gawking at me."

Connor was embarrassed. She was stunningly beautiful and he certainly did his fair share of staring at her, albeit more discretely and not in a creepy way. Or so he hoped. "Good thing we're going home tomorrow. Won't have to see him ever again." He was very relieved by that. But only that. He was too disappointed that he himself wouldn't be seeing Heather again.

She stared forward with no reaction until they reached the first of several bunkies the trainees shared in pairs. "This is me," she shouted.

These former fishing cabins were scattered along a winding trail, each barely big enough to fit two small beds the width of a sleeping bag, a tiny nightstand in between, above which was a single narrow window.

"You gonna be okay? I mean –"

"I'll be fine. I promise." She was grateful for his concern.

"Okay….goodnight then," he waved.

"I'll give you back your t-shirt before we leave tomorrow," she shouted as he walked away.

How that registered in his brain was: *We shall be reunited once again, my hero.*

With a smile, he gave her a thumbs up, then darted away through the meandering path. He felt horrified about what she had just endured, but grateful a bigger catastrophe had been averted. In no small way, thanks to him. He had done something right for a change. Now he just wanted to get to the bunky he shared with George, collapse in his bed, and dream of her all night until they would meet again the next morning.

Dodging puddles that had formed quickly, he raced as fast as he could to beat out lightning that seemed dangerously close. Finally at his door, he flung it open, rushed in and bent over catching his breath as water from his hair dripped to the floor and quickly pooled. He raised his gaze and gasped. Laying naked and intertwined in the equally nude body of another, was George. The glance was brief before Connor instinctively jerked his eyes away. But it was just enough to notice the genitalia of both parties was male. He opened the door, flung himself back outside, leaned over and vomited. Within seconds, the other guy rushed out past him and away into the darkness. Connor never looked up. He neither needed nor wanted to know who it was.

George hurried into a pair of underwear before racing out to Connor's side. He pulled his shoulders up to raise him. "Con, it's pouring, get back inside, man." Ushering him in, he asked, "Where's your t-shirt?"

Connor plunged onto his mattress, wet shoes and all, laying sideways to face the wall. "Never mind that," he replied, while holding back his rebuke of George's own lack of attire.

"Look, it's not what you think," defended George, now sitting on his bed, drying himself off with a beach towel after tossing another over to Connor. "We were just trying stuff. It was stupid. Just a onetime thing." He was doing his best to steer Connor away from any conclusions.

Connor remained silent and still.

After too long a pause, George begged, "Say something, will ya?"

Breathing steadily to calm his nerves, Connor chose not to respond. He had zero interest in talking. It was hard enough for him to know what to think, let alone what to say. The night was long, too long. Horrifying then shocking. He just wanted to turn it all off. Purge the images from his mind and sleep. Then wake up and see Heather. Nothing else.

Uncomfortable with the silence, George wondered, "You're not..." He hesitated before finishing his question. "...jealous, are you?"

At that, Connor rolled over to face him, disgusted. "What? No! Are you nuts?" Before adding anything hurtful, he turned back toward the wall. "Just let me sleep."

"Hey man, you know I was just kidding," George chuckled dryly, trying to act as though Connor's emphatic reaction hadn't hit a nerve. He lay down on his back, knowing he should respect his wishes. They could fix this tomorrow. It could wait. Except it was killing him. They never let things get uncomfortable between each other. He needed to make this better tonight. To find a safe topic; safe, but not trivial. Something to divert them to a better headspace. He had an idea. Hard as it was to imagine, maybe Connor's shirt was removed in a moment of passion. And if it was, Connor would definitely want to share that. He broached it very casually, "Con, I need to know though. Before you fall asleep. Like, was she there?"

"No," replied Connor, sounding defeated. That drama he would keep to himself.

"Sorry, man." George felt bad for asking and worse for being wrong. Unless, "Did you make out with someone else?"

"No!"

"Oh. I thought maybe your shirt —"

"You thought wrong," Connor exclaimed, annoyed.

George was just about ready to resign himself to silence, but, "One last thing."

"What now?" Connor's tone was beyond impatient.

"Promise you won't say anything about, you know, what you saw here?" George pleaded. "I'm a dead man if anyone thinks that's my thing." He was intent on deleting it from Connor's memory.

Equally motivated to delete it, Connor replied, "Trust me, I won't say a word."

With that they both fell silent for the night.

CHAPTER THREE

— 2003 —

"Don't forget your lunches!" I shouted from the kitchen, coffee mug in hand, as my three girls headed out the front door for school. Then, turning to my husband, Nick, who was placing the last bowl into the dishwasher, "And you don't forget you're on dinner duty." I gave him a peck on the cheek to ensure I had his full attention. "I have that meeting at Dad's home, remember?"

"Oh that's right," he replied, walking toward the front door in his usual khakis, button-down shirt and blazer. He, too, was leaving for school, only in his case, as a Harvard History Professor. "I've got it covered." He stopped, then turned back towards me. "What's that about again?"

"Don't know," I shouted from the counter. "But Gloria said she needed to tell me in person. Maybe a change in his meds?" I hadn't really given it much thought other than to wonder why it couldn't wait till the end of the week when I would be visiting Dad per usual.

"Need me to join you?"

"No, no. I'm sure it's fine. Besides someone has to take care of homework and dinner." I winked and blew him a kiss. "I should be home before you're done eating."

He left the front door open for me as I walked down the hall toward the entrance, then slipped into heels and grabbed my briefcase on the way to my Toyota Camry parked in the driveway. Today's fitted skirt-suit was navy with a cream colored blouse. A string of pearls, matching earrings and an updo concluded my quintessential workplace attire.

* * *

"It's 2:45," said Perry while tapping gently on my open office door.

"Oh gosh. Thank you. I completely lost track of time," I said, looking to my watch, then my screen, then the files spread across my desk.

"Don't worry about these," he said, already extending a hand to grab one. "I know where they go."

"You're a lifesaver," I sighed as I rushed to place my laptop and notebook into my briefcase to resume work later tonight. "See you tomorrow!" I waved as I marched toward the elevator.

Perry was turning out to be the perfect junior accountant. Supremely organized and attentive, he ensured our dealings were always in order. No fussing, no confusion, no reading between the lines. Clear, open dialogue with someone whose mind was a sponge absorbing every tidbit of information. A recent graduate, he had learned quickly when and when not to interrupt me, and reveled in the challenge of discovering the slightest error I may have missed. *May* being the operative word. Attention to detail was my super power. At least it was when it came to numbers.

There was just something about numbers that I gravitated to early on. Initially because math came naturally to me, so it was easy and made sense. With time, I developed a real appreciation for its unambiguity. No debate, nor any need for factoring in emotions, political subtleties, nuances or innuendos. Only a logical path to a clear conclusion.

My head remained focused on the annual report I had been immersed in as I drove the thirty minutes to Dad's nursing home. My client's deadline was fast approaching, but I hadn't quite worked out how best to amortize the information technology investment for their global web implementation. More and more companies were looking to do the same, but building this type of infrastructure on an international scale was still in its infancy. Estimating the individual country-specific requirements was a best guess at this stage, and doing so with so little empirical data made me rethink every assumption over and over again.

It was only once I turned into the parking lot at Meadowbrook Homes that my mind switched gears. *Wonder what Gloria needs to speak to me about.* Quick check of the time as I turned off the ignition. Only two minutes late. Make that two minutes too late for someone who prided herself on being punctual. I darted out quickly to make up some time.

"I'm so sorry, Gloria. I didn't mean to make you wait," I puffed as I arrived at her office.

She stood up, waving her arm to signal me over. "Not at all, Jennifer. Please come sit."

Gloria was a woman of refined taste; in her clothing, her demeanor and even in her office decor. During their thirty-five years of marriage, she and her husband had traveled the world, collecting trinkets from each destination, many of which were displayed throughout her main floor corner office. Though tastefully dispersed across shelving, window ledges, end tables and her desk, I admit, it all seemed a little too cluttered for my taste. I preferred a more minimalist design; clean lines and bare surfaces, other than a photo or two of family.

As I sat down, my first words were, "Is everything okay with Dad?"

"Yes, yes, dear. He's fine."

Relief.

"And I'm sorry to have made you come by. I didn't mean for you to worry. I just didn't feel comfortable discussing this over the phone."

"Okay?"

"I'll get right to it," she said, her hands resting on her desk, fingers interlaced. "I received an unexpected visitor for your father yesterday."

"Really?" Dad had no visitors. Other than my family. "Was it Joe Rich by any chance?" I winked with sarcasm.

"Who?" Gloria asked, puzzled.

"Never mind." I waved off the inside joke.

She didn't appear amused. "It was a police detective."

I sat up tense, my eyes widened with shock. "Has something happened?"

Calmly, Gloria proceeded, "No, dear. It doesn't concern Meadowbrook." She paused, then continued, "He asked to meet with your father –"

"Meet with Dad? What on earth for?"

"He believes he may be able to assist with a case he is currently investigating." She raised her index finger the instant my mouth opened, gesturing for me to let her finish. "Don't worry. I told him your father is unfit for an interview."

"Well that's good." I nodded with incredulity. "What kind of case would he think Dad could possibly assist with?" It's not like his experience in construction was an area of unique expertise.

"He wouldn't say. But he was rather insistent. He even tried to get me to elaborate on your father's mental capacity."

"What did you tell him?"

"That it's not my place to reveal any of my patient's confidential medical information." She sounded offended that he had dared to ask.

I relaxed my torso back into my chair. "So that's it then?"

She paused while adjusting her seating, then continued. "Not quite. Once he realized I wasn't going to yield, he asked if he could speak with your father's guardian. He suggested your presence during the interview could be an option. If you were agreeable, that is."

"As Dad's interpreter?" It would seem like a reasonable suggestion for someone who didn't know the extent of Dad's limitations. "I don't see that working either."

"Nor do I. So I repeated to him that your father was simply unfit. I then advised him it was my responsibility to inform you of our exchange." She leaned to whisper as though the detective was in the room. "I thought it would be less off-putting for you to hear this from me rather than to have him show up at your door."

"It is. And I thank you for that." I briefly imagined how surprising that would be, then immediately purged the thought. "Then what did he say?"

"He handed me his business card and asked that I share it to you." She slid it across her desk for me.

I took it from her blindly and opened my purse to place it into my wallet. "Did you give him my name?"

"No, dear," she reassured. "I didn't provide any contact information. Though he is a detective and was able to find your father's current residence. I assume he would have the means to find you as well."

"Good point. I'll call him tomorrow and sort this out... Well, if there isn't anything else? Thank you, I guess?" It didn't seem like there was much more for us to discuss on the matter. "Is it okay for me to see Dad now?

"Of course. Debbie should still be with him." Just as I was leaving her office, she stood up adding, "And Jennifer, I didn't mean for you to be concerned when I asked to see you today."

"I understand Gloria. It isn't every day a detective comes knocking. I would have done the same."

This must seem so intriguing to her, I thought as I headed for the stairs rather than the elevator to get to Dad's third floor room. The mild exertion allowed me to recount this odd development. A short walk down the hallway lead me to room 310. The door was ajar; an indication that Debbie was, in fact, still with Dad. I tapped lightly and announced my arrival.

"Come in, Jennifer. We just finished our snack," said Debbie in her charming Jamaican accent, while gently wiping the butterscotch pudding from Dad's cheek. Within moments, a light glistening of drool would begin to form along the drooping right side of his mouth. The outcome of his stroke two years ago, the paralysis was sadly showing only minimal signs of improvement.

"Hi Daddy," I said with a bright smile as I kissed the top of his bald head and moved to face him. I placed my hands over his as they rested on the armrests of his chair. "How are you feeling?"

He looked into my eyes with his usual inquisitive stare. *Am I familiar to him today?* A smile or an attempt to speak would determine the state of his memory. He squinted and moved his left hand, the one he could control, over mine to tap it repeatedly, "J-j-jen…ny," he labored with a half-smile. This was a good day.

I'm not certain why I called him Daddy. He had always been Dad for as long as I could remember; for as long as he was the one taking care of me. It was odd that I felt inclined to switch to Daddy once he became incapacitated and entrusted to my care. I suppose there was something more endearing about it. In the same way I was his Jenny. He was the only one to ever call me that.

I turned to Debbie with a smile. She knew how rewarding it was to have him respond to me with recognition. Those times he just stared blankly at me for an entire visit were brutal. I could never tell if he knew who I was but was simply unable to express it, or whether I was fading from memory; a thought too painful to process.

"Has he shared anything new and exciting?" I asked Debbie

with a wink. It was a running gag between us since Dad's language was so limited. But on the rare occasion, he became more vocal. That is, more vocal by Dad's standards. A succinct man who spoke in short sentences, he was prone to only the rare bouts of conversation at the best of times. Since his stroke, his speech had become more jumbled. When he seemed intent on sharing, he rambled on about utter nonsense. But it made for something new for Debbie and I to discuss, and attempt to decipher. Otherwise, my routine with Dad was repetitive and uneventful, as was so typical of us. Both creatures of habit, and mostly silence, when it came to how we shared our time together.

"Just the usual," she replied, while removing Dad's bib then fixing his collar. "Oh, and he mentioned Joe Rich again." She shook her head with a smile. The name had come up every so often and when it did, he always seemed so determined to elaborate. But as hard as he tried, it all sounded incomprehensible. He would eventually give up, appearing discouraged and exhausted. "Still don't know who that is, do ya?"

"Nope. And, quite frankly, I've run out of places to look." In truth, I hadn't tried all that hard. There were too few avenues to even explore. Dad never spoke of anyone important in his life. Other than me and my family, that is.

"I remember one lady long ago," Debbie began. Her decades of assistive care had turned her into a treasure-trove of anecdotes. "She did something similar after her stroke. Her family searched and searched for this mystery person she kept talking about." She paused and looked up, thinking, "Nancy I believe it was. Yes, that's it." Then, while continuing to tidy Dad's dining tray.

"When they finally found her in a kindergarten class photo – that's how far ago her brain went – they managed to contact her. And that poor old woman couldn't remember a damn thing about kindergarten." She chuckled as she rolled the dining table away toward the door with her slow, waddling stride. On her way out, she added, "You know, Jennifer? The mind is a mystery. Nonsense can stick, and important things can just fade away."

I agreed wholeheartedly. And wondered just how much of Dad's memory had faded. It was so hard to tell given that the past wasn't ever a topic of conversation between us, even when his mind was sharp. We were creatures of comfortable silence; content to spend our time reading, watching television, playing cards or enjoying a meal with brief conversation based in the moment. *How's your steak? Wonder when the rain will let up. Wanna watch Jeopardy or play Gin Rummy?* Now that he struggled to remember the simplest of details, or to put them into comprehensible words, I confess to harboring a bit of regret at our failure to reminisce. Though it lessened the perceivable impact of his memory loss, at this particular moment, I realized how a discussion with anyone, let alone a detective, would be void of content. As for broaching that specific topic with him, it seemed completely absurd. *Hey Dad, feel like assisting a detective with a case he's investigating?*

I dismissed my fleeting urge to prod, and stuck to our more predictable banter. "So Dad, who's this Joe Rich?" No harm in asking for the umpteenth time. Then I sighed in anticipation of his unhelpful response.

"J-j-joe…R-rich," he stuttered.

"Right. Got it," I replied in jest. And that was as deep as that conversation ran.

I rolled his table in front of his chair, sat across from him, pulled out a deck of cards and began dealing his set of ten, facedown. I placed the cardboard panel my girls had crafted for him between us; it served as a barrier to keep me from seeing his cards as he turned each over, leaving them flat on the table. As soon as we started our game of Gin, half his face lit up with a smile. In response, both sides of my heart burst with warmth and affection.

* * *

I did make it back in time to have dinner with Nick and the girls. A plate of spaghetti and meatballs was ready for me as I walked into the house. "I'm home!" I shouted from the entrance. "Smells yummy. Going to change. Be there in a minute!" I walked toward our bedroom to slip into leggings and a t-shirt.

"I'm going to check if Mommy wants wine," Nick whispered to the girls as he got up to place my plate in the microwave before joining me in the bedroom. As soon as he entered, he asked, "So? How did the mystery meeting go? Everything okay?"

"It was weird to say the least," I replied already slipping into a t-shirt. "Dad's fine though. We had a good visit, which was nice. I'll catch you up after the girls are asleep."

"Intriguing," he replied, following me as we headed toward the kitchen table.

I sat down and began twirling my fork through noodles

drenched in marinara sauce. Before taking my first bite, I looked up at my girls. Each with their olive skin and big brown eyes. Each with their big head of tight curls. Other than height, their one distinguishing feature was hair color. From dark brown, to medium and to light as they decreased in age. "Anyone need help with homework tonight?"

"Yup, me," replied Grace, the eldest, in fifth grade. "I have to hand in my family tree tomorrow." She snuck in a last bite and chewed quickly before adding, "Daddy did some, but I need you for the rest."

"Sure thing, Gracey. That shouldn't take long at all," I mused. Unlike Nick, whose family was massive on both sides, Dad and I had no siblings, and Mom had just one sister.

As Nick and the girls debated who earned today's honorable mention for most interesting day, I marvelled at how much dialogue there was at our dinner table compared to when I grew up. And so much teasing and laughter. Sure there were more of us in this house, but it was just a different vibe. Where Dad brought me comfort and stability in his quiet disposition, Nick did the same for our girls through his antics and animated conversation. I, of course, always joined in. It felt surprisingly natural. But so did silently observing them, in awe of the beautiful humans they were becoming. And though there was no question that mine had been the most interesting day, I let Lisa, our youngest, win the daily honor for her first grade show-and-tell about rock-climbing and how she hoped to one day tackle the highest mountain in the world.

* * *

"Mommy!" Grace called from her bedroom after dinner was done. "I'm ready."

A green sheet of poster board lay on her desk. To accommodate Nick's side, she had oriented it in landscape format and had to place herself way off-centre toward the right, making for a strikingly lopsided family tree. The branches had all been traced with a ruler and marker. Small white rectangular pieces of paper on which names and years (birth and death) had been printed by hand were glued above their respective branch. A few more lay to the side, partially filled in, awaiting my input.

"Ok, let's see what you've done so far," I said as I examined the left side. It was crammed with so many names, the rectangles almost overlapped one another. Half of them Greek from Nick's mother's side, and the other half Haitian from his father's. Moving my gaze over to the notably sparse right side, I had to fend off accountant-brain and its urge to create balance. Fortunately, Grace exhibited no qualms about her tree's asymmetrical appearance.

"First, I need your middle name," she began. "Daddy said it's very important to add it."

Did he now? I was among the many who tried to abolish an otherwise embarrassing middle name where possible. But begrudgingly, I replied, "It's Chastity."

"That's a name?" She giggled and began to write, but needed help spelling it out.

I felt compelled to elaborate on its origin. "It's what my

mommy wanted to call me. But Grandpa really liked the name Jennifer. So they decided to give me both." *Yay Dad.*

Satisfied, or in a hurry to finish her homework and watch tv, she moved on. She took out three rectangles, one with the name Connor. "That's Grandpa and he was born in 1942 right?"

"Yes he was."

"Okay. And these are his parents. Daddy guessed the dates." She turned to me. "Are they right?"

"They look right to me."

She laid out three more rectangles that had names, with only the year of death printed out; and for some reason, it was the same year for each of them. "Okay, so Daddy told me the car crash was in 1972, and that your mommy was thirty right? So that means Heather is 1942 like Grandpa?"

"Yes," I affirmed, though a little perplexed. "I see you put 1972 for Eleanor and Anthony too?"

"Yup. Those were her parents right? They died with her so I know it's the same year. I just need the years they were born."

Why had Nick told her they all died in the crash? Now I needed to check my math before replying. "Let's see, my grand-father, Anthony, would have been seventy when he died so that means he was born in 1902." As Grace filled in that date, I felt a little more conflicted with stating an outright lie, so I chose my words more carefully. "I'm pretty sure my grand-mother, Eleanor, was fifty at the time of the crash. She was much younger than my grand-father. So born in 1922."

We added my aunt, Dawn, and I guessed her birth year knowing she was a few years younger than my mother. We were estranged from Mom's family so I had no idea if she ever married or had kids.

Grace flipped the rectangles over to squeeze glue in zigzag fashion across the back then pressed each into its spot to dry. "Thanks Mommy," she said, while getting up to rush downstairs. She stopped in the doorway. "Wait," she exclaimed, having just done the math in her head. "You were only nine when your mommy died?" Her look of shock was alarming.

"Uh huh." I replied sheepishly. I knew it wasn't an easy notion for an eleven-year-old girl to process about her own mother. Our girls all knew, sort of, but Nick and I deliberately kept the details to such a minimum, nothing really registered with any of them. It didn't need to. Until now apparently.

She walked back toward me with a look of grave concern on her face. "Were you sad?"

"Yes. Very." I squeezed her hands in mine. "So was Grandpa. She was the love of his life. But he took really good care of me so I would be okay."

"What did he do?" Grace couldn't understand how this all worked.

"Well, he thought we would both be much too sad if we were surrounded by reminders of her all over the house, so we moved somewhere new. Somewhere to start new memories." I smiled, grateful for my selfless father, hopeful Grace was a little reassured.

"But what about all your friends?"

"I made new ones. And Grandpa was always there to keep me company." In reality, I just didn't have that many friends.

Dad was my constant. Grace, however, still seemed troubled. I thought adding more might help. "You know, in those days, Grandpa was very active. We packed a picnic lunch then went on long bike rides, or sometimes big hikes. And he loved to swim. Especially in lakes. He took me often." I smiled remembering how he was then. His mind so alert. Something my girls never got to see.

"He did?" Her look of shock didn't surprise me. The grandfather she knew was sedentary and largely incapacitated.

"Yup, he did. He's the reason I have such a wonderful life. Well, one of the reasons." I tickled her belly and pinched the end of her nose with a smile.

She giggled then walked away, satisfied. I hoped.

Relieved that her concern had passed, it otherwise pained me to realize that her image of Dad was in such stark contrast to the man I had grown up with.

* * *

I gave Nick a quick debrief of my conversation with Gloria once we were both in bed for a bit of reading or in my case, work, before calling it a night.

"Wonder what that's about?" he questioned.

"I know right? I can't begin to imagine what would make a detective think Dad could assist with an investigation."

"So are you planning on calling him?"

"I don't know. Honestly, I'd prefer not to." That seemed like one way to avoid the situation. "But I don't want him just showing up here, so I may as well just get it over with tomorrow. I'll call when I need a break from this report." With that, I was about to resume working on it, then thought to ask, "By the way, why did you tell Gracey all three of them died in the car crash?"

He turned away from his book and looked at me with his big dark eyes. "I thought it would just be easier that way. She had lots of questions about how everyone died on my side. I could see that all the cancer was getting to her."

"Thank you," I said squeezing his thigh. "Other than fibbing a little, yes, it did make it easier."

"I trust that wasn't too arduous," he winked, leaning over for a kiss while flexing his bare pectorals.

"I'm going to stop you there, my darling," I said, taming his affection. "I absolutely have to finish this annual report."

"Fine. Fine." He pulled back to his side of the bed, then leaned over to remove something from the drawer in his nightstand. "And when you're done that report, you're going to stop working in bed, and just read a novel like a normal human who needs to unwind." He handed me a hard copy of The Da Vinci Code. "Got this for you. Just released. You'll love it. All about numbers." An avid reader, Nick consumed tons of literature, curating novels for me to enjoy, when I got around to granting myself such leisure time. His favorites were mysteries. "Also," he casually added to entice me more, "there might be the discovery of details that call into question long-standing beliefs."

With that, my curiosity was officially piqued. "Deal."

CHAPTER FOUR

— 1962 —

"Not so tight," Heather pleaded, cringing at her reflection in the full-length mirror, while her mother forcefully adjusted her corset from behind. "We need to breathe," she blurted, unwilling to let her mother forget, for a single moment, the reason behind this imposed nuptial. "I can't believe you're making me wear this stupid thing. I'm not even showing."

"You know your father. He notices everything," said Eleanor, while tugging even harder.

She raised her gaze to face the mirror and looked Heather in the eyes across the reflection. "You will be a well-behaved blushing bride. Is that clear?"

Heather held her tongue.

"There. That should do it." Eleanor released her grip from the corset then made a full turn around Heather to check that her work yielded the perfect unrevealing fit. Satisfied, she grabbed a tissue to gently dab the moisture away from her brow and neck, before leaning into the mirror to check that her makeup and bouffant hairstyle had remained elegantly intact. Emulating her fashion icon, Jaqueline Kennedy, she wore an ice blue gown of celadon silk draped to form a pleated skirt and gathered bust line.

Her only departure from the classic *Jackie look* was her choice of jewelry; the more extravagant, the better. And she encouraged her husband to feed that whim at every opportunity. If not for the color of her dress, one would think Eleanor was today's bride.

"What if I throw-up?" poked Heather. She hadn't experienced any morning sickness, but knew the mere thought of something so unbecoming during this high-profile ceremony would wipe the smug look off her mother's face.

At that, Eleanor flinched. "Fine. I'll loosen it. But ever so little."

Heather relished her small victory.

Time to slip on the wedding gown. Eleanor turned Heather by the shoulders to face her, gathered the ivory lace dress from the base, and placed it over Heather's raised arms. She then let it drop before gently pulling one side at a time to carefully maneuver it over the corset. Giving her a top to bottom inspection, Eleanor nodded her approval then pivoted Heather back to face the mirror. Eleanor's expression softened, her tone turned endearing, and she smiled. "You look beautiful."

For a brief moment, Heather felt like a princess. The dress she had made, and Eleanor approved, was the only part of this affair that she had any say in, and the result was stunning. Simple and strapless, it fit the curves of her slender figure with just enough give to camouflage the dreadful corset.

"Here," said Eleanor, while placing a string of pearls around Heather's neck and securing the clasp from behind. "Something borrowed. It was my mother's."

Surprised, Heather ran her fingertips along the smooth

surface. "I love it." Her mother, not one for sentimentality, delighted instead in showcasing their family's stature during social gatherings. An expensive piece from her signature collection was what Heather had otherwise expected. *She mustn't trust me with something that valuable*, she thought. Regardless, she much preferred this choice. She stepped into her pumps, eager to pick up the final accessory to place over her long straight brown hair that was parted at the center with strands from each temple gathered at the back. It was a floral crown of delicate wildflowers.

"I'm just in time," exclaimed Dawn, maid of honor, who thundered into the room startling both of them. "Something blue." Her hand was raised to reveal a blue lace garter. She lowered her short, large frame to Heather's foot and began removing her left shoe.

"Ever hear of knocking?" cried Heather. "You nearly gave mom a heart attack! Not to mention my condition –"

"We're fine," interrupted Eleanor, refusing to let Heather remind her, yet again, of this pregnancy. "Now look at me both of you," she exclaimed the moment Dawn had finished sliding the garter up Heather's thigh and stood erect. "Today is important. Your father has many business associates here. We need our elegant daughters to be on their best behavior." She waved her index finger at both of them for emphasis.

Heather could not hold back. "Cause there's nothing more elegant than a knocked-up sixteen-year-old," she sighed with sarcasm.

Eleanor advanced to within inches of Heather's face and stared her in the eyes. "Let me make this perfectly clear.

Today, this bride is twenty years old, and very, very virginal. Understood?"

"Yay, we're twins," chimed Dawn awkwardly, trying to cut the tension. The two could not look any less alike.

Eleanor turned to Dawn. "We're lucky you look like you're the youngest." Then she fixed her gaze at both of them. "One day, girls. Just one day is all I'm asking you to play nice in front of these elite strangers. Can you please oblige me that?" She was almost trembling, her tone severe and desperate.

Choosing not to infuriate her, they both nodded in submission.

Outside the west wing of Delano Manor, the sun shone across a clear blue sky as staff fussed over last minute touches for the ceremony. At the front, valets tended to a steady flow of pristine Jaguars, Rolls-Royces and Porches; so many of them, they flanked the entire length of the long circular driveway. A team of ushers stood at the ready, escorting prestigious guests from their vehicles towards the entrance nearest to the grand, opulent living area. Sliding doors at the opposite end opened onto a stone path lined with magnificent bouquets of exotic blooms atop roman pillar pedestals. It weaved its way toward the rear side of the outdoor seating that faced an altar of white arched stone erected earlier during the week. Two hundred gold Queen Anne arm chairs with white upholstered seats and matching chiffon sashes lined both sides of the aisle. As a measure of added refinement, small bouquets of fresh white roses were fastened at the center of each bow. Cream colored marble slabs had been laid just yesterday after Eleanor dismissed the original white carpet as a tripping hazard, or perhaps not suitably ecclesiastical. The result was a veritable sea of white and gold. An exquisite backdrop of purity to mask the darkness of sin.

And there was nothing like a diversion from sin to legitimatize the outdoor setting of this particular wedding. For the staunch Catholic matriarch of the household, anything other than the House of God would have been deemed a sacrilege. Until now. The abomination of a teen pregnancy threatened to tarnish the family image; an ugly blemish that needed to be concealed behind the most auspicious veil. And so it was that the sanctity of today's sacrament now rested squarely on the shoulders of the priest; the one religious element for which Eleanor had remained steadfast.

As for the bride-to-be, this celebration was a farce, a union imposed. Punishment for her latest misbehavior on the continuum of reprimands she endured, regardless of her innocence, and despite her courage. She had been completely upfront, had admitted to the pregnancy. And asked for her mother's support in terminating it quickly, convinced this stain-to-be was unacceptable, unworthy, unwanted. Her mother's unwavering fixation on what others thought, on how her husband would react, would surely prompt her to seek reversal immediately.

But Heather underestimated the power, and the burden, of her mother's beliefs. How tight a hold they had over her. So tight, she could not bring herself to participate in the taking of an unborn life. Not even this one. Nor was she willing to allow her grandchild to enter this world out of wedlock. Rather than rush her daughter to a planned parenthood clinic as Heather had expected, Eleanor marched her straight to church to seek penance. The moment she emerged from the confessional booth, Eleanor exhaled a sigh of relief at the forgiveness extended. She then became immediately determined to persuade the priest to permit a church wedding. Though it was a tall order in the face of such impurity, she pleaded for an exception. He refused. She insisted. He insisted more, until days later, when a very large donation prompted his reconsideration. They negotiated until they reached terms acceptable to all three parties concerned: Eleanor, the priest and God. An abbreviated outdoor ceremony officiated by the priest and registered with the parish, but without the taking of holy communion. Feeling victorious, Eleanor rushed to inform Heather of her successful arrangement. *I'll take care of your father. He will know nothing of this child. Only that you two passionate sweethearts are desperate to seal your love in holy matrimony.* To entice her husband, Eleanor proposed a grand affair to wine and dine the social elite. He had been seduced into agreeing.

As a prominent display of Massachusetts' upper echelon mingled quietly at their seats, a harpist off to the far right strummed Vivaldi's Four Seasons. The gentle breeze did nothing to quell the moisture forming on Connor's forehead from the heat of his black tailcoat tuxedo. Standing nervously in front of the altar, his clean shave and perfectly sculpted hair aged him a little, perhaps even enough. But beneath this polished white-tie façade, hid the frame of a sixteen-year-old trying desperately not to falter. To maintain his focus. If not for his best man, George, by his side, he may have fainted by now. The same George who initially questioned his judgement and cautioned him about the repercussions of this marriage. How could he not? Everything about this situation screamed of disaster. But Connor's mind was made up. And where Heather was concerned, he was resolute. A gentle reminder of his indebtedness to Connor, had ultimately given George cause to back off, to retract his objections. Support from him was necessary, so support from him would be received; by standing by the groom's side, by charming the ladies during the reception, by doing whatever it would take to ensure this ceremony would go off without a hitch.

As they both stood, hands folded, facing the guests, George whispered to Connor, "You good?"

Just at that moment, Dawn, Heather and their father appeared at the opposite end of the aisle.

Connor's heart began to pound, first at the presence of his imposing father-in-law to be, then at the sight of his beautiful bride. "It's actually happening," he said, inhaling a breath of courage.

Anthony Delano was a large man, his broad neck bulging over his collar almost touching his bowtie. Twenty years Eleanor's senior, his gray hair was greased back to give the illusion of thickness. He sported a pencil moustache, freshly trimmed for the occasion; it would feel like pin pricks against every cheek it caressed. He was a man of power and success whose stature, both physical and professional, inspired fear and created envy.

Connor's eyes locked onto Heather's in the distance. It felt odd to do so in the presence of so many witnesses. He couldn't help thinking how, not so long ago, he could only gaze at her in secret. But in just a matter of minutes, she would be his and only his to admire, to linger at. And she looked utterly ravishing; even more stunning than he could have imagined. In a setting pulled straight from the pages of a fairy tale. How he wished they could be transported into one right this moment. Be guaranteed a perfect ending. To live happily ever after. But he knew this was no fable. And yet still, he must be her prince charming. For her, he would be. It's what she had asked. Perhaps even what she needed. Neither of them was escaping this surreal, overwhelming, and uncomfortable day of matrimony. So Connor smiled, with resolve, focused solely on his Heather.

Dawn kissed her sister on the cheek before beginning her procession down the aisle as Eleanor smiled with anticipation from the front row seat. Unlike her sister, Dawn welcomed the corset and how it compressed the many bulges around her waist, no matter how constraining it felt.

After Dawn took a few steps, Anthony turned to Heather, held her by the elbow and pulled her toward him so he could look into her eyes. "You see all this?" He used his free arm to gesture toward the elaborate staging of this ceremony and their extravagant property. "All this is what I provide for you. I give you everything." He tightened his grip. "And what do you do? You rush to you leave."

Heather swung her head to look back at Connor. "You're going to bruise me," she whispered, trying to free her arm.

He lessened his grasp just as the harpist transitioned to

the Bridal Chorus, a signal for him to not keep this important audience waiting. He smiled in the direction of their guests and whispered through the side of his mouth before they began to advance. "Mark my words. You'll be back."

Heather stayed silent, steadying her focus on Connor. A day of decorum and fanfare. Just one more day before her release from this unbearable hold. *Mother had better keep her promise.*

CHAPTER FIVE

— 2003 —

I woke up feeling a greater than expected sense of urgency to get the call with the detective over with. Trivial or not, there was something uncomfortable to me about the idea that Dad was considered useful in his investigation. Unable to afford a distraction this close to an important deadline, my plan was to call him after my morning scrum with Perry. This was our customary start to each day during which we reviewed his progress, and I gauged what he should tackle next. Our session was productive and efficient as always, and had ended over two hours ago.

I still had yet to pull the detective's business card out from my wallet. Each time I glanced at the phone on my desk, I meant to, then immediately reverted back to my report. But it wasn't like me to put something off. The more I did, the more irritated I became. *Just get this over with.* I opened my desk drawer where I kept my purse, unzipped it and removed my wallet to pull out the card. As I was about to dial the number, something glared at me. It wasn't his name, Max Cisco. It was the unit he worked for. Homicide. *Oh my God.*

I held the receiver to my ear then began to type in the

numbers. It rang twice before a voice appeared at the other end.

"Detective Cisco," he exclaimed. No hello. No how can I help you.

"Um, yes, this is…I'm calling…Gloria Thompson from Meadowbrook Homes gave me your number."

"Ah yes. You must be Connor Rivers' guardian. Is that correct?"

"Yes. His daughter." I hesitated before adding, "Jennifer. Jennifer Vincent now."

"Thank you for calling me back, Mrs. Vincent."

"Of course," I replied, eager to get to the part where we both hung up.

"I'll get right to it. As you know I was hoping to speak directly with Connor Rivers. Mrs. Thompson suggested he was not well enough. Perhaps you feel differently? It would be perfectly fine for you to be present if I could I meet with him."

"I'm sorry. What exactly is this about, Detective Cisco?"

"Yes, of course. This must seem…out of the ordinary. In a nutshell, I'm looking into newly surfaced material concerning a case that had been closed for some time. I have reason to believe Connor Rivers might have pertinent information."

"Pertinent information?" I held back the urge to laugh. "Detective Cisco, I'm not sure my father remembers what he had for breakfast this morning. I'm sorry, but I have to agree with Mrs. Thompson. He's not fit for an interview."

"That is unfortunate. And of course, I understand," he sighed.

Does he though? I waited for him to end the conversation. The silent pause was verging on awkward.

He finally spoke. "Might *you* perhaps be willing to speak with me, Mrs. Vincent?"

"I'm sorry. You think I have the pertinent information you're looking for?"

"Possibly. The timing in question occurred while you were still living with Connor Rivers."

Oh my God. He actually thought Dad would remember something that far back? I debated blowing him off completely since this was beyond absurd, but then considered entertaining his request, if for no other reason than to make Nick jealous that I was involved in an actual investigation. A homicide investigation, no less. But the voice of reason emerged. "That was a *very* long time ago, Detective. And I'm afraid I'm just too busy. I'm sorry, but I won't be able to help you."

"I understand," he replied with disappointment. "But just to be clear, it would only be a few questions. It wouldn't take long at all. We could meet here at the station. Or I could come by your office? Or your home perhaps? No need for you to go out of your way." He sounded accommodating, but desperate.

"Could we just do this over the phone? Like right now?" I regretted the suggestion the moment I uttered it.

"While I thank you for the offer, Mrs. Vincent, it's unfortunately a matter of policy that we do this in person. I'd greatly appreciate any time you could make yourself available."

"Can you at least tell me what kinds of questions you would be asking me?" *Why am I suddenly sounding like I'm considering this meeting?*

"I understand this may seem unusual, Mrs. Vincent." He

cleared his throat. "But since I cannot engage directly with Connor Rivers, I would be looking for anything relevant you might recall about a particular time in question. I'll provide more precise details when we meet." He paused as though waiting for my response, then added, "Can I count on your cooperation, Mrs. Vincent?"

"You do realize that my memory of that time is unlikely to be anywhere near what you expect?" This was my reluctant way of agreeing, while letting him know he was wasting both our time.

"Understood, Mrs. Vincent. Shall I come by your office then? I can be there within thirty minutes."

"Um, no." I didn't want to have to explain his presence to my colleagues. "I'll come by the station. I can be there at noon." *Ugh. This had better be interesting.*

"Absolutely. Noon it is. Thank you so much, Mrs. Vincent." He hung up before I could reciprocate the salutation.

I dialed Nick immediately.

"Hey, was waiting to hear from you. How did it go?" he asked, having expected my call much earlier.

"He wants to meet *me* now. Believe it or not, I'm going to the station at noon."

"What? How did that happen?"

"Well, for one, I'm an idiot." Then I thought, "make that a sucker." Before adding, "Doesn't matter. But I did tell him, no, he couldn't meet with Dad. So now he expects me to recall something from when I lived with him." My tone revealed how ludicrous this seemed.

"That long ago? What the hell is he investigating?"

"Yes. I can't for the life of me think of what this could be about. But get this. He's a homicide detective. Can you believe it?"

"Ooh. Maybe one of your many neighbors did something nefarious your Dad witnessed."

"Yeah, cause Dad was so big on mingling," I replied sarcastically. If anything, Dad avoided eye-contact with our neighbors for fear they may engage in conversation.

"He may not have been very good at idle banter, but he was certainly a keen observer. It's possible he saw something. Or maybe," his voice became mischievous, "he was a spy. Connors Rivers, secret agent."

"Yeah. Okay. You read too many crime novels, Nick. Dad hardly fits the profile."

"Oh I don't know. Quiet, unassuming, observant?"

"Please stop desecrating my wholesome image of Dad. Besides our life was way too humdrum. No drama. Just the way we liked it. Our only excitement was moving, which we did cause of his work. In any case, even if he did see something, how would I possibly know, let alone remember? You know me, I have next to no memories from back then." In my defense, there was nothing particularly noteworthy to remember. Other than the one thing Dad and I preferred to forget.

"I wish I didn't have office hours at noon or I would come with you."

One of us was intrigued about the session. It must be killing Nick not to be able to see the inside of a police station. "Trust me. I'll tell you all about it when it's done. Okay, gotta get some work done. See you later."

"Leave a message if I don't answer," he insisted. "Later." He hung up knowing it was unlikely I could get back to him before his 1:30 lecture.

I slipped into my runners and waved at no one in particular as I headed toward the elevator. "I'm going for lunch."

I typically packed a sandwich or a salad on a nice day; something easy to savor from a bench at The Common. Going alone, I would eat quickly then squeeze in a long walk before heading back to work. This is was my quiet time, no files, no calls, no shop talk. I shut it all off and tried to simply focus on my surroundings; smell the flowers, listen to the birds, watch the squirrels as they chased each other along branches, or people-watch if that suited my mood. But at this particular moment, I was stuck power-walking to police headquarters of all places, slowing down just enough to not be completely out of breath upon arrival.

I was ushered into a room that had a rectangular table that seated four, two on each side, and that's pretty much it. The door was mostly glass, there were no windows, and the walls were painted a muted beige-wanna-be-mocha tone. If it had a mirror, it might look like an actual interrogation room. *Now that would make Nick jealous.* I declined the coffee from my police escort in favor of a bottle of water. I waited no more than two minutes before Detective Cisco entered and closed the door behind him.

To my surprise, he was young. And rather handsome. It was unnerving how it threw me off. I don't even know why exactly.

Perhaps because my stereotypical image of a detective was old, heavy and unattractively stern. Meanwhile, Detective Cisco and his million-dollar smile, piercing green eyes, and thick head of dark waves, made me feel like I was being punked.

He reached out to kiss, I mean shake my hand, before sitting across from me, "Thank you for coming so soon, Mrs. Vincent. I know you're a busy woman. This is much appreciated."

The *Mrs. Vincent* sounded so old now that we were meeting in person. "Hello," was all I responded, while still taking in his stunning good looks. *Maybe this meeting won't be so terrible after all.*

"Okay then. Shall we get started?" He had opened a folder containing several pages with hand-written notes. "Some of my first questions may appear personal, but it's part of the protocol."

"Oh. Before we begin, Detective Cisco, I'd like to just say. You know how there are those people who remember a ton about their youth? Some of them in intricate detail?"

He raised his eyebrows in an expression that suggested yes and no.

"Well, I'm not one of those people. I remember pretty much nothing about it. I was more of a live-in-the-moment kinda girl."

His countenance remained unchanged as though waiting for me to finish.

"I just thought I should set your expectations since we're discussing something from so long ago."

He nodded, apparently clueing in to my point. "I appreciate the contextual input. Shall we begin?"

Great. He thinks I'm an idiot.

He rifled through his pile of sheets and lay two side by side. He flicked a pen he held between his index and middle finger back and forth, then looked up. "As a matter of record, your full name is?"

"Jennifer Chastity Vincent, formally Rivers." *Revealing my middle name twice in one week. How delightful.*

"And you were born in?"

"1963." *I could have done without sharing that.*

"Connor Rivers is your father?"

I paused waiting for more. There wasn't. "Is that a question?"

"Yes. Protocol," he sighed, as though equally annoyed with it.

"Yes he is."

"Your biological father?"

"I'm sorry, what was that?"

"Is Connor Rivers your biological father?"

"Oh I heard you the first time. I just don't understand how that's even a question."

"My apologies, Mrs. Vincent. Pro—"

"Protocol. I get it." It was amazing how quickly he was becoming less attractive.

"So for the record, Connor Rivers, born in 1946, is your father. Is that correct?"

"No. My father, Connor Rivers, was born in 1942." Relief. This whole thing was a big mistake. Wrong Connor Rivers.

I was about to stand up when he said, "Interesting." He flicked and flicked looking down at his sheets, then scratched his head with his pen before looking up. "Was your mother Heather Delano?"

Damn. This wasn't over. "Yes."

"The same Heather Delano who married Connor Rivers in 1962?"

"Yes."

"I see." He flicked more quickly, always staring down at his sheets before asking another question. "And do you recall the summer of 1972?"

Oh my God. Really? He's going there? "Yes," I replied, trying to hide my annoyance. "It's hard to forget the summer your mother dies."

He tried to express concern. "That must have been a very difficult time for you, Mrs. Vincent. And for your father of course."

While I appreciated the empathy, it could use some work. Hopefully with more experience, he would get better at it. "It was a long time ago. And not a fond memory as I'm sure you can appreciate." My polite way of urging him to move on. "Why exactly is this relevant?"

"Of course. My apologies, but pro–" he stopped himself, then looked up. "The information I have on file indicates that Heather Delano remained on life support for approximately six months. Does that sound correct?"

"Yes." It seemed so terribly long to hear him say it out loud.

"And during that time, what did you and Con–, I mean your father do?"

"We moped and visited her at the hospital every day. To see her expressionless, still body." This was bothering me much more than I expected. "Again, why is this relevant?"

"The entire six months? That must have felt eternal."

"It did."

My gaze dropped as I was brought back to that time. A heavy, gloomy, depressing time. I immediately thought of my girls and what their world would be like if that had happened to me. It felt even worse to think of it from their perspective. How did I ever get through it? Dad. Thank God for Dad. He just seemed to know how to make it all bearable. And that's when it struck me. *Oh my God. The RV trip!* How could I have forgotten about it?

Detective Cisco noticed the change in my expression. "Are you recalling something, Mrs. Vincent?"

"Yes." *Not that it's any of your business.* I was almost in a trance, wondering how long it had been since I thought about that trip. "That summer, to try to salvage a bit of fun for me, my father rented a camper and took me on vacation."

"I see. You camped in your driveway or a nearby campground?"

Driveway? "No we moved around to different campsites. We followed the sun. Or at least tried to." I felt momentarily transported as brief flashes of it were trying to push their way back into my memory.

"And you still visited your mother every day?"

"No," I replied blankly. "Not while on vacation. We were too far."

"I see. And do you, by chance, recall where these campsites were located?"

"My knowledge of geography at that age was poor at best. So no. But we spent most of our time in the countryside, either in the forest or by a lake. That kind of thing."

"Did you perhaps keep a photo album? Maybe a journal?"

Why so much interest in this trip? Is he trying to distract me from the horrible reminder of my mother's death? "No. Sadly we didn't have a camera. And I wasn't a journal type of kid." A shame really given how poor my memory of my childhood was.

"But you drove far? At least it seemed far? Maybe hours at a time?"

"Yes. There were stretches of highway, but I couldn't tell you which ones."

"It sounds like a wonderful adventure, Mrs. Vincent." He actually seemed pleased to learn of it. At least that's what I assumed the large note he added to his page implied. "And during this trip, did your father ever leave you alone?"

"I was nine, so no. Other than the bathroom. Or a quick run to get supplies at the campsite convenience store."

"But he must have called the hospital or someone else to get updates on your mother's condition?"

He did have a point. And I'm sure Dad did. We just didn't talk about it. So I responded with what seemed most likely. "I believe he did that from the payphone at the campsites."

"And do you recall how long this trip lasted? A few days? A week?"

"Most of the summer break." I replied, grateful I could at least remember that.

He scribbled something else down, then asked, "But you returned before your mother passed away?"

No actually. We had to race back home once Dad found out.

"Unfortunately, she died while we were away. The moment my father received the news, we rushed back."

"I see." He paused. I hoped he wasn't going to give me a judgmental look. "So you were away when Anthony Delano, your grandfather, died?"

"Well no. We were back, but we just didn't attend his service. We had no contact with my mother's family. Sharing brief condolences at my mother's funeral was the only time I recall ever seeing any of them."

He appeared confused. "Give me just one moment to check my notes."

The pause gave me an opportunity to sneak a peek at his files. I watched as he circled certain phrases, underlined others, or maybe crossed them out. He made several annotations in the margins, drew arrows and scribbled between lines already filled with his chicken-scratch. It all looked like a disorganized mess. Another turn-off.

He flipped through several other pages then looked up and asked, "Mrs. Vincent, what is your understanding of the cause of your mother's hospitalization?"

Okay now he's just being cruel. "She suffered severe head trauma in a car accident," I replied robotically. And before he asked, I volunteered the rest. "Her parents survived without injury. And if you're going to ask me the same about my grandfather, my father told me his failing heart couldn't handle the grief of losing her, so he went into cardiac arrest."

"Thank you, Mrs. Vincent." More annotations, then, "One last question."

Finally. This is almost over.

"Does the name Jorge Vasquez mean anything to you? He also went by George?"

"No. Should it?"

"He is believed to be a long-time acquaintance, more in fact, of your father's."

It was almost laughable to think of Dad having a more-than-acquaintance, sad as that seemed. "My Dad was a very private man with no social life. I don't ever recall him with, or talking about anyone named Jorge or George."

He flicked at super speed. I was about to lunge at his pen to make him stop. Then he lifted a few pages and pulled one out from the bottom and handed it to me.

"Perhaps this may look familiar?"

It was blown-up, photocopied image of a photograph. Two men in their twenties facing each other on a sidewalk in front of what looked like a bank or store. One with a beard, ballcap, t-shirt and jeans, while the other was clean-cut and wearing a suit. They appeared to be exchanging an envelope.

The ballcap was Dad. I stared. We had next to no photos from back then. I could barely remember him looking that way. The memory of his beard tugged at my heart.

"That's my father," I said while pointing. "I've never seen the other man." I paused. "Where was this taken?"

"I was hoping you might be able to tell me. It was during the summer of 1972. That's Jorge Vasquez."

"Sorry. Doesn't look familiar." I lied. It did. Much to my surprise. I wondered who could have possibly taken it. And why?

"So it appears your father did leave you on occasion during this trip?"

Great, he's cross-examining me now. "If he did, it was momentary. I have no recollection of ever being alone." *Because of course, I have such a great memory. Does he even believe a single thing I'm saying?*

"I thank you for your time today, Mrs. Vincent. You've been very helpful."

I have?

"That will be all." He closed his folder, stood up and extended his hand to shake mine before leaving. He appeared even more rushed to end the session than I was. On the way out, he added, "Bill will escort you to the exit."

"Detective Cisco?" I asked as he crossed the doorway. "You never said what this case is about."

"Nothing for you to concern yourself with, Mrs. Vincent," he replied in a reassuring tone before turning away.

Easy for you to say. Meanwhile my head was about to explode. I couldn't get out of there fast enough. All I wanted in that very moment was to plunge myself back into my neatly organized, completely fact-based report and forget this entire exchange.

Detective Cisco returned to his desk and turned on his computer. On the floor beside his chair, lay an open cardboard box filled with documents from the original case file: hospital records, photographs of the crime scene, witness testimonies, statements, court transcripts, and the police report from the investigation. He stared at his blank screen, elbows on his desk, his temples leaning into his fingertips. None of the material had been digitized. *This is a complete waste of time*, he sighed with frustration. *Why couldn't this damn evidence have surfaced after Randall turned in his badge for good?* He lifted his gaze to see Detective Randall walking towards him. *Speak of the devil.*

"So, Cisco, how did the interview go?"

Detective Randall was a dark man with a striking gray crown of tight curls. He peered above the reading glasses that rested on his broad nose as he approached Cisco's desk. His voice was deep, the kind that would be perfect for radio; it fit his tall, solid stature. A few months shy of retirement, he had recruited the recently promoted, Detective Cisco, to assist him in the investigation of this curious development.

The original case was among the very first Detective Randall had been involved in after joining the police force as an officer. As high-profile as it was, it had left a big impression. So it was no surprise that he, in particular, took great interest when a shocking new discovery materialized out of nowhere. Dated thirty years prior, a written murder confession had just been received by mail from an anonymous sender. The curve-ball: it was for a crime that had gone completely undetected; perpetrated against the suspect in the original investigation of Heather Delano's incident. Its revelation however, was met with differing perspectives on whether it warranted reopening the case this long after the fact.

"Unfortunately, she'll be of no help, Detective. To Connor Rivers' credit, she was kept completely in the dark." Having recently experienced the overwhelming sense of paternal protectiveness following the birth of his own daughter, Detective

Cisco felt admiration for how Connor Rivers had managed to shield his own from the tragedy, even after all this time. "I don't know how he pulled it off, but he did."

Randall appeared dubious. "Many things can motivate a man to keep a secret, Cisco. My experience suggests there's more to this."

"Maybe so," he replied politely. "But I'm not sure how we can go about finding that out decades later, without direct involvement of the two *actual* persons of interest." While they were captured in the photograph that had been sent along with the confession letter, one was now deceased and the other of unsound mind.

To Cisco, the most this confession justified was a forensic analysis to assess its authenticity. And regardless of the result, its relevance remained purely historical. No punishment could be exacted for the alleged crime being confessed to; the parties were all dead. His intent had been to wait for the report, then update the case archives as appropriate. But Randall was insistent that the very existence of this confession pointed to a serious deficiency in the original investigation. He not only questioned how that could have happened, but whether other significant details might have been overlooked. As for the admission of guilt, he struggled to understand what would motivate the author to preserve something so damning for all this time. If it was a matter of clearing his conscience, was there a reason he hadn't revealed it earlier? If imprisonment, then why write it in the first place?

That Randall could still recall the image of this young,

impressionable man in the throes of a disturbing tragedy, made him question all the more the author's ability to even commit the crime to which he was confessing. Might he have been coerced? Or perhaps blackmailed? Was there some other explanation? His gut told him to look deeper. "Keep reviewing the notes, Cisco. There must be other questions we could be asking her."

"Detective, I'm telling you she knows nothing. She was just a kid. Other than identifying Rivers in the photo, she's of no value. She doesn't know Vasquez, she thinks her mother's coma was caused by a car accident, she had no relationship with her grandfather, and thinks he died *after* her mother. Christ, she even thinks her father's year of birth is four years earlier than it actually is."

Randall had not expected quite so little from their exchange. The gaps in her understanding of the past seemed suspiciously large. *She must be holding back*, he thought. *Or could the trauma have been so big, it suppressed her memory?* "She was believable?" he asked.

"Yes. Very. Her reactions seemed perfectly natural."

Randall raised his hand to stroke the stubble across his chin as he took some time to think. "Okay," he went on, "but she hasn't been nine-years-old for the past thirty years."

"I don't follow."

"The smokescreen worked when she was a child. But surely she asked questions as she got older. What Rivers chose to tell her over time might be relevant."

Cisco was uncomfortable with the thought of an inquisition. In his mind, Connor Rivers had succeeded in sparing his daughter the horrific truth, and what Randall was proposing could undo all of that. Besides, even if Connor Rivers was found to be complicit, which to Cisco was a stretch, he didn't see why Jennifer Vincent should have to suffer a single consequence.

"How? And to what avail, Detective Randall? If this crime was in fact committed, why does it have to concern her? The one absolute is that she's totally innocent in all this." Trying to urge Randall to suppress his need to pursue this case, he took a jab, "Unless, of course, you think she was some kind of child psychopath."

"No. no, of course not, Cisco," Randall replied defensively. Then, in a more measured tone. "I understand your trepidation. And I'm not proposing we interrogate her on the grounds that we can't question Rivers."

Cisco sighed with relief.

"Like I said, I believe there's more to this. Something doesn't add up. And right now, she's our only access to new information. We can't lose sight of that." A reminder Randall felt compelled to point out. "If jarred properly, her memory may contain an important piece of this puzzle." He advanced closer to Cisco and placed a hand on his shoulder. "Try to make her feel comfortable. The more she talks, the more likely she could be to remember something that might help us."

"And if she's unwilling? It's her right to refuse."

"Then she's unwilling," he replied as he began to walk away. "But something tells me, you'll find a way."

Detective Cisco begrudgingly accepted the vote of confidence. But only because he had no choice. Randall was senior, thus the one calling the shots; leaving Cisco to review obsolete documentation, and to pry information out of someone who did not deserve such a disruption. And for what? *It's not like anyone was falsely accused and served time. And it sure as hell isn't because the victim was a saint, or even had long to live. So what gives? Randall's illustrious crime-fighting legacy? Can't dare to see it stained by an embarrassing omission? Or is his caseload so empty that he has too much time to kill?* Whatever Randall's reasons, Cisco knew he wasn't going to let it go without an irrefutable argument. It would be up to Cisco to find one soon. Or to find a way to let this linger long enough for Randall's retirement date to have passed. Either way, he had no intention of dragging Jennifer Vincent any further into this.

CHAPTER SIX

— 1972 —

It had been four months since the tragic accident that left Heather in a coma with no prospect of recovery. Months of unrelenting grief that ate away at Connor's very soul. He struggled to breathe, to wake, to move. If he mustered any strength to function, it was only by convincing himself she was just sleeping. By extracting doses of calm from her steady pulse and the warmth of her skin. But the power of her immobile presence had its limitations. Without mercy, the memory of their haunting last conversation would come crashing back. Over and over again. To consume him, and gnaw away at his core. Why, why, why hadn't he stopped her? His instincts had been right. He should have been more firm. Insisted she stay home. His dear, sweet Heather. His one true obsession. And now his biggest failure, who was reduced to a shadow.

Consumed by his own anguish, Connor hadn't realized he was also failing the only other person who mattered most to him. His Jenny. He had neglected to notice the magnitude of his daughter's suffering. How the light in her eyes was dimming. How she strained to find words; her smile fading from her face. In selfishly clinging to Heather, he was keeping both his girls in this cruel state of limbo; letting Jenny endure false hope of an outcome that would only be tragic. It took a harsh awakening to jolt him when Jenny confessed she no longer wished to visit the hospital anymore.

With each passing day since, it weighed more heavily on his conscience. Until Connor accepted that he could no longer perpetuate the inevitable. The time had come to let Heather go. It was the only way to restore Jenny's livelihood. She had to be his priority now. His reason to move on. *Perform the ultimate act of kindness and bring them both some peace,* he told himself. But he needed to act swiftly for fear of backing down. And that meant confronting the almighty Eleanor Delano beforehand.

With legal authority over Heather's care, the decision to cease medical intervention rested solely with Connor. But it was the fear of repercussion, dare he proceed without Eleanor's blessing, that concerned him most. *She probably thinks it's her decision to make*, he worried. Her insistence on covering the medical bills had rendered her unavoidable. And she had spared no expense for Heather's utmost comfort, as though ignoring her fatal prognosis. *And then there's Jenny.* One month into Heather's coma, he began to suspect an ulterior motive to Eleanor's magnanimity. Her one glimmer of light in all this darkness. Discrete access to someone she had otherwise been forbidden from ever seeing.

Marry Connor and we will stay out of the child's life was what Heather told him her mother had promised. Since Jenny's birth nine years ago, Eleanor had held her side of the bargain; never had the Delano's been in Jennifer's presence. Even after Heather's tragedy, their visiting hours were coordinated to never coincide.

Only once had he noticed Eleanor sitting in her parked car, watching them from a distance, as Connor and Jenny exited the hospital. To his surprise, he actually felt for Eleanor. Somewhere behind that stern exterior was a mother in pain. A grandmother deprived of her only grandchild.

Apprehensive as he was, he built up the nerve to reach out to her and requested they meet somewhere neutral. To his surprise, she accepted without hesitation. So it was planned for the following day at the coffee shop next to the hospital. Now to prepare his announcement. Should he be direct or try to soften the blow? *How do you even tell a mother she has to say goodbye to her daughter? I'll have to keep it simple.* But he knew that however it would come out, she would be devastated; that was the one sentiment, the only one, they both shared.

Eleanor was already sitting at a table by the window when he arrived. She was impossible to miss in that vivid candy red skirt. *Seriously? A cheerful outfit?* he cringed. Only she would dress like she was attending a Children's Hospital fundraising luncheon, when instead visiting her dying daughter in palliative care. But this was Eleanor. Connor understood all too well that it was beneath her to let on that she was suffering, that there was no hope. She maintained her composure as he approached. Any ounce of strain was carefully concealed behind layers of make-up and her forced grin. Though, if he didn't know any better, it almost seemed like she was happy to see him. He chose to interpret that as a sign she might actually be in an agreeable mood.

Connor sat down with the intent of cutting straight to

the chase. His nerves were agitated, so he spoke slowly and awkwardly. He eventually got it out, then braced himself. He knew she wouldn't scream, cry, or have a complete breakdown like a normal person on the receiving end of such tragic news. But would she acquiesce? Accept that this was best for Heather and his Jenny? Respect his selfless decision? No, she would not. Remaining stoic, Eleanor categorically refuted his plan. She would not allow the taking of her daughter's life. Not even if, in every other respect, she was already dead. He tried to appeal to her sense of mercy, for his Jenny's sake, but she could not be swayed. The more he insisted, the more adamant she became. He was not to defy her. Period. And she made certain of it with a threat so cruel, it shocked him into submission. As she stood up and walked away, she left him to ponder her words, to consider the consequence should he tempt fate and see the Delano's go through with the unthinkable.

Stunned, panicked and desperate, he rushed back to his car and drove. Though Eleanor was conniving enough to just be bluffing, there was no way Connor could take that risk. He had no idea what to do next, but he knew they couldn't stay there. He had to figure out a plan, find somewhere safe, somewhere she wouldn't locate them. But where? How?

He raced along the rainy highway staring blankly ahead until he locked eyes on the trailer lot in the distance. He had driven past it hundreds of times before without ever giving it a second thought. But it gave him an idea. Turning the steering wheel abruptly, he crossed over two lanes and screeched onto the exit for an impromptu detour.

The storm had passed and the sky was clearing by the time he had completed his walk-through of the first available Winnebago. He signed a rental agreement right then and there, on condition it be ready for pick-up the following morning. Then, once he arrived home, he marched straight into the park below their apartment building, where his daughter sat somberly on her swing. Standing to face her, he announced, "Jenny, we're going on an adventure. Pack your bags. We leave tomorrow." Within less than twenty-four hours, they would be heading to destination unknown.

* * *

Could this thing be any harder to turn? thought Connor, as he gripped the steering wheel so tightly, his knuckles turned white. *And when did the streets get so narrow?* Advancing at a snail's pace all the way to his neighborhood, he was already second-guessing his choice of transportation. *I should've just stuffed a tent in the trunk of the Beetle.* But he knew it was too risky to turn back now. Especially knowing their departure would not go unnoticed for long. The escape vehicle may not be fast nor discrete, but it was the last place Eleanor, or anyone else for that matter, would ever think to search for them. That alone made it ideal. So he concentrated on arriving home, getting Jenny, and hoping he could count on George to follow his strict instructions. *If she asks, tell Eleanor we've gone on vacation with my parents. Keep it casual like it was planned ages ago. Go to the payphone outside the hospital at 4pm each day. That's when Eleanor's gone. If I need to reach you, I'll call then and only then. If I don't, we're fine. Get me cash. As much as you can. But don't let anyone find out. We'll figure out how to get it to me later.*

George was caught completely off-guard by that call; they hadn't spoken since the accident. He felt elated that Connor had reached out, and grateful to be entrusted with such a sensitive task, even if Connor had withheld the reasons. For that, George would have to earn back his trust. But this was finally an opportunity to start making it up to him. Even if only a little. *Give me your word, George. You can't screw this up. And keep tabs on what they're up to.* George had sworn on his own life that he would keep his word this time. With no other option, Connor had to hope he would come through.

Exhaling with relief that he hadn't dented the motorhome nor any other vehicle on route, Connor parked in front of their house and braced himself for their imminent escape. His heart pounded with urgency to get Jenny and leave as quickly as possible. Just as he stepped onto the sidewalk, she came bursting through the front door with a smile so wide and eyes filled with anticipation. His heart melted at the first sight of joy he had experienced in months. Overcome by her delight, he gestured, "Welcome to your Adventuremobile."

He observed as she marveled at what would be their home for the next little while. She beamed with so much excitement, every horrible feeling wearing on him was momentarily displaced by joy. Such a beautiful feeling. And it gave him just enough courage to believe they might actually pull this off.

An hour into the drive, Connor began to feel more comfortable behind the wheel. The highway's wide, straight lanes made navigating this beast of a vehicle much easier. The plan was to keep going for as long as there was daylight. Initially, they would have to stick to proper campsites. Then, once they were skilled enough, they would graduate to bushwhacking. Which would hopefully be soon, because that's what it would take for them to relax in total privacy afforded by veering off the beaten path.

Having been so focused on keeping steady and gaining distance, he hadn't once turned over to look at Jenny, other than to notice her legs swinging from the corner of his eye. Finally comfortable enough to peel his gaze away from the road, he delighted in seeing her on the edge of the passenger seat. Her hands pressed against the armrests so she could lean further forward. She was smiling, and probably had been since the moment he turned on the ignition. It soothed him instantly. What he would give to keep her this happy. To make it so that as far as she would ever know, this was a vacation, an adventure. Better still, the adventure of a lifetime.

* * *

"Good job, Dad!" Jenny shouted, holding two thumbs up as Connor successfully backed into their first official campsite.

He chuckled at how easy she was to please. He had been struggling to line up just right for at least thirty minutes. And it didn't help that the sun was slowly setting. If not for the unsolicited assistance from the experienced road-trippers in the neighboring campsite, he may have been at it all night.

"Y'all are just in time for the corn roast," exclaimed Bob from #22. Bald, mid-fifties and sporting a well-nourished belly, he was a sight for sore eyes after a tiring first stretch of travel.

"Thanks for the help," replied Connor as he stepped out of the driver's seat. "A corn roast sounds great." They had been driving all day with no time to stop for groceries. The chips, Twinkies and pop they had been snacking on weren't going to cut it for dinner.

"Put them wheel chocks in place, then come on over. Ya can't miss the big campfire over there," Bob said, while walking away and pointing in its direction.

As covert as Connor would have preferred today's travel to be, he felt immense relief at being parked far from home for the night. With the prospect of a free meal to boot. But first, he had a mystery to solve. *What the hell are wheel chocks?*

Appealing to his daughter's sense of curiosity, he exclaimed, "Adventuremobile quiz #1." Once she turned to him, he asked, "If you were a wheel chock, what would you look like?"

"Hmm," she pondered, squinting as she tried to guess. "I know!" She ran to the next site and looked at the wheels of that camper, then ran back. "Is it the yellow triangle things?" Her eyes were wide, hoping she guessed right.

Why didn't I think of that? "Very clever," Connor replied, impressed with her logical approach. As distracted as he had been during the morning pick-up tour, he was glad to have remembered seeing them in the side storage. "Come help me put them in place."

They both scarfed down hot dogs, corn on the cob and smores before Jenny went off to play hide-and-go-seek with the other kids. He could hear her laughing in the distance, a sound he had almost forgotten. The night was capped off with songs by the campfire. The atmosphere felt so pleasant, wholesome, relaxed. Exhausted, Jenny had fallen asleep, her torso draped across his lap on a bench. He coaxed her awake and let her lean on him as they sauntered back to their camper. *Remember flashlights. And bug spray next time*, he reminded himself.

Connor fumbled with the door, then struggled to find the light switch only to realize he had omitted to plug in the motorhome. Too dark to find bedding, they each collapsed on the two dining benches for the night. *Pillows, sheets, pj's,* he thought as he sunk into deep sleep.

* * *

"Ew!" screeched Jenny, reading from the motorhome manual as they drove to their next site. She had discovered it in the glove compartment on day two and decided she should study for future Adventuremobile quizzes. "It says we're supposed to empty our black water tank. It's filled with poop!"

It had already been a week since they had left home, and Connor thought they were doing surprisingly well, considering the endless number of mishaps they had encountered. Apparently, they still had more to learn.

"So that's what all those campers were lined up for when

we left." Connor had felt so clever passing them all. Now they both wondered how much fecal matter they were transporting. "Something does smell funny. I thought it was just you farting because of all the junk food you keep eating," he teased.

"Dad! You're so gross," she giggled.

And this was how week one on the road had been for them. Laughter and teasing. They figured things out as they went. No stress, even when they had no clue what they were doing. Which was often, but thankfully less and less. They were content. Relaxed. Conversation was minimal, but light. They listened to whatever station they could synch until it got too scratchy, then switched to another. No frustration, no complaining, no impatience. The mood between them was comfortable and easy. And if not for this adventure, Connor would never have realized just how much he enjoyed Jenny's company. A gentle soul, so much calmer, trusting and easy-going than her mother. *Perhaps if Heather had grown up in a different home, she too might have been this way,* he wondered.

* * *

"Here's twenty dollars. You get our supplies while I make a quick call," said Connor standing near the payphone that hung on the wall of the campsite convenience store. He let it be implied that it was to check on her mother. They spoke very little about her, both avoiding the sadness it conjured.

He dialed George for the first time since their escape.

The phone barely had time to ring once. "Con! Is that you?"

cried George, who had been standing at attention each day, desperately waiting to hear from him.

"Yeah, it is. You sure no one's watching you?"

"Yes. She's back at the manor. You guys okay? Where are you?"

"We're fine. We keep moving." He paused, worried about the response to his next question. "Is she…is she asking about us?"

"I overheard her mentioning that the doctors hadn't seen you. I said it's cause you were on vacation with your parents. Casual like you said. She didn't flinch."

"Good." Connor was surprised, but relieved.

"She's really agitated though. Way more than usual. Completely out of sorts"

Shit. "Did she say anything?"

"The prosecution has turned up an unexpected witness. Anthony's older brother, Michael. Did you know he had one?"

"No. But what does he have to do with anything?"

"What I read from the discovery was that he was convicted of fraud years ago. It cost him the family business. He was supposed to be successor to Delano Sr., not Anthony. Anyway, he claimed at the time that Anthony set him up. But then was never able to prove it."

"I don't get how that matters."

"He wants the company. Says he's entitled to it if Anthony is found guilty of a criminal offence more severe than his, which was only a felony. Right now, Delano Enterprises goes to Eleanor. She's Anthony's legal successor."

"Holy shit. Eleanor would lose the business?"

"Only if Anthony's convicted. And even then, it would be

a real long shot. But that's not the problem –"

"What is?"

"It's got her scared shitless. Like completely panicked. So the defense team is getting her to retract her statement. Which helps them a lot. She was the biggest hindrance to Delano's defense. Instead, they've got her claiming she was in too much shock and misread the situation."

Shit, shit, shit. "Tell me he won't get off, George." Delano being released would signal a disaster for him and Jennifer.

"Trial starts in two days. I'll get a better feel after the opening statements," George replied, choosing to withhold the fact that a solid defense was being mounted.

Connor's head was spinning. How could he keep Jennifer safe if Anthony Delano was actually going to be set free? And if Eleanor now needed him to be released, there was zero chance Anthony would stay behind bars. Connor and Jenny would have to keep running.

He looked up and saw Jenny at the other end of the aisle, arms filled with food items for dinner. "I need to go, George. Jenny needs me."

"Con, call me tomorrow. Please. Let me help. There's a way. I'm sure of it."

"Okay. I'll try."

"Before you hang up, just one more thing," George added with hesitation. "I passed my bar exam. Two months ago."

"George, I'm dealing with serious shit right now. If you absolutely need my congratulations. Fine. Congrats," he replied tersely.

"God no, Con," replied George, insulted Connor would think he was seeking accolades. "It means I'm even more closely involved. I have direct access to the legal files. But I want you to know that even if I'm officially part of the defense team, I'm on your side. I'll play the part, but only so I can help you. You have my word."

Connor wasn't sure how much weight he could attach to George's word. "Be careful, George. These people are dangerous. Gotta go."

Connor hung up just as Jenny arrived at the cash. The thought of mulling through all this was discouraging. But it would have to wait until after she was asleep. For now, he had a pleasant evening to enjoy in her company.

CHAPTER SEVEN

— 2003 —

"I swear, it's like someone zapped me with that mind erasing thing from Men in Black," I cried, recounting my meeting with Detective Cisco to Nick, now that the girls were tucked away in their beds. I was already on my second glass of wine. The tannins seemed necessary to calm my nerves.

"The neutralizer," he mocked, turning towards me with his hand to my forehead as if holding one. We were sitting on the couch; my back leaning against the armrest, my legs draped over his. It was my invitation for a soothing foot-rub, which he obliged.

"It's not funny," I defended. "Nor is it normal that I forgot so much. Who does that?" I felt like an idiot, and was outright embarrassed.

"You're being too hard on yourself," Nick reassured. "It was a traumatic time in your life. It's probably a good thing that you forgot."

"The bad stuff yes, but why the good?" I stared in the distance trying to remember more details. "Like, get this. Have you ever, I mean ever, heard me mention the RV trip I went on with Dad?"

Nick leaned forward almost spitting out his ill-timed sip of wine, and burst into laughter. "Okay now you're just making shit up."

"I wish I was," I cried in despair. "I mean, I don't wish the trip was made-up. I wish I remembered it before today."

"You're actually being serious right now?" He seemed dubious.

"Yes! Dad showed up with this big honking Winnebago and we hit the road to nowhere. For…like…two whole months!"

Nick's jaw dropped with surprise. But my tone was serious enough for him to believe me, or at least go along with it. He reasoned, "You lost your Mom, for crying out loud. It's only natural that what happened afterwards would be a blur."

"But that's just it. It wasn't after she died."

"You mean to tell me that the mother you describe as completely cautious and paranoid went on a camping trip? Sounds like she was more fun than you let on."

"She didn't come. We went while she was in hospital. In a coma for God's sake. And we had fun. That I do remember." Thinking of it in hindsight, it seemed like such a horrible thing to do. "Were we being completely callous?"

"Hey, come on," he comforted, his hand stroking my shin. "You were Hannah's age."

That fact resonated with both of us in the moment. Our middle child seemed so young, far too young to endure that kind of loss.

After a pause, Nick continued. "Imagine your dad. He had to keep his little girl together while you both waited for the inevitable. Your mom was otherwise gone. He gave you a much-needed vacation. Would you think me horrible if I did the same?"

"No I wouldn't." And though I meant it sincerely, I also knew he would never leave my side. "And you're right," I sighed. "That's actually what I told the detective." Still thinking about it, "You know? It was probably my most exciting summer ever. Until meeting you, of course," I winked.

"So tell me about this trip of yours." He squeezed himself further into the cushions ready to hear the details.

"Gosh I remember so little. I've been wracking my brain all afternoon trying to remember more. Anything really. But I can't name a single place we stopped at, and yet I'm pretty sure there were many cause we drove a lot. What I do remember is the feeling of it. There was such an easy vibe, like everything was so casual, unplanned, fun."

"Well, it had to be a breather from the hospital. And that vibe sounds pretty typical for you two. I've only known you to be chill when you're together." Which Nick, no doubt, found challenging at times. We were a little too sedate for his energy level.

"I know right? And yet, that's what stands out most. I don't know why." I tried to think of a reason. "Maybe cause Mom wasn't there? It's not like Dad and I ever did anything that exciting, just the two of us, before then. I remember her being such a nervous person. Really uptight all the time." I thought of how Dad always seemed to be caressing her shoulder as if to calm her. "Then she was gone. And so was the tension. I mean, we were sad, but Dad never seemed stressed, or emotional. Just quiet. So I was too."

THE BURDEN OF TRUTH

"He was focused on you, just as a loving parent should be."

It was typical of Nick to consider our behavior as perfectly natural. He was nothing but supportive and agreeable where the subject of my mother's passing was concerned. He didn't say so, but I know it pained him to think of it. Which wasn't often since it was especially rare for me to ever bring her up. In fact, I never did. For as inquisitive a person as he was, Nick surprisingly drew the line at the topic of her. He never raised it, never pried. And yet all he knew, for the longest time, was that she had been in a car accident. It was a statement of fact I shared in the same way I revealed my favorite color. It's orange, by the way. It had taken Lady Diana's car accident for me to feel compelled enough to elaborate more. Watching her sons, Princes William and Harry, as they followed her coffin during the royal funeral procession, robotically moving forward without displaying their sadness, had brought me to tears. I became completely overcome with emotion. So much so that I had to share with Nick how much I could feel their pain, and yet how lucky they were that their mother's death didn't drag out for months like mine had. My opening up to him should have triggered a barrage of questions. Had it been any other topic, it would have. Instead, Nick listened in silence, held me close, and simply reminded me he was there.

"I gotta admit though," he added, perhaps to lighten the mood, "it's hard to imagine the two of you roughing it on the road. And, who knows? You might start remembering more now that it's on your mind."

"Maybe." That would be nice. Surprising, but nice. "You

know what's really weird?" I said, staring in the distance, "Dad and I never talked about it afterwards. Not ever." It seemed bizarre to me now, given how big an adventure it had been. Our only adventure, at that. "I guess he must have felt guilty that we left Mom and weren't with her when she passed." I realized in saying it out loud, that Nick didn't know that either, until just now. I'm not sure I ever really thought of it myself until Detective Cisco forced the topic today. I almost wished I could take it back. I had nothing but adoration for my father, and by extension, so did Nick. *Will he think less of Dad because of this?*

"Could be. But that was decades ago now. Maybe you should bring it up to him? On a good day, that is. Let him know it was such a great memory for you. It would make him smile. And if you're really lucky, he might actually be able to share something about it."

Leave it to Nick to just be thoughtful.

"I suppose I could." If Dad had any lingering guilt, it would have passed by now. Assuming he even remembered that time in our lives. It was impossible to tell what the state of his memory was anymore.

I then recalled something else from today's meeting. "Oh, I almost forgot. Detective Cisco showed me a copy of a picture that was taken by I don't know who, while we were on that trip. How he got it, I have no clue. It was of Dad with who Detective Cisco claims was this supposedly close acquaintance of his, Jorge Vasquez. Could you believe it?"

"Really?" Nick seemed very intrigued.

"Yup, and he hoped I could tell him about it."

"He thought you took it?"

"That hadn't occurred to me. Maybe he did. I didn't say anything, but I do remember something about it. It was Dad's beard that reminded me. That was the only time he ever had one. Bohemians that we were."

"You remember Jorge?"

"Not exactly. It's super vague, and I may have made it up in my mind. But I think the sidewalk they were on was opposite a county fair I pleaded with him to take me to when I noticed the ferris wheel from a distance. I feel like Dad maybe went to get some cash from the bank to buy tickets for the rides, and on his way out, he saw the guy in the picture."

"Did he look like he knew him?"

"Not to me. They exchanged briefly, but I think Dad said he just asked him for some change or something. I can't remember."

"And you never saw him again?"

"Nope."

"Wonder what would make the detective think he was a close acquaintance?"

"Beats me. But he wasn't. That I would know. Which is why I didn't say anything. Besides, I was so struck by seeing Dad looking that way, I kinda froze."

"Well I can't imagine it's that big a deal. Plus, how much could he expect from someone who was only nine at the time?"

I appreciated the validation. "The whole thing felt so invasive." And yet I felt oddly grateful to have been pushed to remember this adventure that was now consuming me. "What I'd give to have a real conversation with Dad right now though."

I got lost in all the questions I suddenly felt compelled to ask him. *Oh God, I'm becoming Nick.*

Breaking the brief silence, Nick asked, "Did old man Cisco tell you what exactly he's investigating?" He was still too curious to know more details.

"Nope. Said it's nothing for me to concern myself with." Then I added. "Oh and he's not old. In fact, he seems awfully young for a detective."

"Ah. They put a newbie on it. Can't be very important."

"And a far too good-looking one at that." That just blurted out.

"Is he now?" mused Nick, perhaps a little jealous.

"Oh don't worry. He's totally confused. Actually had Dad's birth year wrong. *And* his notes were a complete mess."

Nick chuckled. In part because he knew how much I loathed disorganization. But also, it likely relieved him to know the impression Detective Cisco had left wasn't merely his good looks.

"Well, if I had to guess, it sounds like this Jorge person was the one involved in something around that time. The photo could've been taken by someone investigating him. And since your Dad was in it, they're trying to cover all the bases."

"Over thirty years later? Seems a bit late. Also, Detective Cisco had information about my mother *and* my grandparents. I don't get how that would have anything to do with Mr. Jorge."

"Hmm. That is weird." Nick seemed as confused as I was.

"I just hope he doesn't contact me again."

"He probably won't. But if he does, can I participate?" That didn't surprise me. Nick had to be curious to see Detective

Cisco for himself.

"Be my guest. As far as I'm concerned, I'd like to forget the whole thing. And as we both know, my mind is apparently very good at that," I smirked sarcastically.

"Okay," he exhaled, lifting my legs off his thighs and extending a hand to pull me up. "Time to get you to bed. You need some rest for more 'annual-reporting' tomorrow."

"That actually sounds delightful at the moment," I replied, while accepting the assist to stand-up.

"Ah, the soothing comfort of numbers," Nick mocked with a wink. "Speaking of soothing," he added, while raising his near-empty wine glass. "A toast to your Dad."

"Okay?" I raised mine, not too sure where he was going with this.

"Since the very first moment I met you in college, you've been the most grounded, together person I have ever met. You could've turned into a complete mess after suffering a loss at that age. It took one hell of a father to push through his own heartbreak and devote himself completely to his daughter's well-being. He's rockstar in my book."

Between the wine, the words, the drain from my time with Detective Cisco, and my pure adoration of Dad, my eyes watered up as I clinked my glass against his and took my last sip. Nick was nothing if not perceptive. And in that moment, his reminder of how much of a saint he felt Dad truly was, meant more to me than I could say.

CHAPTER EIGHT

— 1972 —

"**F**ine. I'll go!" exclaimed an exasperated Heather, as she slammed the receiver against the olive colored dial phone that hung from the kitchen wall.

"Go where?" asked Connor. He had just walked in to grab the bottle of Tang from the fridge.

"You're not gonna like it," she replied, visibly annoyed.

He stopped before starting to pour himself a glass and looked at her. "Who were you talking to?"

She took a deep breath and exhaled. "My mother."

"What? Since when do you talk to her?" It had been years since she last called.

"When she gives me no choice."

"What does she want?" Connor had zero trust in that woman.

"Apparently," she began, while imitating her mother's tone and gestures, "the great Anthony Delano was recently honored for his economic contribution to the city. Since I didn't have the courtesy to extend my congratulations earlier, she thought I might want to do so during the gala she's hosting to celebrate him."

"Wow. She's a real piece of work." Connor looked concerned. "And you said no, right?"

"Of course."

"Good."

"But then she insisted."

"Which the master manipulator does so very well."

"So I reminded her that Jen was to be nowhere near that house."

At that, Connor breathed a sigh of relief.

"But there's some photo op thing. She's begging me to be there for it. Just this once."

"No!" Connor's tone was firm, his eyes wide with intent.

Heather whispered, "Lower your voice. You're gonna startle her. She can hear us from her bedroom."

Connor lowered the volume, but not the resistance. "We're not going. Period."

"You're not." Heather agreed. "You stay here with Jen. I'll go, do the quick poses, then say I have to leave." She tried to make it sound like a perfectly reasonable plan.

"Go alone? Are you out of your mind? That's even worse!" He paused to lower his voice again, his look even more stern. "The road conditions alone are a disaster. As for the destination. I swear, it's a deathtrap." He was fuming.

Heather tried her best to temper him. "The snow stopped hours ago. I'll drive safe, I promise. Plus, both Dawn and George will be there."

Connor sensed something fishy. Heather had gone nowhere near any of her family since Jenny's birth. Not to mention how much she hated being in the car if there was so much as rain or insufficient daylight. She was prudent above all else. *What's this really about*, he wondered. "Is it the money? Did she threaten to cut you off?" As benevolent as Eleanor tried to appear in supporting them for the good of her grandchild, Connor remained leery of the strings attached.

"No, no. Well…maybe." Heather realized this might be the angle that could sway him into letting her go. "She didn't mention it specifically. You know how she is. She prefers to imply things."

"I don't like it." Connor began to pace back and forth across their small kitchen. "Let her cut us off. We'll manage. We can find a cheaper apartment. I'm getting better contracts now. More money will come in without us owing anyone anything."

"Conway," she sighed, reaching out to hold his arm. She used that term of endearment to get him to relax. "It'll just be this one time." She waited till he looked up at her, then added, "I know what I'm doing."

"Wait." The look in her eyes caused him to worry. "You're not planning a confrontation are you?"

She turned away.

"No, no, no!" he pleaded, pulling her arm firmly to prevent her from walking away. "I forbid you from going!"

She whipped back to face him, a look of shock and anger in her eyes. "Don't you lay a hand on me! How dare you!"

He released it immediately, took a few steps backwards, hands raised as though she was pointing a gun at him. "I'm…I'm sorry. I know. I never should've. Really, I'm so sorry."

"You promised."

"I, I know. It won't happen again. I swear. I'm so sorry. I

just can't let you be in his presence. It's too dangerous." He was almost on the verge of tears.

She seized the moment. "It's okay." She advanced and caressed his arm. "But I need you to let me do this. Please, Conway."

Though every fibre of his being was sending warning signals, he could tell her mind was made up. No matter how convinced he was that he would regret it, he knew she wouldn't stop until he resigned himself. "I hate it. I'm going to be sick with worry the whole time. But you have to promise me here and now that you'll stick close to Dawn or George at all times. Promise."

"I promise."

* * *

It had been hours since Heather had left the house. She looked so stunning in her red gown. The gown everyone but Connor was now admiring. She also looked so vulnerable; like a target entering the bullring draped in a red cape. And the bull in question was ferocious. Connor's sole consolation was George, who he had finally managed to reach. Having joined the Delano staff after charming Eleanor at Heather and Connor's wedding, he was Connor's one access to intel on all the goings-on at the manor they otherwise avoided. Ever intent on repaying his debt for Connor's silence, George dutifully responded to the call for protection, and assured Connor he would keep an eye on Heather until she left the gala.

For hours Connor tried to keep himself occupied as he impatiently awaited her return. If not for his Jenny, he may have gone mad. Luckily, she was a big fan of board games and could play for hours. He had even let out the odd chuckle as he watched her fiercely try to beat him. But despite the distraction, he couldn't shake the feeling that Heather had taken too big a risk; that thought was eating away at him. By dinnertime, he whipped up some grilled cheese, heated Campbell's tomato soup, and let his Jenny eat while watching game shows on tv. He waited until she was fully engrossed before leaving the room to try reaching George for more reassurance. But before he had completed dialing the number, the doorbell rang.

He rushed over breathing a sigh of relief. *Heather must have forgotten her key.* Upon briskly swinging the door open to celebrate her safe return, his heart sank at the presence of two police officers, each removing their caps as they greeted him.

"Mr. Rivers, I'm afraid there's been an accident. Your wife is in the hospital. We can escort you there now."

Connor's heart pounded so hard he could feel it in his ears. He was about to vomit, or faint, but then, "My daughter. She's in the living room watching tv."

"It might be best if she did not come, sir. Is there someone who can stay with her? We can wait until they arrive."

Connor had to think quickly. His parents lived three hours away; too far to get there fast enough. He rushed to the phone and dialed his neighbor, Mrs. Jane, the only other person to babysit Jenny the few times she got home from school while both Connor and Heather were out. She arrived within moments.

Connor sat in the backseat of the patrol car stunned. *Why, why, why did I let her go?* He needed to know more. "What street was she on when the accident occurred?"

"It wasn't a car accident, Mr. Rivers," replied a young Officer Randall in the passenger seat. His voice seemed so deep for his age. "There was an incident at Delano Manor. The investigators are looking into the details."

"That animal!" His worst fears had come true. An altercation with the devil himself. *How could George let this happen?* Sweat had built up over his brow, his face was pale with worry. He felt like he was suffocating. "Tell me she's going to be okay," he pleaded.

"The doctors will be the ones to discuss the details with you, sir," replied Officer Randall in the gentlest of tones.

The patrol car had barely come to a stop when Connor lunged out the back door and ran into the entrance of Massachusetts General Hospital. He was directed to the surgical floor waiting room where George was already pacing feverishly. His tuxedo jacket was draped over a chairback in a feeble attempt to unburden some of weight from his shoulders.

"George! What happened? Is she gonna be okay?" panted Connor, rushing into the room, grabbing George's forearms for support as he caught his breath.

"Come sit down, Con. I'll tell you what I know." George was visibly shaken. His eyes red from crying.

"What do you mean *what you know*? You were supposed to stay with her the whole time!"

"I know. I tried. I'm sorry," he cried. "I tried. Really. But it's complicated in that place —"

"Cut the crap and tell me what happened."

George insisted they sit down, then struggled to speak of the trauma that occurred, fully consumed with guilt for not preventing it from happening. But once again, the urges he yearned to control had gotten the best of him. And once again, Connor was paying the price. He stuttered and sniffled trying to explain that Heather had fallen and hit her head on the marble floor of the foyer. At least that's what he understood. Eleanor had insisted he return to the guests so he hadn't seen it happen. He only heard the screech.

"So who was with her?"

"She was with her parents at the top of the stairs. Dawn was in the foyer."

"At the top! She fell from up there?! Oh my God, oh my God!" Connor bolted up, pacing while rubbing his temples raw. "How the hell can she survive that? That's two flights high." He visualized the grand entrance with its rounded staircases on either side, connected by a railed mezzanine at the top. "I knew she shouldn't have gone. Why did I let her go?" He pounded his fist on the back of a chair.

"Mr. Rivers?" called the elderly surgeon, who walked into the waiting room, his scrub cap moist with sweat.

"Doctor, how is she? Will she be okay?" cried Connor, racing to within inches of him.

"Mr. Rivers, I'm Dr. Benson, neurosurgeon. Your wife suffered massive head trauma. I just performed a procedure to relieve some of the internal bleeding in her brain. She's now resting and is under careful observation. The next few hours will be critical."

"Can I see her?" begged Connor.

"I'm afraid that isn't possible just yet. She needs complete rest while we monitor her closely. We'll advise you immediately of any change in her condition."

"Just please tell me she's going to be okay."

"We're doing everything we can for her, Mr. Rivers. We'll know more in the next few hours."

Dr. Benson walked away. Who knew how many similar announcements he had made over the course of his career; the bearer of news that came as a sledgehammer to the gut.

Connor dropped into a chair, his head falling forward in despair.

George sat beside him and placed his arm around Connor's shoulders.

Connor shrugged it off aggressively. Without looking up, he said, "I've always, always, *always* kept my promises to you, George." He then raised his head to look him in the eyes, his tear-filled gaze piercing through George's soul. "Are you ever gonna do the same for me?"

George's head fell forward as tears of regret began to drip onto his lap. "I will make it up to you, Con. I promise," he sniffled. "Whatever it takes. I'll do it. I mean it." He sobbed as his shoulders bobbed in anguish.

Connor didn't say a word. His silent tears rolled down his cheeks as he stared blankly toward an uncertain future. He thought of his Jenny. What would he tell her? *Heather has to be okay. My little girl can't lose her mother.*

Connor was jolted out of his trance the moment Eleanor

entered the waiting room. Still dressed in her ballgown, her hair looked uncharacteristically disheveled, her demeanor just as uncharacteristically deflated. Following her was a police officer.

She looked at Connor in a state of utter panic. "What did the doctors tell you?"

He had no energy nor appetite for an inquisition or confrontation with the person responsible for Heather going on this suicide mission of an event. Almost robotically, he responded, "They relieved some bleeding in her brain. The next few hours are critical."

"How many hours? What's the doctor's name? I'm going to find him," she asked, while storming to the closest nursing station before he could respond.

"Mr. Rivers?" asked the police detective, who just arrived in the waiting room. "Might I have a word with you? In private?"

"Want me to come, Con?" asked George, desperate to support his friend in his time of need.

"No. You to stay here. Come get me the second the doctor comes back with more news."

George stood up and nodded emphatically, almost in salute to his commander, ready to stand at attention for as long as needed.

"What do you mean I can't see her? She's my daughter for God's sake?" yelled Eleanor from down the hallway. One of the officers who had escorted Connor to the hospital had been stationed outside Heather's room to prevent anyone other than authorized medical personnel from entering.

Once in a quieter room, Connor and the detective sat down in chairs leaving one between them. The middle-aged investigator of broad girth, pivoted toward him, his small flip pad opened ready to take notes.

"Mr. Rivers, I'm very sorry about your wife's situation. We're actively investigating the cause of her accident. To that end, I just have a few questions for you, if that's okay?"

"Yes. Of course." No one was more interested in knowing what happened than Connor.

"I understand you did not attend today's affair at Delano Manor. Is that correct?"

"No, I was home with my daughter."

"Why is that exactly? Was it not an occasion for both of you to attend?"

An occasion neither of us should have attended. "We both agreed it was not an appropriate event for our young daughter, so I stayed with her."

"And where is your daughter now?"

"Home. With a sitter. She's only nine and doesn't need to see her mother in this condition."

"So you've seen your wife then?"

"No, not yet. But I can only imagine how scary the image of her mother in a hospital bed would be for her."

"Of course…Going back to the event. Why didn't you have your daughter stay with the sitter so you could join your wife?"

I should have. But could I trust myself with that monster? "To be frank, I didn't want either of us to attend. But Heather insisted. Or should I say her mother did."

"Why is that? I mean, why didn't you want either of you to attend?"

"Anthony Delano is an aggressive man. He took out his frustrations on my wife while she was living there. We had kept our distance since we got married almost ten years ago. And would've kept it that way, if not for this event."

"I see." The detective scribbled some notes. "So while you believed Mr. Delano to have been aggressive with your wife in the past, you preferred that she be in his presence without you?"

Put that way, Connor felt like a complete failure. "No! I just…didn't want her to go at all. She insisted. And she didn't want me there." He was fumbling. It was impossible to make this appear like sound judgement on his part.

Sensing that Connor was getting flustered, the detective moved onto a different line of questioning. "Was your wife ever hospitalized in the past as a result of Mr. Delano's alleged aggression?"

"No. He seemed to have just enough restraint to stop before hurting her to the point of hospitalization."

"No prior medical intervention," the detective dictated out loud, while adding to his notes. He looked up at Connor. "And did you ever witness this alleged aggression yourself? Or perhaps see any physical evidence on her person subsequent to the said aggression?"

"Witnessed no." *I would've beaten the shit outta him.* "But she did show me her cuts and bruises before we were married."

"And you did not urge her to file a complaint?"

"Yes I did. But she refused. She was convinced he would just get away with it. His money gave him power. And she worried he would just beat her even more afterwards."

"Would you say she feared Mr. Delano?"

"Yes absolutely. He was horrible to her."

"And yet she insisted on being in his presence today?"

"Like I said, it was her mother who insisted. Heather felt obligated, but also knew she would be surrounded by many guests."

"So she did not appear concerned?"

Bizarrely she didn't. "She appeared dutiful. And just wanted to get it over with. For some photo op."

"Did you ever hit your wife, Mr. Rivers?"

Connor bolted up from his seat. "Oh my God! What? No! Never! I would never!"

"I'm sorry, Mr. Rivers. I had to ask. It's not unheard of for victims of aggression to pursue relationships with abusers."

"Or with the complete opposite! Like the good guy who wouldn't lay a finger on her!"

"Please, please sit down. I apologize, Mr. Rivers. I had to ask. It's part of the investigation. Understanding motive, patterns of behavior…But let's move on to other questions shall we?" He quickly changed gears. "Is your wife on any medication?"

"No she isn't." He was trying to calm himself down. Trying not to appear aggressive himself.

"Might she have been drinking or perhaps have taken a narcotic today knowing she was going to be in the presence of someone who made her uncomfortable?"

Connor had no idea where he was going with this, but there was no way anyone was going to make his very clean Heather appear otherwise. "My wife neither drank nor smoked nor took anything that would limit her faculties. She was a supremely cautious and alert person."

"Might she have taken a sip of champagne at an event like today's?"

"Yes. That she might do. For a toast. But she never finished a glass. That wasn't her thing." Connor was getting tired of the questioning. "Look. I'm worried and exhausted. But I still don't know what exactly happened. Can you at least tell me that."

"Of course, Mr. Rivers. And thank you for your patience with these questions," replied the detective as he flipped the pages of his notepad back to the earlier entries. "It seems your wife fell from the mezzanine of the grand foyer. She was in the company of both Anthony and Eleanor Delano at the time of the incident. Her sister, Dawn, also witnessed the fall from below. Each gave their testimony at the scene, then Anthony Delano was taken into custody for further questioning."

"Oh my God! That monster tried to kill her!" Connor rose to his feet, beside himself.

"He is denying any wrongdoing –"

"Of course he is. He's above the law!"

"Forensic evidence is being gathered for analysis. Medical reports will also be reviewed. We'll get to the bottom of this, Mr. Rivers. In the meantime, I sincerely hope your wife will make a complete recovery."

Connor soldiered back into the original waiting room, completely drained from the interview. The image of Heather falling over the railing tortured him. Hard as he tried, he could not keep his mind from imagining her body lying on the ground.

How badly were her limbs contorted? How long did she lie in a pool of blood? Will she survive? Will that villain pay?

George and Eleanor interrupted their heated exchange the moment they noticed Connor arriving. George rushed over to him immediately and let Connor know the doctor had not yet come back.

"How did it go? Do you want coffee or something else to drink? To eat? At least come sit down." George tried his best to tend to whatever Connor might need.

"Can't eat or drink till I know she's okay," replied Connor, dropping himself down into a chair.

The three sat quietly, stunned, numb, until Connor broke their hour of silence. Turning toward Eleanor, who sat at the opposite corner of the room, he asked almost blankly, "Where's Dawn?"

It only just occurred to him that she wasn't there. She had once been so close to her sister. Today would have been the first time they were together since the wedding. How horrible it must have been for her to witness the fall. He expected she would be with them by now.

Nervously, Eleanor responded, "She was a complete mess after the police interview. Couldn't keep it together. Far too frazzled to handle more trauma. I sent her to bed and instructed the maid to give her Valium to calm her nerves."

George cringed at the thought of poor Dawn. He was certain the sound of her deafening shriek would be etched in his memory forever. Never had he heard a human cry so loud, so filled with terror. He had sprinted to her side trying to hold her arms while she trembled. But Eleanor cast him aside the moment she got to her, pulling her into the other room, away from the sight of her sister's mutilated body surrounded by a growing pool of blood.

CHAPTER NINE

— 2003 —

"Here's the forensic report you were waiting on, Detective Cisco," said his colleague, June, as she set the manila envelope onto an over-flowing paper tray at the corner of his desk. A chatter of voices and keyboard strokes echoed across the open office. Buzzing with activity on this midweek morning, a scent of stale coffee and boxed doughnuts filled the air.

"Great. Thanks, June," Cisco replied, picking it up almost immediately. He unwound the string from the button, lifted the envelope flap and pulled out the report produced by the forensic document examiner. It contained several pages stapled at the top corner.

Alright. Let's see if there's anything unexpected in here, he thought to himself, hoping to find actual evidence to support Detective Randall's fascination with this case, or more likely, the absence of cause to pursue an investigation of any kind.

Dated 1972, the letter of confession was compared with the original copy of Jorge Vasquez's own witness statement from the incident report following Heather Delano's accident of that same year. Per Randall's orders, Cisco had pulled it from the existing case files to expedite the analysis.

Cisco thumbed through the initial paragraphs, looking for any indication of inconsistency between the handwriting samples, then turned to the conclusion of the first section. All unique qualities; spacing, slants, baseline alignment, connecting strokes, formations and other attributes, were invariable between the two; validation that both originated from the same author.

Not a forgery. He then flipped to the next section wherein ink dating approximated the age of the document at thirty years. *Date is legit.*

The following section applied to the envelopes themselves; the original marked *private & confidential* containing the letter of confession, and the other into which that envelope had been later placed for mailing. While the original envelope remained sealed along the remoistenable gum strip, the top crease had been sliced open by way of a letter opener or similar sharp object. The document examiner described the texture and appearance of the fibers along the cut edges as showing minimal evidence of wear; the condition of the envelope itself, not indicative of multiple reinsertions.

So the letter was opened recently. Likely after Vasquez's passing. Possibly by whoever discovered it while sorting through his personal effects, deduced Cisco. *That must have been a shocker.*

As for the postmark imprinted on the outer portion of the stamped mailpiece, the report confirmed its authenticity; expedited last month, from New York.

Wait a second, Cisco paused. He had dismissed the packaging as irrelevant upon learning of its dated content; an uncharacteristic oversight and harsh reminder he should have been more thorough in his examination. *Why didn't the sender mail it to a local station?* That the confession letter made its way to New York where Vasquez resided until he passed away was not suspicious. That it was directed to this specific police station however, hardly seemed coincidental. The implication was that the sender was aware the original investigation had been conducted in Boston. *Or maybe they researched it? Given Delano's notoriety, that information wouldn't have been too difficult to find,* he reasoned. *Either way, it's deliberate.*

Cisco turned to the final section which pertained to the photograph of Jorge Vasquez and Connor Rivers. Inserted in the outer envelope, it was the one he had shown Jennifer Vincent a photocopy of during their interview. Why the sender had included it with the confession letter remained unknown. To Detective Randall however, it was cause for immediate questioning of Connor Rivers, rendered unfeasible due to his mental state. Analysis of the photograph yielded the following results: an original with characteristics of darkroom development, absent of any trace of a date stamp. Attributes of the card stock were consistent with those used in the early 1970's. Identifiable elements of the image namely landscape, building markers and flora, were emblematic of the west coast. Handwriting on the back side, *Connor July 27, 1972,* matched that of the confession letter.

In his haste to dismiss the anonymous package as obsolete, Detective Cisco had also neglected to inspect the backside of the photograph before submitting it to forensics. The date inscribed on it drew his attention. Chastising himself for yet another omission, he bent down to reach through the files in the box still beside his desk and pulled out the one confirming Anthony Delano's fatal heart attack. He recalled from his notes that it had occurred on July 28, and had prompted the automatic abatement of the criminal court proceedings. *Why would Vasquez place himself on the west coast the day prior?* That only made sense to Cisco if Vasquez needed an alibi. *Clearly he wasn't looking for one since he not only wrote a confession, he wasted no time drafting it.* The letter was also dated July 28. And as for any suggestion that Connor Rivers was somehow implicated in the confessed crime, the time-line of the photo put that to rest. There was no way it was feasible to trek to the opposite coast in a motorhome, with a child, in less than twenty-four hours. That was enough justification to exclude Connor Rivers, and by extension Jennifer Vincent, from any further involvement. *At least there's one positive to come from this report. Unless of course, the date on the photo was fabricated. Who the hell took it in the first place? And why?*

Damn this case, Cisco sighed, his mind now racing with more questions than answers. Something definitely seemed off. What that was had yet to be determined. And whether it was relevant thirty years later had better be the case, because while it pained him to admit it, Randall's suspicions no longer seemed quite so exaggerated.

Whoever found the confession letter, chose not to destroy it. They intended for this police station to obtain it. Even though Vasquez is dead. Why? And why remain anonymous? And what's the deal with including the photo? Cisco could only surmise that someone had an ax to grind or something significant to gain from this murder being revealed. But in provoking this inquiry, the sender had effectively positioned themselves as a person of interest. *Looks like we're heading to New York.*

* * *

Determined to beat out traffic, Detective Cisco had departed before dawn to the sound of his tearful infant daughter gently cradled in his wife's arms. He waited until after her 4am feeding, selfishly unwilling to forego his precious alone time with her while mommy got some extra sleep. It was a moment of deep admiration to memorize every bulge and curve of her skin, every crease in her tiny fingers, the tresses of hair that had suddenly sprouted. All to the sound of her suckling as he held a bottle of breast milk to her eager lips. It was the first time since her birth that he would be away overnight; tomorrow he would miss their morning ritual. And a mere hour into the drive was all it took for him to start regretting his decision to leave. Already, the distance seemed too great; the farther he traveled, the more irresponsible he felt. *This trip better bear fruit.* If he was sacrificing moments with his child; a waste of time wasn't an option.

Having sipped his last drip of coffee from his oversized travel mug, he welcomed the eye-relief afforded by the sunrise behind a veil of thin clouds as he drove southbound along Interstate 84. To his surprise, this was not a road trip for two. After appearing so pleased with Cisco's new findings, Detective Randall had decided to pass up on the opportunity to accompany him. Instead, he relegated this portion of the exercise entirely to Cisco's direction, who in turn, wasn't certain whether to feel flattered by this show of confidence, or concerned that Randall was only letting him reach a dead-end like some rookie learning experience.

Left to strategize alone, Cisco's first thought had been to identify immediate family from Vasquez's obituary. Unfortunately, it was void of any kin that still had a pulse.

Jorge "George" Vasquez, 57,
of Manhattan, New York,
passed away on August 3, 2003.
Prominent attorney and philanthropist,
Jorge was predeceased by his parents Manuel and Maria,
and his brother, Victor.
He leaves behind a legacy of support to various charities.
A small private service will be held in his honor.

As for directory listings for *J* or *G Vasquez* in New York City and surrounding areas, the tally exceeded one hundred and fifty. Before putting June to the task of contacting each one of them, he found a more promising path, made possible by an internet search of legal offices. It turned up Manhattan-based, *Vasquez & Associates*. Two days later, Cisco was on route to their offices.

He initially debated calling ahead, but quickly decided against it. For one, he couldn't ask to speak with a dead man. Secondly, it seemed more prudent to avoid tipping anyone off – in particular the sender intent on remaining anonymous – that a detective was snooping for information.

By 11:30am, he was stepping off the elevator opposite the floor-to-ceiling, double-glass doorway of the fifth floor occupant of the historic building at the intersection of Tribeca and City Hall. An expansive, renovated hallway of dark mahogany was visible behind a matching reception desk; *Vasquez & Associates* etched in gold on its facade. Cisco pulled the large brass handle of the heavy door, while admiring four plush leather club chairs in the reception area, each with its individual round, gold-rimmed glass end-table, surrounded by oversized planters bursting with abundant palms. Not a sound could be heard other than the tapping of keystrokes from a women in her mid-forties, who was seated behind the desk. Her tight brown perm and geometric-patterned fuchsia and black sweater mounted over prodigious shoulder-pads was a blast from the eighties. As he approached, the thickness of her eyeliner became more apparent over thin reading glasses perched on the end of her narrow nose.

"Can I do something for ya, sweetheart?" she asked, not lifting her gaze from her screen to notice Cisco's drab navy suit and tie. Before he could respond, she raised her index finger to gesture for him to hold on while she answered the phone that had just rung. "Vasquez and Associates." She paused to listen to the caller. "Uh huh….uh huh…right. I'll get that to you shortly." She hung up and looked up at Cisco. "Sorry 'bout that, sweetheart. Do you have a meeting scheduled?"

"No actually." He took out his badge and raised it. "My name is Detective Cisco. I'm investigating a matter that concerns an old case Jorge Vasquez was involved in —"

"Say no more," she interjected. "You're here for the Delano

file. Am I right?"

What did she just say? Trying to withhold his shock, he replied, "Uh…yes. Yes, you are."

"I'll go get it for you. Be right back."

"I'm sorry, but…" He was tempted to ask about it, but stopped himself.

She halted. "What was that?"

"I'm just sorry for your loss, that is. Must be a difficult time for your firm."

"Yes it is," she grinned politely, before turning toward the hallway in the direction of the storage room. "Might have started with that," she mumbled to herself as she marched away. Her sweater hung so low, her black leggings looked like two pegs inserted into her ankle boot pumps. "These young whipper-snappers got no manners." She entered a room filled with wall-to-wall file cabinets, and pulled open a tightly crammed drawer, reaching for the envelope squeezed at the far back. "Glad to finally be getting rid of you," she said, looking at it.

As Cisco awaited her return, he stood dumbfounded. The best case scenario for this visit was to get a lead on one of Vasquez's close acquaintances. Instead, he was about to become the recipient of a file he knew nothing about, that concerned the victim of the decades-old case he just so happened to have re-opened. *What the hell is going on?*

"Here you go, Captain." She handed him the thick sealed envelope as though passing him a hot potato. "Bye now." She waved him off, eager for the document to exit the perimeter of the office.

"It's detective. But thank you, ma'am." He looked down at the inscription across the envelope, *Delano file,* and recognized the penmanship immediately. It was written by Vasquez.

Seeing that he hadn't yet turned to leave, she looked up, raised her eyebrows and leaned her head forward, waiting for him to speak.

He hesitated. "Might I ask how long you've had this file?"

"Too long, if you ask me," she replied, exhaling pent-up frustration. "This is no place for documents that don't concern the firm. That was always George's rule." In defense of her acceptance of the file, she added, "But how was I supposed to know when that kid with his bicycle helmet and tights came rushing in all sweaty delivering a box I wasn't expecting? I had half a mind to decline it, but he played the bleeding heart. Said he needed the money for college. So I caved."

"So...am I to understand you had no knowledge of this document until you received it?"

"That's correct, Captain. Turns out it was mixed in with material George was transferring from home. Couldn't blame him for forgetting to tell me. He was already in bad sorts by then. Explains why he was so confused when I called him. Took him a while to understand what I was talking about. Then he got real upset. I suppose I should've been more flexible given his condition, but I was just following his own rule." She paused to sip her coffee. "I offered to bring it back to him. But he said he didn't want me seeing him that way. He did sound like he aged twenty years. Voice all croaky. Spoke real slow. And when I said I'd get it delivered, he refused that too. Insisted it shouldn't have been handled by a courier in the first place. Too sensitive, I suppose. Promised he'd arrange for someone proper to pick it up." She fanned both arms outward, and smiled. "And here you are." She dropped her hands flat onto her desk and turned serious. "Bout damn time too. Sure as hell wasn't expecting to have to store this thing for so many months."

She's a talker. This is good. Cisco wanted to keep her going while he tried to make sense of all this. It seemed best to play along, to act as though he was in fact part of the plan. "I'm very sorry it took so long for me to get here. I have a newborn daughter, you see. It's hard to pull myself away from her. But I'm grateful you held onto it." While true, Cisco's real intent was to get into her good graces. "No need for you to inconvenience yourself any longer."

"Is she your first?" she asked with motherly calmness.

"Yes she is. Jade is her name." It felt awkward for Cisco to share personal information with a stranger, but an opportunity to express paternal pride was hard to resist.

"Magical isn't it? And that's a beautiful name. I got three kids. Everyone says it, cause it's true. They're the best part of life. You go on now, Captain, and get home to her."

"I will. Thank you once again. You've been very helpful." He turned to give the appearance he was leaving, then stopped and asked, "Would you happen to know where I might reach Mr. Vasquez's next of kin? In case…there is something contained in here that they may want to keep."

"Well, it's not for me to say, but since you're law enforcement and all, George never spoke of kin. Lived alone. Or so he said."

Her last comment intrigued him. He wanted her to elaborate. Perhaps she would with a little flattery. "You strike me as someone very…perceptive, ma'am."

"It's Fern, Captain," she smiled. "And yes, you could say that."

"Fern it is," Cisco smiled. "But I'm still a detective," he winked. "A good one at that. And my senses are telling me you know something."

"Now don't be trying to butter me up. I get enough of that at the pub," she batted her arm. "And I'm not one to get into people's business. But when you work long enough with someone, you can't help but know things."

"Anything you think might be important for law enforcement to know about?"

"Now I see what you're doing," she said, waving her index finger. "Using that police-type probing. Except that won't work with me. Not one to gossip."

"You got me," he smiled. "There's no fooling you." *It was worth a try.* He pulled out a business card from his lapel pocket and handed it to her. "Here's where you can reach me. If ever something should come up."

She took it and read, "Max. That's a strong name."

"Take care of yourself, Fern," smiled Cisco, before turning toward the elevator. *She knows something.*

He pressed the down arrow and was tempted to open the envelope the moment he stepped inside and the doors merged, but waited until he was in his car parked below. Sitting behind the wheel, he rolled the window down one inch then ran his key along the crease of the envelope to unseal it. Inside was a thick assortment of documents, many on Delano Enterprise letterhead; some handwritten, others typed, all photocopies. He flipped through the pages quickly seeing what appeared to be notes on the defense strategy for the court case and other related material. But the sheer volume of information would require a more thorough review better suited to the privacy of his motel room. He fanned a few more pages and landed on one containing a grid of headshots, numbered one through twelve by hand. *This must be the jury,* he assumed. Anthony Delano died prior to delivery of closing arguments, thus they never had cause to render a verdict. He was about to count the Y's and N's inscribed by hand on the squares, when he heard a loud knock at his window.

"Captain Max!" Fern blurted through the crack.

Startled, he let out a yell, dropped the pages and instinctively reached for his gun before realizing who it was. He exhaled while throwing his head back, then bent over to gather the documents that were sprawled at his feet.

"Come walk with me." She motioned for him to follow, an unlit cigarette adhering to her newly-applied bright pink lipstick.

He quickly reached for his briefcase on the passenger seat and stuffed the pile of documents inside before getting out to catch up to her. He carried it with him, unwilling to leave it out of sight.

"You got a light?" Her pace was quick, as though she was seeking cover.

"Sorry no. I don't smoke," he replied, now matching her stride.

"Good for you. These things will kill ya."

"So, where are we going exactly?"

"That bench." She pointed. "We're gonna chat."

She exhaled as she sat down, neither lighting nor removing the cigarette from her mouth. "Okay. So here's the thing. I mind my own business. I'm not one to judge or to gossip."

"Understood," Cisco reassured her, eager to hear what was to follow.

"George was my guy. Solid, you know? A generous soul. Always looking out for others. Sometimes too much, if you ask me. Did lots of pro-bono for folks he thought were good people stuck in bad situations they never chose. And it's not like he needed to do it. Made himself a great living. But he insisted on it. It was like he couldn't help himself. It seemed a bit much to me, but I don't judge."

Her pause compelled Cisco to fuel her chatter, while he amazed at the cigarette staying in place while bouncing as her lips moved. "It isn't just any attorney who dedicates his time to helping others for free. Sounds like he was a very generous man."

"Oh that he was. And his clients were grateful. Most of them at least. Steered a whole lot of them back on the straight and narrow. Some, mind you, fell off the wagon. But certain types can't be helped, you know?"

"I do." Agreeing seemed like the best approach.

"I got why he helped the illegals. I mean he spoke Mexican and all. Hell, he was born in Guadalupe. But the druggies were a messy bunch. I warned him to be careful, but he just kept at it. Said they were broken, not dangerous."

Where is she going with this? "I'm sorry, Fern. I realize that I never asked how Mr. Vasquez died." He hoped she wouldn't find this question unusual coming from the detective mandated to pick up the mysterious envelope.

"Pancreatic cancer. The cruelest one if you ask me. Diagnosed then dead in less than a year." She paused and looked away, her eyes appearing misty.

"That's horrible." He wasn't sure if he should place his hand on her shoulder for comfort. Not that she would feel it under the thick shoulder pad. Instead, he tried to move the subject along. "Has anyone taken over his pro-bono cases?"

"Nope. But if the druggies find themselves back in rehab, there'll be plenty more room for them now," she replied derisively.

"What do you mean?"

"George left half his estate to the Mount Sinai Rehabilitation Center. That's how much it mattered to him."

"Really? That's extremely generous." It also explained the philanthropic reference in his obituary. "And how is it that you know this?"

"Captain Max," she replied in a sing-songy voice. "I reviewed the damn thing ages ago. That's my job. It was drafted at the office."

That means she knows who the rest went to. "Yes, of course. I should've known," Cisco pretended to blush. "You said he had no next of kin, but surely the other half went to someone close. A girlfriend? Or a distant relative?"

"Now you're starting to connect the dots, Captain Max. Let's put those detective skills to the test, shall we?"

"Okay then," he obliged. "Game on, Fern." If she was willing to share, he was more than willing to play along.

"Now I don't judge, you know that about me. And I mind my own business. But ya can't help but notice things when you're…perceptive…like you said. So here's the thing. George always had a handful of clients who kept him on retainer. They came and they went. Sometimes they came back later on. That's all normal. For each of them, there were meetings for me to book or documents to put together or court cases to arrange. Something for me to take care of other than just transferring the line. Except for one. Called pretty regularly, for years in fact, right up until the end. But never came into the office, never needed a single document put together, never a court case to speak of."

"You're not making this easy for me," said Cisco to keep her going. "But I'm guessing you suspected there was something going on between them. And it wasn't necessarily work related. An affair with a married woman perhaps?"

"Look at you, Captain Max," she said with pride as though commending her pupil. Then immediately turning serious. "No. A few times, George would head out right after they spoke. Said he was meeting someone, but never said who, and it was never marked in his calendar. Ever."

Since his first guess was wrong, Cisco tried another angle. "So…you think he was involved in illicit activities?" He wondered why she had painted Vasquez as a saint if she suspected something nefarious. Unless she took issue with this particular someone.

"I suppose that's one way to look at it," she gestured her disapproval.

"What would be another way?"

"Now it's real hard not to judge some things. Especially when they're unnatural. But like I told you before, George had a soft spot for certain types. He was drawn to the wrong crowd if you know what I mean. Makes my skin crawl just to think about it."

"I see many kinds of crowds in my line of work," Cisco replied. "Too many to count. Of course, you already know that. Which kind of crowd are you referring to exactly?"

"The kind that kept George from having kin!" she blurted. "You know?" She stared at Cisco waiting for his next guess, then continued when he didn't respond quickly enough. "You're gonna make me say it out loud, aren't ya? Fine. He was a gay. I'm certain of it. Brandon Wong was no client. That's for damn sure."

Cisco had to contain himself. Learning of someone that close to Jorge Vasquez was a major victory. "I see. That is very interesting, Fern. So am I to assume the other half of Mr. Vasquez's estate went to Brandon Wong?"

"Nope," she declared. "Not sure what George was thinking when he decided the rest was going to the National AIDS Foundation. Like I wasn't gonna put two and two together? Seriously? Guess he didn't realize how perceptive I am, the way you do. Anyhow, this poor Brandon, he got nothing."

Now that's interesting. Was the secret gay lover expecting an inheritance? "Fern, would you by any chance have contact information to share?"

"I'm one step ahead of you, Captain," she boasted, pulling out a note from her purse. She had memorized the number from seeing it repeatedly on her telephone screen over the years and had transcribed it for him.

"Thank you," he replied, accepting this coveted detail. "I'm curious though. If George kept it a secret, why are you telling me about Brandon?"

"You asked for next of kin," she reasoned. "In case something in your envelope should be given to them. From what I can tell, Brandon is the closest thing. Deep down, I think that's what George would want. Bless his soul."

"It seems George Vasquez wasn't the only generous person in your firm. You've been very kind, Fern. I'm grateful for all your insight."

"Pleasure, Captain Max. Now go on home to your baby. That file's been sitting here for months. It can wait a little longer for you to read it."

CHAPTER TEN

— 2003 —

"What did you get Daddy?" Grace whispered into my ear as we were getting ready to leave the house. She and her sisters were always amused by how creative we were with our anniversary gifts. The *we* being a tad generous; Nick was notoriously ten steps ahead of me when it came to ideas. In all likelihood, Grace's question was really intended as a nudge for me to do better.

"It's a surprise," I replied with a devious smile, while grabbing my tote bag by the front door. His gift, which was tucked away in my office drawer for safe-keeping, was going to be transferred into it before heading out to our romantic dinner.

The girls hounded me for clues during the entire drive to school, but I kept my lips sealed. Sadly for them, they would have to wait until tomorrow to find out, because they would be fast asleep by the time Nick and I got home.

As far as my past purchases went, I personally considered them quite thoughtful, but the girls' impression suggested otherwise. It's true that I lacked Nick's originality. His were the kind of gifts you didn't find on retail shelves. He was more inclined to seek out those one-of-a-kind, sentimental items I never even knew existed. So I had given up on even trying to compete with his creativity and instead stuck to my comfort zone; something practical. But not this year. This was my time to shine, and I was ready to make a big splash.

I acted very matter-of-factly as we parted ways this morning. That alone probably made him suspicious. But I didn't care. I knew his face would drop once he'd unwrap the book. There was no way he'd ever guess it. Nor could he possibly have come up with something more shocking. And lord knows, he was planning something special because he'd been acting especially secretive all week.

As soon as I arrived at my desk, I took a peek inside the drawer to double-check that it was still there, then imagined the look on his face when he would unwrap it. I almost felt giddy, I was so excited. Knowing Nick, he would think it was something to read at his leisure. A picturesque tribute to his heritage that would adorn our coffee-table. Little would he know until he opened the hardcover that two airline tickets to Athens were sitting in an envelope, accompanied by a one-word note: *Honeymoon?* It was our thirteenth anniversary after all. And high time to go big.

Ours had been such a simple, intimate wedding that a honeymoon was never in the cards. We had careers to focus on, then came the girls. The only time the topic had ever been intimated was in utter jest after Lisa's birth. I recall him saying as we both were over-joyed, completely sleep-deprived, and without an ounce of time to ourselves, that we should stop making excuses for that honeymoon we never took. We both shrugged it off with a guffaw, then never brought it up again.

I wasn't sure what would surprise him more. The fact I came up with the idea or that I had time to plan it all without him knowing. Surprisingly, it was that session with Detective Cisco that thrust me into over-drive. I bulldozed through my annual report with so much productivity, I completed it well ahead of schedule. A detail I chose not to share with Nick, while I instead worked in consort with a travel agent.

* * *

Nestled in the heart of Harvard Square, we had first discovered this flagship farm-to-table gem on our very first date. Since, Harvest had become our anniversary tradition, a familiar yet special treat, in celebration of the new milestones we had reached over the course of the past year. The fancy clothes and gifts were the added touch, a staple for the occasion.

I could see Nick sitting by the stone fireplace at the far end of the interior courtyard. It was the best table in the house when al fresco dining was possible in early fall, and we had made sure to book it early. Along the outer perimeter was a pale fence contrasted by topiary hedges dispersed throughout. Matching posts and beams, wicker chairs and white table cloths completed the cozy coastal feel.

A bottle of white was chilling in the wine bucket standing next to him; no doubt a pinot grigio. As I crossed the patio toward my handsome husband, who was too deep in thought to notice my arrival, I inhaled the scent of competing delicacies.

The sound of soft jazz and clanking of silverware could be heard over the hum of conversation.

"I see you're not even waiting till we've made a toast," I said, announcing my arrival with a kiss on his cheek and quick glance at the package. A gift-wrapped box, the size of a paperback novel was sitting on my place-setting.

"Hey," he replied, a little startled. "How was your drive?" He bolted up to give me a proper kiss and hug before pulling my chair out for me to sit. He looked so dashing in his light gray suit and black shirt, unbuttoned at the collar.

"It was fine. And thank you, Mr. Debonair." Nick never wasted an opportunity to be chivalrous, particularly when dressed the part.

Our waiter was already at the table, wiping the condensation off the bottle with the cloth that was draped over his forearm before pouring a glass for each of us.

"And your annual report? Meeting went okay?"

"Yup. It went really well." A few days ago, but he didn't need to know that part.

Our glasses were filled halfway. We gave them a quick swirl by the stem before picking them up and clanking. "Cheers," we said in unison with a look of celebratory affection.

"Shall we read the menu before I open this?" I asked, glancing at the gift.

"How 'bout we start with what you got me first?" he winked, implying that what he bought would be the bigger surprise.

"Only if you're ready to be blown away," I declared with casual confidence.

"I don't know," he replied with even greater confidence. "Pretty sure you'll be floored by what's in front of you."

"Then I guess we'll just have to wait and see," I said, picking it up to stake my claim.

As I was about to run my nail across the tape along the fold at the back, he placed his hand on my arm. "I need to warn you," he said, looking into my eyes. "My curiosity got the best of me. I came across something while snooping. This is just one of two surprises."

"I see," I replied, having slowed down my unwrapping. What had he come up with this time? "And just so I'm prepared. Where might this rank on the sentimental scale?" Nick took it upon himself to awaken that part of me, which he politely referred to as dormant rather than deficient. Though I may never attain his level, his mission was more successful than he realized.

"It's pretty high up there," he grinned, pleased with himself.

I removed the lid from the box and set it to the side, then opened the two folds of white tissue paper that were joined at the center. My jaw dropped the moment I saw the photograph. I had no words. Nick looked at me, smiling, waiting for me to speak. I couldn't. I was too stunned.

"Do you like it? I had to have it doctored a bit so it would look good in that frame."

He had the edges burned and the image tinted like an antique portrait. Set against a cream-colored mat, he had placed it in a vintage oval frame.

"How Nick?" I cried. "Where did you find this?" I couldn't believe my eyes. I was actually staring at a photograph of my parents on their wedding day. Never had I seen one before. They were dressed like royalty heading to a glamorous ball.

"That's my next surprise."

"Okay...give me a minute." I needed to catch my breath and just admire it for a while.

He got up to stand behind me, rested his hands on my shoulders and whispered into my ear. "Can't believe how much you look like her, Jen. She was stunning."

"She really was." And so young. But sadly, she felt like a stranger to me. Just a part of my DNA. Dad on the other hand, was a real shocker. "I can't believe he's in a tux! And look at his hair. So much of it. And it's groomed!" I almost laugh-cried imagining him suffering through a ceremony looking like that.

The waiter arrived to share the daily specials. His interruption felt disruptive and yet welcome. I needed to pull myself together to focus on food. Relieved that the lobster and shrimp fondue was still on the appetizer menu, we didn't hesitate to order it. We had been drooling just thinking about it since making our reservation a few weeks ago. As for the entree, I was tossing between the crab-stuffed ravioli or the seared Atlantic salmon. The dilemma was solved by ordering each so we could share.

"Well, true to form, you got me something precious. Again. I don't know how you do it, Nick Vincent."

"It's to keep you coming back for more," he winked.

"Oh, you're never getting rid of me, honey." I smiled and sipped more wine, having fully regained my composure. "So dare I ask what else you have for me?"

"Ah. Yes," he said, reaching for a piece of paper from his lapel pocket. "So…you know how I've been doing internet searches to update my lecture material?"

"Yup."

"Well, I may have used some of my library computer time to run a search on…are you ready? Mr. Jorge Vasquez."

This was not at all where I thought our conversation would be headed. In fact, I was happy to have deleted that name from my mind. I looked at the folded paper in his hand with trepidation. "Okay? Do I want to know what you found?" To be honest, I wasn't so sure that I did.

"You're never gonna believe this."

"And you're not gonna make me guess. I have no idea where you're going with this."

"Well, imagine me scrolling down. Scrolling, scrolling to see what I could find, and then suddenly I land on a pic of your parents' wedding." His look of shock was no doubt intended to mimic his reaction at the time. And he was probably waiting for me to do the same.

"You found my parents' wedding picture on the internet? While searching for Jorge Vasquez?" This seemed inexplicable, and very creepy.

"Believe it or not, their wedding was referenced in a heading of the 1962 Post-Gazette. So I had to check to see if I could find more info. If there was anything, it would be in the microfilm. The projector was vacant, so I sat for over an hour and half and went through images of pages till I finally landed on it. Not only did I find the wedding announcement, it had a picture. He unfolded the one he was holding and held it up for me to see. "This is it. I made a copy, had it cropped to isolate just your parents, then tinted it to create the one in the frame."

The photo I was looking at included another couple. She was standing beside Mom and he beside Dad. To my surprise, the guy looked vaguely familiar.

"Jen, this is Jorge Vasquez. He was your Dad's best man!" Nick smiled as though he had just won the lottery. Or the award for most clever sleuthing.

Meanwhile, I was now more stunned than I thought possible. Looking more closely, the gentlemen did look similar to my memory of the photo Detective Cisco had shown me at the police station. But why did I know nothing about him? Or even get introduced when he met Dad on that trip? Maybe I did and completely forgot?

Seeing that I was at a loss for words, Nick continued. "The minute I saw it, I thought you might wanna show your Dad. You haven't asked him about your trip yet, and since you don't have a copy of the picture the detective gave you, maybe this one would trigger his memory."

"It might," I agreed. "Or upset him." Such an overt reminder of Mom might seem a bit harsh to Dad.

"Yeah I considered that too. Anyway, I thought you'd find this cool."

"So where is this Jorge now?"

"Dead." Nick's disappointment was palpable. "Just a few months ago. Saw his obituary on the internet. He was a prominent attorney. I'm guessing he was working that old case the detective was looking into."

"That would make a lot of sense. Though how Dad could assist with the investigation still doesn't."

"Who knows what other photos he had in his file? He saw one of your Dad and maybe hoped he could help identify something. We'll never know."

The waiter returned with our appetizer. The smell was divine. We were both famished and wasted no time spearing the mouth-sized pieces of lobster then submerging them into this delectable creamy, gruyere-based lobster-bisque goodness before savoring a bite.

"Yum," I sounded before even beginning to chew. I felt the need to let the flavors permeate my taste buds before sending them down my throat. "This is so good."

We were silent while working our way through the remaining lobster, shrimp and crackers, soaking up every last drip of fondu as our spears dueled for those few morsels that had dislodged themselves.

"You know what I could do?" I said, while licking the last drop from the tip of my spear. "I could bring it to Dad and ask him who the other two people are. Pretty sure the woman is my aunt, Dawn. If that goes well, then I'll bring up our trip."

"Good idea." Nick then looked back at the picture with an air of surprise. "Is that really your Mom's sister?" There was no resemblance whatsoever. Dawn was much shorter, heavier with a thick head of ringlets and features that looked disproportionately small for her round face.

"I know right? I could be wrong. But I feel like I remember her from Mom's funeral. She seemed so gentle and concerned for me. Behind all her tears, that is."

"Ever think of reaching out to her?"

"No. I don't even know what we would talk about. Plus I have no idea if she's even alive."

"I can help with that," he smiled, eager for another internet search.

"You missed your calling, honey. You should've become a detective. But I'd prefer to just leave things be where Mom's family is concerned...Now, if you're desperate for another mystery to solve, knock yourself out finding Joe Rich. With a photo, please."

"I'm on it," he replied with a wink. "Do you think he's real?"

"Nope. But if he is, I'm sure you'll find him." I winked back.

That seemed like the perfect segue for my turn to present his gift. But not without putting him through the mandatory guessing game he liked to torment me with before letting me open one of his. "All right, honey. It's that time. Are you prepared to be shocked?"

"Okay. What did you get that's made you so smug?"

"Well...try your best to guess." As eager as I was to show him, there was no way he was bypassing the tedium he had put me through so many times before. "Good luck. The clock starts now."

By the time we had ended dessert, he had exhausted his guesses. And I realized in listening to them, that my prior gifts may have been generous, but somewhat short on sentimentality. An accessory for the office, or his car, or the house, or an item of clothing, or sports gear. Fortunately, I would be more than making up for all of it today.

"Okay I give up," he resigned.

I reached down into my tote bag and pulled out the gift-wrapped book and handed it to him. "Here you go, my love."

"Ah ha. A book. I should've known," he said, while taking it. "It's huge. So not a novel. Something non-fiction?"

"Just open it," I said, disinterested in another reminder of my penchant for all things cerebral.

"Wow," he said, seeing the gorgeous beach behind the title: Images of the Greek Isles. "This looks beautiful. Thank you, Jen." I waited, hoping he would open the cover, but instead he set it down and looked at me. "I can't wait to look through it with my feet up on the couch and a glass of wine. It's going to be spectacular."

"Or…" I added, because of my own impatience. "You could maybe open it for a quick peek right now?"

His reaction showed that he got the message. "Oh. Okay. Absolutely."

He picked it up and turned to somewhere in the middle. I was about to lose my mind, until the envelope containing the tickets slipped out just enough for him to notice. He pulled it out, flap side up, and opened it. His eyes grew wide with shock. Mission accomplished.

"Turn the envelope over," I instructed, knowing he hadn't seen what was inscribed on it.

"Jen." The look on his face became serious. "I don't know what to say. This is…unbelievable."

"I know right? And don't worry. I thought of everything.

The dates coincide with spring break."

His complexion reddened and his eyes became teary. I hadn't expected this emotional a reaction. Maybe I should've waited until we got home to give this to him. It was, after all, a drastic leap from anything he would have expected.

"Jen, I –"

"Are you amazed?"

"Yes. Completely," he sniffled, wiping a tear with his knuckle. "I'm just…not sure we can go." His look was serious. Too serious.

"What do you mean? Is it the girls? They'll be fine. Your sister is thrilled to come stay with them."

"It's not that."

"Then what is it, Nick? I don't understand."

"I didn't want to say anything. Not tonight. I was gonna wait till tomorrow. But I didn't expect you to do this incredible, extraordinary thing. God Jen, there's nothing I want more than to go on our honeymoon –"

"Nick, I swear, you're starting to scare me. Spit it out."

"The doctor called this morning. He wants to see me right away. I'm going in first thing tomorrow." His face dropped, knowing he had just thrust a dagger into my gut.

"Did he say anything else? Tell you what he wants to talk about?" I could feel my heart rate accelerating and tried not to sound worried, knowing what he needed from me was calm support and reassurance.

He was staring down. "Nothing. But Jen…" He looked up at me. "He wouldn't ask to see me if my results were normal."

"I'm going with you."

"That's not —"

"Yes it is. I'm in this with you. And damn it, Nick, I want another thirteen years. Then another after that. So we're not gonna panic. Everything will be fine. Do you hear me?"

"Okay," he exhaled.

"You get regular screenings so if the results aren't normal, whatever they show should be manageable. Let's just take it one step at a time, starting with the doctor tomorrow. As for the trip, don't worry about it. If – and that's still an if – we can't go during spring break, it can be postponed. But the minute we can, we're going." I squeezed his hands so hard, I thought I might cut off his circulation.

He smiled and took a long deep breath. "Thanks, Jen. For everything."

I wanted to burst into tears, scream at the top of my lungs, rip the pages of this damn book. Nick's family history was a reality we would always have to contend with. One that he thought was too unfair to subject me to. But I was in from the start. Come what may. So we made smart choices for diet and exercise. Ensured regular screenings out of prudence. Nick was the picture of health. The one who was going to defy the odds with endless normal results, so we could grow old together. I was certain of it. I had to believe it.

And as these thoughts raced through my mind, I saw the photo of my parents and thought, *My God, Dad, you lost her out of nowhere. Denied anything close to growing old together.*

CHAPTER ELEVEN

— 1972 —

S itting on a rock at water's edge, listening to the gentle lapping of waves as the sunlight danced over smooth ripples, Connor thought of the words he would use to describe this serene view to Heather. It had been so long, too long, since she had needed him to do just that. He had tried to while she was in hospital, wishing it might soothe her into awakening, even though he knew that the only interruption to her slumber would be the halting of her heartbeat. But he still hoped she could hear him. And that if she did, he was bringing her some measure of comfort.

He recalled that very first time she had asked. It was the moment that had sealed their relationship. Over the phone of all places. After the horrors of yet another beating at the hands of her father. She had been lying in bed, battered, bruised demoralized, and then thought of her sweet, gentle Conway. They had met only six months prior, by the lake, at life-guard training camp, where out of nowhere, he had rushed to her rescue and saved her from a vicious attack. The only person to have ever protected her. And now the kind soul who restored her faith that not all men were evil. They had spoken over the phone every few days since, but only when she was well. Each time, he was so kind, attentive and always made her laugh. Then, in the aftermath of that particular altercation, she chose not to suffer in silence as she had done each time before. Instead, she picked up the receiver by her bedside and called her Conway, entrusting him with her dark secret; making him her confidant. He wanted to rush to her side, call the police or swing a baseball bat, full force across Anthony Delano's head. But she urged him not to, and said that all she needed was calm. *Describe the forest to me, Conway. Then a sunset, and a campfire.* So he did as she asked, for as long as she needed, until her breathing slowed and the horrors of what she had just endured slowly faded from her mind as sleep took hold; just like a child lulled by a bedtime story.

His thoughts were interrupted by the spinning of the reel. Jenny had just cast her fishing rod from a few feet away, barefoot, pants rolled up, her tongue sticking out as she concentrated. With every attempt, she narrated her self-evaluation to his amusement: *Nope, released my index too quick. That was better, but my motion wasn't fluid enough. Ooh, that was a good one.* And on and on she went, having practiced over five-hundred times since receiving the pole last week. She was nothing if not persistent. Which was convenient, since they had exhausted all their food supplies.

She insisted on one final catch before they left. And he was more than happy to prolong their time in this hidden lakeside gem, nestled within dense foliage. They had spent the last three days there. Three days with nothing but tranquility and nature; not another human being in sight. And now that they had mastered life off the beaten path, courtesy of Everything You

Need to Know About Camping, they wanted for nothing. The size of an encyclopedia, it had been purchased at her insistence once she completed the Winnebago manual. And it was paying off quickly. Quietly Jenny absorbed the facts, pleased to put her skills to use whenever the situation called for them.

If it was up to Connor, he would stay there forever. Seeing how easily Jenny acclimatized to this lifestyle, it was tempting to give up life in the city all together. Homesteading seemed so alluring. *I bet if I got her the guide book, we'd be set,* he mused. But Jenny would grow up, need an education, her own life, and in the more immediate term, a pair of shoes that actually fit.

"Dad, is the fire just right? I'm gonna catch one soon. I can feel it." She needed their campfire to be down to embers – so said her book – in order for the fish to cook just right.

"Yes ma'am. And I've got the fish net in my hand," he replied, as instructed. *Watch her become a survivalist one day,* he chuckled.

"Oh and you're letting me filet this one by myself right?"

"Yes I am."

"But I'll let you cut off the head."

"I think a real angler would leave it on," he teased.

"Yuck no. I can't eat it if it's staring at me," she smirked, while side-arming her next cast.

With a swift kick of dirt to smother the last of the flames, Connor and Jenny had packed up the motorhome and were ready to head into town. In truth, neither wanted to leave. As with so many other stops along their journey, they wondered whether they would ever see this place again. But Connor reassured her that there was still plenty more for them to discover. Until then, they took one last look to try to commit the image to memory.

Once they reached the highway, and Jenny had settled on a radio station, his mind began to wander to a place it had been resisting all day. The trial. In a court of law, miles and miles away from them, Jenny's grandfather was finally facing a grand jury after months of detention. And as far as Connor was concerned, this fact was one his Jenny would never ever need to know. He would make it his mission to shield her from both her mother's tragedy and her grandfather's aggression no matter what it would take.

* * *

"George! What the hell? This is the third time I dialed," accused Connor, expecting him to be at the ready for their 4pm call. He had timed their travel specifically to be at a payphone for their chat.

"Sorry Con," George replied, out of breath. "We only got started at 1pm. I had to scramble to make our call."

"Another delay?"

"Prison doctor keeps saying Delano's failing his medical exam. The judge got fed up and gave us an ultimatum on whether he was fit enough to stand trial. She was a hard-ass at the bail hearing. Pretty sure she suspects he's faking. The defense insisted he was okay. Finally got the go-ahead after a three hour wait. He looks like total shit, by the way. If it's only an act, he's convincing."

"With him, it could be. Or prison life is killing him,"

hoped Connor.

"He looked even worse after hearing the opening statements. The prosecution are painting him as a hostile, physical aggressor. He went pale and looked like he was about to collapse."

"So this is good, right?"

"Yeah, so long as they can prove it. Not sure if they have enough evidence to convince a jury."

"What do you mean not enough? She's lying in a coma for God's sake!"

"And if she could come in and testify, things would be completely different. Without her testimony, the evidence will be refuted as circumstantial. It helps Delano a lot that there's no official record of prior abuse."

"What about Dawn? She knows he's an abuser."

"She's been holed up in her bedroom since the incident. You should hear her shrieking from the hallway. It's hair-raising. Her maid said that's how she sounds when her meds wear off. There's no way she's stable enough for the witness stand."

"So now what?"

"The prosecution has listed his brother as a character witness. But he needs to survive cross-examination, and it looks like they have enough to discredit him. Plus the defense team has a much bigger slate of character witnesses. Most of them were at the gala and will say Delano is nothing but charming and cordial."

"Does that mean his brother is no longer a threat to Eleanor's succession? Will she go back to her original statement?"

"She's pretty much lost all her family at this point. And their glowing reputation is in the toilet. She won't risk losing her fortune, even if it's a complete longshot."

"Damn it, George. Is he really gonna get away with this?"

"I have an idea. You may not like it. But hear me out okay?"

"What is it?"

"You come in and testify –"

"No way!"

"Hear me out, Con. You're the one who can not only speak to the history of abuse she shared with you, but how he was kept from your daughter her entire life because he posed such a threat to her safety. That's powerful."

"And you just said it. He poses a threat. I'm not putting Jenny anywhere near him. Period."

"Leave her with your parents. They're hours away. She won't need to know anything about this."

"George, no! Eleanor will figure out where she is, and God knows what she'll do."

"There's nothing she can do, Con."

Connor wasn't willing to divulge what Eleanor knew and what she was threatening to do with that knowledge. But he needed for George to understand what she was capable of. "Knowing her, she'll accuse me of kidnapping my kid to deflect attention."

"You're her parent, Con. Kidnapping doesn't apply."

"She falsified mine and Heather's birth records, George. She would be perfectly capable of doing the same with Jenny's."

"And what, Con? Change the name of her father? Look, I get that you're paranoid. But trust me, Eleanor has much bigger preoccupations at the moment. Disrupting Jenny's life sure as hell isn't one of them."

"Fine. But I'm still not testifying. Find another way, George. One that doesn't involve me and Jenny being anywhere near there."

"There's another possibility. But it's extreme, Con."

"George, I literally escaped with my child with no plan to return. Is that extreme enough for you?"

"Alright, I get it," he paused. "Con, what are the chances of Heather waking from her coma?"

"None. She's brain-dead."

"You know that, Eleanor knows that. The doctors do too, and yet they won't declare it officially. I saw the hospital records. They exclude any reference to life-support."

"Okay? How does that matter?"

"So long as there's a possibility Heather will survive, the charge against Delano is attempted murder, at most. That changes if she's declared brain-dead because the line between that and actually dead is super thin. So we'd be talking first degree murder. With a much more severe penalty."

"So they're paying the doctors to lie? Jesus, these people won't stop at anything."

"It's more of a bribery. Eleanor is dangling a massive donation to fund a new shiny cardiac institute."

"She has one daughter in palliative care, another in mental breakdown, and a husband in jail but she's focused on a new project? Get to the point, George. Not sure how much more of this I can take right now."

"She's got the hospital thinking that it's between them and

another one for her donation. Whoever makes the better case will be rewarded. Massachusetts General's case is tied to holding off on changing Heather's records until after the verdict. Eleanor wants it to be a grand announcement. If he's acquitted, they get to say it was one big mistake, here, look at our big donation. And if he's indicted, they will say he feels remorseful and the donation is their way of restoring the Delano name as synonymous with community support."

"Jesus, these people," Connor sighed. "How do you even know this, George?"

"Well, you asked me to get you intel. And Eleanor gets very chatty when she drinks. I'm trying to be a shoulder for her to lean on. Seems to be working."

"Be careful, George. She could just as easily be playing you."

"She's incriminating herself, Con. She literally said there's nothing like philanthropy to mask a crime."

"Okay so what's your extreme idea?"

George hesitated before saying, "You issue a directive for the doctors to terminate life-support. You have power of attorney and I can get you the paperwork."

"No, George. Not that. I can't do it."

George felt horrible for even suggesting it. "I understand, Con," he replied. "Look, I'm sorry. I'll find another way. I promise."

"Please George. I'm counting on you."

"You have my word, Con. Whatever it takes." Now if only he could come up with an idea. In the meantime, a change of subject was in order before ending their call. "By the way, how long before you need cash?"

"Two weeks, tops. Can you get it?"

"Yup. Where do you think you'll be by then? I mean, can you at least tell me the state so I can arrange delivery?"

"California. Assume northern. Won't know where exactly until sometime next week. Can you work with that?"

"I'll make it work, Con."

"Okay good. Is that it? I've left Jenny for too long."

"Just curious, Con. Are you really not planning on ever returning?" The thought of never seeing Connor again felt gut-wrenching.

"I don't know, George. I just can't. Not while he's alive."

"Okay I get it. We'll find a way, Con. I promise. Just don't despair, okay? The day will come when their money can't buy power, and their luck runs out. And when that day comes, they won't know what hit them." *There had better be a way,* thought George. He couldn't fathom a life without Connor.

CHAPTER TWELVE

— 2003 —

"Okay, Vasquez. What is it that I'm supposed to find?"

Cisco laid out the pages contained in the newly acquired Delano envelope across the vacant second mattress of his lackluster motel room. This unexpected treasure, entrusted to him by Fern, filled the entire surface in a quilt-like pattern. *Is this even the right order?* he wondered. However they were compiled originally was unknown; his altercation with her at his car window caused them to scatter. The best he could do was to sort them by date, and infer where those without one should be placed.

He stood at the foot of the bed, arms folded, hoping the bird's-eye view would make one stand out; a title, an image, a name, even a word more glaring than the others. Clarity as to why Jorge Vasquez had held onto them all this time. It had to be deliberate, he reasoned. Perhaps it hinted to the motive for murder that his confession letter otherwise failed to reveal; a motive so strong, it compelled him to take such extreme measures. Better still, the rationale for why any of this mattered thirty years later. The burning question to Cisco was: who had what to gain from revealing this now?

Failing to gauge their relevance at a glance, he gathered them up, sat on the edge of the bed and read each one individually again, trying to glean the key themes. Most, but not all, were tied to some facet of the litigation for Anthony Delano's trial. So he began by sorting them into piles. The notes on defense tactics were separated by charge. In the case of Heather Delano, he created three piles: aggravated assault, attempted murder, and murder in the first degree. Another pile contained all material pertaining to his brother, Michael Delano, including his lawsuit against Anthony claiming fraud that led to his wrongful conviction years prior, the draft denial of those allegations, a lengthy character assassination, and what appeared to be an excerpt from Delano Enterprise bylaws that outlined reasons for disqualification of business succession: conviction of fraud, felony or crime. In reviewing this material, Cisco surmised that after the death of Michael Delano Sr., founder of Delano Enterprises, the business should have been transferred to his eldest son, Michael Jr., but his prior fraud conviction cost him that title, which instead went to Anthony. Michael's defence attorneys had argued that he was set-up by Anthony who stood to profit from his incarceration, but the burden of proof proved unsuccessful. Having served his time, and with Anthony facing far more serious legal woes, Michael had resurfaced demanding his rightful seat as head of the enterprise. Cisco thought for moment. Michael had been referenced in Vasquez's confession letter. *Could a member of Michael's lineage be seeking their dues?* Money was always a big motivator. Especially when dealing with the very rich. *They may think they were entitled to it had*

Anthony been convicted.

Other pages included reference to the Delano donation to Massachusetts General Hospital, a copy of the invitation to the gala event where the incident took place, Jorge Vasquez's original employment contract, the list of jurors for Delano's trial, newspaper clippings of the incident, and a variety of business contracts, some typed, some hand-written. It was a veritable cornucopia of documents that appeared more random and unintentional the more Cisco reviewed them. But not a single one was from after Delano's death.

Cisco stood up and taped a blank sheet of letter-sized paper onto a bare wall. Since he thought better while standing, he positioned it at eye level. His best investigating was done when he paced, especially while clicking the retractable plunge of his pen. With no colleagues around for him to annoy, he could roam and click to his heart's content. *Okay, so how do I split this up?* He paced a few more minutes then stopped to face the sheet while running through what he considered to be the most pertinent input to capture. He then wrote three words across the top: convicted, acquitted, deceased. His plan was to populate each column with the names of the parties who stood to benefit or lose from either outcome. If Vasquez had an accomplice or was acting on someone's behalf, this might help narrow down the prospects.

Before he began, his Motorola cellphone rang. "Cisco," he replied curtly.

"Detective Cisco, this is June. I have the information you requested."

"Great." So focused on these documents, he had almost forgotten he had asked her for intel on Brandon Wong as soon as he left Fern. "Let me grab my notepad." He walked over to the desk by the window, pulled it from his briefcase and sat down. "Okay. What have you got?"

"Nothing suspect," she began. "Brandon Wong, fifty-one, sales rep for Dell. No spouse, no kids. Travels once or twice monthly, always domestic. Last flight was to JFK three days ago so he's in town. Goes into the office on the lower east side most Mondays, otherwise works from home. I'll send you both addresses when we hang up. No priors. Bank records are clean."

"Okay got it. Anything else I should know?" Cisco replied as he jotted down notes.

"Nothing."

"Thanks June. That's all I need for now." He hung up and waited for the addresses to appear on his cellphone display, then transcribed them onto his page.

"Okay, Mr. Wong. Seems I shall be paying you a visit tomorrow. For now, let's see what else I can decipher from these documents."

He walked back to his chart and began with the conviction column. It seemed to Cisco, that Michael would have the most to gain, assuming he had a legitimate case to win back the business, and that it would be heard, and then won. Three really big ifs. Anthony had the most to lose, followed by Eleanor should Michael succeed in claiming the business. Not to mention the reputational damage to her family, which would also impact Dawn whose name he added too. He wrote *business partners* followed by a question mark. As for Vasquez, he wasn't certain. Would a conviction have benefited or hurt him?

He then moved to the acquittal column. The material suggested possible jury tampering so Vasquez may have assumed Delano would be released. Anthony was obviously the one to gain the most from his freedom. Similarly Eleanor. His legal team, including Vasquez, would get a big win and associated compensation. Business partners would pursue engagements per usual. Everything would go back to normal, barring of course, the grief over Heather's tragedy. *So did Anthony pose a threat to someone? Vasquez? Could he have blackmailed him? With what?* None of the documents referenced Vasquez other than his employment contract. *Or did Vasquez get wind of something criminal Delano was involved in and was worried about being implicated somehow? Was Delano blackmailing someone close to Vasquez?*

Cisco scratched his head then moved to the last column. *Who gained from Anthony dying?* Financially, Eleanor as successor to the estate. Possibly anyone who may have been threatened by him. And possibly business partners if an unfinished arrangement had fallen through. But most of them would have to be dead by now. *So what stays relevant thirty years later? It has to be tied to the survivors and the money.*

Cisco dialed June. She picked up on the second ring. "June, I need you to find out what transpired after Eleanor Delano inherited Anthony's estate. And find out what became of Dawn Delano. Also, look into Michael Delano, specifically his kids and what they've been up to."

"Okay," she replied. "Anything specific you're looking for?"

"Start with the money. I wanna see where the trail ends. Thanks." He pressed the end-call key, then resumed his pacing. "Money," he said out loud. "It's got to be the money."

* * *

The following morning, Cisco arrived at Brandon Wong's address, a flat in the heart of midtown Manhattan. Take-out coffee in hand, he walked several blocks through the bustle and sunshine of a crisp fall day.

"Dell business is good," he said to himself as he walked up the steps to reach the doorbell. He had always been curious to see the inside of one of these stone townhomes so often featured in New York-based films.

An Asian, middle-aged man answered the door. Fit, well-groomed and sporting a stylish button-down shirt with fitted jeans, he asked, "May I help you?"

"Brandon Wong?"

"Yes. And you are?" Wong asked with a sway, his voice somewhat nasally.

"I'm Detective Cisco, sir." Raised his badge, he immediately detected what it was about Wong's diction that had raised Fern's suspicions. "Might I have a word with you? It concerns Jorge Vasquez. George as you might know him."

Brandon's pale complexion went flush. His expression intimated discomfort. "George is dead. If it's all the same with you, I'd rather let him rest in peace."

Cisco considered offering his condolences, but held back since he wasn't supposed to know Wong and Vasquez were in a relationship. "Yes. I'm sorry. I mean no disrespect, Mr. Wong. But there is a matter under investigation. And I have reason to believe you might be in a position to shed light on some recent findings."

Wong hesitated for a few moments, then said, "Alright, but I'm working. I don't have much time." He then opened the door further and gestured for Cisco to enter.

"This shouldn't take long," assured Cisco, as he followed Wong into the kitchen, glancing all around to see if a photograph of Vasquez may be on display. He saw none.

"If you don't mind, I was making myself a caffeinated beverage. I see you have one, but I'd be happy to make you another," offered Brandon Wong, as he walked toward the barista-style espresso machine on the counter.

Used to a simple drip brew, Cisco had only seen devices of this scale in specialty coffee shops. "No. No thank you. I'm fine," he replied, taking a seat at the dining table then pulling out his notepad.

He noticed how Brandon Wong's flat was pristine, his taste impeccable. From what he could tell, most of it seemed renovated within the past few years.

Wong sat down across from Cisco, cupping his glass mug with both hands, while swaying his shoulders ever so slightly. When Cisco looked down at it, he declared, "It's a macchiato. I'm all yours now, Detective."

Cisco noticed how quickly Wong had regained his composure. Oddly, in fact. He even smiled, faintly, his eyes firmly on Cisco's through thick-rimmed designer blue frames. "Thank you, Mr. Wong. Okay let's get started." He looked up. "Can you tell me how long you knew Jorge Vasquez?"

"Let's call him George, shall we?" Wong released one hand from his mug to motion gracefully as he spoke. "And the answer is…" He placed his index over his lips as he thought. "Over twenty years."

"And how did you meet?" Cisco maintained a serious, unaffected tone.

Wong paused. "At an NA meeting here in New York in 1981."

"As in narcotics anonymous?"

"Correct." Wong looked as though he was anticipating a judgmental reaction. None was offered.

Interesting how that tidbit never made its way into Vasquez's document assortment, thought Cisco. "And to your knowledge, did Mr., I mean George, struggle with drugs since that time?"

"After being in and out of rehab for nine years, I am pleased to report he became clean as a whistle after our fateful meeting. Both of us did. Probably wouldn't have had we not met."

"How is that?" Cisco was intrigued.

"When you put a group of broken people into a room where it's safe to divulge their weaknesses, their vulnerabilities, a connection can build that is unlike any other. George and I had that. Started from the first meeting we were both at. We chatted well into the night and quickly became each other's sounding-board, then support-system then cheer-leader. Before we knew it, we were both encouraging each other to get back on our feet."

"And how did he do that exactly?" Cisco needed to reconcile the addict in rehab turned prominent defense attorney.

"He was certain he'd never be able to practice law again. Wasn't even going to try. But I felt he was passing up a chance to make a real difference," explained Wong. "It was my idea for him to start with the low hanging fruit, defending other addicts. It's not like attorneys were lining up to take those cases. It started with minor misdemeanors, then felonies and before he knew it, he was establishing himself as a criminal defense attorney. Back to his original roots. I was so proud." He wiggled with delight.

"That's quite a success story," said Cisco, surprised to be learning this side of Vasquez. "Would it be fair to say that George owed you his career?"

"Oh gosh no," he said with a swoosh of his arm. "No more than I owed him mine. We just found a way to believe in each other when we had otherwise given up on believing in ourselves."

Nicely put, thought Cisco. "Mr. Wong, since you clearly understood George's vulnerabilities, could you tell me what it was that caused his addiction in the first place?"

"Now you're getting to the ugly stuff, Detective Cisco. We don't like going there at all. But what I recently discovered – the hard way, might I add – is that it had to do with a case he was involved in early in his career. Twisted drama, tragedy, grand jury, the whole shebang. And it sent him reeling."

Cisco dug into his briefcase and removed the now-unsealed envelope he had received from Fern. He showed the cover with *Delano files* inscribed on it to Brandon Wong. "Mr. Wong, does this look familiar to you?"

Brandon Wong flung from his chair and turned his back toward Cisco. "Oh my God! I can't believe you have that! That was such a mistake!"

"Mr. Wong, what can tell me about the contents?"

He kept his back to Cisco, holding his hands over his face. "Nothing. I never opened it."

"Then what is it that's upsetting you?"

"It was never meant to be sent to his office. I screwed up. It was an honest mistake. I apologized to George. Profusely." Brandon Wong turned toward Cisco in despair. "But he was so upset with me. Refused to let me do anything. He insisted he would get it back himself. And I was certain he did." He shook his head back and forth, then looked up. "Clearly he didn't."

"And do you know why George was so upset about it?"

"Detective, recovery from substance abuse is a lifelong process. No matter how long an addict stays clean, there's no guarantee they won't get triggered again. What you're holding references the case that triggered George's addiction. Something he kept for his own very personal reasons. But I had never heard him mention the name Delano. Ever. It was among the things he kept private. If I had known, I would never have sent it to his office. But I saw an envelope with the word *file* on it, while he was packing up his apartment after being diagnosed with cancer, so I added it to a box of items going to his office. I found out my mistake when he tore a strip off of me after his secretary called him to ask what she was supposed to do with it. I literally threw his trigger right in his face while he was dying.

I felt horrible." Brandon Wong's eye reddened. He pursed his lips and tried to stop his chin from quivering.

"Mr. Wong, from what you've told me, you were George's biggest supporter. Your mistake was an honest one. I'm sure he understood."

"Tell that to the pile of boxes cluttering my basement. I'm afraid his spirit will haunt me if I dare get rid of anything."

"You mentioned that George kept certain things private. Can you elaborate on what those might be?"

"Well us, for one. God forbid anyone should know we were together. As if it wasn't obvious. But he insisted it was best that we keep separate addresses and only one name on each lease. Never appeared at social events together. We had to be one big fat secret."

"That must have been difficult."

"You have no idea. At least it was for me. George never seemed to struggle with it. I guess he was better at denial. Or he had other reasons."

"What might those be?"

"If you were in a relationship with someone and she insisted on separate living arrangements for over twenty years, might you become suspicious?"

"I guess that would depend on the nature of our relationship. If it was intimate and we were committed to each other, then yes, I would expect that we would build one life together."

"We loved each other. We were committed to each other. We were exclusive. That much we shared. And we built our lives in this home. Mostly. If George just wanted to hold an address because of the optics, I would understand. But he would stay there. At first, only when I was traveling on business. But during the last five years, it became more often, almost weekly, sometimes more."

"Did he say why?"

"He'd say he was working late and it was less of a commute. Which was true. But it seemed like more. Like he was hiding something."

"Did you confront him?"

"Yes. In the heat of the moment I even accused him of having an affair."

"And how did he respond?"

"He denied it. Then apologized for making me even suspect that. He then explained there was a part of his past that was still troubling him. And that he just needed time alone to work through it."

"And then what?"

"I had no choice but to accept it. He wasn't doing drugs. That much I could tell. And he said he promised he wasn't having an affair. Eventually, I assumed he was pining over someone."

"What would make you assume that?"

"I always suspected there was someone special to him before we met. Always had a gut feeling about it. He was, after all, thirty-five by then."

"But he never mentioned anyone?"

"Never. He kept it secret."

"But you're certain there was someone."

"Well I am now."

"I don't follow."

"There were a few things he never got around to packing up by the time he was admitted to the hospital for good. So I went to his apartment to make sure it was empty before letting the landlord sign a lease with a new tenant."

"And you found something?"

"A shoe box. Under his bed, way at the back. Covered in dust. Filled with photographs of some guy and this young girl. Tons of them. By a lake, in the forest."

Cisco's curiosity was piqued. "Was this someone you had seen in pictures before?"

"Nope. Had no idea who the guy was. Nor the kid. And they weren't identified. So I closed it and looked under other furniture, the closet and all the drawers. That's when I found the one in his nightstand." Brandon Wong paused to bite his lip. He was visibly upset. "Just as I suspected. A special someone. Together in a picture with him. And that one had a name on it. Connor."

"Really…" *This just got interesting.*

"I was fuming. I still hadn't gotten over how angry he had been with me about the file I sent to the office. So I brought the picture to the hospital to show him." He looked at Cisco, "Petty I know, but I, too, was under duress. And there was a sealed envelope under it marked *private and confidential,* so I brought that too. I wasn't going to live without knowing the truth. That much he owed me."

He read the confession? And isn't batting an eye? "And what did he say?"

"Keep in mind he wasn't all that well when he had reamed me out, but that didn't stop him. He was worse once he was at the hospital. Weak, but still completely lucid. Lucid enough to answer my question."

"And?"

"I marched into his hospital room. Made sure he was awake, fed, and his doctor had completed her rounds. I didn't want to be interrupted. Then told him I had a very important question and needed him to promise me he would give me an honest answer. He said he promised. So I took out the picture and asked him who the hell Connor was." Brandon Wong then paused.

"Then what?"

"He burst into tears. Sobbing like a child. I was in complete shock. I had never seen him George cry before. He was the only unemotional Latino I had ever met. Go figure. It was as if I had opened the floodgates. He was inconsolable. So I held him, cradled him in my arms and swayed until he calmed down. It took a while, but eventually he did."

"Did he say anything?"

"Once he was able to, I asked him again. Only this time, I used a more gentle tone. Who is he, I asked him." Brandon Wong held his hands to his heart. "His response broke my heart. He said, *my Connor*, in his labored voice. *My very best friend. I failed him, Brandon. He never forgave me.* I was tempted to ask more, trust me. But that level of emotion was more than I could handle."

"What about the envelope? Did you show him?"

"Yes. Then I asked if he wanted me to find Connor to give

it to him. He said it wasn't for Connor. That if I absolutely wanted to, I could read it, but only after he died. Then I could do whatever I wanted with it."

"So you read it?"

"I wasn't going to. Didn't care about it anymore. But then it started to eat away at me. So I did."

Cisco found it odd that he had no reaction to it. "Then you sent it to the police station?"

"What? No! Why would I do that? It had no business going to a police station."

"What business did it have?"

"It was deeply personal and concerned a matter that only one person had the right to know about. So I searched for her. And once I found her, I gave her the letter along with the photo it had been kept with."

"Might I ask who it was that you gave it to?"

"Her name is Dawn Delano. I presume from the file you brought along that you know who that is."

"I do," replied Cisco, rubbing his forehead, while wondering whether she had been the one to send them the letter or if it had passed through more hands first. He flipped through his notes to check for a question he had written down earlier. "One more thing Mr. Wong. Whatever happened to the shoe box of photos?"

"It's in the basement."

"Would you mind if I had a look?"

"Be my guest. I'll go get it for you," said Wong before walking toward a door that opened onto a lower staircase.

While he did that, Cisco wondered. *How did Vasquez fail*

Rivers? By murdering Delano? Did Rivers have something to lose because of it?

Brandon Wong reappeared, box in hand, wiping some of the remaining dust off the top. "Here you go."

Cisco opened the lid. The box was filled with dozens of photographs that had clearly been taken around the same time as the one of Connor Rivers and Jorge Vasquez. He noticed how in not one single picture were Connor Rivers or Jennifer Vincent posing. *They had no idea they were being photographed,* he deduced. "Mr. Wong, would you mind if I took these with me? Unless of course you have reason to hold onto them."

"None whatsoever. They're yours, Detective."

"Thank you, Mr. Wong," said Cisco, while standing up. "Before I leave you, I have to ask. I understand George donated his estate to charities. Did it bother you that he didn't leave you any inheritance?"

"I wanted George, Detective Cisco. Not his money. I earn a good living, as you can see." He gestured toward the furnishings in his house.

"Of course. I didn't mean to imply otherwise." Preferring to change the topic, Cisco asked, "Is there anything else you think I should know about George?"

"He was one of the most giving people I ever met. But also, among the most troubled. For as long as I knew him, I believed it was his brother that had been his greatest loss. He was only six when he died, from an illness his parents hoped could be cured in the US. It was the reason they had migrated from Mexico. But it turns out that it took a confrontation while he was on the brink of death to learn he had been carrying all his guilt for a friend he had failed. It pains me to know he lived with that. And that he didn't think I could help him through it."

"Perhaps he worried he might fail you too?"

"I suppose. I can be handful," he jested.

Wishing to end their session on a kinder tone, Cisco said, "Mr. Wong, I know there are many who feel strongly about who it is we're allowed to love. But for what it's worth, I'm not among those who judge."

Welcoming the acceptance, Brandon Wong replied, "Then I shall let my flamboyant-self walk you to the door."

"Thank you," he replied. Before stepping outside, Cisco added one more thing. "And Mr. Wong, I'm deeply sorry for your loss."

CHAPTER THIRTEEN

— 1962 —

"**H**ave you completely lost your mind?" cried George in defiance upon learning of Connor's plan to wed Heather. They were sitting on the floor, backs leaned up against George's bed, listening to the newly released The Jazz Soul of Little Stevie album playing on his turntable. A self-proclaimed music afficionado, George had insisted Connor rush over the moment he got home with the latest addition to his growing vinyl collection. They were three songs in when Connor blurted out that he and Heather were getting married.

"Look. I know it seems…quick, but it's meant to be," replied Connor as he attempted his best show of confidence for this life-changing decision.

"Quick? We're sixteen for God's sake! You've barely explored what's out there. Just go move in together!" George shouted, appalled by the idea of Connor settling down this soon.

"It's not an option." Connor had expected that suggestion and already thought of what he would respond. "Her parents are way too Catholic, remember?"

"Yeah. Real Catholic," George said dryly, in reference to the one parent he learned recently was far from the picture of piety. "There has to be another way to get her out of there." He paused while thinking. "Can't she go away to a design school or something? Somewhere far enough that he can't get near her?"

"George, it's complicated. I just need you to trust me on this. Please. Can you do that?" The fact that George was even referencing Heather's abuse worried Connor. He had shared it in confidence, in a moment of weakness, and had been worried ever since that George might slip up even though he vowed he would never tell a soul.

George questioned whether it was Connor who objected to the notion of Heather leaving. His obsession with her was clearly clouding his judgement. "Con, for Christ sake, you're asking me to be supportive of your marriage into a family that has way too much power and… and a serious violent streak! I know you need to get her out of there, but how the hell is this the only option?" George buried his hands in his hair. "And what about your parents? Do they even know?"

"Yes, of course they do," replied Connor, weighed down by their disappointment. "They're not thrilled. But they're supportive. Something I need you to be."

"They're supportive? Really? How is that even possible?"

Connor didn't want to have to give George the real reason for the emergency nuptials. It was hard enough to trust him with one secret, he felt another would be too much for George to contain; discretion was not his strong suit. But the more the conversation went on, the more adamant George became about changing Connor's mind.

"I'm not letting you go through with it!" George bolted

upright up and stared down at Connor. "You're my best friend, damn it. I'm not gonna stand by and watch you throw your life away. Sorry Con, but if you go ahead with this, we're done." George threw his hands in the air before turning away. And it nearly crippled him with anguish to have made such a declaration.

George's words pierced right through Connor's core. He had expected a strong reaction, a challenge, an argument. But not an ultimatum. Even for George, this was excessive. And as trying as George could be, as impossible as he was to trust, as judgemental as he was about Connor's choices, he was always by his side. Always. The thought of losing him had never crossed his mind. But Connor had no other option. He had to marry Heather. That he knew. So he tried to put himself in George's shoes. Tried to imagine how he would react if the tables were turned. That's when he realized there was only one way to get George onboard. Which meant bracing himself for an even bigger reaction.

"I got her pregnant." Connor's gaze lowered as his hands rubbed his thighs. He regretted saying it almost immediately.

George swung around to face Connor, then froze. "Jesus, Con." His shock was paralyzing. "I…I don't know what to say."

Connor looked up. "Say nothing. To no one."

"Okay, but," George hesitated. "She wants to keep it?"

"Catholic," reminded Connor.

"And…you're okay with that? This is big, Con."

"Yes. And don't ask me that again."

George sat back down, facing him, legs crossed, filled with worry. "Her father's gonna kill you. You're a dead man."

"He doesn't know. Only her mother does. And she's keeping it from him. Wants a quick wedding so we can announce our 'honeymoon pregnancy' afterwards," he said with air quotes.

"Do your parents know?"

"Yes. They were shocked. Not too happy with me. But I told them I wanted to do the responsible thing. That's the only reason they're being supportive."

"And what about her father? He isn't suspicious about why she's in such a hurry to get married? I mean, don't these people plan year-long engagements with all the fanfare that goes with it?"

"Her mother has dealt with him. Heather says she sold him on the idea of making the wedding a big affair. You know, so he can invite all his elite business partners. They'll use the event to help secure some big contracts he's working on."

"Selfish pig," George uttered with disgust.

"Which is why he can't be near Heather. Or our child."

George flinched at the mention of *our child*. Heather had already had an impact on their friendship; pulling Connor farther and farther away. How much less time would Connor have for him once he was knee-deep in diapers? "How are you two gonna even manage on your own?"

"I'll find a job. And…" Connor hesitated to reveal the rest. "Her mother will help with money till we're on our feet. "

"That sounds dangerous, Con. They'll have a hold on you."

Connor shared George's concern. "I know. I don't like it either. But her mother says if that's all Heather will allow her to do for her grandchild, then she has to accept the money. Neither of them will ever meet the baby though. Heather made that a firm condition of our marriage."

Shit. He's leaving, thought George. "So where will you go?"

"Not sure, but won't be far. That was her mother's condition."

George was relieved, and yet not. "How does that guarantee they won't interfere with the baby? You really think they'll stay away."

"I know. I thought that too. But Heather threatened her mother that if they ever tried, we would escape without a trace. We've already discussed how we would do it."

"Damn it, Con."

"I know. I know. But Heather is certain her mother will keep her promise. And she never has anything good to say about either of them. But on this, she's convinced. So I have to trust her."

"Okay…Then…I guess I have to trust her too. But if ever, and I mean ever, you have to escape, promise me, you'll tell me, Con. And let me help you."

"I promise, George," he replied with a forced smile. "But it won't happen, okay?"

"Okay."

The conversation paused as another song faded before the next began. Both sat silently, absorbing the reality ahead of them. And how their respective lives were about to change.

George interrupted the quiet, still shaking his head in disbelief. "And to think. You're the one between the two of us having the shotgun wedding. Bet no one saw that coming."

Connor looked at him with a wan smile. "Well, it's not like you're ever getting anyone pregnant."

"Who says?" George defended.

"Really?" Connor challenged. "Come on, George." He ended it there, choosing to leave George to his denial. And the assurance that Connor would never reveal his secret.

Grateful for Connor's discretion, George returned the kindness with affection. "You know, Con. You're gonna be a great dad."

Whether George truly meant it or not, Connor was touched by the sentiment, particularly so soon after his earlier objections. But it should come as no surprise how ill-prepared Connor was to be a parent. He had always assumed it would happen. Someday. In the distant future. At minimum, when he was a grown-up. But this timing and these circumstances were a far cry from anything he could have dreamed. And yet, as Connor sat in the presence of a friend whose inclinations might be a hindrance, he felt grateful for the possibility of fatherhood. He wondered how that would work for George, should the time come when he yearned for a child. Would he be willing to live a lie for the sake of fatherhood? He felt for his friend and what struggles lay ahead for his future.

"Thanks George," he replied. "And I bet you'll be a great uncle. Until then," he added, hoping it would mean something to him, "I think you'd make a really great best man."

* * *

It was only a matter of days before both Connor and George were relegated to one of the twenty bedrooms at Delano Manor to get into their formalwear ahead of the pending nuptials. Somewhere at the far end of the building, was the bride and her entourage tending to her preparations. George's angst over Connor going through with the marriage, now paled in comparison to his fascination with all the pomp and circumstance that oozed from every room, every hallway, every furnishing. He was immediately enchanted by all the glitz that surrounded him and how unexpectedly comfortable he felt in such an artificial setting.

"Con, come check this out. You can see the set-up from here. It's huge!" George marveled as he pressed his head against the window of the third floor to peek over to the far right at the guests who were beginning to arrive. Their room, meanwhile, looked like the kind of presidential suite he had only ever seen in movies. He had already tested every chair, couch, mattress, opened every drawer, closet and cabinet. And especially delighted when staff knocked at the door to deliver pre-ceremony refreshments.

Connor emerged from the majestic bathroom, having dressed himself to the best of his abilities. He gave up on trying to figure out his white bowtie, leaving both ends to dangle around his neck. "Could a tux be any more uncomfortable?" he complained, looking down at himself. He still had yet to put on his tailcoat.

"Damn. Look at you," smiled George as he walked toward Connor, whose hair was coiffed for the first time ever. "But let's tuck you in properly." Too much of Connor's shirt was bulging over his pants. "I'll do the back for you." George moved behind him and slowly slid the shirt in below his belt, careful not to leave a crease. Connor's tight, slim waist against his touch gave George goosebumps; a feeling that caught him off-guard. He paused and swallowed deeply before moving to tighten the strap at the back of Connor's white vest. He then stepped over to face Connor and said, "There. Much better."

"Thanks. You have any idea how to tie this thing?" Connor asked, while waving one end of his bow tie.

"Allow me," replied George with confidence. "I've been practicing." George advanced to within inches of Connor's face as he held both ends and began by folding the longer over the shorter, then pulling it up through the hole. As he focused on getting it right, he noticed how clean shaven Connor was. And how he had to resist the impulse to caress his cheek. *Focus George,* he urged himself, frustrated to be feeling this way. "Is this too tight?" he asked as he pressed it into place.

"No more than the shirt collar," replied Connor. "Can I take a look?" He brushed past George and walked over to face the mirror. "Well done, George," he smiled with relief.

"And now for the final touch." George held Connor's tailcoat from behind. "Hold out your arms." He raised the jacket over Connor's shoulders, then turned to admire the full package. "You look unbelievable, Con." George stared in amazement at how much more grown-up he appeared in his formal attire.

"And you look pretty incredible too, George." His was a black tie and vest, with a dinner jacket instead of a tailcoat.

"Do you really think so?" he asked, pulling at his lapels and turning to the side as if posing for a men's fashion magazine.

"Too good. Heather's gonna come down the aisle, take one look at you, then say she changed her mind and wants to marry the best man instead," he smirked, knowing George was no threat in that regard. No matter how much more handsome he was.

George appreciated the compliment despite its platonic nature. "Not a chance, Con. She'll be so captivated by you, she won't even notice I'm there." *Nor will you,* he thought with regret.

"Okay, enough with the compliments. Time to go over the rules," urged Connor. He needed George to be on his best behavior.

"I know, I know. No getting drunk, keep an eye on her parents. Dance with her mother and her sister. Be charming. Don't worry, Con. You can count on me, okay?"

"Thanks, George," he replied with appreciation. "And you are allowed to have some fun. It's a celebration after all." Connor forced a smile then looked down to check his watch. He took in a deep breath then exhaled. "And on that note, it's show time."

* * *

By the time he was escorting his new bride to the dance floor, Connor's recollection of the ceremony was a blur. Only the sensation of his wedding band as he squeezed Heather's hand, while they walked beneath the ornate chandelier of sparkling crystals at the center of the grand ballroom, served to remind him they were officially married. He held it tight as he pulled her gently to face him for their first dance as Mr. and Mrs. Connor Rivers. The moment the live band began strumming Harry Nilsson's Without You, he swayed then leaned in to whisper into her ear. "Alone at last."

The lights had been dimmed with only a spotlight shining

above the newlyweds. Dozens of tables surrounded the dance floor, filled with guests who paused their conversations to watch as the young couple enjoyed their moment. Along the wall that lined the dance floor was the honor table, where both sets of parents, Dawn, and George sat and watched intently. Disbelief, admiration, relief, envy, disappointment, and hope were among the emotions they experienced as Connor and Heather embarked on their new life together.

"I still have to get one dance over with," Heather replied with a look of despair in her eyes.

"He won't dare do anything with everyone watching. Be strong. We're out of here as soon as it's over." He kissed her cheek. She then rested her head on his shoulder.

The moment the song ended, Anthony Delano, father of the bride, was announced. Connor stood with Heather, holding her hand, as Anthony walked over, his arms held wide to acknowledge the crowd that was cheering him on like a superstar stepping onto the stage. Anthony took Heather's hand from Connor. Both men gave each other a curt nod before the theatrics were about to begin. *At least it isn't a slow dance,* thought Connor, walking to the edge of the dance floor.

Within seconds, the band switched gears to the classic Italian wedding song, Luna Mezzo Mare, while Anthony and Heather showed off their brisk tarantella. Eleanor watched with delight and anticipation, like a choreographer admiring her performers. The guests clapped to the rhythm, shouting their cheers as Anthony displayed his cultural prowess. Heather forced herself through the motions, kept up with his aggressive lead, and did

THE BURDEN OF TRUTH

her best to avoid the sight of his sweaty grotesqueness.

George, who came to stand next to Connor, could feel his tension as he watched this spectacle. "It's almost done, Con."

"We're out of here the second it ends. And I need you to come with us."

"Oh, okay," replied George, surprised.

Anthony attempted to end their performance with a bow, but was constrained by his expansive waistline. Holding Heather's hand, he raised it to his adoring crowd.

Connor rushed over immediately and interrupted them by grabbing her hand and waving a thank you to everyone and shouting, "Time to take my bride on our honeymoon!"

What's he gonna do now? wondered George, who knew better than to think he would be joining them.

Connor and Heather rushed out of the ballroom as George followed. They made their way to the room that was set aside for them: their change of clothes and luggage had been stored there earlier in the day. Once inside, Connor turned to George. "We're leaving tonight. Staying at a hotel. I need you to stand guard while we get changed."

"Okay," replied George, having clued in to his role.

Connor and Heather barged out within moments, dressed up in their travel attire. "Here. Take our luggage down through the back door at the end of that hallway. A cab is waiting for us. We'll go make our final appearance before we leave. They don't need to know we won't be coming back to this room tonight to consummate our wedding vows."

George proceeded as directed, while Connor and Heather

returned to the ballroom to make their farewell round to all the guests. The moment Eleanor gave her nod of approval, they were free to retire for the evening, her expectations having now been met.

George was standing by the taxi when they arrived outside. He opened the back door and gave them each a hug goodbye. "Have fun, you two. And be careful," he said before closing the door.

"Thanks for everything, George. And please don't tell them we left."

"I won't, Con. Don't worry."

"Now go back and remember to dance with the Delano ladies, okay?"

"Fred Astaire is ready to dazzle," smiled George.

The driver pulled away. George watched as the taillights disappeared from view. His heart felt heavy, maybe even a little fractured. Would their friendship survive this marriage? He preferred to not even think of it. For now, he had a job to do. And what better distraction from sadness than an abundance of music and a dance floor.

"Might I have the honor, Mrs. Delano?" asked George, while bowing forward with his arm extended to take her hand. She had just returned from the powder room to the sight of her guests engaged in a waltz.

"Oh my. Such a gentlemen," she replied almost giddily. If ever there was a way to impress Eleanor Delano, it was most certainly with gallantry.

He held her hand raised up as he escorted her, then placed the other high up around her waist before beginning the steps. He had asked his father to teach him over the last few days. Whether his interpretation was acceptable to Eleanor, he would soon find out. And just in case his movements weren't quite up to snuff, there was always flattery.

"If I may say, Mrs. Delano, this event is spectacular."

"Why thank you, George."

"And might I add that you look positively ravishing." All those movies he had watched with debonair leads were paying off.

"So you're a charmer, I see." Eleanor looked at him inquisitively.

For all he knew, he had made her blush. "It's easy when you're in the presence of such beauty. Now I know where Heather gets her looks," he winked. By all appearances, she hadn't been flattered in a long while, or simply enjoyed lapping it all up.

"And why is it that a handsome young man like you is without a date today?"

"I take my best man duties very seriously, ma'am. Today is all about Connor. And Heather of course."

"And he's loyal," she said, speaking of George. "You're quite the catch, aren't you," she mused.

"If there is anyone who's loyal, it's Connor. Heather is in very good hands."

"That's wonderful to hear." Eleanor appeared relieved by his comment.

"Is Dawn here with anyone?" he asked casually.

Eleanor seemed shocked by the question. "Oh. No. No,

she's not."

"Would it be okay if I asked her to dance?"

Her eyes widened with joy. "Yes. Yes, of course. I'm sure she would be delighted."

George bowed as the waltz ended. "Thank you for dancing with me, Mrs. Delano." He smiled, then walked in the direction of Dawn.

"It is I who thanks you," Eleanor mumbled to herself as he walked away. It had been a very long time since she was last in the company of such a handsome and charming young man.

Dawn was standing alone a few feet from the bar, in her poofy baby blue gown, staring into the crowd, while swaying to the more current tunes.

"Can I offer you a drink?" asked George.

"Oh," replied Dawn, looking around to see if he was asking someone else. "I'm fine for now, thanks." She was fidgety and awkward, clearly not expecting the attention.

"Okay, then how about a dance?"

"Really? With me?"

He reached for her hand and walked her slowly to the dance floor, turning his head over his shoulder and said with a wink, "Come on."

Dawn wasn't sure she even knew how to dance. In public, that is. In the privacy of her room, she danced in front of the mirror almost daily, unsure if to others she would look ridiculous.

George stopped in a tight space between other couples, and began to sway. The beat was quick, the volume too loud to chat, so he took her arm and urged Dawn to spin. She hesitated the first time. Then slowly, with his encouragement, began to let loose. She had a natural rhythm about her that intrigued him. He kept his gaze steady on her eyes, showing his beautiful smile, melting her heart.

Once the band slowed the pace, he pulled her closer and whispered into her ear, "How come you don't have a date?"

At twenty years old, Dawn had yet to receive anything close to an invitation from a male suitor. As the pretty sister, Heather got all that attention. It only made it worse that their mother was also stunning. Much to Dawn's displeasure, she was cursed with her father's beady eyes and oversized frame. Her thick mass of unruly curls also gave her grief.

She took offence. "Don't tease, George."

"What do you mean?" he asked, surprised by the insinuation.

"Look at me. I'm no Heather. Or Eleanor Delano," she blurted, then lowered her gaze, visibly upset.

"Hey, come on, Dawn. Don't say that. You have such a beautiful smile. Let me see it, will you?" He placed his thumb under her chin to raise her face. She looked into his eyes then forced a smile. "There, that's better," he said with affection.

When the song ended, he walked her over to the bar and ordered two drinks before they sat down to chat. He listened as she talked about how she hoped to become a school teacher, and then described her obsession with music. From there, they compared notes on different artists, and who had what album in their respective portfolios.

"You're welcome to come listen to them one day," she offered.

"I'd like that a lot," he replied, relishing the discovery of someone equally passionate about music. Meanwhile, in the back of his mind, he imagined Connor being pleased by how he was connecting with his in-laws. And with Dawn, it didn't even feel like the least bit of effort.

They spoke for what seemed like an hour before George got up to go to the washroom. As soon as he left, Eleanor, who had been observing from a distance, sauntered over toward her daughter. "You seem to be having a nice time, dear."

She better not be here to tell me he's too Hispanic, or out of my league, thought Dawn, expecting her judgement and criticism. "I am," she replied firmly.

"I'm delighted for you, dear," she smiled, while briefly touching her arm. Expressions of affection were not natural for Eleanor.

The gesture caught Dawn off-guard. *You are?* she thought. She felt speechless.

"Oh, don't look at me like that. He's absolutely charming."

She actually likes him. Dawn's mind began to race. She had an idea. A self-serving one. She acted very matter-of-factly as she stated, "You know, Mother. He fits in perfectly here. You should consider hiring him."

"Hmm," thought Eleanor, surprised she hadn't thought of it herself. It was her style to pillage new staff whenever she encountered a young person that showed potential. Not that she expected such a discovery on her daughter's wedding day. "That's not a bad idea," she said, walking away.

CHAPTER FOURTEEN

— 2003 —

From the way Nick was pampering me, you would think that I was the one to have received the heart-wrenching diagnosis. Admittedly, my reaction after leaving the oncologist's office did little to disguise my struggle with the news, let alone the treatment plan. The moment we sat in the car and closed the doors, I wailed without restraint, gripping the steering wheel, while pounding my forehead against my knuckles. Meanwhile he, who had just been confronted with his worst nightmare, sat quietly stroking my back, saying it would be okay, until I pulled myself together. I wiped my snot-and-tear-drenched face and told myself to just keep breathing, until I slowly regained my composure. That's when I tried to convince him I was fine. That I was letting it out. Just this once. But then I thought about the girls, and the tears returned. Then the treatment, and they started up again. Quiet, pathetic tears of despair. Discouraged, Nick ended up kicking me out of the driver's seat and drove us home himself. I felt ashamed about my devastation, and promised I would do better after sleeping on it.

We held off on telling our daughters for a few days to give us time to process and to get ourselves organized. They were still so young. We needed to craft the proper messaging; words that were truthful but void of doom and gloom. Nick quickly recruited his teaching assistant to cover his lectures for the duration of his chemotherapy treatments. It was killing him to have to abandon his students mid-semester, so he worked out a plan to remain available remotely, if and when possible. As for being stuck at home until he was out of the woods, he was less than thrilled. My offer to relinquish all control of the kitchen was met with only modest receptivity. He did however appreciate that my sense of humor was returning.

Keeping him distracted had become my mission; I sought out a variety of ways to occupy his time, at his own leisure, from the comfort of our bedroom. Beginning with the library, I signed out the maximum allotment of books. How soon he would get through the first five didn't matter; I was prepared to return as often as necessary. I also, finally, purchased the home computer he had been begging for. Knowing he would be deprived of the ones at Harvard library, it seemed only fair to enable his internet searches from home. To make it accessible, I moved a table and chair into the bedroom under the corner window, with the stipulation that this set-up was only temporary; relocation to the basement would follow once he was all better. Finally, there was that box of old photographs to sort through. Envelopes upon envelopes of print copies set aside to one day be neatly organized in chronological order, then placed into albums. I bought a few; the kind with the clear adhesive film. He merely had to pull it away, before placing photos on the page, and then press it back down and smooth out the air bubbles.

If he was feeling really creative, he could crop the photos with a pair of scissors and even add commentary on the color paper pad with markers I had also included. Sentimental man that he was, he could enjoy the trip down memory lane in the process.

Where his treatment was concerned, the doctor wasted no time getting it underway, and felt confident that given the early stage-one detection of his leukemia, Nick's prognosis was favorable. His first chemotherapy treatment would be administered by intravenous injection tomorrow morning. Thereafter, the pill form should suffice. While we were both reassured, sort of, we also understood that Nick would never be truly cured. The quest for remission would be followed by constant screening, and constant breath-holding as we awaited results of whether the cancer was keeping at bay or creeping its way back into his blood stream. If it did, would an even more aggressive treatment plan be required the next time around? Or worse, a bone marrow transplant? The thoughts weighed on both of us. As did his family history. An ongoing cause for concern that suddenly became reality. As painful as it was to acknowledge, he now joined the ranks of kin saddled with this horrible disease, for which some – too many – had been extinguished by its cruelty.

The hardest part for me was to watch my upbeat, glass-half-full husband lose his spark. He tried not to show it. For my benefit, I'm sure. But I could see in his eyes the emotional pain. Would he be able to mask it from the girls? How much would they be able to handle at ages seven, nine and eleven? The responsibility fell on me to ensure Nick kept up hope, felt supported, and believed that I and the girls were okay.

* * *

"I'll tell Gloria I won't be there to visit with Dad today. And ask her if Debbie can spend a bit more time with him," I said to Nick, while folding laundry at the end of the bed. He was lying down, depleted after the ordeal of his first ever chemo injection.

"No, Jen," he objected with a weakened voice. "I don't want you to miss that. Go see him. I'll be fine. I promise."

I stopped folding and looked at him. "Nick. Come on. Don't ask me to leave you. Not today."

"Jen, I'm exhausted. I'll be asleep the whole time. Trust me, your Dad will be better company. Plus, you have the picture to show him, remember?"

In all the drama since our anniversary dinner, when Nick disclosed his call from the oncologist, I had forgotten about the photo he had printed of my parents' wedding with Jorge Vasquez and my Aunt Dawn. It was true that it would be a wonderful distraction for me if Dad remembered something. Even better, if it brought him joy. But I wasn't sure how I would feel if it triggered no memory whatsoever. Or worse, one that made him feel sad.

I stared at Nick who was clearly forcing himself to stay awake. "You're absolutely sure?"

"Yes."

"And you'll call the second you need anything?"

"Yes. But I'll be fine."

I could see he needed me to believe that. Hovering over him was never going to work for him. Certainly not beginning on day one. "Okay. I'll go. But I'll make it quick." I set aside the rest of the folding and went to the closet to grab a sweater.

"Don't forget to bring the picture."

"Right." I looked right and left. "Where did I put it?"

"Behind the framed one of your parents."

"Yes." I turned to my dresser and picked it up then stopped to look at the one he had framed. *You were able to get through so much worse, Daddy. Let's hope I can be just as strong.* I walked over and gave Nick a kiss, pulled up his covers then left.

I made my way to the elevator doors upon entering Meadowbrook Homes. Just as they opened, Gloria stepped off.

"Jennifer dear. I've been wondering how you've been," she smiled.

We were not in the habit of crossings paths during my visits, so I let the doors close to wait for the next elevator.

"Hi Gloria. How are you?"

"Fine dear. But it's you I'm curious about?"

Did Nick call her? He wouldn't have, would he? "Why is that, Gloria?"

"Well, I assume you contacted that detective?"

"Oh. That." Of course, she would be curious. We hadn't spoken since she had told me about his unexpected arrival in her office. And she had surely noticed he was a homicide detective when she received his business card. "Yes we spoke. It's all good." I waved it off with relief.

"Oh, lovely." She appeared disappointed I didn't have something more juicy to share. "Well then, I don't want to keep you from your father. Debbie says he's very chatty today." She smiled and pressed the up button for me, then walked toward her office.

"Great. Thanks Gloria," I said with my head turned as I watched her leave before entering it. *Dad is chatty? That's hilarious.* I chuckled to myself as I took the short ride up.

As I stepped off onto the third floor, I could hear laughter coming from the direction of Dad's room. And it was a hearty belly laugh. *Is that Debbie?* I realized that, as cheerful as she was, I had never actually heard her guffaw before. It was a marvelous sound of pure happiness. *She can't possibly be with Dad*, I thought as I neared his doorway. He just wasn't a funny kind of guy.

I arrived and there she was, wiping the tears from her eyes, she had laughed so hard.

"What's going on with you two?" I walked in and smiled. It was infectious. Even Dad's face was all lit up. Make that the left side he could control.

"Oh, your father is saying very silly things today," replied Debbie, still letting out the odd chuckle.

If there was something that Dad was not, it was silly. Or chatty. *What's happening?* Whatever it was, it seemed far too fun for me not to play along. "He is, is he?" I turned to give him a kiss on the top of his head. "What did you say now, Daddy?"

Debbie chimed in while raising herself. "Can you imagine he said I reminded him of Oprah?" She burst into laughter. "Oprah Winfrey!"

No I cannot. That seems like way too many words for him to string together. "That's quite the compliment." I smiled, while looking at her inquisitively.

"Compliment? Damn girl. She's…the…Oprah…Winfrey!" she boasted. "My life can end right now." Debbie puffed her chest with pride, then began to walk out of the room mimicking a debutante's stride. As she passed by me, she whispered into my ear, "That's what I chose to hear him say. He's in a lovely mood. Enjoy yourself."

Her words felt like a warm hug after days of cancer strain. I turned to him. "You have no idea how much I need this right now, Daddy."

"J-j-j-enny…c-c-ome…s-sit."

Wow. He really is doing well today. I pulled up a chair and sat across from him, our knees touching. He reached out his hand to signal for me to hold it.

"Daddy, I brought you a surprise."

"S-sur-p-prise?"

"Yes." I smiled. It was so wonderful to see him this alert. "But it's gonna bring back memories. Of Mom. Is that okay?" I crunched my face, worried he might get upset. It felt so weird to even mention her.

He barely hesitated. "Y-yes..p-please."

Surprised, relieved, I pulled the paper from my purse, unfolded it then held it up to face him.

His mouth dropped open, his eyes fixed it intently.

"Daddy? Are you okay?"

He lifted his hand toward the photograph and gently stroked

the image of my mother.

"She was beautiful, Daddy. And look at *you*," I exclaimed, still shocked to see him so dapper.

"B-b-beau-ti-f-ful…l-like…J-J-enny." His eyes glistened.

I could feel my eyes well up. "You're gonna make me cry," I said, dabbing my eye with the tip of my finger. *Why hadn't we ever done this before? He's completely mesmerized.*

We sat quietly as he stared at the photo. Eventually, I asked, "Daddy, is the other girl her sister, Dawn?"

He nodded faintly, "Dd-dawn. Y-yes." He could not pull his eyes away.

"And the other guy. Do you remember him, Daddy?"

"J-j-oe-r-r-ich."

Oh my God! No. This can't be. "Daddy, wait here. I'll be right back." I put the picture in his hand and rushed out into the hallway to find Debbie. I peeked into three other rooms before I found her.

The moment she noticed me, she paused feeding her other patient and asked, "Everything alright, Jennifer?"

"I'm so sorry to interrupt. But I need you to come to Dad's room as soon as you can. You won't believe this."

"I'll be right there," she replied, then turned with a smile to her poor, probably hungry patient, whose spoonful just got pulled away. "I'll just be moment." Then she got up to join me. "What happened, Jennifer? He was doing so fine."

"Just come with me." I pulled her by the hand and rushed back into Dad's room. Once inside, I said, "Debbie, stand here and listen. Carefully. Just listen."

Debbie frowned and looked around, confused. "Oh okay. I'm listening."

"Daddy, I need you to tell me who the guy is again. Can you do that for me?"

There was a slow pause as he prepared to speak. Then out it came. "J-j-oe-r-rich," he stuttered very seriously.

"Well I'll be damned," marveled Debbie.

I looked at her. "That's it right? He just said Joe Rich. Right?"

"That sounded like Joe Rich to me." She smiled in agreement.

"But it isn't Joe Rich. I mean, it is. At least, it's how Daddy has been saying it all this time. But it's actually George. This is George!" I jumped up and down with excitement, like a winning contestant at a gameshow.

"And who is this George?" asked Debbie, equally amazed the mystery man had finally been identified.

I was about to respond that it was his best man, but saw that Dad was ready to do so himself.

"B-bes-st…f-fr-ie-nd," he replied.

My heart sank a little at hearing that. I sat back down and took his hands. "He was your best friend, Daddy?"

He nodded. His eyes brightened. "W-want…s-ssee…h-him."

Shit. He looked so happy. How could I possibly tell him he had died? *Why didn't we ever talk about this stuff before? I would've done anything to find George so they could meet again.*

He squeezed my hand, and added, "P-pl-ease…J-j-enny…s-s-see…hh-him.

I dropped my head and took in a deep breath before looking into his eyes. "Daddy, I'm so sorry. But George…" *God this is harder than I expected.* "George is gone. He died, Daddy."

"N-n-o…n-n-o…n-n-o…" He shook his head, his face turning red, his eyes tearing up. He looked so upset, so heartbroken. "N-need…s-say…s-sor-ry."

"I'm so sorry, Daddy." My eyes were teary too. They must have had a falling out. I hated that he was so upset.

As soon as he noticed my tears, he calmed himself. "J-j-en-ny…n-n-oo…c-cry." He patted my hand. "I…h-ha-ve…p-pic-ture."

Typical Dad. Always the one to comfort me. "You want to keep the picture, Daddy?"

"Y-y-es," he smiled.

"Of course, Daddy. It's for you." I squeezed his hand.

"G-g-ood…s-s-ur-p-prise, J-j-enny," he said, a tear rolling down one cheek.

"I'll leave you both," whispered Debbie, squeezing my shoulders from behind. In the magic of the moment, I had forgotten she was still there.

* * *

Dad was exhausted from all the emotion by the time I had left him. We had played a game of Gin Rummy so I could be sure he was more settled. He seemed fine but insisted on keeping the photo in front of him the whole time. I then made sure to find Debbie again on my way out. She had reassured me she would check up on him a few more times.

Having just pulled into the driveway, it was time to prepare dinner and think of what to say to the girls. My moment with Dad made me realize that delaying telling them about Nick was unfair. It would only make the shock worse later. How avoiding topics, like Dad and I always did, might cost them in the end. His friend I knew nothing about, passed away only a few short months ago. A few months too late for them to reconnect. For Dad to apologize for whatever it was that had obviously preoccupied him with all his Joe Rich talk. So I resolved to tell them, to find the right words, and to bear their reactions.

"Mommy, is Daddy still sick?" asked Lisa, rushing to greet me as I opened the front door.

"Yes he is, sweety," I replied, while bending down to give her hug. "I'm going to check on him. Then I'll come make dinner okay?"

"Okay," she said with a lopsided grin before turning back to join her sisters who were sitting on the couch watching That's So Raven.

I spared them the inquisition on whether their homework was done. That was the prerequisite for pre-dinnertime television. I chose instead to give them the benefit of the doubt. Just let them unwind so they would be in the best frame of mind for what I was about to announce. I walked upstairs to find Nick sound asleep. I changed into leggings as quietly as I could. My news regarding the infamous Joe-Rich-turned-George-Vasquez would have to wait.

"What do you mean he has cancer?" cried Grace. I kept all three at the table after we were done clearing the plates away.

"That means he's gonna die!" she shouted, immediately upset.

"No! I don't want Daddy to die," cried Lisa.

"He's not dying, sweethearts," I said calmly, reaching out to take their hands from around the table. "I promise. The doctor found a teeny tiny small speck of it. The medicine will help make it go away."

"That's not true. People die, Mommy. Even in our family!" shouted Grace. The image of her family tree was still fresh in her mind.

"Yes. You're right. Some people do. But not all. Not those who get treatment early on. Like your Daddy, who, by the way, takes really good care of himself. He's very strong and will fight this."

"Is it contagious?" asked Hannah, who had been quiet.

"No, sweetie. It's not," I assured her.

"So why can't we see him?" barked Grace.

"He had his first dose of medicine. It's very strong so it can fight the cancer quickly. But it's making his body work very hard, so he's really tired. He needs complete rest to build up his strength."

"But for how long?" cried Lisa.

"He'll start getting his strength back soon. And the minute he can, he'll join us for dinner again, watch tv with you, play board games."

"He'll be allowed?" she replied.

"Yes he will, sweetie. Not every day. Sometimes he'll be too tired. But that's when we can all help take care of him."

"But we're so little? How can we take care of him?"

I could see that Lisa was going to need a lot more convincing.

Each of them would. To help process this in their own way. For now, at least they had the truth. "By keeping him company when he's awake. Bringing him a drink when he's thirsty. Maybe making him a special snack if he gets hungry. But mostly just by telling him we love him and giving him lots and lots of hugs."

Nick finally opened his eyes after I entered the room to get into pyjamas.

"It's dark out? Are the girls already in bed?" he asked. I could tell his mouth was dry.

"Yes they are." I went into the washroom to fill a glass of water and brought it to him.

He sat up. "Thanks." After a few gulps, he asked, "How long was I out?"

"A few hours. How do you feel?"

"Like I'm going to vomit this water." His face went pale as he swung his legs over the edge of the mattress to stand up.

I helped him to the bathroom and stroked his back as he regurgitated over the toilet bowl.

When he was finished, I dampened a facecloth and wiped his chin. "Think you can handle brushing your teeth?"

"For both our sakes, yes."

I didn't bother to offer him food. I wasn't even sure I wanted to discuss any of the day's big news. So I tucked him back into bed and lay down beside him, holding his hand.

"I'm going to get through this, Jen," he reassured me, squeezing my hand while staring up at the ceiling.

"I know," I replied, squeezing it back. Then, changing

my mind on at least one bit of today's developments. "The girls do too."

He turned to look at me, his eyebrows raised. "They know?"

"I told them after dinner. They needed to know. I couldn't let them think this was a flu."

"Are they okay?"

"They will be. It will help when they can each spend some time with you. When you're ready, that is." I pressed my index finger against his chest. "And don't even think of rushing it. You take care of *you* first. That's how we'll all get through this. Understood?"

"Scouts honor," he replied, raising three fingers.

He turned his head back to lay flat, then asked, "So how did it go with your Dad? Did you end up showing him the picture?"

I wasn't sure if this was the right time to share such big news, so I tried to feel him out first. "It was a nice visit. He made Debbie laugh, believe it or not."

"Really? How did he do that?"

"Told her she reminded him of Oprah. At least, that's how she chose to interpret whatever it was he actually said." I grinned thinking about her proud moment. "Pretty sure he made her day."

"No kidding. It would make mine if a student ever told me I reminded them of Oprah."

"Hate to tell ya, honey. Your look is all wrong," I mused.

"Is it the hair?" he jested, tapping the spot at the back that recently started thinning out.

"Yeah," I nodded sarcastically, "it's the hair." Since he seemed alert, playful and not as nauseous, I decided to spit it out. "So….

the picture."

"You showed him?" he turned over, eyes wide.

"Yup. I did."

"And?"

"Stutter the word, George, the way Dad stutters, will you?"

"You want me to imitate your dad's speech?"

"Uh huh," I replied with a sneaky look on my face.

"G-g-eo-r-ge," he tried, but too quickly. "Like that?"

"Yup. Now do it really slowly and listen to yourself.

He obliged. Repeated it a few times, then realized it. "No Way!"

"Yup. Joe Rich is George Vasquez."

"Wow. That's crazy. So it's his best man that he's been mentioning all this time."

"His best friend, Nick. That's how he responded when Debbie asked who George was. Can you believe it?"

"You must have met him before, Jen. At least on your trip that summer."

"Honestly, I don't think I did. I have absolutely no memories of him. And yes, I know, my memory sucks."

"So how did your dad react when he saw the picture?"

"He loved seeing Mom. Kept stroking her image. Then he said he wanted to see George. He seemed so happy. It broke my heart to tell him he was gone. He actually cried, Nick."

"Ouch. That's sad." We both paused for a minute before he asked, "How was it that the detective had described their relationship?"

"That. Oh. It was odd and formal." I tried to recall. "I think it was a more-than-acquaintance."

"Well…turns out he was right."

I nodded. It bothered me that I was only just learning of George now that it was too late. And that a random detective knew he had been close to Dad before I did.

"You know, Nick. This whole George thing is making me think I should reconsider finding my Aunt Dawn."

"Really?" He seemed pleasantly surprised.

"It's like I don't want to find myself suddenly wanting to meet her one day only to learn that she's dead. Though for all I know, she already is."

"I would be happy to find that out for you," he declared, delighted with the prospect of a new project.

"Well we do need to put that eyesore of a computer to some use. But only when you're really up to it. This isn't a rush."

"I promise."

"There was something so nice about actually talking about Mom with Dad. I mean, we didn't really say much. But it was more than we ever did. And it felt good, you know?"

"I get it."

"He won't be around forever. And we should be able to talk about the people that mattered." I turned to Nick. "Right?"

"Yes you should. And I hope your aunt will have lots to share with you," he yawned.

"Who knows? Maybe I have a whole bunch of cousins I have yet to meet." With that, I leaned in to kiss him goodnight, then closed my eyes to let my exhaustion take over.

CHAPTER FIFTEEN

— 2003 —

Cisco was relieved to be back at his desk in Boston. While his time in New York had been more productive than expected, it was his glorious reunion with his baby girl that brought him the greatest satisfaction. How grateful he felt to know he would be going straight home to her at the end of the work day.

The new trinkets he acquired on his trip sat on his desk: an envelope filled with Delano documents he had yet to draw a conclusion from, and a box of photographs of Connor Rivers and Jennifer Vincent. But by far, the biggest revelation was discovering that Jorge Vasquez's long-time secret lover, Brandon Wong, had not only been the one to uncover the letter of confession and photograph of Rivers and Vasquez, but he was also responsible for giving them to Dawn Delano. *Now to figure out why she sent them here.*

June approached his desk, wearing her usual white blouse and navy pants, her hair tied back in a ponytail, her stride assertive and purposeful. "I've got the information you were asking for, Detective Cisco. There's a free meeting room we can use to go over it." In her early forties, she was reputed for getting to the point and being very thorough.

"Find anything interesting?" Cisco asked, while standing up, collecting his pad of lined paper and coffee mug.

"I think so."

They entered the same spare office Cisco had met Jennifer Vincent in. "Did you ask Detective Randall to join us?"

"I did. He said for us to go ahead and to debrief him later. He's out on another matter."

Interesting, thought Cisco, who expected Randall to be chomping at the bit, wondering what had transpired in New York. *Unless he's skeptical about my findings.* "Okay so what have you got?" he asked, while placing his pad on the table before taking a seat across from her.

"Let's start with Michael Delano," she began her point-form account. "He got married a few years after serving his time in prison. Worked in construction. He and his wife eventually had a child. A boy. Had Down's Syndrome. Died at age twenty. Heart malformation from birth."

"Damn," uttered Cisco, shaking his head. He could only imagine how devastating that would be for the parents.

"It gets worse," added June. "His wife committed suicide the following year."

Cisco's expression went blank.

"I know," she frowned, acknowledging the tragedy. "Michael died of a heart attack the year after that. Like Anthony, he too had a heart condition, which was no doubt exacerbated by the loss of his family."

"No kidding," exhaled Cisco. "Did anyone in that family have a happy ending?"

"Hard to say."

"Alright," he resigned. "How about something less depressing? The money."

"That's where it gets more interesting." June closed one folder then opened another.

"Good." Cisco reclined, arms folded, his curiosity piqued.

"There are two pieces: Anthony Delano's personal estate, and the business assets. I'll start with the personal. Per his will, the manor, cars and all his personal effects went to Eleanor. In the case of his life insurance policy, it was split between three beneficiaries, his wife who got fifty percent, and both his daughters who each got twenty-five percent. So that's two million to Eleanor, and one million to Dawn and to Heather."

"But Heather was in a coma."

"Correct. It was Connor Rivers who had power of attorney over her affairs. But get this…" Her eyes widened. "He disclaimed the inheritance."

Cisco's eyebrows rose. "Connor Rivers turned down one million dollars?"

"Yup," June nodded.

"What the hell would make him refuse that amount?" He ran one hand through his hair. "So what happened to Heather's portion?"

"Hold that thought," June urged, while raising her index. "Let's move on to Anthony Delano's business assets." She pulled out yet another file. "As sole heiress, Eleanor succeeded Anthony as chair of the Delano Enterprise board of directors. Instead of nominating a new president, she assumed an interim role and proceeded with an immediate divestiture of all company assets." June looked up at Cisco. "I checked the records. All sales were on the books. Mostly to businesses with whom Delano had long-time real-estate ventures. Everything closed quickly, possibly to take advantage of positive market dynamics." Her keen interest in financial markets made June eager to explain further. "The Dow Jones had gone up fifteen percent in 1972 and 1973 was expected to be even better. So it's conceivable that the transactions were rushed to leverage that growth."

"I see," replied Cisco. He assumed the detail was pertinent. June was not one to insert random facts for no reason.

"But things didn't quite pan out as expected. The stock market took a downturn. As in, it crashed. Between the Nixon Watergate scandal and the oil crisis, benchmark indices lost over forty-five percent of their value by December 1974."

"So Eleanor rushed the sale of the company to invest the proceeds in a market upturn, only to lose close to half its value in less than two years?"

"Sort of. There's more." She looked at Cisco to ensure she had his undivided attention. "As part of the Delano Enterprise bylaws, Eleanor, as new chair, was immediately mandated to name her successor. And it had to be formally documented before exercising the sale. Care to guess who she named?"

"Don't tell me it's Vasquez?"

"Nope."

Cisco shrugged and lifted his hands palms up, "Dawn?"

"Heather." June's eyes lit up.

"What?" Cisco questioned, a line appearing between his

brows. "Wasn't she dead?"

"Not yet. The papers were finalized two days before she passed away."

"While she was in a coma? So…they were redone after she died?"

"They should've been, but never were. Possibly because Eleanor considered it moot given her imminent sale of the company. Or?"

"It was deliberate?"

"A portion of the proceeds from the sale of the company were placed in trust. Under Heather's name. That was months after she had died."

"Okay, wait a minute. Could she even do that?"

June shrugged.

Cisco stood up and began to pace, arms folded, one hand over his chin. "If Eleanor set money aside in her deceased daughter's name, it had to be because she wanted to hide it. But from who? The IRS?" He stopped and looked to June. "How much money are we talking about?"

June pivoted the sheet in front of her and slid it across the table. It outlined the summary of five transactions that concluded the sale of all Delano Enterprise assets. "About ten million in total."

Cisco stood above the sheet resting on both hands gripping the edge of the table. "That's a fortune. How much of it went into Heather's trust?"

"Five million."

"And do we know what ever happened to that trust?"

"From what I can tell, it's been active since 1973. Oh and the starting amount of the trust? It was six million dollars, not five."

"An extra million…Just the amount Rivers disclaimed. That can't be a coincidence."

"Nope."

Cisco resumed his pacing. "So you said the trust is still active. Who's withdrawing from it? And what's it worth now?"

"I didn't get that far. But just for fun, let's say that initial amount had remained untouched. It would be worth about twenty-two million dollars today."

"Well now, June, I think you just found us the end game."

"I hope so. But it'll take some time to access the transactions. I've got thirty years' worth to sort through. And the early years would all be paper-based."

The reminder of how old this case was made Cisco cringe. But he now realized that with so much time having elapsed, someone could have uncovered the massive interest accrual and wanted to get their hands on it. Which made Cisco question, "Wait a second. If Heather Delano was made trustee after she died, who the hell has been managing the account? And on whose authority?"

"Good question. I wondered that too, and I have some theories, but they still need to be vetted."

"Shoot."

"Scenario number one: Connor Rivers exercises his power of attorney."

"So he declines the inheritance but accepts responsibility for disbursement of the trust... That would gain him way more at less of a tax burden…Except that his own affairs are now being managed by his legal guardian, Jennifer Vincent. Presumably, she would have become trustee as part of that transfer."

"Easy enough to check. Ready for scenario two?"

"Let me have it." Cisco hoped it excluded anything to do with Jennifer Vincent, which would make Randall's suspicion right all along.

"In setting up the trust, Eleanor names herself as successor to Heather."

"Seems a little roundabout. Couldn't she have put it in her own name to begin with?"

"Yes. But then she would have to absorb the full tax burden. Combined with the balance of her inheritance, that would be high. And don't forget, she had lost a big chunk of the initial proceeds in the market downturn."

"Okay, but Heather would've been the one to have to name her as successor, which she couldn't do."

"True, but it wasn't beneath Eleanor to falsify documents. Or at least, it wouldn't have been the first time she did something of that nature. Unless of course, Dawn and Heather were twins."

"What do you mean?"

"Well, you asked me to look into Dawn. I'll get to that later, but suffice it to say, her birth year stood out. It's the same as Heather's. I was sure I had it wrong, so I searched some more."

"And?"

"Heather Delano's hospital and death records reference her birth as being in 1942. However, when I obtained the original birth record for Heather Chastity Delano, daughter of Eleanor and Anthony Delano, it was produced in 1946.""

"What the hell?"

"I have theory. The very first record I can find of Heather's birth year as 1942 instead of 1946 is in 1962. The year she got married. That would mean she was only sixteen at the time. Meanwhile, any entitlement to the Delano estate, by either of their daughters, could only occur at age twenty-one."

"So what? It was precautionary? To ensure Heather had access to her share in the event of Delano's death? Was anyone else planning to murder him?"

"Not sure about murder, but Delano Sr. died of a heart attack at age fifty-six. Anthony would have been sixty by then. And not particularly fit. Longevity may not have been presumed."

Cisco thought back for a moment to his meeting with Jennifer Vincent, and how it seemed odd that there was confusion over her father's birth year. And if he remembered correctly, the difference between what he had on file and what she claimed to be her father's year of birth was four years. The same four years as Heather Delano. *So if Heather Delano's birth records had been falsified at the time of her wedding, was it also the case for Connor Rivers?* Turning back to June he asked, "Got any other scenarios?"

"Yes. Just one more. A trustee's legal representative could facilitate the issuance of directives to the bank. And the central figure in this investigation just so happens to be a lawyer."

"Vasquez. Hmm. Not bad, June. He could have acted on behalf of Eleanor. Or even Rivers. I'll need you to explore that further."

"I'll get right on it after I give you the last piece you asked me about. Dawn Delano."

"Right." Cisco shook his head. He had almost forgotten about her.

"Well, I'm fairly certain she's the one who was actually born in 1942. She was twenty at the time of Heather's incident. And went quiet for years thereafter. The next record of an address for her, other than Delano Manor, turns up in 1983. Small condo in Boston that's still in her name. No record of marriage or children. She was listed in a retirement announcement from Datacube Inc. just last year, after twenty years of service."

"What was her occupation?"

"Technical writer, from what I can tell."

"Is her condo the penthouse? She did inherit one-million dollars."

"No it's a one-bedroom unit."

"Seems a little lackluster compared to her lavish upbringing."

"An upbringing that resulted in tragedy."

Cisco nodded in agreement. "Do we know what she did with the money?"

"I'm looking into it, but some definitely went to charity."

Cisco stared down at his hands. "Interesting how there was all this money, and yet each one of them seems to have refused it, lost it or given it away," he said, having added Vasquez's handling of his own estate to the mix. "Meanwhile there's this mystery trust. Someone has dibs on it. We need to find out who." He paused, then looked up. "Do we know what happened to Eleanor?"

"Died in a nursing home in '98 at age seventy-six."

"So who took over the manor?"

"I'll have to confirm that." Closing her folder, she said, "That's all I have for now. Unless you have anything else, I'll start tracing the money."

"Good work, June," Cisco replied, while raising himself and sorting his files. "Oh, do you have the address for Dawn's condo?"

"Yes. I meant to give that to you." She flipped through a few pages then handed a sheet to him. "Here you go."

"Looks like I'll be paying Miss Delano a visit."

CHAPTER SIXTEEN

— 1972 —

"**M**ake me a copy of this, will you, Georgie," instructed one of the senior members of the Delano legal team.

A group of six, including George Vasquez, had been occupying a large office in Delano Manor since Anthony's incarceration. Operating as a makeshift war room, it sat at the far end of the east wing, across the hallway from Anthony's private den, which remained off-limits. They had been holed up in there, day and night, in an effort to get the charges dropped after their failed performance at his arraignment. Having aggressively – perhaps too aggressively – pressed Judge Willis to set the date immediately after his arrest, she had obliged, only to then deny him bail. Describing Delano as a flight risk, she remanded him to prison custody, leaving his legal team scrambling, and Delano infuriated.

Following that fiasco, Anthony Delano issued an edict to his legal team. If the exorbitant sums he was paying their collective genius didn't result in his acquittal, there would be hell to pay. They now had no choice but to build a bullet-proof defense strategy. And there was no way they were going to risk offending Judge Willis with pressure to rush the trial date. In fact, they orchestrated just the opposite to buy themselves more time to strategize. And all it took was some carefully disguised intimidation directed at the prison doctor to ensure he'd be especially vigilant before giving Delano the okay to appear in court. The repeated delays however, nearly backfired. The time the legal team had gained was to the detriment of Delano's health, patience and state of mind. His anger toward the situation, and toward his lawyers was tempered only by his slow deterioration.

"Right away sir," replied George with military obedience, bolting up to rush toward the photocopier that was tucked in behind a partition at the far corner. He fully understood the toils of working his way toward a more senior status, and was up to the task no matter how menial or how repetitive it was. After a decade of serving as a glorified gofer under Eleanor Delano, he was more than prepared to meet the demands of his new bosses. If anything, he considered them tame in comparison to her volatility.

George often thought back to that fortuitous moment, ten years prior, that had launched him on a path toward law. It was just after Connor's wedding ceremony had begun, when instructed to flirt with the ladies, and to play especially nicely with Eleanor and Dawn. Feeling awkward but unwilling to disappoint Connor, George had embraced the glamor of the event and unleashed the full force of his charm. He shone so brightly, he earned himself an invitation directly from Eleanor to join the Delano staff. At the time, the allure of life in the manor was both enticing and fascinating, making it easy for George to fit in, and even easier to keep tabs on Delano dealings to report back to Connor. Never would Eleanor be suspicious while he was executing his duties with such enthusiasm. As an added bonus, there was always at least one other person on staff who shared his persuasion, along with an abundance of space in which to act on his physical impulses in total privacy. George was in his glory, satisfying Eleanor's, Connor's, and his own needs with full discretion. As more time went by, legal affairs began to pique his curiosity. Not the content per se, but the navigation of contracts, the crafting of iron-clad clauses meant to address even the most unlikely scenario. The means, as it seemed to him, of legally getting away with the impossible. He toyed with the idea of studying law. Joked about it with Eleanor to see what she would say. One thing led to another, and before he knew it, she was flexing her social muscle to assist with his admission into Harvard Law School. In the years that followed, his life revolved around studying and working, and the odd tryst when a consenting partner presented himself. When Eleanor offered him the promise of a better future with a seat at the Delano legal table, he did not hesitate to pass his bar exam.

Following the briefest of celebrations after achieving this milestone, George was immediately relegated to coffee duty and varied administrative tasks requested by each of the five senior attorneys. The moment he dared to intimate that he could take on more than what he felt should be assigned to a paralegal, they graduated him to updating Anthony Delano on their progress. In person. In prison. And that was two days ago. Within moments of that encounter, George realized none of his rehearsing had prepared him for such a confrontation. Never had he felt more nervous or been on the receiving end of more verbal abuse in his life. Anthony Delano considered his months of continued detainment an abomination, an abject failure of his incompetent lawyers. *You mean to tell me my team of idiots put a child in charge?* he fumed. *Are they waiting till you're out of diapers before getting my trial underway? Give them this message for me, Vasquez. Get me the hell out of this shithole. Now!* When George reported back Delano's reaction, they immediately recognized the error of their ways, working even more feverishly on their strategy. As for twenty-six-year-old George, he realized he had much to learn before attaining the status of his colleagues twice his age. So he accepted his reassignment to photocopy duty without objection, a task for which he had developed a newfound appreciation.

His altercation with Delano intensified George's mission to find a way to keep him far from Connor and Jennifer. Permanently. His sense of urgency increased after seeing The Godfather in theaters; Anthony Delano was literally the reincarnation of Vito Corleone. *I'm going to wake up to a dead horse head in my bed,* feared George. Of equal concern was his intimate knowledge of the defense strategy; the likelihood of a conviction seemed more and more improbable. But he remained determined. He had to, if he was ever going to see Connor again, and earn back his friendship. What he needed was to come up with an angle, then find a way to get it into the prosecution's hands. Something the Delano team could not defend. So far, he had but one idea, and it was so drastic, so risky, he questioned whether he could even pull it off. Meanwhile he gathered intel, as much from the office as he could get, hanging on to hope that a solution would manifest itself. To do so, each time he was asked to make copies of material, he bumped the number up by one and let the extra page slide in behind the photocopier. Then, on the nights he was last to leave the room, he collected the scattered sheets and brought them home to add to the growing array of documents he had accumulated. *Somehow, somewhere, in all of this, has to be the secret to Delano's demise.*

It was 9pm by the time the last of the lawyers was leaving for the day.

"I'll lock up," George told him. "See you tomorrow."

Moments later, he walked over to the photocopier, rolled it far enough away from the wall so he could reach in behind it and pick up the pages he had let fall. He placed them in his briefcase, pushed the photocopier back into place, turned the light switch off before locking the door on his way out. He walked down the carpeted staircase that lead to the main floor corridor. The manor was perfectly silent with most of the staff having retired for the evening. The dim lighting that emanated from sconces dispersed along the walls illuminated his path toward the grand entrance. Before reaching it, he passed the lounge; a large room with scattered seating throughout: club chairs, sofas, cocktail tables with stools, and an impressive bar along its back wall. It was used predominantly by Anthony and his business associates to celebrate the signature of another new deal.

"Long day for you, George," said a voice from within.

Startled, George recognized the sound of another invitation.

"Ma'am," he acknowledge, while stopping in the double doorway. "Just doing my job."

"You're working too hard. Come make yourself a drink," said Eleanor, speaking very slowly. She was sitting in a leather chair by the wall, swirling the ice cubes in her glass. Half her face was discernable from the light of a small gold lamp on the end table just next to her. Other than the under-lights along the shelving above the bar, the room was perfectly dark.

George could tell from her diction that she had refilled her glass several times before his arrival. And while she was still wearing a glamorous outfit, the usually poised and calculated Eleanor Delano was now without her defenses, without her filter. Reluctantly, he rested his briefcase on the floor against the chair next to her before walking toward the bar and scanning the well-stocked shelf. He noticed his reflection in the mirror backsplash just beneath it, and avoided eye contact with Eleanor who was staring directly at him.

"Why don't you open a bottle of champagne," she suggested when he failed to make a quick selection.

"Are we celebrating?" he asked. Only Eleanor would find reason to do so while her three family members were in misery.

"Massachusetts General has agreed to the terms of my donation," she replied with ambivalence. The lisp and unsteady pace of her speech confirmed her state of inebriation.

She's going to be very chatty, thought George, who though tired, knew to seize this opportunity. "So you succeeded in getting them to hold off on declaring her brain-dead until after the verdict?" This was far too twisted to deserve an actual

THE BURDEN OF TRUTH

congratulations. But he popped the cork off the Veuve Clicquot nonetheless, poured some into two flutes with elongated slender bowls, then walked over to her. "For you." He extended a glass before sitting into the supple leather chair, resting his free hand on its cushioned armrest. He placed his flute on the lamp table that sat between them, intending to sip it very slowly.

She downed hers in one take. "More please," she slurred, while handing him her empty glass.

"Maybe we should save it for another time, Mrs. Delano. I can go get one of the maids to help you to your room?"

"Champagne doesn't keep, George. You know that." She waved off his suggestion. "Just bring the bottle here."

He drew in a long breath and raised himself to walk back behind the bar. Returning with bottle in hand, he took her glass, choosing the steadiness of his own grip as he filled it before handing it back to her.

She took a gulp and set it down with exaggerated effort. "I hear they sent you to meet with Anthony."

They told her? George's brows snapped together. He nodded, bracing himself for more criticism.

She slurred her way through her frustration. "Can you believe that ungrateful bastard? He actually dared to boast about it. To me! The nerve of him!" She shook her head, utterly appalled that Anthony had unleashed his frustration on poor George. As she slouched deeper into her chair, she turned to him, waving her index with every word. "Don't you worry, George. He won't dare lift a finger to you next time."

George unclenched his jaw with modest relief the information had originated from Anthony rather than his colleagues. That it caused her to drink herself stupid however, seemed a bit extreme. *This whole situation is getting to her more than she wants to let on,* he surmised. "Thank you, Mrs. Delano, but I doubt there'll be a next time." The senior lawyers were intent on resuming the daily prison meetings.

"That's very unfortunate," she mumbled, while trying to muffle a burp.

"How so?" George tried to appear as though he hadn't noticed.

"He'll be too busy…berating each and every one of them. He won't hear a word they say. But with you," she paused and pointed, "he has no choice but to listen. Cause I said so."

George neither responded nor reacted. A perfectly sober Eleanor Delano was difficult enough to read. This drunk, she was an enigma.

"You don't think he listens to me, do you?" she scrutinized.

"Oh, yes. I'm sure he does," George exclaimed, realizing his silence had offended her.

"I'm gonna let you in on a secret, George," she uttered with her index over her lips. "Sh."

Please let this be good, thought George as he leaned in closer. "Okay, I'm listening."

"That man would be absolutely nothing without me," she began, while gesturing with one arm, her motions very uncoordinated. "If he didn't see the inside of a prison cell until now, it's thanks to me. But then…then…he goes and does this. The fool! Put everything we've built at risk."

George opened his mouth to respond then snapped it back shut. He knew Eleanor thought highly of herself, but in her alcohol-induced stupor, she sounded even more inflated. Curious as to whether she was preparing to divulge more, he focused on keeping her talking. "For what it's worth, Michael Delano's testimony will be dead in the water with cross-examination. Between the statute of limitations on his fraud claim and his own record of behavior, he really doesn't pose a threat."

"Michael? Pfft," she said dismissively. "He was never a match for his little brother. Too gentle. Not cut-throat enough."

"Okay. Um…I wasn't sure if you were still worried about him."

"Ha! Dear heavens, no, George," she grimaced. "There was no way he could waltz back in and take what he wanted."

"Well, we're doing everything we can to get Mr. Delano acquitted. The prosecution's case is pretty circumstantial so it's looking good for him." Speaking truthfully, George tried to hide his displeasure with the likelihood of an acquittal.

"George, if it was going so fine, it wouldn't be taking this long." She took another sip.

George didn't know how much more she could consume before completely losing her faculties, but he remained serious. "Failure isn't an option, Mrs. Delano. The team just wants to be sure we have what we need to cast enough doubt when refuting whatever evidence they present in front of the jury."

"Blah, blah, blah. I know, George. And I'm tired of your lawyer talk. Let's change the subject." Drops of spit, reflected by the light, spattered as she spoke.

Without any benefit in pursuing this dialogue further, nor interest in seeing Eleanor even more intoxicated, George proposed to defer their conversation. "I think we should save that for another time, Mrs. Delano. I really do need some rest and should probably head home."

He was hoping for her nod of approval before standing up to leave. Instead, she picked up the bottle and attempted to pour herself another glass, spilling it as she struggled with her aim. George reached over to help her. "You know, George," she began. "You and I are more alike than you realize."

This should be good, he thought, sitting back down. "How do you figure, Mrs. Delano?"

"We're both trapped," she blurted.

"Trapped? How so?" George found it ridiculous that she would consider herself confined given the circumstances surrounding the rest of her family.

"We both yearn for a love we can't have." She stared him in the eyes to capture his reaction.

Her love-hate relationship with Anthony was interesting to George. To a point. And only if it led to information of value. The notion of her yearning for him however, was jarring, if not nauseating. "Well, hopefully you won't have to miss him for much longer." He really wanted to wrap this up quickly.

She spat the sip of champagne she had just taken and guffawed. "You think I'm referring to Anthony? Oh George, there's absolutely no yearning where he's concerned. Ha! But you did make me laugh." She wiped the tears from her eyes as she tried to regain her composure. "Haven't done that in a while. Thank you."

"You're welcome?" George was certain she had entered the nonsense stage of her drunkenness. "But you've lost me, Mrs. Delano."

She took in a deep breath, then sat up to twist toward the table on the opposite side. She pulled a paper from on top of it and moved her hand under the light of the lamp and held it to face George. "This George. This is who we yearn for."

George held back a gasp. His eyes widened. Eleanor was in possession of a photograph of Connor and Jennifer. Both were splashing in a lake in the sunshine, smiling from ear to ear. He took it from her to stare at it more closely. Connor had facial hair. He hadn't shaved in weeks. The picture had to be recent.

"Could they look any happier, George?" she stated with envy.

Keeping his gaze fixed on the image, he asked, "Where did you get this, Mrs. Delano?"

"I may be forbidden from seeing my grandchild, George, but I'm certainly not going to keep myself from watching out for her." She paused to give George the time to process it all. After a moment, she added, "You miss him, don't you?"

George reminded himself that she was not of sound mind at the moment. *Did she mean to show me this? Will she even remember that she did come tomorrow?* But he had to know. "Who? Who took this?"

"The same person who took these." She flailed her arm over to grab the five other photographs sitting on the end table, handed them to George then watched as he looked at each one individually: Connor and Jennifer sitting up against a tree reading, Connor and Jennifer building a campfire, Connor and Jennifer packing up a motorhome, Connor and Jennifer entering a convenience store. As the last one was revealed, she asked, "Was he talking to you, George?" It was a picture of Connor standing at a payphone, receiver against his ear.

Shit. She's having them followed. George could feel his panic rising. How could he not have known this? And what could he respond without jeopardizing her trust? She was waiting. He had to say something. *Answer with a question.* "Where are they?"

"Vacationing with his parents," she replied, staring at him. "Isn't that what you said, George?"

Keep your cool, George said to himself. *Don't let her get to you.* "I did, but he never said where. Exactly."

"You should've stopped him when you had the chance," she warned. "Who knows how far he'll go? Or if he'll ever come home." She dropped her head, visibly distressed. "Unless."

"Unless what?"

"Go to him, George."

George looked up at her with confusion.

"You want him back, don't you?"

Don't respond. Don't respond.

"George, he needs you too."

Oh how I wish that were true, thought George with a heavy heart. "Look at them," he finally replied, while raising the pictures. "They're happy. They're obviously fine." Like Eleanor, George struggled with seeing their joy and not being able to share in it. "Connor will come home when he's ready."

"I'm disappointed in you, George. I was certain you were a

better friend than that."

How dare she! The last thing George needed was another reminder of his failure as a friend to Connor. *God she's good. Even drunk, she's a conniving bitch.* George stood up and extended his hand out to return the pictures to her. "It's time for me to leave now, Mrs. Delano. It's been a long day."

"Keep them," she replied, while waving them away. Then, reaching into her purse by her side, she pulled out a prescription bottle. "And here. Take these. You might need them tonight." It contained two Quaalude tablets. "They work for Dawn. They'll help you with the strain of being away from Connor."

She has real nerve, he fumed, while wishing he could throw them at her forehead. But he refrained himself. He had to. "Thank you," he said, picking up his briefcase. "Good night, Mrs. Delano."

"And George," she added as he turned away. "Let me know if you change your mind."

* * *

As soon as George got back to his apartment, he sat on the edge of his bed and planted his forehead into his palms. The bombshell revelation that Eleanor was having Connor followed was catastrophic. All this time, he had been telling Connor she wasn't asking about them. *No wonder. She's known all along.* What would George tell him now? *If he finds out, he'll blame me. Then he'll hide even farther. I'll lose him forever.*

He pulled the pictures out of his briefcase, and stared at

them again. But they only made him realize just how badly he missed Connor. How selfish he was for wanting him to come home. How jealous it made him to see him this happy without him. He worried that Eleanor was right; Connor would never return. Why would he? There was nothing for him here other than his psycho in-laws, of whom one was watching his every move. Who knew what else she was capable of? *But is he in more danger if I don't tell him?* George was sweating, his legs shaking, his mind was racing. *And how on earth does she know how I feel about him?* George had never told anyone, not even Connor. He barely acknowledged it to himself, preferring to ignore the attraction that would never be reciprocated. But his feelings were real, and at the moment felt agonizing. As tempting as it was to go to Connor, George knew it would jeopardize ever earning back his trust. *It's just a trap. She's dangerous. Connor always said it.*

He wanted to do the right thing for his best friend. But how could he now that the witch was onto him? *God only knows what she did to make him run.* George unleashed his rage by yelling at the top of his lungs. Maybe the volume could override the nagging sound of his thoughts. Stop the tension from building up even further. He was desperate for some rest, some clarity. He tried convincing himself that tomorrow he would know what to do, he would find a way to keep Connor safe. He had to.

He removed his shoes, jacket, tie and belt, before dropping his pants and unbuttoning his shirt. He lied down in his briefs and undershirt and tried closing his eyes. He bolted right back up and began to pace. Then he remembered Eleanor's parting gift. *Damn her,* he grumbled. Against his better judgement, he reached into his briefcase for the pill bottle, then rushed to the sink to pour a glass of water before washing one down. He then collapsed back onto his bed, and waited for the calming effect to take hold.

CHAPTER SEVENTEEN

— 1962 —

Connor lay on his bed, staring up at the ceiling, unsure of what to think or how to feel. He was aching for Heather's company, as he did each time he retreated to his bedroom. But tonight, he was consumed by far more.

Since their very first encounter two years ago, he obsessed over how long he could hold onto her. How long it would take before she realized he wasn't good enough. But as of today, he could put an end to trying to avert the chance of their relationship failing. Soon, Heather would be his forever.

And so would their child.

Stunned, he processed this sudden, new reality. It wasn't the cause for celebration that it should be. These were circumstances intended for much farther into the future. Circumstances that should have been foreseen – at minimum, discussed ahead of time. Instead, they were mandated. And a celebration there would be, with plans already underway. Grandiose and glamorous. In only a matter of weeks.

In the living room outside his closed bedroom door, he could still hear the faint sound of his mother's sobs. She was reeling in agony over the loss of her son's innocence. How all the promise he showed was completely cast aside at such a young age. A careless moment of temptation. A night of seduction carrying a lifetime sentence of parenthood. And the innocent child that would follow, entrusted to the care of immature teens.

Connor took a little solace in his father's reaction. He had held his tongue, comforted his wife, and applauded his son's sense of responsibility. Though Connor still felt his deep disappointment, he was grateful to have been spared his judgement. Which would not be the case tomorrow, when telling George, who most definitely was incapable of such restraint.

As he lay there, Connor relived today's conversation over and over. He had been prepared for it to be serious; Heather never insisted they meet so early. So as always, he was worried that she didn't want to be with him anymore. Even though, not once in two years, had she ever said a word, or implied anything to that effect. At times, she would go silent. Possibly for days. That's when his anxiety would intensify. But not only for fear that she was leaving him. Of greater concern was how badly she had been hurt. That he might have to defy her demands, and call the police to have her father apprehended.

But Heather was neither crying nor panting when she had called him last night. Nor did she need him to soothe her in any way. And yet, her voice sounded different, distressed. She seemed guarded, and insisted they needed to speak in person.

It was just after dinner when the phone had rung. "Conway, we need to meet. But not at your place. How early can you be at the park tomorrow morning?"

"As early as you want," he had replied. "Is everything okay?"

"I'll fill you in tomorrow. Let's meet at nine."

That conversation had ended quickly. Too quickly. Which had made Connor immediately question whether it had to do with their first sexual encounter. Maybe she hadn't enjoyed it; even though she had been the one to initiate it. But it was unplanned and too hurried. Not romantic like he had hoped. Then before he knew it, they were done and she was rushing back home. Did she now regret it? Was the sight of his scrawny body with pasty white skin and a tuft of auburn public hair a complete turn off?

Those were the thoughts going through his mind earlier this morning when he sat waiting for her by the pond at Boston Public Garden. The park was still quiet with only a few young families and dog walkers strolling along the paved paths under a cloudless summer sky. He was fidgeting with his hair and fingernails when he saw her arriving in the distance. Jumping up from the grass to go greet her, he held her tightly after she ran into his arms for a hug. Just one kiss was all it took to bring him instant relief.

She sat down on the grass by a large tree, tucking her sundress around her bent knees that rested to one side. "Conway, I have to tell you something. But I…I don't know how," she stated with a look of deep concern.

Facing her, legs crossed, he took both her hands in his. "Did he hurt you again?" He looked around her bare skin for any evidence of bruising, but saw none. "You can tell me. You know that." He tried his best to sound reassuring.

"Conway. This is different. I really don't want you to be

upset with me." She couldn't even bring herself to look at him.

"What? How? No, Heather," he reassured. "I could never be upset with you. But you're scaring me so please…please just say it." His heart was beginning to pound.

"God. How do I say this? Conway…" She looked into his eyes. "I…I'm pregnant."

Connor couldn't breathe.

He stared blankly, trying not to faint, not to vomit, not to say something stupid. It took a few seconds for him to realize that in their haste, he hadn't worn a condom. He had been too caught up in the passion of the moment to even think of it. How careless he had been. But was it possible for her to know this soon?

"Please, Conway. Say something," she begged, her eyes welling up with tears.

He inhaled deep breaths over and over, until he finally found the words. "Are…are you okay?"

His reaction of concern relieved some of her tension. "Yes. I am. I mean, physically yes. And, I need you to know…" She dropped her head. "I told my mother –"

"You what?"

"I know. I know. But, I thought…I was sure she would make me get an abortion. I…I wanted to do that for you. For us."

Connor let go of her hands and pressed his against his skull. Within the space of one minute, he learned of the existence of this pregnancy, followed by the intent for it to be terminated. This was a lot. More than either of them was prepared for. And while a part of him obviously wanted to make this go away, an abortion made him nervous. What would it do to Heather? How would she be after that? And how would he feel? Would he be too scared to touch her again? But then, did they really have a choice? Clearly they were unfit to raise a child. He felt weak, pale, and on the verge of passing out.

"She won't allow it, Conway. She's insisting we get married."

Connor raised his eyes in shock. He was stunned, baffled. "Your mother…wants you to marry me?"

"Yes," she replied, before lowering her gaze. "Right away."

This seemed like pure insanity. "And you? You want that too?" he asked, uncertain he was more afraid she'd say no or say yes.

"It's not that simple. There's more, Conway." It was the worst part of what she had yet to share.

"Okay?" He couldn't imagine what else there could be after that bombshell.

"It's really awful. I'm afraid of –"

"Shit, Heather it's okay. Please just…just tell me." Connor didn't know if he could take more, but he needed it out so he could try processing it all.

She hesitated, her eyes red. "It's not yours," she cried, bursting into a deep sob.

Connor nearly fell backwards. Had he been standing, he would've fallen to his knees. He tried to keep it together. Tried to understand how she could have been with someone else. Or why she was so determined to be with him just recently, if she was already intimate with another. How could she do this to him? How long had this been going on?

He felt hurt, angry, betrayed. He couldn't hold back. He

needed to know. To understand. "Who Heather? Who else did you sleep with?" His face was crimson. His eyes bloodshot.

"No! Conway. It's not like that. There's no one but you. I….I promise."

"Heather…" Connor felt enraged, but chose to abort his sentence. He couldn't think of anything to say that wouldn't be hurtful. He lowered his gaze, shaking his head, wishing this was all just a terrible dream.

"Conway, I…I was raped."

Those words descended on Connor like a boulder crushing his chest. He could feel the tension building within him as his mind went straight to the lake where they had first met. How vividly he recalled happening upon someone that was ready to violate her. How he had been able to interrupt the act that time. Been able to rescue her then. So why did this have to happen when he wasn't there to protect her?

His eyes filled with tears of failure. Looking into hers, he asked. "Who? Who Heather? Who did this to you?"

"One of my father's business partners," she cried, her head planted in both palms.

"How? Where?" he agonized. He knew her to be so safe. If she wasn't at home or at school, she was with Connor. And even then, only if Dawn was going out and let her tag along so the driver could drop Heather off and pick her up.

"I had another stupid argument with my mother….A really big one….So I stormed out of my room. It was really late. I was sure no one was around." She paused to wipe her tears, catch her breath.

Connor squeezed her hands. "Take your time, Heather."

"I went to the lounge to grab a drink from the bar. I was gonna bring it back to my room...I crossed him in the hallway just as he was leaving –"

"Who was he?" Connor was struggling to remain calm.

"I don't know. I never saw him before. My father has so many partners. But this one was really angry. More than I was."

"Okay, then what?"

"I was embarrassed to be seen in my nightgown so I ran. He was so hurried, I thought he didn't notice me. I was sure he was gone when I reached the bar. The lights were so dim while I poured my drink. Then..." She burst into tears.

Connor moved in beside her. Wrapped his arm around her shoulder and pulled her head against his chest, rocking her back and forth. He tried hard to hold back his own tears, his deep anger. He couldn't say a word through his tightly pursed lips.

She eventually composed herself enough to continue. "Then he approached me from behind. He covered my mouth and said something like he was making my father pay for backstabbing him –"

"Where the hell was your father?!" shouted Connor.

"I don't know. In his den. On the phone or with someone else. The guy obviously knew he wasn't coming down soon."

"It takes a special kind of creep to rape someone's daughter in his own damn home. Did you call the police?"

She couldn't look at him. "He said if I told anyone, he would destroy me and my family... And I was afraid if I told you...you would never want me."

"When did this happen, Heather?"

Her head dropped in shame. "Almost a month ago."

"But, but, why? Why didn't you tell me?" cried Connor with compassion, unable to believe he had been kept in the dark. That he hadn't noticed it in her behavior. Until he realized. "We made out, Heather. Did you even want to?" He couldn't help but think that for her, their intimacy was just an attempt at masking what had happened. Or worse, a cruel reminder of it. Meanwhile for him, it was so much more.

"Yes, Conway. I wanted to. I hated having this, this, horrible experience of it. I know it was selfish of me. I know. But I wanted to just be with you. To be touched by…by someone who loves me, someone gentle. But Conway, I didn't know I was pregnant. I would never have –"

"Never have what? Been with me? Ever?" He pulled his arm away from her.

She grabbed it back. "No, Conway. I would never have had sex without you knowing."

He waved her off. "We did have sex without me knowing. Knowing that you were raped!"

"Would you still want me if I had?" A fresh set of tears rolled down her cheeks.

"Yes…No…I don't know, Heather. Maybe not right away. I'll be honest. As stupid as it sounds, I feel violated too. You're mine. I don't wanna share you," he replied, defeated, a tear finally escaping.

"If I wanted the abortion, it was so I could be with you, Conway."

"Shit, Heather. Does your mother even know? I mean, know the father isn't me?"

"No. All she cares about is that we get married. She's insisting. Like right away. To make it look like I got pregnant on our wedding night. She's determined for her grandchild to be legitimate."

"This is crazy, Heather. And dangerous. What if this guy shows up again. Decides he wants to claim his kid?"

"Conway, no. Never. He'd never dare come back. And he'll never know about the baby. No one will. It will be your baby. That's if…you want it to be."

"What about your father? There's no way he's okay with you getting married."

"My mother's taking care of it. He doesn't know I'm pregnant. And he won't. He'll only be told after, and that it happened on our wedding night. She'll find a way to sway him with a big event for his sake. He falls for that shit."

"Is he too stupid to know pregnancies last nine months?" Connor exclaimed.

"We'll just say it's premature. It's not that rare. But that's why she wants the wedding to be soon. And super fancy so it doesn't look like it was a last minute thing."

"Then what happens after we're married? Your parents will be awful to me. And…And I don't want your father anywhere near this baby." In that moment, Connor recognized his very first impulse to protect this child.

"They won't go near us. My mother told me so. She made me a promise. If we get married, they'll stay away. Always.

She swore it. They won't be in the baby's life. Ever. Her only contribution will be money so that we can, you know, get an apartment and stuff."

Connor wasn't sure if he was more shocked by the situation itself or that Heather was amenable to it. "And you believe her?"

"Yes Conway. I do. She was really, really serious. This is her grandchild and she wants to protect it."

"I don't know how you can trust her."

"I don't have a choice."

"But…is this what *you* want? I mean a baby? And…and me?"

"Conway, I'm sixteen, pregnant from rape, and have been beaten by my father for the last four years. I don't want any of that. None. I don't know how much more I can stand. But maybe, if I can have you, then I get to live in a home where I'm just safe and loved. A place I can keep this baby away from all the bad stuff."

"Jesus, Heather."

"So yes, Conway. I want to marry you. Only you. But if I can't. If this isn't what you can accept. I'll understand. I will. I mean it. Cause absolutely none of this is your fault. It's all mine. I don't even deserve to live."

"Wait." Connor held her shoulders and looked her in the eyes. "No. Don't say that. Don't you ever say that. None of this is your fault."

She shrugged herself away. "Just leave me, Conway. This isn't fair to you. You should find someone who isn't damaged."

"No, no, no, no, no, Heather. That's not an option. I'm not going anywhere. And neither are you. Do you hear me?"

"It's pointless, Conway. I don't even know why I bothered coming into your life. I'm a complete mess. You don't deserve that. All you deserve is goodness."

"Heather, stop. Please. Let's just keep talking. This is big, you know? I just need a minute to think about it. It's a lot to digest. But I love you. That's all that matters right now. So come here and let me hold you."

He scooted in beside her and pulled her head against his chest and began to rock her gently. She could feel his heartbeat against her ear. They sat quietly, staring into the distance as two swans drifted across the pond. Instinctively he began to describe the surface of the water as a trail of ripples followed behind the elegance of their bold white feathers. How their smooth advance masked any hint of the vigorous paddling of their webbed feet beneath. How their graceful long necks were held high and steady, always focused forward. As he spoke, he could feel the gradual release of tension in her posture, the weight of her head sinking more deeply against his shoulder. Slowly, he brought her toward a place of calm. Even if momentary, it was a reminder of how he had that ability with her. Which made him realize she could never go through this alone. Nor could he let her.

He broke their long moment of silence. "Okay. So if we're gonna do this, I have two requests."

Surprised by his consideration, she replied, "By *do this*, you mean what exactly?"

"I mean…get married."

"Okay?" She felt encouraged. Surprised, but encouraged. "What kind of requests?"

"No one – and I mean no one – not even this baby, will ever know it isn't mine." He turned towards her. "I'm the one who got you pregnant. Okay?"

"Yes, Conway. Of course. Your name will go on the birth record. No one will even question it."

"As for you, you have to promise me you'll never do anything to put yourself at risk. You'll never go near him, no matter the reason. And you'll never go anywhere alone unless it's like… the hairdresser, or the grocery store, or someplace crowded and super safe."

"Yes, Conway," she replied, like a young child obeying the house rules.

"I mean it Heather. I can't. I won't spend my life worrying that my wife is in danger. I'll go mad."

She giggled.

"This isn't funny, Heather. I'm being very serious right now."

"I know you are. It's just funny. More like sweet to hear you say *wife*." She smiled for the first time today. "Got any other requests?"

"I want a lifetime, Heather. None of this *I don't deserve to live* shit. Till death do us part means we grow old together. You have to promise me you'll never hurt yourself. Ever."

She lowered her head, uncomfortable with the inference, even if it was justified. But she was too relieved by the lifeline he had just thrown her to give him any reason to believe she would waver. "I promise."

"Good," he nodded. "Then, I guess I need to get you a ring."

It had felt like a pleasant conclusion to an otherwise intense conversation. But from the moment they parted ways, Connor's mind began to race. And hours later, he was still thinking and processing the magnitude of the commitment he had made, while letting it slowly sink in.

Could he and Heather really do this? Or were they making a horrible mistake?

One minute his confidence waned, the other he relished the idea that she was really going to be his and only his. There was only one way for Connor to maintain his resolve. To stay focused on his unwavering love for Heather, and on his determination to protect her and their child.

CHAPTER EIGHTEEN

— 2003 —

I should have seen this coming. Been more prepared. But that just wasn't how I was wired. I lived in the present, perfectly fine to leave unnecessary stress for another day, well into the future, as close as possible to never ever. But that day had not only come, it pulled me into unchartered territory.

At first, the thoughts of Nick, of Dad, and surprisingly of Mom, came in waves. They swept in quickly then subsided with enough of a distraction. But as they persisted, they grew in intensity, whirling rampantly through my mind, making me feel vulnerable, rudderless. Before long, they morphed into a full-on storm of preoccupation that engulfed me. So here I was, overcome with the impulse to reflect, to question, and, if I was being completely candid, to indulge in self-pity, while stranded on the isle of overthinking.

It was bad enough to be consumed by the eventuality of confronting a life without Nick, but I was also plunging into the recesses of my mind in search of memories of my youth that may not actually exist; which, of course, made no sense, and only served to generate a growing number of questions likely to remain unanswered. I needed time to stop. To have a moment to myself. To settle. But between tending to Nick and worrying about his battle, trying to hold the fort for the girls, and keeping up with work, there wasn't much left in a day. And, of course, there was Dad. *God, I really need a spa day.*

Sadly, my me-time didn't involve much pampering. It was relegated to the aisles of Star Market where I sifted through fresh produce, trying my best to ignore the tear-provoking lyrics of Shania Twain's, You're Still The One. I felt like shouting out in frustration, *That don't impress me much!* I may have even made myself chuckle with that one. That is, if I wasn't so focused on trying to keep my defective shopping cart straight. Yes, on top of everything else, I was today's lucky shopper assigned the wonky wheel cart intent on veering to the right.

As I gauged the ripeness of avocados, while surrounded by an army of impatient midday-Sunday shoppers, I envied their functioning carts and resented that their worlds weren't being disrupted by cancer. Okay, maybe I was being a little unfair. Perhaps everyone here was dealing with something undesirable. Why else would we be breaking up a perfectly good weekend with such a mundane task? Were we all secretly hoping our troubles could be resolved in the junk food section? Would a pilgrimage to the freezer aisle numb our brains? I suppose the one upside to my state of mind was that I didn't feel pressured to remember everything on my food list. Forgetting would give me another excuse to submit to more grub-therapy.

It was the thought of losing Nick that was a trigger like no other. And while that loss may be a long time away, another suddenly became equally preoccupying, and possibly more imminent. What would I do without Dad? He was my constant. Stable, even when his mind was not. Comforting, even when his heart was crushed. But my perception of him seemed different now. I had taken so much for granted where he was concerned. How despite his own needs, whatever those might be, he always made me feel like I was all that ever mattered. And it was still true even now with his limitations. No matter my mood, my fatigue, or how busy I was, his company made me feel better, calm, reassured. It shamed me that it had taken our 'chat' about Mom and George for it to occur to me how much he had suffered without ever letting on. Not even a little. Was that all for my sake? Did he feel I couldn't handle it? Or was he truly just that selfless?

As for Mom, she was by far my most confusing topic. I was struggling with this in a way I never imagined that I would, feeling guilty for not ever exhibiting even the slightest curiosity, and disappointed in myself for never asking Dad how he felt after losing her. I may even be somewhat intrigued about how our lives would have been had she not been in that accident. It was as though a void appeared out of nowhere, prompted by a bizarre inquiry from a detective, that I was now compelled to fill. Perhaps this yearning was also motivated by my obsession with Nick staying in our girls' lives come what may. I had to believe that no matter how broken I might feel after losing him, I could never erase him from memory, never remove him from our future. I felt very strongly that I would make every effort to keep his spirit alive for them, to talk about him, to have pictures of him throughout the house, to uphold family traditions that he had begun. And I would do the same after Dad would one day pass. Meanwhile, when Mom died, she simply ceased to exist. How horrible that seemed to me now. How wrong. How sad. Perhaps the gap I had never felt before was always there, lying dormant, completely unobtrusive, waiting for me to reach this epiphany. But it felt so cruel that it was manifesting itself now of all times.

What I was struggling with most was why I knew so little about Mom. My memories of her were vague at best. Not a single conversation nor moment really stuck with me. I just had brief flashes of her at home or in the hospital. Nothing that pulled at the heartstrings. Nothing that I could say I really cherished. She was a presence bereft of personality. Like a background figure. Or an extra cast in a film; essential to the realism but not critical to the plot. Or wait staff in a restaurant; keeping the wine glasses full but never joining in the toast or the conversation. She was the type of person who didn't draw attention; at least not mine in any event.

I trudged along to the next aisle, resisting every temptation to kick my defective cart forward to release some aggression. Maybe later, I would take my adrenalin to the streets with a good run, but for now, I resolved to remain well-behaved and collect my items in an orderly fashion. I glanced across shelves of condiments and spices, hoping to simply stay focused on what I needed. But no, my mind immediately went back to Mom and how bland she was. Neither flavorful, spicy, sweet or savory. Even her facial expressions were dull. Her smile was never from ear-to-ear, her laughter never from the gut, her anger

THE BURDEN OF TRUTH

was controlled, if not muted. As for her gestures, they, too, were tame. All I could recall was that she swung her leg when she sat and had a twitch in her finger. I hadn't really noticed it until I held her hand while she was in the hospital. I subconsciously anticipated the sporadic movement, but she had remained completely still.

While I was beating myself up for not showing interest in learning more about her, my real question was targeted at Dad and why he never initiated a single discussion. There had to be a reason and it had to be something big enough to make the topic so taboo. I was a logical, rational person. Surely I could figure this out. So I considered the plausible reasons. The first was what I had always assumed; he was too heart-broken and couldn't bring himself to talk about her without falling apart. That seemed acceptable. Until now. Faced with the possibility that I might become a single parent one day, I was adamant that grief alone was no excuse for relegating a spouse to the past. So there had to be more to it.

I thought about Mom's behavior and considered the possibility that she might have been unwell. She seemed to always have something on her mind. And she was obsessed with safety, almost paranoid. Our front and back doors had dead-bolts. No matter where I went, she insisted Dad accompany me. We couldn't travel anywhere other than to Dad's parents because she only saw risks. The minute we got into the car, we had to press down the lock buttons. I had to come straight home from school. Sleep-overs weren't permitted. Could it be that she suffered from some sort of anxiety disorder? It would explain why Dad might feel uncomfortable talking about her. At least while I was too young to understand. But wouldn't he one day feel that was something I should know? Or had we just reached a point of no return on the topic?

"God, I'm literally spiraling."

"Good one!" laughed the random shopper crossing me in the aisle.

I hadn't realized I had said that out loud nor that I was holding a box of rotini noodles. The unintended pun did cause me to grin.

Back to Mom and her behavior. She wasn't an affectionate women by any means. At least not with me. Dad was more touchy-feely, always sitting in the middle of the couch, wrapping his arms around us so we could both rest our heads against his shoulders. She wasn't big on one-on-one time either. I had more of that with Dad. He's the one who read me bedtime stories. She only came in afterward to kiss my forehead and wish me sweet dreams. He played board games with me and seemed interested when I spoke about something that happened at school. Meanwhile, she was very quiet, reserved, disengaged. Could it be that I was the issue? Maybe she wasn't into kids. Dad certainly wouldn't want to tell me that.

I rounded the bend, relieved it was time for a right turn and arrived in the junk food aisle to grab a bag of nachos. The chips, pop and marshmallows triggered a memory. The one time Mom had actually seemed excited, albeit momentarily. We were eating dinner when, out of nowhere, she had suggested we go on a camping trip. She wanted to be lakeside, swimming and sitting by a campfire. I was mesmerized by her enthusiasm and the prospect of this dream vacation. It may have been the happiest I remember seeing her. Then, just as quickly as she had hatched this wonderful plan, she reverted back to her cautious, boring self, and ran off all the reasons we shouldn't go in one fell swoop. From unpredictable weather, to getting lost, to crowds, to not being safe in a tent, to bugs; each element was a strike against moving forward. So naturally we never went. Not until she was in hospital, that is.

Then something else came to mind. Mom rarely went anywhere without Dad. So where on earth was she going when she got into her accident? It couldn't be a doctor's appointment or the bank or a store, because she had left in the evening. And if I recall correctly, which of course is hit and miss, I feel like she was all dressed up.

I stopped dead in my tracks. "Oh...My...God...." I figured it out. "She was having an affair." My jaw dropped, my eyes probably bulged out of my head.

"Everything okay with you, dear?" asked an elderly woman, who released her cart to place her hand on my forearm.

"Oh. Yes. Yes. I'm fine. Thank you. I...just realized I forgot something in the dairy section," I replied dismissively.

Did I just uncover the big fat secret? The reason for all the silence? It explained everything. She was cheating on Dad. She went out to be with her lover and was killed in the process. Dad found out and was doubly devastated by the tragedy. Had he been suspicious before then? Or did he only discover the affair while at the hospital?

My poor father. How horrible for him. That would totally justify his lack of interest in talking about her. He'd have to lie; paint a picture of a wonderful mother to me, while feeling jilted, betrayed, used. This had to be the reason. I was certain of it. And as terrible as it was, I felt this odd sense of relief in having arrived at a rational explanation.

Before I knew it, I was pulling into the driveway. And though my mind was still swirling, my sanity felt partially restored by my successful deducing. I parked then popped the hood open. Too lazy to make a second trip into the house, I divvied up the bag weight so that it was equal in both hands, then made my way to the front door. I could hear Nick and the girls inside so I didn't bother putting anything down to pull the knob and just leaned my forehead against the doorbell.

Lisa came rushing to open it and greeted me with the most heartfelt welcome. "Yay, guacamole is here!" she cheered, turning toward her sisters and Nick in the living room.

They were all sporting their New England Patriots jerseys to watch the game that was underway. A coloring book was on the coffee table, to keep Lisa, who wasn't quite as interested, occupied while they watched.

"I prefer it when you call me Mommy," I replied with a wink.

She hugged me as I extended my bag-carrying arms outward. "Okay Mommy. Oh and Mommy, Mommy! Tom Brady is gonna take us to the toilet bowl!"

"Super Bowl!" Grace, Hannah, and Nick shouted in unison to correct her.

"Oopsy," she giggled. Her mischievous grin suggested her mistake was deliberate.

"I'm not so sure about that, sweetie." I replied, walking toward the kitchen to set the bags onto the counter.

Thrilled as I had been when our young quarterback earned us the coveted championship title in his second season with us, I was the more realistic Pats fan of the household and didn't hold out much hope for a repeat performance.

"You just wait and see, Jen," Nick shouted from the couch, his eyes fixed on the third down conversion.

"How 'bout we start by making the playoffs." I shouted back, while placing items into the fridge and cabinets. Following our big win, came a lackluster season; another reason for my lower expectations.

"Mark my words," said Nick, emphatically. "This kid is something else. We're going back. I can feel it." He was in great spirits today, his enthusiasm was palpable. As was his apparent man-crush on Tom Brady, who, I admit, wasn't too hard on the eyes.

Nick joined me in the kitchen during a commercial break and gave me a kiss on the cheek.

"Looks like you're feeling better today," I smiled.

Four perfectly ripe avocados sat in a mixing bowl, peeled and ready for mashing and spicing.

"My girls, the Pats, and no puking. What more could I ask for?" he grinned, grabbing a serving bowl into which to pour the bag of nachos. "Oh and I should probably tell you. The trailer for Return Of The King aired earlier. Told the girls I would take them during Christmas break."

I paused my prep and looked up with deep concern for the expectations he was setting. "Nick, you need to be careful making promises like that. They'll be so disappointed if you can't go."

"I know, I know. I wasn't going to, but I just...feel so good today. Like I'm back to normal. And it made them so happy. Even Lisa."

"I get it," I sighed, "And I hope it works out." I then pointed my avocado-infused potato masher at him. "But you're on nightmare duty if she's traumatized by all the disgusting creatures."

"She'll be fine. I'll watch the other episodes with her first. Her sisters said they'll join us too." He paused and walked in behind me. "Also, I kinda told her the orcs were like cancer."

"You did what?" I turned to face him, leaving my masher on the cutting board.

"Hear me out," he said, his hands on my shoulders. "Like you said, they're disgusting. Plus they're mean and they attack –"

"Exactly what she doesn't need to see."

"Yes, but we know that they get destroyed in the end. By Frodo. He's the chemo. Get it? It's a perfect visual image. Admittedly a bit graphic. But it works."

I didn't know whether I wanted to smack him or take pity on him, so I refrained from uttering an explicative and instead replied, "You had better hope Peter Jackson didn't take creative liberties with the ending."

"He would do no such thing." Nick frowned, insulted by the mere inference any director would dare tamper with something as sacred as The Lord Of The Rings. "Honor the trilogy he shall," he stated with his fist against his heart. With that, he grabbed the bowl and marched back into the living room. He paused part way and added, "Oh before I forget, I found something for you. It's on your nightstand."

"Okay. I'll get it when I change into leggings."

He was already at the couch when he added, "No need to rush. Stay upstairs as long as you need to."

"Okay?" I wasn't so sure I actually wanted more time to myself. My head needed a break. Fun family time seemed like the better choice. I wiped up the counter before bringing my freshly made bowl of guacamole to the family. "Here you go, team. I'll be back to join you in a minute."

All four swarmed in to scoop nachos into it and replied, mouths full, "Thanks, Mommy."

As I walked into our bedroom, I noticed my jersey was prominently displayed across our mattress; a friendly reminder to get into uniform before heading back down. I threw it on over my t-shirt, then swapped out of jeans and into leggings. I was just about to walk out the door, when I remembered to go to my nightstand. Nick had placed a folded piece of paper on it. I dropped onto the side of the bed to open it, expecting blood test results, a medical bill, a list of items he needed from the drugstore. But not this. Even though he had said he would find it, I didn't expect it would be so soon.

On the page he had written a phone number. It was for my Aunt Dawn. And the area code was local. I stared at it and waited for my mind to begin its theatrics. Right on cue, the questions started to open fire. Should I call her? If so, when would be a good time? Will she answer? What would I even say? Will she be happy to hear from me? Is she even curious about me? It wasn't lost on me that she would have answers to at least some of what was eating away at me. Like, how my mother was as a child, whether they were close, did I have cousins? And of course, did she have any idea about the affair? But would she volunteer any knowledge of it if she did? That's assuming she would even entertain my call. It's not like she ever tried reaching out to me before. And why was the family estranged in the first place? *Here I go spiraling again.*

I really wasn't made for this type of internal debate. I preferred clear, straight-forward logic. So I broke it down to the worst that could happen: no answer or she would hang up on me. Was that so terrible? It's not like she was in my life. Losing the potential of her being in it wasn't that tragic. And yet, the thought of dialing made me feel so nervous.

"I have zero chance of getting an ounce of sleep tonight if I don't do this." So I picked up the wireless receiver and began to press the numbers, then stopped. "I should pee first."

I bolted up and walked a few steps to the ensuite bathroom to relieve my bladder. When I returned, I sat back against the headboard, legs outstretched on the bed. I even placed my hair behind my shoulders; a comfortable pose seemed best before picking up the receiver to dial the numbers. The phone rang five times before she picked up.

"Hello," said a voice that sounded mildly out of breath.

"Oh. Hi. Is this Dawn?" I asked, my heart already pounding.

"Yes. Who's this?" She sounded justifiably leery.

"Um. It's Jennifer. Heather's daughter. Your niece." The need to be this elaborate seemed so awkward.

She didn't reply.

I moved the receiver in front of me to look at it before placing it back against my ear. "Hello?"

"Sorry," she responded. "You…" She paused. "This is… unexpected."

"Oh gosh, it is right? I'm so sorry to bother you. I just –"

"Just what?"

"Just thought it might be nice to talk?"

Silence again.

I resisted saying anything. It was only fair to give her time to speak.

She eventually replied, "Why?"

Not what I expected, and I didn't have a coherent response ready. "I don't know. I guess because I never got to really know my mother. I thought maybe you would be willing to tell me about her."

"Oh," she replied with hesitation. "Can't you ask your father?"

If ours was a different dynamic, I could. But that wasn't how he and I rolled. Nor did it seem ideal in light of what I had just uncovered. "I just thought her sister's perspective would be different. That you'd have some juicy girl stuff to share –"

"What is that supposed to mean?" She sounded offended.

"Oh. Um. I guess I thought maybe you'd know things about her that no one else might. Stuff that would be nice for me to know." I wasn't sure if that even made sense.

"Okay," she said. "So you're curious?"

"Kind of, yeah." I smiled, hoping we were making headway.

"I'm not going to be able to help you."

"Oh." That felt harsh.

She may have sensed my tone. "I'm...too busy."

"I understand....I'm sorry I bothered you." It was hard to explain how disappointed I felt.

"You take care of yourself."

"Before you hang up." I was unwilling to completely close the door on a possible connection. "Can I leave you my phone number? In case you ever get...less busy?"

"Sure," she replied.

I dictated it slowly. Even repeated it. Though for all I knew, she probably only pretended to be writing it down.

I stayed seated on the bed for a while after hanging up. Did this woman have a heart? Or did I just drag her back to a place she preferred to forget? Was I being selfish thinking she'd want to get to know me?

Slowly, my eyes began to well up. I wasn't sure why exactly. I guess I was too overwhelmed. Or the rejection hurt more than I expected it would. I was reaching my tipping point when tears began to flow. Before I knew it, I was engaged in a big fat, ugly cry, to the sound of cheers below, signaling a touchdown. I knew that I should pull myself together and join my family in the celebration. Laughter, idle banter, snuggles on the couch would bring such relief. Relief I should be drawn to. But I couldn't stop crying, couldn't move. I felt heavy, broken, sad. Just like when my girls cried for their Mommy. Like I was suddenly crying for my own. It made no sense. It was embarrassing. I was a grown woman for God's sake. A cancer-free one, who lived an extraordinary life. One who needed to be strong. Should be strong. So what was happening to me? Was this how Mom was? Troubled to the point of not experiencing joy? I didn't want to be like her. I had no reason to. I lived with the man I loved. And I wasn't saddled with any guilt for wanting to be with anyone else.

That's when it hit me. And it was so much bigger than just an affair. "Oh my God!" I screeched. The realization struck my brain with the force of a bullet. "Am I Dad's child?"

My mind raced. Mom's affair could have begun long before she met him. If it did, was Dad just a pawn? Did she even want to marry him? And what about Dad? If this was true, did he only find out after her accident? Then worry my real father was coming to take me away.

"Holy shit! Detective Cisco asked if Dad was my biological father. He must know that he isn't."

I bolted up and ran to the bathroom to wipe my eyes and clear my nose. I stared into the mirror. "Tell me there's a resemblance somewhere." But the image staring back at me was all Mom. "Okay, how about my earlobes, my elbows, my toes, anything? There must be something physical that we have in common." I examined every inch of my body despite knowing full well that there wasn't. "It doesn't matter. Lots of kids don't look like their parents." I thought about my personality, my character, my mannerisms. About how often Nick said Dad and I were so alike. Then I stopped and looked back into the mirror. "Who cares? Biological or not, he is my father. Period. Nothing else matters." I stomped back into the bedroom, picked up the paper with Dawn's number and ripped it to shreds. "I have enough family without you," I exclaimed, tossing the pieces into the trashcan.

I stormed out of the room and stopped myself partway down the stairs. Is this something I needed to share with Nick? Would telling him make it matter more than it does? Make him worry about me? Nope. He didn't need to know. Like each of my parents, I was prepared to keep that secret safely tucked away.

* * *

It was a relief to be back in the office, surrounded by busy worker-bees, hyper-focused on their work. Drafting financial statements, planning out deadlines and overloading my agenda was delightfully unemotional.

Another yawn escaped; the result of a very fitful sleep. But my mind had stopped racing. It had come to a grinding halt, weighed down by unexpected and shocking truths. What a difference this discovery had made. I felt more numb than curious, more still than agitated. Hopefully this feeling of heaviness would dissipate over time. It would have to because I remained determined to keep this carefully guarded secret to myself. It seemed like the right way to honor Dad's unrelenting devotion. As for Mom, well, whoever it was that she truly loved must have brought her joy; a good person, I'm sure, but one I had no interest in knowing anything about. I had made the mistake of overthinking and suffered the consequence. Now it was time to shut down that thought for good.

"I'm heading out for a bit," I exclaimed, while stepping out of my office toward the elevator. Some fresh air seemed in order before the rain would start.

A crisp fall breeze had begun to dislodge leaves of red, orange and yellow from the maple trees throughout The Common. They brightened an otherwise dull, grey day, and lined the footpath with a crunchy carpet of color. I dragged my walking shoes, relishing the rustling sound as I kicked the leaves forward. I stopped as soon as I came upon a bench. It was enticing me to sit in tranquility.

As I let my head fall back, a flock of geese migrating south were honking loudly in v-formation directly above me. Lower to the ground an industrious chipmunk was gathering acorns in its extended cheeks, building a stockpile in preparation for its hibernation. The wonders and peacefulness of nature. A trusted respite from the emotional stirrings of the past few weeks. This gift from Dad, borne out of a motorhome adventure; his escape from tragedy and devastation, of a magnitude I now better understood. That journey toward the calm and magic of the natural world had not only sealed our father-daughter bond, it defined our relationship going forward. I hope it helped to heal his pain the way it made my own sadness disappear completely. If only there was a way to properly express my gratitude without upsetting him, without revealing that I now knew what he fought so hard to keep secret.

I let my eyes wander aimlessly throughout the park as I

listened to the wind blowing through the trees. The air already felt damp beneath dense clouds soon to release their moisture. A strand of hair tickled my cheek. I would tuck it behind my ear if not for the weight of my arms that rested comfortably across my lap. Students and workers crossed from various directions, some strides were hurried, others more casual. A gentlemen in a dark trench coat was approaching from the distance. Hands in his pockets, staring at the ground as he walked. He lifted his gaze my way momentarily. It didn't register immediately but when it did, I couldn't believe it.

"This can't be happening," I said to myself, quickly looking down and away from him, hoping he would turn back, or walk past without recognizing me. I waited without budging as the sound of his footsteps grew louder. Too loud. I was not in the mood for this. I debated getting up and rushing back to the office but I had missed my window of opportunity.

"Mrs. Vincent?" said Detective Cisco with a polite smile. "I thought that was you."

Trapped, I feigned a smile. "Oh. Hello. It's Detective Cisco, right?" I had forgotten how good looking he was. His one redeeming feature.

"Yup. That's me." He seemed to find our encounter equally awkward. "You've been well?"

Now that was a loaded question. In no small way thanks to him. "Fine, yes." I chose to withhold a polite reciprocation and instead looked away.

"Okay, well, I guess I'll move along." He seemed to be getting my drift. "Have a nice day."

Then, for reasons I could not explain, I blurted out, "So? Did you solve that case?" The case I wasn't supposed to concern myself with. The case that launched a chain of events leading me to Dad's best friend who's now dead, to Mom's sister who has no interest in speaking with me, oh and to the reality that my DNA isn't shared with the man who raised me with love and devotion.

"Oh, uh, still on it." He seemed surprised or uncomfortable, which made me feel better. A little payback for disrupting my life.

I was tempted to ask him about the picture of Dad and George now that I knew they had been close at one time. Why he had it. Where he got it from. But I resisted. My conscience quickly sounded the alarm. The impact of yesterday's reveal had me feeling extra cautious. There was risk in learning what might be best left unknown. Not to mention the fact that, where my secret was concerned, the one person who could expose it was standing right in front of me. I needed him to just walk away.

"Well, good luck with that. Have a nice day." I waved him off.

He nodded then continued along his way.

I watched as he faded from view, hoping that with his disappearance, all memory of Detective Cisco would be purged from my mind for good.

CHAPTER NINETEEN

— 2003 —

"Ms. Delano, when was the last time you saw George Vasquez?" asked Detective Cisco, while maneuvering his way around the clutter spread across her condo. He sat at one end of her l-shaped couch and rested his briefcase over his lap to avoid disrupting the disorder on her coffee table; a mountain of empty food cartons and wrappers was close to toppling over.

Dawn Delano appeared indifferent when he and Detective Randall arrived unannounced, just moments ago. Welcoming them in without a greeting, objection, or expression of any kind, she merely half gestured for them to take a seat in the living room. If she had been expecting them, the state of her household suggested otherwise. As for its natural light, it was dim for such a sunny morning; her large windows obstructed by blinds closed three-quarters and over-sized shelving jammed with floor-to-ceiling CD's. A bit of airflow would do wonders for dispersing the scent of stale chips and sitting garbage that permeated the room.

Exhibiting no discomfort with the condition of her home, their morbidly obese host sank herself right into the plush fabric at the opposite end and let her head of unbrushed, thick grey curls lean back as she caught her breath. "Let's see," she replied. "It's been a few years. He showed up when my mother died." She then turned toward Cisco and Randall. "Speaking of Mother, where are my manners? I should offer you a cup of tea." She placed her hands flat against the couch to thrust herself forward.

Manners? Cisco sensed they weren't a going concern of hers.

Detective Randall, who remained standing, palms resting against his lower back, responded, "No thank you, Ms. Delano. Kind of you to offer." He then returned to the topic at hand. "Was that unexpected? George Vasquez showing up at that time?"

Relieved to not have to further exert herself, Dawn leaned back, then interlaced her fingers and rested them above her belly, her eyes raised to the ceiling. "I was surprised. Until I learned he was the executor of her will." The middle finger of her left hand twitched as she spoke.

"Had you expected someone else to be? Yourself perhaps?" inquired Randall.

She inhaled before responding, the act of speaking appeared taxing. "No. Mother didn't inform me of such things. George, though. I would've expected him to be more forthright. But… it's not like it was the first time he kept something from me." She showed so little emotion, her finger twitching drew more attention than did her facial expression.

"Might you be referring to his confession, Ms. Delano?" asked Randall, cutting to the chase.

Cisco felt his question was too rushed. He had expected a more subtle approach to ease her into admitting to it herself. Ideally, along with her motive.

"And what confession is that?" she asked, with neither a look of surprise nor hint of denial.

"The one you sent us. Anonymously," replied Randall.

"Well, well, well." She finally turned her gaze toward them. "I suppose I have the two of you to thank for my long lost niece's sudden desire to connect?"

That comment came as a surprise to Cisco. From his recollection, Jennifer Vincent had no relationship with her mother's family. The timing of her reaching out seemed too coincidental to not have been prompted by his meeting with her.

"I'd say you're the one responsible for that, Ms. Delano," asserted Randall.

"Is that so? Do tell, Detective," she replied in a provoking tone.

At that, Cisco felt the need to interject. He did not want her thinking them antagonistic. Keeping their exchange cordial, he declared, "I met with Brandon Wong, Ms. Delano. He informed me that he gave you the letter. So…unless you then transferred it to someone else, we assume you were the one who sent it to the station."

"Well how 'bout that?" she smiled dryly. "I got played yet again. When will I ever learn?" Her sarcastic tone failed to mask her displeasure.

"I'm sorry?" Cisco didn't understand what she was implying.

"I never heard of Brandon Wong before," she began. "He finds my number and calls me out of nowhere, crying over his lost love, and how he's sorting through all his things. I, of course, want nothing to do with any of it. I don't feel the slightest remorse for the fact that poor Brandon felt as though he only had half of George. That's half more than I ever got, by the way. So I'm about to hang up when he tells me about this letter. Private and confidential. And that it's for me." She paused to catch her breath. "I should've just hung up. But no, I was always a fool where George was concerned. I actually thought it might be the apology he owed me. So I took down his address and drove my ass all the way to New York." She caught her breath again, then began to chuckle. "I swear, I laughed myself silly when I read it."

"Did I hear you correctly, Ms. Delano? George Vasquez's murder confession made you laugh?" frowned Cisco.

"Yes, Detective, it made me laugh," she exclaimed boldly, glaring into his eyes. "Oh, don't look at me that way. You never knew my father. The things he did to Heather. Said to me. George could've stabbed him with a pitchfork right in front of me and I would've cheered him on."

Noticing that Randall was about to reply, Cisco signaled for him to hold back. The incriminating nature of her comments was not lost on Cisco either, but he couldn't just dismiss the inference she had made regarding Anthony Delano's behavior toward his daughters. "So you're not upset to learn George Vasquez murdered your father?"

"No."

"Then may I ask what you hoped to accomplish by sending his confession to the station?" asked Cisco.

"To set the record straight. Let the files show that the despicable Anthony Delano deserved to be murdered," she explained as though it was blatantly obvious.

Both men looked at each other before Randall spoke. "I'm not sure you understand how law enforcement works, Ms. Delano. You sent a murder confession to the homicide department. It made your father the victim. The criminal was George Vasquez."

Disappointed that neither was capable of deducing the real truth of the matter, she proceeded to elaborate. "Gentlemen, does either of you have any idea what it's like to watch your sibling get beaten to a pulp because she's pretty?" She glared back and forth between them as they shook their heads uncomfortably. "Or to be told how very lucky you are to be fat because you're not the one getting hit?...Heather got the physical assault, I got the verbal thrashing, and it went on for years. Yes years." The look she gave them was so piercing, it was as though they were to be held personally responsible for what she and her sister had endured.

The men remained silent, both sensing that she wasn't quite done.

"Could we ask for help? Speak a word of it to anyone? No...I mean I wanted to, but then he threatened to hit her harder....That's right. It would be *my* fault. And I'm pretty sure he threatened her with the exact same." Her finger twitched feverishly, her cheeks became flush, and moisture began to form around her hairline. "So with all due respect, gentlemen, don't you dare tell me I don't understand how law enforcement works. I understand it just fine. And it's nowhere to be found when innocent girls are being abused in their own homes. I guess you're all too busy handing out parking tickets to the real criminals."

Fearing Randall's impulse to correct her, Cisco felt the need to stop him. This was not the time to explain the difference between patrol officers and detectives. Nor was it the point. She revealed something deeply personal, terribly horrific, and brutally shocking. "Ms. Delano," Cisco began, "I am terribly sorry for your suffering. Truly, I am. What happened to you and your sister is simply unforgivable. So I can appreciate why George Vasquez's actions brought you relief. That they felt like justice to you rather than a crime."

"Oh Detective, it would have felt like justice if I had actually known about it. Or if he had done it for my sake. But he didn't," Dawn replied with regret.

"What makes you believe that?" inquired Randall.

"After Heather got married, our father lost his favorite target. To make up for it, he flung double the verbal abuse my way. For nine more years I suffered. And George knew about it the whole damn time. So if it he had really wanted to protect me, he would've taken me away or killed that bastard much sooner."

The more she spoke, the more Cisco could tell her pain was still raw. That her feeling of powerlessness in the face of their abuse had left her bitter towards those who should have protected her. From his perspective, that was justified. What was even more frustrating was knowing there was nothing they could do for her.

Randall, however, suspected there was a hidden motive she wasn't revealing. And his years of experience had hardened him enough to look past her emotions. "Ms. Delano, you said you expected an apology from George Vasquez. An apology for what exactly?"

With her guard now lowered, she replied in a more compla-cent tone. "Abandoning me, among other things…Also, George knew I had feelings for him. But instead of telling me he didn't feel the same way, he let me believe that he did…I suppose the signs were always there. Maybe I did turn a blind eye. But we were really close. So I didn't appreciate being misled…I thought maybe he felt bad about that. Enough to put it in writing." After a brief pause, she added, "I suppose it was worse for Brandon Wong. He actually believed George reciprocated his love. But just like me, that poor fool learned long after the fact that George's heart belonged to another."

"Oh? And who might that be?" asked Randall.

"My dear old brother-in-law."

"Connor Rivers?"

"The one and only," she replied.

"Are you suggesting your father's murder had something to do with Connor Rivers?" asked Cisco, now wondering whether Randall's suspicions had been correct.

Staring blankly, she replied, "There was always something between the two of them. At first, I didn't question it. I thought it was sweet. Childhood buddies that were still close. But something seemed weird –"

"Weird how?" interrupted Randall.

"George talked about Connor all the time. I mean, all the time. It was obsessive. Every conversation we had, turned to the topic Connor. Connor this, Connor that. Connor everything. Meanwhile, I never saw them together. As in never ever. So I didn't think much of it…Until Brandon Wong went and gave me that stupid picture of them." She became more agitated as she continued. "I mean, what was he thinking giving me *that*?"

"Did you ask him?" inquired Cisco.

"Of course I did," she exclaimed. "Know what he told me?"

They both shook their heads.

"That George had kept it in his damn nightstand! After all these years! With his precious letter!" She was becoming enraged. "Slap in the face proof that while I was jacked up on sedatives so my mother wouldn't have to deal with my screeching after Heather's fall, he was out galivanting with her husband, who took off while his wife was dying in hospital."

If she was suggesting both men were having an affair, which is what it was sounding like, it still didn't explain why Vasquez would murder Anthony Delano. Nor how he could do so given the timing of the photo, which Randall felt inclined to point out. "Ms. Delano," he stated calmly, "the date on the back of the photograph places them at the opposite end of the country the day before your father's death."

Dawn creased her brow. "So?"

"Do you know who took it?" asked Randall.

"No," she frowned. "Why would I even care?"

"You sent it to us. So I'm confused. Was it intended to incriminate Connor Rivers?"

"What? No! Did you not get that I was left completely in the dark on all this?"

"Perhaps I should rephrase the question," stated Randall. "Do you believe Connor Rivers benefitted from Anthony

Delano's death? Enough to have coerced George Vasquez into murdering him?"

Her eyes darted back and forth in disbelief. After everything she had told them about her father, they still weren't getting the point. He was the criminal. Yes, it was impulsive, and probably misguided, to have sent them George's letter and the photo. But never did she mean for Connor to appear guilty. His only sin was being the object of George's desire.

"We all benefitted from that monster's death," Dawn eventually replied. "He was oppressive and needed to be out of our lives. And yes, Connor hated him for what he did to Heather. Wouldn't you hate the guy who beat up your wife?" She stared at them both in judgement. "But did he orchestrate his murder? No way. Not his nature. He would never risk any impact to Jennifer. He was much too devoted to her." Eager to end their exchange, Dawn finally admitted, "Look, I was really pissed at George when I read his precious letter. And that stupid picture…It made me fume. So I got rid of them both. If it was a mistake sending them to you, then forget it. George is dead, so who the hell cares?"

"He is, Ms. Delano. But Connor Rivers is not," stated Randall, almost impulsively.

He did not just say that, thought Cisco, disappointed.

"So what then? You're pursuing *him* now? Even though you literally have a confession from another man? Well there's law enforcement for you," she said, spreading her arms wide, before setting them down on the couch to raise herself. "I think it's time you both leave."

Cisco was certain Randall was about to object, so he stood up. Leaving was the least they could do for her. "Of course, Ms. Delano. Thank you for your time. And once again, I apologize for everything that you've been through."

As they approach her door, there was one matter Cisco needed to get off his chest. He stopped and said, "Ms. Delano, with regard to Jennifer…" He paused, unsure of how to phrase his request. "You should know. She's completely unaware of everything that transpired. The cause of her mother's passing. Or any of your terrible history. I realize that it's none of my business, but is it your intent to divulge any of this to her?"

"Detective, you're right. It's none of your business. And no, I'm not a witch. That would just be cruel."

Cisco nodded with relief before exiting her condo.

The moment Dawn closed the door behind them, she leaned against the backside and exhaled. "God damn you, George. Look what you went and made me do!"

She was ready to blare some music, grab a snack and binge, to try and push the conversation as far out of her mind as possible. Instead, she waddled into the kitchen and rummaged through the trashcan by the telephone. The note she had reluctantly jotted down was still there; a benefit of never throwing things out. She hadn't expected to ever need it, and yet here she was, dialing the number inscribed on it.

"Hello," replied Jennifer after a few rings.

"Hi, this is Dawn. Your aunt."

"Oh. Hi. Um. How are you?"

"I changed my mind. I'd like us to meet."

A history of abuse. This is what Cisco was coming to realize had provoked the incident causing Heather Delano's accident and Dawn's understandable lack of remorse over the confessed murder of her father. Both victims of his aggression, suffering in silence, while the institutions designed to protect them were none the wiser. He understood that in her eyes, George Vasquez hadn't committed a crime. He had terminated the abuser. His failure was that he hadn't done it sooner, hadn't told her when he did, and that he pined over Connor instead of her. What she had sent them was driven by resentment, betrayal and jealousy.

He considered her tortured soul, hidden and hoarding in her cluttered condo. Her counter lined with snacks so she could devour her feelings. And the apology she wished for that would never be received. Slamming the door after getting into the driver's seat, he turned to his boss in frustration. "Detective Randall, I know this case made an impact on you back then. And I appreciate you giving me the opportunity to take the lead, but I need to know. I mean really need to know. What were you expecting? Because from what I can tell, all that's been accomplished is uncovering a series of crimes that went undetected and can't be punished. And finding a trail of broken hearts left behind by George Vasquez. So please tell me. What are we doing here?"

"I wasn't expecting this, Cisco. And I understand that this has been upsetting to you."

"To me? What happened to Dawn and Heather Delano should be upsetting to everyone. Our system is flawed. It fails to protect innocent victims in their own damn homes."

"I don't disagree, Cisco. But there's more to this. You've done well in putting the pieces together. Now let me explain why I felt so strongly about it in the first place."

Cisco shook his head, trying to regain his calm as he drove them back toward the station.

"Your very first case can leave a lasting mark. For me, it was Heather's accident. I was one of the two officers who informed Connor Rivers. I watched as his face went from expecting her at the door, to living a nightmare. The moment he entered the patrol car, he assumed she had been in a car accident. When he learned it was an incident at Delano Manor, he was convinced Anthony Delano was at fault." He paused and turned to Cisco whose eyes were steady on the road. "If your wife had an accident at her parents' house, would you think it intentional?"

"Of course not."

"And yet that's exactly how Rivers felt. No other consideration…I was assigned to guard the door of Heather's hospital room. Tried to keep my cool as her mother berated me for denying her access. Watched as Connor Rivers and George Vasquez sobbed, one in despair, the other feeling like a failure. These boys were just kids, completely broken. Then months went by as Anthony Delano's trial kept getting delayed. When it finally began, I couldn't believe my eyes when I saw the young George Vasquez sitting among senior attorneys whose reputations were built on defending the dregs of society."

"You were at the trial?"

"Part of it. As one of the officers present, I was asked to testify. I was just a kid myself, so the whole thing felt very intimidating."

"I bet."

"Maybe because I was young. I don't know. But it seemed to me that Vasquez had no place being there. He didn't fit. Didn't seem cutthroat at all. And then he completely disappeared after the case was aborted…I was sure his corpse was going to wash up on a riverbank or be found in some abandoned hideout."

"Shit."

"Had nightmares about it for years. Then landed myself in homicide, go figure. I eventually forgot all about him. Until this damn confession appeared. I swear to you Cisco, there is no way that young kid could orchestrate that crime. He may have been someone's pawn, but he was no murderer. Of that I'm certain."

"And you think he was Connor Rivers' pawn?"

"No. I do not."

"So whose then?"

"Delano was a high-powered business mogul with many questionable relations. With that much power, he had enemies, not to mention probable involvement in organized crime. But these guys are experts at hiding their tracks. They get away with crime after crime. So I suspected the person who sent us the letter might actually lead us to an active player. And because of the photograph, I thought whoever was hired to tail those boys might know something."

"So what you're saying is that Anthony Delano was involved in some kind of crime ring? And you didn't think to tell me that from the get-go?"

"Cisco, it's a suspicion that could never be proven. And it may even have been wrong. I needed you to follow the evidence with your untainted perspective. Not steer you in a direction."

"But you did steer me. You insisted I meet with Jennifer Vincent. How was that fair to her?"

"You're right. That was wrong of me. I got caught up in the memory of that little girl who was about to lose her mother. I guess that, selfishly, I wanted to know what had become of her."

"Bullshit...I mean... sorry, Detective. You just don't strike me as that...sentimental." Cisco regretted the insubordination, and yet not.

"Okay, you got me. That was only part of it. Connor Rivers was away during the duration of the trial. He was rumored to have left before it even started. No one could say why or where he was. And no, Vasquez wasn't out galivanting with him, because he was involved in the entire proceedings. But Rivers' absence raised questions. Some wondered if something had happened to him and his daughter. So I was surprised when I saw that photo was included and thought he might possess information of value. Then, when you said he couldn't be interviewed, I assumed his grown daughter would know something. That he might have confided in her – or even just inferred something – about her grandfather's dealings."

Cisco pulled into the station parking lot. They exited the vehicle and entered the building. "Well Jennifer Vincent doesn't know a thing. So unless you think Dawn Delano, who we know sent us the letter, is part of her father's crime ring, can we please return this case to the archives and call it a day?" Cisco's tone was more assertive than an open question.

Randall nodded in agreement.

Both were interrupted at reception. June had asked that they go to her desk upon arrival.

"Do you wanna be the one to tell her she can abort mission Delano-money-trail?" Cisco asked Randall.

"Let's at least give her the courtesy of showing us what she found first," he replied.

June had her eyes fixed on her screen as they approached. "Come take a look," she said, scrolling to the top using her mouse, while Cisco and Randall moved in behind her. "This is the transaction history for the Heather Delano trust. Or at least the portion that's digitized. Everything older is on paper." She pointed to the heap on her desk.

The display was filled with rows of transaction confirmations; an endless number of them. She was scrolling too fast for either to read the names, but they could tell the dollar amounts were in the three to four-digit range. In the top right-hand corner was the balance, which totalled approximately one-hundred-twenty-thousand dollars.

"We just came back from meeting with Dawn Delano. Unless you found something glaring, we don't need you to spend any more time on this," exclaimed Randall.

"Did she happen to mention the Angel Fund?" asked June.

"No, why? What's that?" asked Cisco.

"I didn't think so." June moved the cursor to the bottom of her screen to select the next tab. She opened it to reveal another account, whose transactions were strictly deposits. "I'd like to draw your attention to the balance," she said. It exceeded six-million dollars.

"Okay? So I'm guessing there's a relation between the Angel Fund and the Delano trust?" At this point, Cisco was hoping there wasn't, or that it didn't matter. As for Randall, his curiosity was piqued once again.

"Yes. Regular transfers from the trust into the Angel Fund. The transactions are buried among all the others."

"By others, you mean recipients of the Delano trust?"

"Yes. Here. You can see them all." She scrolled slowly so both could lean in and read them. "Three recipients are named individuals: Dawn Delano, Connor Rivers, and Jorge Vasquez. Their payments are listed as pension payouts. Not sure why exactly, but it could just be to distinguish them from the rest which are directed to twenty different charities."

"I'm gonna assume there's a logical reason for Vasquez being on this list. And that all those payouts were legit?" questioned Cisco.

"The trustee determines the recipients. In this case, Eleanor Delano would have made that call when she launched it in 1973. The transactions themselves seem to be in order. Set-up for regular disbursements rather than a single lump sum to each beneficiary. Possibly to prevent someone from blowing the whole thing with an extravagant purchase. You know, splurge on a yacht?"

"I get it," replied Cisco. "It also seems very controlling."

"True. But from a long-term perspective, it slows the depreciation, so it pays out for longer. And since her recipients were young, she may have wanted to ensure the funds would last."

"But didn't Connor Rivers refuse his inheritance?"

"He did. But long before Anthony's death, Heather had been receiving a monthly allowance. It was deposited into a joint bank account she shared with Rivers. That account remained active after she died – only her name was removed – and it was used for these pension payouts. Maybe Rivers preferred the monthly disbursement, so he declined the rest."

"Maybe. But it was still a million dollars he turned down." Regardless, Cisco was intent on moving on. "So the original six-million dollar Delano trust is down to one-hundred-twenty-thousand dollars. What happens to it now?"

"Unclear. I should also point out that, if not for the drain by the Angel Fund, it would have been a much larger amount."

"And what do you know about this Angel Fund?"

"Not much yet, since it's an offshore account. I do know it's sitting in a tax haven. Different beast entirely from the trust that it's pulling from."

"So a six-million dollar trust is set-up in 1973 and distributes monthly sums to over twenty recipients, most of them charities. Meanwhile on the backend, an offshore fund has been syphoning it all this time?"

"Maybe not all this time. I still need to confirm when it was set-up. For now, all I can tell is that there has never been a single withdrawal from it."

"Okay, so what's its purpose?"

"That would be a question for its trustee."

"Who is?"

"George Vasquez."

"Naturally," moaned Cisco, discouraged.

"Also, he was the last trustee of the Delano trust. Presumably as of Eleanor's death in 1998."

"And we just found out from Dawn Delano that Vasquez was the executor of Eleanor Delano's will." Cisco was about to lose his mind. Instead of closing the case, he felt obligated to validate whether Eleanor Delano had been swindled by the suave and mysterious George Vasquez. "Okay. Here's what I propose. June, you look into the Angel Fund and see what more you can find out. Meanwhile, I'll contact Vasquez's old firm and see if they have a copy or notes regarding Eleanor Delano's will. If he was working there when it was drafted, it's possible they have a trace."

"I'll get right on," she replied.

Randall nodded then left the room without adding anything further. He didn't need to; his foulplay suspicion was now on the table.

The moment Randall walked away, June grabbed Cisco's arm.

"What is it, June?"

"I just thought you should know. But please keep it to yourself."

"Okay?"

"Randall's wife has been in hospital. That's the reason he's been out so much. He's not talking about it."

"Shit. I had no idea."

"No one does. Mary took a few calls from her doctor. She told me in confidence."

"Do you know if it's serious?"

"No I don't."

"Poor guy. Just as he's about to retire…"

CHAPTER TWENTY

— 1972 —

Wearing her silk rose bathrobe, Eleanor sat facing the mirror of her chestnut vanity, removing the rollers from her auburn-dyed hair. An assortment of blush brushes, eye shadows, lipsticks, and mascara were laid out in front of her like surgical instruments on a sterile tray. Ready to begin her morning ritual, she dabbed a layer of foundation over her face and neck, carefully concealing blemishes and fine lines. Then, ever so methodically, she evened out her complexion, creating the perfect canvas upon which to work her magic. With each stroke of color and highlight she slowly began the transformation; brightening her skin tone, contouring her lips and features, accentuating her brown eyes and cheekbones. It was a well-rehearsed routine, masking as many traces of age, fatigue and distress as possible, completed by teasing her wavy curls. After a generous amount of hairspray, she marveled at the result; a projection of resilience, poise, and control.

Only months ago, her morning preparation had to begin much earlier in the day. Eleanor's attendance was in too much demand. Charity and board meetings, museum or art gallery exhibits, and a myriad of other fashionable events filled her agenda. If popularity was measured by the number of invitations received, she had long surpassed the point at which her regrets had outpaced her confirmations. And the busier she was, the greater the priority of hosting lunch-ins and soirees at Delano Manor.

For decades, the trajectory of her status had climbed, at a pace that seemed unstoppable. Until it all came crashing down. No sooner had news of Heather's tragedy and Anthony's incarceration reverberated throughout the media was she relieved of all socialite engagements. Four months later, the mailbox that had once been filled with invitations was reduced to a trickle of support. If not for the paparazzi on the lookout for the next bombshell, Eleanor was no longer a going concern.

She felt restrained, ashamed. And would be for as long as the criminal investigation was underway. But it was not within her DNA to let it show, to admit defeat, to brake. Somehow, some way, she would adapt and restore her status.

Determined to prevail, she remained steadfast in her daily grooming. Keeping up appearances was essential to preserving a modicum of their family image. As its only member not condemned to a bed or a jail cell, Eleanor took it upon herself to salvage their reputation. And she did it by putting her best foot forward.

On guidance from her legal counsel, she respected a cadence of prison visits necessary to avoid negative press. Meanwhile, her staff was kept on high alert for any mention of the Delano's in the papers. If what Eleanor read was unfavorable, a strongly worded statement to the editor would follow, along with the suggestion of a more forgiving tone that may lead to a monetary reward. Vigilantly, she exerted what influence she still possessed to control the optics surrounding the drama.

If only she could wield enough power to heal her daughters. Heather, fortunately, remained stable, which was the most she would hope for. But where Dawn was concerned, the situation had become volatile.

It was just yesterday that Eleanor was thanking the head psychiatrist, grateful he had been persuaded into admitting Dawn to the institution's care. To ensure that her presence was never to be divulged, Eleanor had cemented an agreement; financial reward in exchange for their discretion.

"There you go," Eleanor had said, breathing a sigh of relief, as she tucked Dawn's bedsheet over her shoulders. Weeks of planning and negotiating now behind her, the orchestration of her transfer to the institution had been conducted in complete secrecy.

Lying almost lifeless within the walls of this barren room, Dawn stared into her mother's eyes with a look of shame, hurt and abandonment. "You put me in an insane asylum?"

With her best attempt at tenderness and comfort, Eleanor had replied, "No dear. Of course not. These doctors are specialists. They will make you better. You'll see."

"By drugging me? Or will they just tie me down? I bet you want them to starve me so I get skinny. Is that the real reason you put me in here?" Dawn's face was flush, her chin quivering as tears escaped from the corners of her eyes. "How could you do this to me?"

Recognizing Dawn's growing agitation, Eleanor knew

her words would only trigger an assault of scathing remarks; comments that would undermine the effort she had put into securing this facility for her daughter's care. So she had done as advised, and signaled to the nurse. Within moments, two orderlies had entered the room, one on each side of Dawn to restrain her as the injection was readied.

Dawn had flailed, while screaming profanities and horrible accusations. But in no more than a few seconds, her battle had subsided, giving way to the numbing effect of the drugs.

"I know that was upsetting to watch, Mrs. Delano," had said the psychiatrist once Dawn was fully sedated. "But it's necessary to keep her calm. She will resent you at first, but in time, she'll come around and such measures won't be necessary."

Eleanor knew that to be true. Just as she knew her daughter could not appreciate that this was in her best interest. How the situation had become too dire back at the manor. Her screeching too out of control. Ranting absurdities at the top of her lungs, Dawn had scared staff to the point of rendering them fearful of entering her bedroom. And it's not like Eleanor hadn't tried to keep her home. She had begged the doctors for stronger sedatives. But they refused, insisting Dawn should instead be weaned. Eleanor disagreed. It was too soon; she needed Dawn to remain tranquil until the family situation was settled. Taking matters into her own hands, she had solicited a private mental institution.

There had been only silence upon her return to the manor last night. Which should have felt peaceful, an affirmation that Eleanor had done right by Dawn. But the look of rage and despair in her daughter's eyes continued to send chills down Eleanor's spine. The sound of her harsh words kept pounding in her ears. It was so unsettling, Eleanor hadn't even noticed when the maid had entered her room.

"Ma'am. Mr. Rivers is on the line for you," she had repeated, waiting for Eleanor to respond.

Eleanor was snapped right out of her daze. It was so unexpected; Connor never called. And though their discussion had been brief, it was just the antidote to get her through the night, to focus on pleasant thoughts other than Dawn. Because in only a matter of hours now, Eleanor's world was about to change.

Though Connor hadn't said it, she had figured it out on her own. And she was beaming at the prospect of what he was about to ask her. So with hair and makeup completed, she proceeded to her final step; what to wear.

"A bright color. Something cheerful," she said to herself, trying not to smile too broadly and ruin her makeup.

It felt like a reward. For keeping her promise, which she had done with resolve from the moment of her granddaughter's birth. In accepting to not exist in Jennifer's world, she had protected Heather and Jennifer from all exposure to Anthony. But doing so came with immense sacrifice and a sense of indescribable loss. Never had she held her grandchild or so much as exchanged a simple glance. Until that moment, only weeks ago, when she finally saw Jennifer for the very first time. It was but a chance glimpse, while seated in her parked car, just as she and Connor were leaving the hospital. And it had made Eleanor yearn all the more for the opportunity to be in her life. How her heart ached for just one hug, one kiss, one hand hold. Her pain repeatedly released through silent tears shed in the privacy of the empty, dark lounge with a stiff drink in hand. But soon, the need for tears would be no more.

Vindicated, Eleanor would finally be rewarded for her ultimate sacrifice and generosity. She would at last be invited into Jennifer's life, to become the maternal presence that her mother could no longer be. Connor knew he couldn't do this on his own. Who better than Eleanor to fill that important void. So a celebratory outfit was in order. The most playful outfit in her wardrobe.

"A candy red skirt it shall be," she asserted to herself.

It was unlike Eleanor to be anything but fashionably late. But after nearly a decade, she could not endure a minute more. She sat by the window of the coffee shop next to the hospital, while glancing at waitstaff filling mugs and serving baked goods from the display behind the counter. Noticing how many folks were reading the newspaper, she was relieved they contained no mention of the Delano's nor Dawn's covert relocation, which she made sure to check before leaving the manor.

She stared out the window, hoping Connor would be on time. The light drizzle had turned to a downpour, distorting the view, blending images into blobs of moving colors. Already halfway through her latte, she had been glancing at the door each time the next person walked in, hoping it would be him.

Finally he arrived. She could feel her heart begin to race with excitement. She took in a deep breath to maintain her composure, intent on withholding any indication that she knew what he was about to ask. Even in this instance, a show of emotion was beneath her.

"Eleanor," he said with a nod of salutation, while pulling his chair to sit across from her. His hair and shirt were damp, his appearance understandably distraught. These were trying times and, unlike her, his universe showed no prospect of improvement.

"Connor, how are you?" She forced a serious tone.

"You know. Not great." His eyes moved from Eleanor down to the table and back again as he rubbed his hands against both thighs.

"I do. This is a nightmare."

Sweat was beginning to form on Connor's already moist brow. "About that," he began. "This is getting really difficult, too difficult for Jenny, I mean Jennifer."

Eleanor found him to be even more awkward than he had been over the last four months. Possibly because their prior conversations, though few, had been initiated by her and only addressed Heather's medical requirements. This topic was completely different. Perhaps, in his state of duress, he worried that she would be reluctant to help. Meanwhile, she hoped he would just spit it out. The anticipation was killing her. "I can't imagine how this must be for the poor child."

"Yeah. It's really bad. She can't take much more of this."

"Of course."

"She, uh, told me she's not comfortable going to the hospital anymore. It makes me sad. Really sad. But I understand. She's so young. This isn't a life for a child."

Eleanor leaned in, her eyes wide. Was he going to ask her to stay with Jennifer while he visited with Heather? "Is there something I can do to help?"

"Yes there is."

"Go on."

"You won't like it."

Eleanor straightened her torso and resisted a frown. Did he actually think she would take issue with spending time with her granddaughter? "What would make you say that?"

"It's time –"

"I agree," she exhaled, unable to contain herself.

"You do?" Connor was confused.

"Of course I do. Why on earth wouldn't I?"

"Because you've done everything possible to keep her alive."

"Well of course I have," she exclaimed defensively. Then, wondering what that had to do with his question about Jennifer, she asked, "It's time for what, Connor?"

"Keeping Heather alive, when there's zero chance she'll ever wake up, is torturing Jenny. It's time to take her off the ventilator. I'm going to inform the doctors tomorrow. It'll give you time to say goodbye. We can let her go peacefully. And let Jenny move on with her childhood." There. He got it out. Now he held his breath and locked on her eyes, waiting for her reaction.

Eleanor could not believe her ears. Surely he was too distraught to think straight. There was no way the man who was so obsessed with her daughter was actually considering condemning her to death by suffocation. She fixed his gaze. "The situation has become too much for you, Connor. You're saying absolute nonsense. You need some rest."

"Eleanor, I'm upset. This is a lot. But this isn't about what I need. It's about what Jenny does." In a desperate tone, he added, "We all need to let Heather go."

She was beside herself. This could not be the reason for their meeting. What was he thinking? "How dare you make such a suggestion? You think killing her mother is how to care for the child? Have you gone completely mad?"

He took a deep breath, intent on holding his ground. "I know this is hard, Eleanor. Believe me, it's killing me too. But there's nothing we can do for Heather. We're keeping her alive for our sake, not hers. That may have been okay before. Only now, it's making Jenny suffer, and that's not fair."

Eleanor could see that he was convinced. And that in some regard he was right. But she hadn't planned for this. Nor ever imagined he would suggest it. And the timing was unacceptable. She needed to think fast and make him change his mind. Leaning in with her pointed index, she exclaimed, "Young man, you listen to me very carefully. My daughter's life will not – I repeat, will not – be cut short by any means. Is that clear?"

Connor began to feel anger mounting within him. He bit his lip trying to remain calm, thinking of how best to respond. Staring down at the table, clenching both hands together above it, he spoke slowly. "Eleanor, I'm sorry. I really am. But…this is not your decision to make. I'm her husband. It's my responsibility."

A look of contempt swept over Eleanor's face. She felt duped by the purpose of this meeting and provoked by his audacity. If this was, in fact, the entire substance of what they were to discuss, he had another thing coming. "That you are, Connor Rivers. But if I understand correctly, you were discussing the child's best interests, were you not?"

Connor looked up. "Yes. Of course. Jenny is the reason. The only reason for my decision."

"I see." Eleanor glared straight into his eyes. "And in this grand decision of yours, have you considered what becomes of Jennifer? After her mother is gone?"

"Yes. Of course. That's all I've thought about for months. I'll try to…we'll have to rebuild our lives. Move forward. I mean, she needs to play, interact with friends, grow up normally. Her life can't just be about the hospital anymore, nor her dying mother."

Eleanor paused. She knew Heather would hate her for what she was about to do. But there was no other way to dissuade him from his position. If money had power with Connor, this would be easy. But it didn't, so she would have to appeal to his weakness. "And is it your presumption that she would be entrusted to your care?"

"Of course she would," he frowned with confusion. "I'm her father."

She stared at him without saying a word. The corners of her mouth turned slightly upward. Whether it was a moment for her to reconsider whether to hold back, or to simply watch him grovel, she waited. He could figure it out on his own.

Connor's heart sank. The color drained from his face. He couldn't breathe. She knew. How was it possible? When had she found out? What would she do? He was in a state of utter panic, trying to resist the urge to vomit.

Eleanor could see his distress. And while Connor may believe it was in Jennifer's best interest to let Heather go right now, he was wrong. If he was intent on forcing her hand, Eleanor had to draw the line. She had to prevent him from making a decision that would ultimately cost Jennifer. Even if it gave her no pleasure. Even it meant being cruel.

Connor was overcome with dread. He couldn't bear her silence, and what it might imply. Never had he imagined the possibility of anyone knowing Jenny wasn't his. "I...I've been so good to her. Always. I've only ever had her best interest at heart." His eyes were glistening with despair.

Finally, Eleanor responded. "Yes, you have," she replied with control. "So let's make sure you can continue to, shall we?"

"What are you saying?" he cried, desperate to keep his daughter.

Eleanor knew she had the angle to sway him. And no matter how horrible it would be for him to hear, she had to put the fear of God in him. "I'm saying that if Anthony Delano were to outlive Heather, you had best be prepared for a custody battle. And trust me, you would lose."

Connor's eyes widened with shock. He couldn't believe his ears. "What? No! No! No! He's in jail for Christ sake!"

Calmly, she fixed his gaze, refusing to flinch. "He'll get out. You can be certain of it. That man gets away with everything."

Connor struggled to hold back tears of rage. "And you? You would do this to Jenny? Take her away from, from...from the only father she's ever known? The father she loves? The father who adores her? Who would do that to an innocent child?"

His words cut through her very soul. It hurt Eleanor to be pegged as heartless where her granddaughter was concerned. It was never the easy decision. But at times, like now, it was the only way. "I will do no such thing, if you, in turn, do what's right."

"What? Tell me. I need to be the one to care for Jenny."

"You shall not curtail Heather's life."

"Okay. Okay. I won't. I promise. But…for how long? She's literally wasting away."

"For as long as I say so." With that, Eleanor raised herself before she, too, might become emotional. She then leaned in to speak into his ear with one last threat. "And don't you dare cross me, Connor. Or you will pay the price." She then walked away and didn't turn back.

The moment she stepped outside, she opened her umbrella and exhaled, closing her eyes tightly to hold back the tears. She felt shattered, foolish, dejected. How had this meeting gone so wrong? Was she so desperate or delusional to have fabricated a fantasy wherein Connor would actually invite her into their lives? Instead he forced her into threatening the unthinkable.

If she was a weaker person, she would breakdown, right then and there on the sidewalk, for all to see. But Eleanor showed no weakness, ever. For as long as she could appear fine, she was fine. So she sucked her emotions back in, stood tall, chest outward and marched toward the hospital, leaving her disappointment to fall to the ground, to be washed away by the rain.

Fifteen minutes later, she entered Heather's hospital room, in her usual stride, as though nothing had transpired. Before sitting down on the chair beside her bed, Eleanor reached for the blush and cotton pad in her purse and gently dabbed her daughter's still, gaunt face. This was the ritual that began their daily communion.

"Let's give you a bit of color," she said, contouring her cheekbones. They seemed more and more prominent as her features slowly melted away. Even the bridge of her nose seemed wrong, so much narrower. "You're getting so thin, my baby. But I need you to hang on. Please. Just a little longer. Okay?"

As she massaged her face in slow circular motions, she let herself imagine its once pudgy, innocent expression. The one with no trace of harm, of hurt. Taking this time to reminisce had become Eleanor's way of finding her words. To share with her daughter what had always remained unsaid. Clearing her conscience, speaking with affection, entrusting her to secrets no one else knew. There was a closeness in these moments of intimacy that had never been shared before.

She leaned in to stroke Heather's forehead, unable to ignore the tiny scars Anthony's anger had left behind. The stubborn evidence of each instance Eleanor had failed to keep her daughter safe. No matter how faint the mark, no matter how hard she had tried to heal the wound, these were the remnants of Heather's anguish. The same anguish she saw in Heather's eyes on that fateful day. The truth she and Eleanor carried, now a burden she alone had to bear.

"I need to confess something to you. And you won't be happy with me. But I had no choice." That Eleanor could utter such a statement was a testament to the bond she had now developed with her daughter. Her level of comfort in being this open and vulnerable. Heather had become her safe space, an audience with whom Eleanor could veer far away from the outward image she projected with everyone else.

"I had to break my promise with you." She was so ashamed, she couldn't bring herself to look at Heather. "And now I can't take it back." She lifted her gaze and caressed Heather's arm as she spoke. "I don't know what Connor will do now, but I had to stop him from going through with taking you off this ventilator." She sighed deeply. "It's been so lovely having you back. And I'm so sorry if you hate this. I know he's right. You must be ready to go." Her eyes began to water. "It will break my heart when you leave. And you will one day…soon. I promise. But it can't be just yet."

Though Heather had sworn her to secrecy, had gone through with the wedding on condition her mother never reveal that secret, Eleanor admitted to implying to Connor that she knew he wasn't Jennifer's father.

"I didn't say it outright, mind you," she defended, as though it lessened the violation. She paused, her head lowered, like a child forced to think about her actions. "But it gets worse," she added, before lifting her gaze. "It's awful. I know. But I had to stop him, Heather. And there was only one way I knew to make him change his mind." Eleanor dreaded telling her, fearing Heather's rage may shock her back to life. And if it did, she would lunge forward to choke her mother to death. But still, Eleanor needed to get it off her chest. "I threatened that your father would take Jennifer from him."

The moment she finished, she bolted upright and turned

to the window, arms crossed, her hand pinching her chin. It was easier to defend her actions while staring blankly toward the sky as storm clouds slowly began their retreat than to be looking right at Heather. "I had no choice. It was the only way to keep you alive…It has to be this way. For Jennifer's sake. She's why I've sacrificed so much." She turned and walked back to Heather's side. "But just until your father's gone, my sweetheart. Which will be soon. I promise. After that, you have my word, I will let you go."

As Eleanor stared at her daughter, she imagined how Connor would be relaying their conversation if he was the one in the room. The horrible picture he would paint of her atrocious mother. That's assuming he would even visit. After her threat, she may have scared him enough to take Jennifer to his parents; the ones allowed to be in her life.

"I don't know if he'll come see you today, sweetheart. And it isn't his fault. You understand don't you?"

The nurse's arrival interrupted their moment. It was time to check on Heather's vitals.

Instantaneously, Eleanor switched gears. "If it's best for you to bathe her now, I can return a little later," she said with an exaggerated smile. "I've been talking her ear off. She could probably use the break."

And just like that, Eleanor stood with her head held high, and walked out of the room. Once again, everything was perfectly fine.

CHAPTER TWENTY-ONE

— 2003 —

"Well if isn't my most favorite law enforcement officer in the whole wide world," cheered Fern upon hearing Detective Cisco announce himself over the phone. Sporting her bumblebee sweater of black and yellow stripes, she pulled the gum out of her mouth before continuing. "And to what do I owe the honor, Captain Max? Oh, but before you get to that, how's that darling baby of yours? It's Jade right?"

Cisco smiled. There was just something about Fern. She was a far cry from the strictly-business formalities typical of his workplace interactions. "Jade gets more adorable each day," he replied, flattered she had remembered her name. "Thanks for asking."

"I bet. If she looks anything like her daddy, she must be quite the beauty. Not that I mean to make you blush or anything."

"And yet somehow, I feel like that's exactly what you mean to do," he jested.

"Okay, you got me. But tell me, does she have those big green eyes of yours?"

"No, my genes are no match for her mother's. She's Chinese. Those eyes are turning brown as we speak."

"Aw, you got yourself a little pot-luck. I'm imagining an even more gorgeous child. Good for you, Captain Max. Now, unless you're calling just to catch me up on your little one – which is perfectly fine – I'm guessing you need something."

A little pot-luck. I'm definitely bringing that up over dinner, Cisco smiled to himself. "I do. I'm not sure if you can help me, but it has to do with a document George Vasquez would've worked on a few years ago."

"Alrighty then. What do you need?"

"I'm looking for information regarding the last will and testament of Mrs. Eleanor Delano –"

"I'm gonna stop you right there, Captain. There was no Delano material in this office other than that…that envelope you picked up." She spoke of it as though it had been germ-infested. "Can't help you, I'm afraid."

"I do recall you saying that. However, I'm told that Mr. Vasquez would have been her executor. I thought perhaps he might have kept some record of it on file."

"Well he did work on some wills, but not Delano. I'd remember."

"I figured you would." The flattery didn't mask his disappointment. "Any chance he kept some of his documents, like his pro-bono work, elsewhere?"

"Unlikely. George wasn't good with admin. I took care of all that for him." She was thinking through past work as she spoke. "What year was it from, anyway?"

"Not sure when it was created, but she passed away in 1998."

"And tell me that name again? The first name?"

"Eleanor."

"Hmm. Give me sec. Something's ringing a bell." Fern put the receiver down and marched back toward the document storage room. "Where did I put that file?" she asked herself as she ran her fingers across the top of tightly squeezed folders in a wide cabinet drawer. After a few moments, she returned to her desk with one in hand, picked up the receiver and exclaimed, "Captain Max, I think you're in luck."

"You found it?"

"I found a file for Eleanor Angelini," she replied, while flipping through a few pages. "I think there might be something here." She zigzagged her index along one paragraph. "Ah. There it is. A beneficiary. Named Dawn Delano."

"That's Eleanor's daughter."

"Well I'll be damned. There was a Delano in my files after all. I'm embarrassed that I missed that one." Fern shook off her momentary disappointment, closed the document before concluding, "Looks like Angelini was Eleanor's maiden name."

"You're the best, Fern. Can I ask you to send a copy over to me?"

"Right away, Captain Max. I'm sure I kept your card in here." She rummaged through her desk drawer to find it. "Yup. Here it is. I'll take care of that now."

"Excellent. Oh and for the record, I doubt anyone would remember as small an annotation as a beneficiary's name from that many years ago. Your memory is sharper than the best of us. If ever you're interested in a career change, you should consider detective work."

"Ha! I wouldn't be suited for your line of business, Captain Max. But I may be looking for a new job soon." She appreciated his uncanny timing.

"Really?" Cisco was surprised, and yet not. George Vasquez's passing surely provoked a change of course for their office. "Is the firm being sold?"

"Nope. The other partners are fine to keep it going. Business is good. They just have a different philosophy than George did. Won't be as good a fit for me."

"How so?"

"For one, they're a bit too tied to the rule of law. George was too, mind you, but he had a conscience. And a soft spot. He felt conflicted when the burden of proof lead to injustice. Wasn't the type to feel proud just because he found a loophole to get the bad guys off."

"But he was a defense attorney. Wasn't that his job?"

"Yup. And he was real good at it. But it bothered him to win when his gut told him his client was probably guilty."

"But he did it anyway. So…was the money too good to resist?" That may have sounded crass to Fern, but Cisco knew of a large fund for which Vasquez was the trustee. Money had to be a motivator.

"That it was. But not for personal gain. And that's the difference. If he could get them cleared, he took their money and channeled it for good, like charities and his pro-bono work. But that won't be happening anymore. These partners will be celebrating the victories by furnishing their mansions."

Cisco couldn't decide if Vasquez was a saint or a con artist fooling those closest to him. "Wish I had the chance to meet him."

"It's a shame you didn't. He would've liked you. In fact, I sense something similar about the two of you," she replied with a hint of nostalgia in her voice.

"Really? And what might that be?"

"I think, like George, you won't always feel like all that rule-following and evidence- gathering has necessarily led to justice. There'll be times when your gut tells you otherwise. Good guys can't help it." She paused, then added, "At least, that's what my gut's telling me. But what do I know?"

"Well, I'll take that as a compliment." Which he knew was her intent. "But let's not tell my boss, okay?"

"Deal." She cleared her throat. "Anyway, it's been lovely talking to you, Captain Max, but I should get back to work. Oh and if you need anything else, try to get to me quick. I don't expect I'll be here for much longer."

"Noted. And thanks again for your help, Fern. Not sure what I'd do without you." Cisco meant it. There was something genuine about her that he relished. "But can I ask one more favor?"

"Sure thing, Captain."

"Let me know where you end up working."

"Aw, Captain Max. You wanna stay in touch? I'm flattered," she smiled, sounding sarcastic yet moved.

"Just looking out for you, Fern. Good luck. And take care of yourself."

"You give that adorable baby of yours a big hug."

"I will. Bye Fern." As he hung up the phone, he wondered

if their paths would ever cross again. He hoped they would.

Fern's document was received at the station the following day. Cisco had given it to June before opening it. His only implication had been to consult a colleague of Italian decent, curious about the meaning of *angelini*. Though he was hard-pressed to believe it was just a coincidence that the fund in question bore such resemblance to Eleanor's maiden name, he didn't want to jump to conclusions. But as expected, its origin was confirmed to be a nickname for angelic or little angel. And to a homicide detective, that could just as easily be the devil in disguise.

It took June no time to review the file, pleased that it helped to fill in some of the gaps in her research. She brought the results to Detective Cisco's desk as soon as she had what he needed.

"Are you ready for this?" she asked, standing in front of his desk.

"I don't know. Am I?"

"Well you're sitting, so that's good."

"Alright. Tell me what you found."

She walked around his desk to stand beside him and placed a folder in front of him. "Okay, so everything seems to be on the up-and-up regarding the Angel Fund. I checked for any evidence or ties to ponzi schemes, money laundering, tax evasion, you name it. Everything is clean."

"Okay," he replied, unsure of what was coming next. "So why is it good that I'm sitting down?"

"First, George Vasquez wasn't named trustee of the Delano trust when Eleanor died. That happened years earlier when she gave him power of attorney over all her affairs. She was placed in a nursing home shortly thereafter."

"Now that's interesting…Does that means her will was also updated?"

"It does. She had first updated it in 1973 to reflect the changes following the transfer of her husband's estate. In that one, she had named Vasquez as trustee but only upon her death. The version I just received was dated 1990, which coincides with her move to a nursing home and his power of attorney."

Cisco leaned his face into both his hands, elbows resting on his desk. "He certainly made an impression on her. Was her trust in him misguided?"

"Well you tell me. The Angel Fund was created in 1998. By George Vasquez. After Eleanor died."

"What the hell? And it's reached six-million dollars in five years?"

"No. Get this. It went by a different name before that. Chastity. Lumped in with so many charities, I honestly misread it to be another one. So that's on me. But I checked the original records and it was there from the start of the Delano trust in 1973. Monthly payments were deposited into a bank account in Jennifer Rivers' name. Because she was a minor, Eleanor had given herself power of attorney. Why it wasn't Connor Rivers, I don't know. Maybe he had refused? Anyway, as of 1998, it hadn't been touched and had grown to over four-million dollars. Then, after Eleanor died, Vasquez closed it, switched it to the Angel Fund, moved it offshore and increased the deposit amounts."

"So Mr. Philanthropist embezzled his client's granddaughter's money without either of them knowing? Very classy."

"That's what I thought too. Until I noticed a change to the beneficiaries."

"I'm not even gonna try to guess."

"Jennifer remained, but he added three more: Grace, Hannah and Lisa Vincent."

Cisco placed both his palms over his face before asking, "Relatives of Jennifer I presume?"

"Her three daughters. They're all minors, by the way, so Jennifer holds power of attorney until they reach twenty-one years of age."

"You've got to be kidding me. So she's in on this?" He shook his head, feeling foolish for believing she didn't know George Vasquez. Then he wondered whether someone else knew about this. "I bet Dawn Delano found out when Vasquez was handling her mother's estate."

"I'm not so sure either Dawn or Jennifer actually know about it."

"How's that possible?"

"Remember when you asked what happened to the manor? It was donated. Along with most of Dawn's generous inheritance from Eleanor. Doesn't sound like someone too interested in someone else's money."

"No it doesn't." It also suggested that Dawn's modest lifestyle was by choice. "But what makes you think Jennifer doesn't know?"

"Her signature is nowhere to be seen on any of the documents. There is literally no trace of her involvement whatsoever."

"Okay…let's say she's not aware. So what's Vasquez's angle? Did he even have the right to withhold Chastity from her once Eleanor died?

"The language of Eleanor's will stipulated that Jennifer was not to receive the funds until after her death. That, by the way, was unchanged from the 1973 version. What was not however stipulated, is how long after."

"That sounds like a bullshit legal loophole if ever I heard one. So who's the trustee now that Vasquez is dead?"

"The fund is frozen until Vasquez's large estate is resolved. That said, I can find out pretty quickly to whom the Angel Fund will be transferred. Unless it's to anyone other than Jennifer, I don't see that we have anything to investigate."

"Agreed. But be honest with me, June. You actually think there's a possibility Jennifer Vincent doesn't know a thing about this?"

"Well if she did, wouldn't she have wanted access to her money before now? Unless you think she's like her father and refused it, so it's just sitting there for her girls."

"I can't see her refusing it. Hell, I've got one daughter who's only an infant and we've already spent a ton on baby stuff. Three older ones would cost a fortune."

"Not to mention she's an accountant. She literally manages money for a living."

"True."

"The bottom line is that, other than accruing for thirty years, there's been no other activity, illegal or otherwise."

"Also true. But it's been managed by a lawyer. Nothing

would look illegal."

"A lawyer who died without withdrawing a cent."

"Yeah, but his condition deteriorated quickly. Too quickly to even get rid of his murder confession. It's possible he was building himself a nest egg but never got around to using it."

"I suppose."

Cisco scratched his head. He couldn't figure out George Vasquez. One minute he appeared generous, the next he appeared conniving. It didn't help that Cisco had no real image of him other than a dated photograph. Or that he had never had a single conversation with him. What he did know, based on others' accounts, was that he cared deeply for Connor Rivers; too deeply, it seemed, to steal from his daughter. And then there was Fern's perception of him. She believed pro-bono was his purpose. Whether it was his passion for Rivers or to make amends for however he had failed him, it seemed possible Vasquez killed Delano, then mindfully oversaw the inheritance funds for Connor Rivers' progeny. "Robin Hood Vasquez."

"What was that?"

"Never mind." He shook his head. "Keep tabs on Vasquez's estate transfer. If the Angel Fund goes to Jennifer Vincent and her daughters, this case is closed."

"You mean until another confession letter appears out of nowhere," she winked.

"Not funny," he laughed dryly.

"I should have a confirmation shortly," smiled June before turning to walk away.

"Oh. Before I forget. Any news on Randall's wife?"

"I haven't heard anything new. I'll keep you posted if I do."

"Okay thanks." He grabbed his trench-coat from the coat stand near his desk. "I need some air."

Cisco walked in the direction of The Common. His pace was quick as he shuffled along the busy sidewalks, dodging people to reach the park's perimeter as fast as he could. The sound of car engines seemed to fade the moment he reached it. He slowed his pace, took in a deep breath and looked up.

The deciduous trees were completely bare. Their leaves now scattered across the ground in thick clumps, compacted by previous rain and footsteps. The sun shone brightly. And though the air was still, puffs of white clouds drifted across the blue sky, propelled by thermals undetectable this low to the ground. Here, Cisco would take a moment to catch his breath. To sort through all that was going through his mind.

What was the point of all this?

His opinion when first presented with the confession letter remained unchanged. Had he been more experienced, more confident, perhaps he could have argued against it more forcefully. Or persuaded Detective Randall to chase it on his own. It was, after all, his decades old intel that had him convinced something current was at play. Instead it was Max's first stab at homicide. Which was doing nothing other than causing him a growing sense of regret.

He considered all the effort involved in uncovering who and why the letter had been sent to the station. None of it felt like it had resolved anything. As for the questions that remained outstanding, they left him more troubled than curious.

Maybe I'm not fit for this.

He knew he was letting his emotions get the best of him. Or it was his gut, as Fern had predicted. But how could he not when each person he had encountered during the course of this investigation was left feeling worse for having spoken with him. He hadn't protected anyone from harm. He didn't prevent a crime. Nor did he bring anyone to justice. He just poked and prodded, for the sake of solving a mystery that should have been left alone. And in the process, he forced each of them to remember a loss or to relive a trauma for which he had no power to make amends. Would this really be the lasting impression of his first homicide case?

This isn't gonna work for me.

CHAPTER TWENTY-TWO

— 1972 —

It had been three days since Dawn's desperate plea. *George, please. I beg you. I'm going to die in here. You have to kidnap me.* For almost a month now, she had been relegated to the mental institution.

George was still stunned. What was Eleanor thinking? Even for her, that move seemed heinous, too cold-blooded. And how had he missed all the clues for something that significant? Had he lost his touch or was Eleanor finally onto him? With her, only one thing was certain; nothing was ever as it seemed. It took being a long-time student of her school of manipulation for George to understand her methodology. Better still, an invitation to her masterclass, offered only during evenings of alcohol-induced revelations. As he observed, listened, and cautiously probed, he gathered tidbits of knowledge, slowly learning just how elegantly she covered her tracks. She was an artist who transformed imagery with the simple stroke of a paintbrush, until it projected the appropriate hue. If she was generous, she was stealing. What she destroyed, she was in reality salvaging. When she appeared evil, it was to disguise an act of kindness. A period of grief was no reason to pause; instead, it created the perfect window of opportunity. So the moment it appeared she was losing her mind, he had to wonder. Was she actually at her sharpest? Sharp enough to realize she had a protege who had been secretly learning this craft from the grand dame of manipulation herself?

He marvelled at how Eleanor had been able to execute Dawn's move in complete secrecy. *Of course she did,* he thought to himself. But now, it was his turn to do the same. He should be working his charm, doing everything in his power to get Dawn out. She deserved nothing less. For ten years her company had filled a big part of the gap left behind when Connor wed Heather. From their shared passion for music had emerged a comradery that developed into an unexpected and reliable bond; more, he suspected, from her point of view. He knew that if the tables were turned, Dawn would stop at nothing to fight for his release. But she caught him at an impossible juncture. He had too much momentum to stop for anything. He needed to stay focused, not back down, not lose his nerve. The plan for his own escape was near. And it would mean abandoning Dawn forever.

It's not that he didn't care. Nor that he couldn't reciprocate her feelings. It's that after all these months of gathering intel, of playing the role of dutiful soldier, of learning the inner-workings of the establishment, he realized there was only one way to truly help her. And it was the same way in which he would help Connor. He had to neutralize the Delano venom once and for all. The snake must be destroyed. Having been pushed to the brink, George had found the will to take matters into his own hands.

It began when Eleanor had cruelly outed him, revealing his very weakness. She had disarmed George completely. What little resolve he had left began to collapse. The sound of her taunt reverberating in his ears, *Go to him, George.* How dare she throw that unrelenting temptation in his face? Was it not enough to know that he would never enjoy Connor's affection? He had held back his rage in the moment, but couldn't keep it from brewing within him. He should have known better. Not let her get to him. He knew how much she derived pleasure in wielding power. But she kept waving it like a sword, over and over, and wouldn't stop until she either broke skin or he took a knee. He eventually caved, submitted. Let her push him over the edge to hit rock bottom. Finished, depleted, broken, he would use his last bit of strength to dig deeper. To burry himself under the guilt that had been oppressing him since that fateful day when his lust distracted him from preventing Heather's demise. But something happened while he festered in that state of darkness and despair, ready to end it all. He realized that he no longer had a single thing to lose. Absolutely nothing. And it felt liberating.

This new perspective was like a super power. Unobstructed by barriers. Unclouded by the fear of consequence. It brought clarity to George's thoughts and changed their focus. Suddenly, he was reminded of someone else's weakness. Eleanor's. Viewed from this lens, her heart's desire presented an opportunity he could exploit. He knew she would never allow any harm to come to her grandchild. So by extension, no harm would ever come to Connor either. It wasn't George who was best suited to watch over him, it was Eleanor herself. And George was prepared to let her do just that.

George was free. To rid himself of guilt. To be bold. To end the Delano reign that cursed them all. And if his plan went off without a hitch, not a single one of them would be any the wiser. In only seventy-two hours from now, he could finally lay his anguish and longing to rest for good.

The time had come to put the wheels of his plan in motion. He had assembled all the necessary documents and separated them into three piles, one for each step. He stood in his apartment, staring down at the papers across his desk and ran through them one last time. "Plane ticket, money transfer, clause from the will, representation agreement. Check," he said, while placing those into his briefcase. The balance went into his drawer for his return. Before closing it, he picked up the prescription bottle and shook the Quaalude tablets it contained. "That better be enough." He had accumulated two-thirds of a bottle, courtesy of his many nightcaps shared with Eleanor. He put them back and closed the drawer before putting on his shoes. It was time to head out for an important phone call.

He paced in circles around the phone booth by the hospital awaiting their call. A daily ritual he faithfully observed, and for which Connor had thankfully become more regimented.

Like clockwork, it rang at precisely 4pm. "Con, hey, how are you?"

"We're good. What's the news on the case, George?"

"We're nearing closing arguments. After that, it'll be up to the jury," he replied, knowing that if his plan worked, the proceedings would never actually make it to deliberations.

"George, be honest. Is he gonna get out?"

"No Con. He won't. Trust me."

As hard as that was for Connor to do, he was relieved that George sounded so confident. "Okay. I hope you're right. In the meantime, were you able to get me money? I'm almost out."

"Yeah I got it. I'm arranging a transfer. You in northern California?"

"Yeah I am."

"Good. Can you make it to Plymouth by 3pm tomorrow?"

"I can try. But does it have to be 3pm sharp?"

"If you wanna be in and out quickly, then yeah."

"Okay, I'll make it happen. Where exactly do I have to go?"

"Write this down. You gotta pen?"

"Yeah. Shoot."

"I need you to get to El Dorado Savings Bank on Main. It's near State Route 49. Should be easy to find. I chose it cause the Amador County Fair is just around the corner. I thought it would be a fun destination for Jenny. You know, make all this driving more worth it for her. You think she'd like that?"

"Good idea, George. Yes, she would." Connor sounded pleased, if not surprised by the thoughtful location.

"Great. Just go in at 3pm. They'll be expecting you."

"You gave them my name?" Connor asked with concern.

"No. Sorry. Mine. But I gave them your description."
Careful, George.

"Hope you told them I have a beard."

"I did."

"Oh?" Connor sounded surprised.

"Uh…yeah, I just figured. Cause you're camping." *Shit. Is he gonna get suspicious?*

"Yeah. Not easy to shave out here. Besides, Jenny likes combing it out for me. Says it's soft. Like I'm her pet," Connor chuckled, while rubbing his fingers along his chin.

George imagined her tenderly grooming her father. Then imagined himself stroking Connor's beard. He shook the thought out of his mind. "Still wearing out your Red Sox ball cap?"

"You know it," he replied with a smile. "Anything else?"

"No that's it."

"Okay I gotta go. Lots of driving if I want to get there on time. And good luck with the case. I need good news."

"You'll get it, Con." He almost said *see you soon*, but stopped himself in time. "Be safe."

"Oh and George?"

"Yeah?"

"The fair could be fun. You did good."

George hung up feeling pleased, guilty, relieved. Step one was complete. Later that night it would be time for his visit with Dawn. A meeting that was unlikely to end with anything close to an accolade.

George had learned of Dawn's transfer the day after it occurred. Sipping a mocktail, he had listened as Eleanor slurred through her justification, in praise of her astonishing maternal sacrifice. He had withheld a reaction, too shocked by this unexpected twist, mortified that he hadn't picked up on any hint of Eleanor's plan beforehand. Spilling vodka with every wave of her glass, she had rambled on about how Heather was holding on strong, and even threw in a snide remark about Connor who couldn't possibly understand. George wondered if she had seen another photo. If there was something else he should know. He had tried his best to decipher her gibberish, pluck out the snippets that may have held value, probe for more. But by then, Eleanor was well past the point of coherence to divulge anything useful. But he hadn't let the evening go to a complete waste. Leveraging her drunken state, he had easily swayed her into granting him permission to visit with Dawn. And he had faithfully respected their daily appointment ever since.

Dawn lay waiting for her prince charming to release her from her dungeon of despair. Once again, hoping she was well enough for him to announce he would be taking her away. It's what she begged for during each visit, wishing he would finally give in. To appear her very best, she had just bathed. Her usually full head of curls was still wet and combed flat against her scalp. She pulled the bedsheet up to her neck to cover the hospital gown she was embarrassed to still be wearing. The doctors promised she could get into street clothes once she could go a full day without sedation. For now, her doses were smaller and less frequent, but still necessary to temper residual shaking, sweating and occasional vomiting.

Since his very first visit, George had urged her to follow the doctor's guidance, to be brave, to control her tongue. To focus on herself and not on Eleanor. He tried to build up her confidence, her hope that things would get better. She mattered to him in a way that no one else did and he genuinely wanted what was best for her. Sadly he knew that could never be him. Which now made him worry that all his kindness would serve only to amplify her outrage after he was gone.

Arriving at the designated hour, he went straight to her side and took her hand. "Hey."

"George, thank God." Her features appeared more and more weathered, but still revealed how pleased she was to see him.

"Let's raise this bed so you can sit up." He looked along the side to find the lever. "It might take two people. Let me get someone."

"No, George. Don't leave," she pleaded.

"I'll be right back," he said, stopping to look at her before walking out of the room. *Shit. This is gonna be way harder than I expected.*

This was his last visit. Their final moment together. A decade of trusted friendship would culminate in betrayal. Would he find the right words to make it okay? And could he do it within the short window before her signs of withdrawal would kick in?

He returned with a nurse. Each held one side of the bed, then raised it so that Dawn was now sitting upright. "Much better. Now I can look at you," he smiled, while joining her on the edge.

And just like that, her tension began to subside. She smiled and placed her hand on his. Her finger twitched.

"What's with that?" George asked, raising her hand.

"Happens when I feel nervous sometimes."

"I never noticed it before." George seemed surprised.

THE BURDEN OF TRUTH

"Guess that's cause you make me feel calm," she grinned, her eyes slightly glazed. Her speech was slow, but her mind was present, enough.

George smiled with affection as he stared into her eyes, feeling speechless. And fearing he might lose his nerve.

"When are you taking me home?" she begged, worried his silence meant it wouldn't be today.

"You need to stay here a little longer –"

"How long, George? I can't take much more." She squeezed his hand harder. Her look of pain was unbearable.

"You can do this, Dawn. I know you can."

"No I can't." She looked down and began to tear up.

He lifted her chin. "Yes you can. Look at me, Dawn. It won't be easy, but we need to get you off this crap. Completely. You're already getting better. I can see it. Let the doctors finish what they're doing. You just keep fighting through this the way you have been. Don't give in. No matter how hard you want to. No matter what happens, okay?"

"I'd rather do this from home. With your help."

"I know you would. But this is something you need to do on your own."

"But why?"

"That's the process, Dawn. You know that," he said, caressing her cheek. "Hang in there, okay? Before you know it, this place will just be a distant memory." *And sadly, so will I.*

"Fine," she replied, turning away from him. "Can you at least stay a bit longer? Our visits are so short. Or…are you too embarrassed by me now?"

"Hey, don't say that. I wouldn't be here, if that was true." He regretted that statement the moment he uttered it. Wished he could take it back. He didn't want her to make that leap come tomorrow when he wouldn't be there anymore. "All I want is for you to get better."

"I'll get better if we spend more time together." Then Dawn thought of something that might entice him. "There's a lounge with a record player. Maybe you can get the doctors to let us do our visits there so we could listen to music." She smiled at the thought of such a prospect.

"That would be nice. But…Dawn, there's something I need to tell you."

She stared into his eyes with a look of concern and chose not to reply.

"I won't be able to see you…tomorrow." That seemed less harsh than saying *anymore*.

"George, please. You're the only thing I look forward to. How else am I supposed to get through the day?"

He needed to say something that wasn't an outright lie, nor too upsetting. "I'm gonna do something. Something very important. Something that's gonna make things better. You might not understand it at first. But one day you will. I promise."

"What George? What are you gonna do?"

"I need you to trust me, Dawn. Can you do that?"

"No. Not until you tell me what it is."

"It's something that needs to be a secret. Please Dawn. Don't ask me again."

"Fine. But why can't you come see me after you're done?"

"Dawn." This was killing George. He couldn't do it. He couldn't look her in the eyes and say goodbye. Tell her he was never coming back. So instead he said, "I love you." With that, he leaned over and kissed her on the lips. A long, soft kiss. The first he had ever given a woman. As he sat back up, she opened her mouth to speak, but he placed his finger over her lips to stop her. He didn't need to hear it back. "Shh, Dawn. It's time for you to rest now."

The twitch in her finger had stopped. Her body was numb, drained of all its defences. She watched as he walked away, hoping it wouldn't be too long until he returned. *He actually loves me,* she smiled.

George walked out of the institute and ran straight to the side of the building to crouch down and wail, tortured by his cowardice and cruelty. Leaving the one person who was actually going to miss him without even saying a proper goodbye. She was the only soul in this world who genuinely cared for him. He hated that he had no choice but to abandon her.

Barely recovered from his devastating non-farewell with Dawn, George went straight to Delano Manor to share a nightcap with a tipsy Eleanor. *And now for step three,* he thought, shaking off his sadness, while marching toward the bar and pouring himself a glass of soda water on ice. He was so bold as to not even have acknowledged her presence when he entered the room.

"You look like shit," she stated. "I take it Dawn did this to you?"

He wanted to lunge at her. He was so done with her provocation. But he held back, sat down, made himself

305

comfortable. *Keep it together,* he urged himself. "She's actually made a lot of improvement." He feigned a smile and tried to perk up.

Eleanor appeared surprised. Or annoyed her dig hadn't bothered him more. "Good. That's exactly why she's there."

"You know," he added, "if you really wanted to do something good for her, get a record player for her room so she can listen to music."

She stared down at her glass as she swirled the ice. "I'll consider it."

Now was the time for George to catch her off-guard. To see if he could beat her at her own game. "Also, I've given it a lot of thought, and I've decided to meet with Anthony again."

"Is that so?" she frowned. "And what would make you want to do that?"

He knew that to sell a lie, it was best to insert some truth. "A few reasons," of which the real one would be withheld. "Mostly because he's gonna get out soon. I didn't handle my last meeting with him very well. I'd like to leave a better impression for when he gets out."

That made her smirk. "So you're going to kiss the ring. I wouldn't expect this of you, George." Her expression didn't reveal whether that was criticism or praise.

"But neither will he." For George, that was the whole point.

"Just don't expect a pat on the back."

"If anything, I'm expecting the opposite. Though based on how the team has described him, he seems like a man whose days are numbered." Precisely two if there were no hiccups in

George's aggressive time-line.

"That's what he gets for never following doctors' orders," Eleanor sighed, ready to move on to any other topic but Anthony.

George got the message. Time to tease up surprise number two. "Also, I've decided to take you up on your offer."

Eleanor looked at him, puzzled. She recalled no offer, nor was she in the habit of making them. "And what offer is that, George?" she asked, seemingly nonplussed.

"I'm gonna go to him. Like you suggested." He waited for her reaction.

At first, it was clear she had no idea who he was referring to. Nor how that constituted an offer. So she, too, waited. The classic signal for him to elaborate.

He chose not to. Instead, he threw in another surprise. "I'd be happy to put in a good word for you. If you like." He wondered how she felt about being on the receiving end of her own methods.

"George, I don't have time for games. If there's something you'd like to share, do tell."

"I'm sorry." No he wasn't. "I thought you understood." That was a dig. "I'm going to Connor." Before she could process that news, he added, "and I'll need you to do me a favor while I'm gone."

She lifted her gaze directly toward him the moment he mentioned Connor. "What kind of favor?"

"Can you tell the team you asked me to take care of something for you so they don't wonder where I am? It'll just be for one day."

CHAPTER TWENTY-TWO

"And when are you planning this visit?"

"Tomorrow. I've booked an early departure and the red-eye back."

"So soon?" It almost looked like she hadn't meant to say that out loud.

"He's a moving target so I have to catch him while I can."

"And he agreed to this?"

"No. He doesn't know I'm coming."

"So you're going to casually bump into him?"

"Something like that. It's a long shot, I know. And it might be a complete bust, but I wanna at least try."

"To convince him to come home?"

Finally. This is exactly what he was hoping she would ask. "No. He's never coming back. That I'm sure of."

"I see. And you're okay with that?"

"Nope. But it's his life, not mine. And after seeing those pictures you showed me, he's clearly very happy now. I want him to stay that way." That was a little payback, disguised as a thank you, for how she led him to his change of heart. It was, after all, what she deserved for having them followed then boasting about it with the photos. The part he chose to leave out was that Connor was obviously happier without George in his life. There was no place for that show of weakness in this conversation.

"But surely you'll be tempted to sway him?"

George knew he would be tempted by many things where Connor was concerned, but it wouldn't change the purpose of his meeting. "No Mrs. Delano. I know I'll probably never see him again. And I also know that only you can understand that kind of sacrifice." Unlike Eleanor, George chose to point out her weakness in a far less antagonistic way.

"So why are you going, George?"

"To offer to handle his affairs. You know, empty the apartment, store his furniture, sign off on the lease transfer. That kind of thing. And, of course, to say goodbye."

"You're helping him stay away?"

"That's not quite how I see it. But yes, I suppose you're right," he replied, pretending to agree. "To be honest, it's reassuring to know that you're looking out for them. At least this gives me something I can do for him too."

She paused and swirled. Her eyes were locked on his. "So he won't see Heather?"

It was a fair question, which deserved an honest response. "That part I can't figure out."

"What do you mean?"

"He's been infatuated with her from the second he first laid eyes on her. I don't get how he's not savoring every last moment while she's still alive." *Come on, Mrs. Delano. Tell me why he ran.*

After a long moment of silence Eleanor exclaimed, "I'll take care of telling the team you're away on an important errand." She chose to keep her secret, and George would keep his too.

"Thank you, Mrs. Delano." He stood up. "I'd better get going. I've got a very early flight to catch." As he walked away, he stopped and turned back. "Oh and I meant it, by the way. I'll put in a good word for you." He wondered whether she expected he would tell Connor that she was having them followed. He wouldn't, but she didn't need to know that. She could stew about it just like he had done for months.

Eleanor didn't reply. She just stared as he walked away.

* * *

George entered the El Dorado Savings Bank at 2:45pm the following day and stood behind two other customers waiting their turn for the next available teller. If he could choose the one who would best succumb to his charm, it would be the middle aged, over-weight woman on the far right in the bright blue blouse.

Alas, he was lucky. "Hi," he smiled, while raising his briefcase onto the counter. He pulled out a business card and placed it for her to see. "I'm Jorge Vasquez. I believe you have an envelope for me."

"Oh yes. Of course, Mr. Vasquez. I'll get that for you right away."

"By the way, that blouse looks lovely on you…Nancy," he said, having checked her name plate. "Really brings out your eyes."

"Why thank you, Mr. Vasquez," she blushed, before going to get his envelope from a room behind the counter.

George glanced around to get the lay of the land while he waited. There were six other customers inside, of which two were seated at open desks with bank representatives. Conversations were held to a relative whisper, interjected only by the sound of knocking from handheld date stampers as the clerks pressed them against ink pads then applied them to deposit or withdrawal slips. The glare of the sun through large windows was partially obstructed by beige vertical blinds.

Nancy returned quickly. "I just need you to sign here for me please, Mr. Vasquez," she said, sliding the slip toward him. She then handed him the thick envelope. "Here you go. Is there anything else I can do for you today, Mr. Vasquez?"

"Yes, actually there is. More like a favor really." He winked, leaned in and spoke just loud enough for her to hear.

"Of course. How can I help?"

"I'm meeting with a client soon and was wondering if it would it be okay if he and I spoke over by the window? You see, I'm traveling on business and I don't have access to an office in town. Your bank is the perfect meeting spot. It should only be for a few minutes."

"Why of course, Mr. Vasquez. Stay as long as you like."

"Thank you, Nancy. Much appreciated."

"The El Dorado Savings Bank is pleased to serve you, Mr. Vasquez. You have yourself a wonderful day now."

"And to you as well."

George walked over to the right side of the entrance. By the window was a private enough spot to wait for Connor to arrive. Wearing a full suit on a sunny July afternoon in California was already a sweaty venture. The stress of seeing him again, of wondering whether he would be happy or angry George was here, was even greater cause for perspiration.

The Winnebago pulled up across the street about twenty minutes later. Moments after, a black Cadillac DeVille pulled in behind it. *Fancy wheels like that must be Eleanor's spy*, thought

George, who would have expected her to employ a more subtle vehicle. He watched as Connor crossed the street sporting blue jeans, a t-shirt and his Red Sox ballcap. He loved the rugged look of his bearded face and couldn't wait to see it up close.

The second Connor crossed the doorway, George called him over, "Con. Over here."

Taken aback, Connor almost froze, but darted quickly over to George. "What the hell are you doing here, George? Someone could've followed you." He looked all around for suspicious behavior.

"Con, relax," he whispered. "There's nothing to be worried about. We're in a bank. I didn't even give them your name. I gave them mine. Here." George handed him the envelope of money, while smiling and looking around to make sure Connor's reaction hadn't surprised anyone. Nancy, in particular, who was still staring at him. "You should have enough to last you a while."

"Shit George. You could've told me you were coming." Trying to get over the shock, Connor failed to express his thanks for the boost to his dire finances.

"I know. But I wasn't sure if I could make it. It was a last minute thing. It's good to see you, though. You look good."

"Thanks George," sighed Connor. "And sorry. You just caught me off-guard. So how are things?"

George knew the question was not directed at how he was doing. It was always about the others. "Heather's stable. Eleanor is Eleanor. Oh and Anthony is really sick."

"What? Like in the hospital?"

"No still in jail, but I doubt he'll last much longer."

"You're kidding?"

"His pride is the only thing keeping him going at this point, but soon that will die too."

"Wow." Connor seemed relieved but unsure of what would follow.

"Look. There's something else. Something I wanted to show you," George said, removing an envelope from his briefcase. "I know Eleanor is cruel, infuriating, and has the moral fiber of a screwdriver, but somewhere deep down, I think there's a bit of good in her."

"I don't know what you're smoking, George, but it's making you hallucinate."

"Here," he said, handing him a document.

Connor took it. "What's this?"

"It's a page from Anthony's will. I know you have your reasons for wanting to hold onto Heather, but I think maybe Eleanor has her reasons too, and they might actually be generous."

Once again Connor had a look of panic. He worried what this page would reveal. Glancing at it quickly, but unsure of what he was supposed to glean, he asked, "What am I looking for?"

"It's what's not there. You and Jenny. Anthony's beneficiaries exclude you both. The will states that if he's predeceased by any one of his three beneficiaries, their amount gets divvied up between the remaining two." Hoping he had uncovered a meaningful detail for Connor, he added, "It's possible Eleanor wants to keep Heather alive as long as possible so you and Jenny can access her inheritance." He pulled out another document from his briefcase. "I drew up a representation agreement, just in case."

"What's that?"

"It's a contract. You hiring me as your lawyer."

"What do I need a lawyer for?" Once again Connor began to panic.

This document was purely for posturing. A back-up in case George's plan fell through. But he could see Connor's discomfort, which was not what he had intended. "When Delano dies, Heather will be entitled to her inheritance. You'll need to sign for it as her power of attorney. This agreement lets me do that on your behalf."

"I'm not sure I want to."

George did not expect that response. "What do you mean?"

"Their money. I don't want it."

Of course you don't, thought George. *I should've known better.* And yet, he couldn't let Connor give that up just on principle. "I get it, Con. But think of Jenny. You're not expecting her to spend her teenage years hanging with her dad in a motorhome are you? Her education, her future, everything would be taken care of. You'd never have to worry about money. Ever."

"I'm not interested in having her grow up like a spoiled rich kid."

"Fat chance of that happening with you as her father. Besides, she doesn't need to know anything for as long as you don't want her to. Put the money in a trust. It will be there when you need it."

"I hear you, George. But I don't think I can get past the fact that it comes from filth."

"It does. That's true. But you can take that dirty money and use it for good. Jenny is good."

"I'll think about it." Turning to the window to check on her, he asked, "Can we take this outside? I don't want Jenny to start looking for me."

George nodded.

They stepped out onto the sidewalk, in full view of a camera-wielding spy hiding behind tinted car windows. And there, sitting in the passenger seat of the motorhome, was Jenny reading. She seemed so grown up to George.

"Con, there's one last thing," George began. He took in a deep breath. "I'm going away."

"Away? Where?"

"I won't have a job soon, you know, after Delano is convicted or dead. And you're gone now, so there's nothing really left for me…in Boston."

Connor knew to expect surprises from George, but this was different. George was a staple in his life. It was true that they hadn't spent much time together since Jenny's birth, but he was always close by. And for all the blame he placed on him for not protecting Heather, it never occurred to Connor that George would ever leave. It felt oddly upsetting. "So where? New York? I remember you used to always say we should move there." In hindsight, Connor realized how different their lives would have been had they followed through. Before Heather's pregnancy and its life changing impact, that is.

Connor's sudden nostalgia was pressing George to accelerate his departure before becoming too emotional. "I think I just need to disappear for a while. You know?"

"Oh. Okay." Connor actually felt sad.

"Do you think you can start calling the hospital yourself for Heather's status?"

"Um, yeah. Of course. So that means you're leaving soon?"

"Yeah. Very. I've been making the arrangements."

Suddenly Connor realized that he knew nothing about what George had been going through. Since Heather's incident, every discussion they had was about Connor and his needs, his disappointment, his fear, his demands. Never was anything about George. "I'm gonna miss you, man."

At that, George had to hold back tears. "Me too, Con. It's been quite the ride. Wouldn't have wanted to go it with anyone else."

A moment of awkward silence followed what was sounding more and more like a final farewell. Connor tried to think of what to say next. George was always the one to try to pick up the mood. In this instance however, he felt it was his turn to return the favor.

"So…speaking of rides. Care to join me and Jenny at the fair before you go? Pretty sure she'd like to meet her Uncle George." They hadn't seen each other since she was a baby. Heather didn't want him around her once she was old enough to speak. Or anyone else with ties to the Delano's. She was too afraid of what her daughter might overhear. Couldn't take the risk of having to explain something to her then have to lie in the process.

George hadn't expected the invitation. He was used to being excluded. But it was tempting. To spend actual quality time seemed long overdue. And a fitting way to say goodbye. But he couldn't do it. Not to himself. Nor to them. "That would be such a blast. But…I can't. Got a flight to catch. Duty calls."

"Too bad," replied Connor, disappointed. "Look George, I –" Connor couldn't find the words.

So George did. "I know." He leaned in to give him a bear hug.

"Oh wait," exclaimed Connor. "You gotta pen? I'll sign that thing. For when I need a lawyer." Or to ensure there was a way for them to keep in touch.

With the exchange of that envelope, they parted ways. For the very last time.

* * *

Apparently, George's return flight was very smooth. Or so said the passengers with whom he traveled. He hadn't noticed through the turbulence of his thoughts. While he may have foregone the county fair, he soared up, down and around through the roller coaster of his mind, bouncing between his conversation with Connor, what was said, what wasn't said, what should've been said, and his upcoming conversation with Anthony. He rehearsed for every conceivable reaction he might face, then refined his responses accordingly. It fired him up. Like a jet engine. But he had so much adrenalin coursing through his system, sleep had eluded him completely. Before he knew it, it was time jump in the shower, shave and dress for his last day.

Document pile number two securely in his briefcase, George made his way to prison, the place he would commit his crime.

"Didn't think I'd see the likes of you here again, Vasquez," Anthony Delano mocked, while having his handcuffs removed after being escorted into their meeting room. Even in his blue jumpsuit, Anthony appeared more menacing than vulnerable.

"To be honest, neither did I, sir," replied George, already perspiring. He breathed calmly, focused on restraining all facial expression and body language. *Let him think I feel intimated,* he thought, as he waited for the guard to leave and close the door behind him. The moment they were alone, he declared, "But there's something you need to know." He lifted his briefcase onto the table, opened it and removed a document-sized, sealed white plastic envelope.

"And they sent you? This better be good, Vasquez."

In the weeks since George had last seen him, Anthony had aged considerably. His features were more worn, his skin tone had turned to a sickly pale grey. The prison menu was absent of the calories and alcohol that normally kept his rosy cheeks full. They sagged, tugging so hard at the bags beneath his bulging eyes, they caused them to droop over his cheekbones like overflowing pouches of un-cried tears.

George chose his words carefully. He knew Anthony did not like to be caught off-guard. Particularly by such an unequal adversary. "They don't know I'm here, sir. In fact, they would kill me if they knew what I was about to show you."

Anthony leaned back and glanced around the room to feign disinterest, exactly as George expected. Eventually he stated, "Spit it out, Vasquez."

George slid the envelope across the table. "Please open it, sir."

Anthony paused, annoyed he had to rip the plastic open himself. But he did with a gesture of frustration, then pulled out another sealed envelope. "What is this? Fort Knox for fuck's sake?"

"I wanted to make sure that it didn't get tampered with, sir. You wouldn't want anyone seeing this." In truth, George just didn't want to expose himself to the substance while it was near him.

He watched as Anthony tore the flap off and pulled out the dozen-page document. Now a master of the photocopy machine, George had spent weeks doctoring photographs, cutting, pasting, fabricating the most disparaging notes possible, all appearing legitimate, and all with the intent of ensuring Anthony Delano's undivided attention.

"What the hell is this, Vasquez?" he exclaimed, while looking at a picture of his wife dancing with his brother, Michael, on the very first page.

"Sir, you're not gonna like this," George replied, "but you need to know. Your wife is having an affair with your brother."

The bate was set. Now to keep Anthony fully engaged. Because George absolutely needed him to turn every single page.

"This is bullshit!" he shouted, pushing the document away and throwing his hands up in the air. The mere suggestion of her infidelity was an utter insult.

George began to panic. The success of his plan rested entirely on Anthony physically touching the pages. "Sir. I know it's shocking, disgusting actually. And an absolute betrayal." Anthony still wasn't budging, arms-crossed like a pouting child. George needed to push harder. "But it gets worse. They were plotting against you, sir. The details are all in there. You need to go through it."

Anthony grabbed the document back and began to pant with rage. George watched. Hoping. Trying not to lean forward as he waited to see if Anthony would start reading. Then, he finally did it. He licked the tip of his sausage-like fingers and turned the first page, grunting as he breathed. So heavily, George thought smoke might blow out of his nostrils.

Encouraged, George now needed for Anthony's blood pressure to rise even more, to work him up as much as he could, while ensuring he read through every last page. "The team didn't think you could take it, sir. They said your heart was too weak. But I know you're not weak, sir."

Another page, another lick, another swallow, as Anthony unknowingly ingested more and more of the trace amounts of cyanide laced onto each corner.

Midway through the document, Anthony's strain was so intense, he grabbed at his heart, short of breath. The pause worried George. He had calculated the right number of pages, the exact dose needed for Anthony's system to collapse in about four hours. But it was imperative that he get through the last few. Less might not work. To entice him, George had deliberately reserved the most compromising material for the very end.

Nearing it, Anthony spoke. His face was flush, sweat was dripping from his brow. He clenched both fists then whispered through gritted teeth, "I'm going to kill them both for this."

"As you should, sir. That's what they deserve," rallied George in fake allegiance to the man he was two pages away from extinguishing.

"And you, you little prick," said Anthony, fixing his gaze, while panting in anger. "I bet you think you're real clever right now, don't you?"

"What? Sir, what do you mean?" George's eyes widened, his heart pounded. There was no way Anthony could know. How could he? George just had to remain calm. Try his best to not lose control.

"You think I'm a fool?" he exclaimed. Then speaking very slowly and furiously, he continued. "Bringing me this shit, acting like you're some kind of hero. That's exactly what the guilty do. They deflect. So Vasquez, tell me. Do you enjoy screwing my wife?"

George nearly fell off his chair. "What? No! Never sir. Never would I touch Mrs. Delano." The thought repulsed him completely. As would any woman. But Anthony couldn't know George had the perfect defense. The incontestable one. One he had never said out loud. To declare it here of all places, with Delano of all audiences, seemed surreal, desperate. But George needed to steer him away from that assumption so he could finish reading the document. Reminding himself that he had nothing left to lose, that it didn't matter who knew anymore, he declared, "No sir. No…I, I don't like women, sir."

Anthony looked surprised. Then disgusted. "A fucking homo." He fumed as though in the presence of the worst possible scum. "A fucking homo comes in my face to tell me my wife is screwing my brother. You're a dead little sissy, Vasquez. Get the fuck outta here!" He repeated over and over, louder and louder, clenching his heart without letting go.

George pulled the handkerchief from his pocket, placed it over the documents and envelopes and slid everything into the briefcase he held by the edge of the table. He closed it quickly then shouted, "Guards!"

The guard entered immediately and rushed in to handcuff Anthony while he continued to shout and sweat. A second one followed, who George pulled aside by a firm grab of his arm.

"The doctor should never have cleared him for this meeting. What was he thinking?" challenged George, faking his displeasure. "Mr. Delano's heart is frail. He nearly had a heart attack right in from of me. Do you have any idea how bad that is? Get him back into his room and leave him alone so he can rest. No stimulation of any kind. At most, a sedative to relax him."

"Yes, sir. Will do," replied the guard nervously. "I'll escort you out and make certain that Mr. Delano is taken care of."

George took a long countryside detour before driving back into the office for his final act. He had found this stretch of dirt road years ago. It was a quiet place he escaped to when he needed to run away from it all, scream at his own demons at the top of lungs, grateful for the absence of prying ears. Today, it was a fitting place to destroy the evidence. He parked the car, placed his briefcase on the ground and pulled the gasoline container out from the trunk then began pouring. He stepped back, lit a match and threw it. It ignited immediately, turning his masterpiece, his weeks of crafting, falsifying, and plagiarizing provocative material, into smoldering flames, never to be read again.

"May you burn in hell, Anthony Delano," he said as he watched. "I'll be joining you soon." A tear rolled down his cheek as he thought of Heather, Connor, Jennifer and Dawn. Lives broken because of his temptations, his weakness. To them he said, "This is it. The best I could do to make it up to you. It doesn't make it right. But I hope it makes it better." He stayed for as long as it took for the pile to reduce to ashes, then kicked some dirt over it to cover every last trace.

He stopped at a gas station on the way back to refill the container and use the washroom to wash his hands, throw water over his face, try to cover up the parts of his day that needed to remain secret.

He entered Delano Manor and went straight to the war room. The team were all there, sitting around the large conference table, working on their own documents, tweaking closing arguments.

"Gentlemen," he declared, "I screwed up real bad."

They all looked up. "What Georgie?"

"I went to see Mr. Delano. Tried to make up for my shitty visit last time. You know, so I could get into his good graces for when he gets out."

"That was brave. But pretty stupid, Georgie. What happened?"

"It's like my presence was an insult to him. He got completely enraged. I had to call the guards cause he was pulling at his chest and got all sweaty. I swear I think I gave him a heart attack." George was trying his best to sound remorseful, like he was the innocent bystander who had visited Delano with the best of intentions.

"Shit."

"The doctor had cleared him first. I made sure to check. But I'm, I'm worried because he was gone for the day. I…I don't know if he was able to examine him after I left." But George knew Delano wouldn't be examined. He had timed his visit precisely for that reason. And if the guard had done as he was told, Anthony should be resting peacefully.

"I'll call the prison. Make sure they watch him. Thanks for telling us, Georgie."

George nodded, then took his seat and immediately started to review the files that had been laid out for him.

Moments later, his colleague confirmed, "Looks like Mr. Delano is sleeping. They gave him a mild sedative after your meeting and he's been out ever since."

"Thank God," sighed George, relieved that Anthony was being left alone while the poison could work through his bloodstream. Now, all George had to do was act natural while he waited.

It took no more than five hours before the telephone rang. George's chest was beating with anticipation. After his colleague hung up, he walked in behind George, rested his hand on his shoulders, and informed them that Anthony Delano was pronounced dead just moments ago.

"Don't go thinking this was your fault, Georgie," said one colleague. "His heart was done. It was only a matter of time."

"I'm going to check on Mrs. Delano," said the most senior. "Let's call it a day and reconvene tomorrow morning."

George dropped his head. Relief, sorrow, liberation. There was no expression to capture how it felt to know he had freed those dearest to him from this monster for good. Now, he had but one final curtain call before he would excuse himself permanently from their lives. "I'd like to go see her first, if that's okay?" he asked.

"Okay Georgie. But please. Don't beat yourself up over this."

Eleanor was in her office, wearing a navy dress and pulling files out of a cabinet behind her desk. Her movements seemed hurried, nervous. If she planned on reading, she would soon have to turn on the lamp. Only minimal light was cast from the large window as the sun was setting. He noticed the two photographs at the corner of her desk. Her two daughters, school-aged, in uniform, probably taken on class photo day. He wondered whether it captured a moment in time before the beast had begun to unleash his anger. Did it bring her any relief to know he was gone? Or was it still too soon to process?

George never interrupted her while she was in there. They only ever met in the casual ambiance of the lounge, to unwind, and at times, unravel. Perhaps she would have preferred that he wait until later to meet her there. Today of all days, she would need his company. But he was too drained to keep up the hypocrisy. His performance was over and it was time for him to bow out. This was all he could muster for his final encore.

"Mrs. Delano," he said as he crossed the doorway. "I need to confess."

She turned quickly, startled by his presence, and even more so by his comment. "George? Oh. I didn't see you there. Come in." She gestured for him to take a seat.

Sitting on opposite sides of her desk seemed unfamiliar, so formal. That, and she was sober. But he obliged, hoping this would be quick. "I think this is my fault."

"Why George? Because you saw him last? Don't be ridiculous." She waved off his comment.

"He really looked like he wanted to kill me for being there. My presence set him off. I'm sure of it."

"George, we talked about it two days ago. The man had a heart condition. That killed him. And should have long before today. It certainly wasn't your presence that did him in. So please stop with that nonsense."

"Okay," he sighed. "But you? You're okay?" He felt an odd sense of concern for her. Perhaps because he realized he had just gotten away with murder.

"I'll be fine. After we get through the service, and put his affairs in order. This needs to get done quickly. Put it all behind us." She moved the files on her desk as she spoke, in a hurry to get the wheels in motion. She then looked up at George. "I've already informed the coroner not to bother with an autopsy. No need to prolong the process for no reason, wouldn't you agree?"

Whether the cyanide would be detected or not was debatable. And though George felt strongly that Delano's heart condition would be to blame, if poison was revealed, he didn't care. He would be long gone by then, his punishment already taken care of, self-inflicted. But still, he replied, "Yes I agree. It seems pointless." Then, preferring to move the subject in a forward direction, he said, "Besides, I'm sure you're eager to get your life back."

"Precisely. I'll finally be able to start focusing on doing some good for the community. Get back to charity functions. I've missed them so." She looked up at him. "You'll help me with that won't you, George?"

He didn't see that coming. "Oh, uh. I, I…have no real plans now." If not for the fact that his life was on the verge of being cut short, he would have just lost his employer. Where he would have taken his law practice from there was never a consideration. As he nervously looked around, he landed his gaze on the girls' photos.

Eleanor noticed and picked up the one of Heather and ran her fingers across it. "She's next," she said with sadness, her eyes beginning to shine. "She won't last much longer." Before becoming too emotional, she set it back down, inhaled, and asked George, "Tell me. How did it go with Connor? Will you be handling his affairs while I deal with Anthony's?"

It seemed like weeks ago since he had seen him. Meanwhile, it was only yesterday, the day before George chose a life of crime, became a murderer. "Good. They're doing great. Happy." He felt no desire to elaborate, other than to add, "and I did throw in a good word for you. Just like I said I would."

She brushed it off. Perhaps it triggered more emotion that she was able to handle. Or she didn't believe him. Either way, George was indifferent. "You look exhausted," she said. "Go get some sleep. We can discuss all this tomorrow."

"Good night, Mrs. Delano." He stood up and walked away, knowing there would be no such discussion, because there would be no tomorrow.

Back in his apartment, George was ready to collapse. Drained of his last bit of energy, he still needed to muster just a bit more. It would be unfair to not leave a note, to not explain his actions. Mostly, he needed them to know it was because of how much they meant to him. So he sat at his desk and pulled out the last document. The one that had yet to be written. Two blank sheets for two letters. He didn't want to call them suicide notes because that seemed weak. For once he felt strong. Tired only from expending his power. He had done what no one else had been brave enough to do.

Minutes ticked by and the pages were still blank. He struggled to keep his thoughts straight with so little energy. He had tried starting Dawn's, then aborted and tried Connor's. Thinking of a first sentence, changing it, almost putting it to pen, then retracting it because nothing sounded right. How could it when what he believed deep down, was that they would never understand no matter what words he used. They would hate him for leaving whether it came with parting words or not. Maybe he was just too tired. His mind too exhausted to compute. His body too drained to sit straight. He wanted to rest. To let the contents of the pill bottle in the drawer above his lap bring him relief, lead him toward his final breath.

"I can't just leave without writing at least something," he sighed to himself, rubbing both hands against his face. He then placed them flat against the desk, took the pen in one hand and said, "Write George. Just write."

And so he did.

Unplanned, unexpected, and possibly ill-advised, these were

the words he put to paper.

July 28, 1972

I, Jorge (George) Vasquez, confess to the murder of Anthony Delano. During our attorney-client meeting today, I deliberately aggravated his heart condition by implying his wife and brother were having an affair. To convince him, I fabricated a document with compromising photos and notes. The pages he handled were laced with trace amounts of cyanide meant to mimic cardiac arrest within a few hours. I summoned the guards to take him away once he appeared sufficiently agitated, then burned the document in a field after leaving him. He was pronounced dead hours later.

My self-inflicted punishment should not to be construed as remorse.

He added his signature, folded the page in three, inserted it in a letter envelope, licked the flap, sealed it and inscribed *private & confidential* on the front.

He got up and placed it face down at the bottom of his sock drawer. Then returned to his desk with a glass of water, removed the Quaaludes from the bottle and swallowed them down before lying on his bed for his final rest.

CHAPTER TWENTY-THREE

— 2003 —

"So?" asked Nick, while rubbing my shoulders from behind as I stood in front of our bathroom mirror. "How do you feel?"

I was brushing my hair, letting it hang below my shoulders for a more casual look. An updo felt too formal and a ponytail too casual. "Weird. Nervous. Excited." I wasn't sure how I was supposed feel about meeting my aunt for the very first time. Excluding my mother's funeral, of course, but that was too long ago and blurred behind tears and grief. I turned to face him and asked, "I look okay, right?" I was wearing a pair of jeans, a buttoned lilac blouse and flat shoes.

"You look beautiful," he said with a kiss. "And don't be surprised if she stares. You look an awful lot like her sister."

"True. I guess this is weird for her too. Right?" I wondered if she was as nervous as I was.

"And exciting. Now, stop worrying. It'll be fine." He ushered me into the bedroom straight to the doorway. "I suppose you have a list of a thousand questions?"

"So many. I don't even know where to start."

"Try not to bombard her," he urged with kindness. "She probably has just as many."

I took a deep breath, ready to leave. "Okay."

"Oh and Jen?" he said as I crossed the doorway. "Maybe have some herbal tea instead of coffee," he winked.

He made a valid point. Caffeine avoidance would be better for my nerves.

I arrived at the coffee shop way too early. I couldn't wait, despite feeling oddly conflicted. Was this going to be a life-enhancing reunion? Or the worst idea ever? Like a little girl on Christmas morning, I was impatient to see what Santa brought me, but worried that I wouldn't like what I had asked for.

Though it was hard to imagine how this introduction would go, one thing was clear, I was overcome with curiosity. From the moment Dawn agreed to meet, my mind had been spinning with excitement and it surprised me to feel this way.

To keep from overthinking about our upcoming conversation, I overthought instead about where to sit. There were twenty or so tables, with varying degrees of sunlight cast from each of the windows along both facades of the corner establishment. A steady flow of people was coming and going, most ordering to-go cups before heading right back outside. As for the seated patrons, I waited till they vacated their tables, then immediately darted over to test a new one. Admittedly, they were all pretty much the same in this small space, but it kept me occupied while I waited with anticipation. My real target was the corner banquet for its privacy, but the foursome of students washing down doughnuts with mega-sized beverages didn't appear to be in any hurry to leave. So I pursued my game of musical tables for another thirty minutes until an obese woman with an abundant head of gray curls walked through the door.

That must be her. She wore a black, pleated, flowy top that fell past her wide rump and light grey leggings. The handles of her large charcoal handbag hung over her bent forearm that rested against her tummy. *She's wearing earrings. Why didn't I wear earrings?* I waved to signal to her. "Dawn?"

She acknowledged me with a short grin, then manoeuvred as best she could between tables that were too tightly configured for her girth.

Crap. I should've picked one closer to the entrance. It was painful to watch but she eventually made her way toward me. I stood up to greet her. *Do we hug?*

She nodded with another short grin before immediately dropping onto the small wooden chair, then exhaled loudly.

I sat and looked at her without a clue what to say. So I held back and let her catch her breath; her complexion was already moist from the effort. But when the pause began to feel awkward, I needed to break the silence. "Can I get you coffee?" Clearly I wasn't going to expect her to wiggle herself over to the counter.

"Sure. Black. Thanks," was all she replied with a huff.

I got up and went to place our order, choosing to follow Nick's guidance and stick with tea, then stared at her backside as I waited the interminable two minutes for it to be prepared. Finally, my name was called. Returning to our table, I placed the mugs between us. She was breathing more normally by the time I circled around to take my seat across from her. Time to ask questions. Where should I start?

Dawn beat me to it. "So how did you find me?" she asked, with neither a smile to show she was pleased that I did, or a frown to suggest that she wasn't.

I cupped my mug with both hands for comfort. "My husband, Nick is his name, he gets the credit. I was looking at a photo of my parents' wedding recently with Dad. I had never seen it before. Well, if I did, I was too young to remember. Anyway, you were in it. Dad pointed you out." *Stop rambling.* "I later mentioned to Nick that it would be nice to connect with you."

Still no reaction. A moment of silence was interrupted by her next question. "So what's Connor been up to?"

"Not a whole lot. Started struggling with his memory a while back, then had a stroke a few years ago. Suffered paralysis on his right side. So he's in long-term care now. But, other than that, he's his usual pleasant self." *She's not smiling. Am I smiling too much?*

Her next question came quicker. "Did he remarry?"

That caught me off-guard. The thought seemed absurd. "No. Never even dated. Mom was his one and only." Oddly, I suppose. Had he been too scarred after Mom's adultery?

She appeared surprised. Sort of. Her eyes narrowed; a first facial expression. "He was the best thing that ever happened to her. And to you too." She stared more intensely. "You look a lot like her, you know?"

"So I've noticed," I smiled sheepishly. "What was she like? Were you close?" I was going to add a third question but held back to pace myself.

She took in a big breath. "We were very different. Not just physically." Her forehead creased to show she was stating the obvious. "She was the young princess, and I was the clumsy big sister."

I furrowed my brow. "But she was older."

"Oh right. Yes," she shook her head as though she had forgotten. Then she explained, "I was such an old soul. Always felt like I was the oldest." Her eyes shifted as though embarrassed.

The response seemed unusual to me, but what did I know? As an only child, I couldn't relate. Perhaps one day, the order of their birth wouldn't dictate how old my own girls felt relative to each other. "Do I have cousins?" I blurted to change the subject.

"Nope. Never married."

I couldn't tell if that was by choice, but I did sense some discomfort. So while I was disappointed there wasn't a bigger family out there for me to discover, I reverted back to my own. "I have three daughters." Not that she asked. "I brought pictures. If you'd like to see."

"Sure," she replied, as I was already reaching into my purse to pull out the envelope of color prints that had yet to be placed into a photo album.

They were from Grace's last birthday. I glanced through a few before selecting one that had the three girls in it and handed it to her. She looked at it, then reached for her reading glasses in her handbag to take a closer look.

"That's Grace, in the middle. She's eleven. Hannah, nine, is on the right, and Lisa, seven, is on her left. They have your curls," I smiled. Then immediately felt like an idiot. Their skin tone left little doubt that their father did as well.

Dawn's eyes softened. A real smile began to form across her

face. "They are really beautiful."

"Thank you," I smiled, feeling that we were making a breakthrough.

As she handed it back to me, she said, "Show me more."

Wow. Better than I expected. We looked through the whole pack. They were mostly of the girls and their friends being all kinds of silly. I also showed her Nick and found one with Dad when we all brought him his piece of birthday cake. "There's Dad," I pointed. With a half-smile, wearing a party hat, he was waving the hand he could control.

She stared at it for a long while, with a look that seemed so serious. It was hard to tell if she was nostalgic or just surprised by how much Dad had aged. Then, out of nowhere, her mood changed. She handed it back to me, and placed both her palms on the table to pull herself up. "Well. This was nice. But I should go."

"Oh? Already? But...we just got here." *Was it something I said? Was I talking too much?* I stood up confused.

She reached out one hand, palm facing upwards. When I gave her mine, she placed her other hand above it and squeezed tightly. The moment I felt her finger twitch, my heart sank. Just like Mom's. "You have a beautiful family, Jennifer," she said, her eyes glistening. "Heather would be proud." Her voice cracked, then she let go and turned away.

I stood dumbfounded as I watched her leave. Was that it? No *let's get together again*? I wasn't okay just leaving it like this, so I called out to her. "Dawn?"

She stopped and turned toward me.

"Here," I extended a photo to her. "Keep it as a souvenir." It was of the five of us just after Grace had blown out the candles on her chocolate birthday cake.

"Thank you." She accepted it with a sad kind of smile, then waddled away.

Later that night, I still hadn't shaken off how Dawn and I had parted. The finality of it was so disappointing. She had been a stranger my entire life, and in only a matter of minutes, I let myself feel that we were close. Or that we could be. I suppose it's that I wanted to be.

"It was a bad idea. I shouldn't have reached out. I obviously upset her," I said to Nick as we were lying in bed.

"I think you're wrong."

"You didn't see her, Nick. The way she looked at the pictures. It was like she got lost in them." I shook my head. "I probably shouldn't have brought them. I bombarded her with too many of us. We should've just continued talking about whatever she wanted." Nick let me pause for a bit while I ruminated. "She never married, you know. Never had kids." I turned to him. "And she referred to Mom as a princess. Maybe she was jealous of her," I reasoned. It was possible that it made her feel worse to see Mom's lovely progeny when she had none of her own.

"Jen, come on," assured Nick, while stroking my arm. "This was emotional for her too. Just seeing you had to bring back tough memories. Give her some time to get over the initial shock. She'll reach out to you again when she's ready."

"I hope so."

Why I cared so much was bizarre. Maybe having so little family on my side made the idea of gaining a new member that much more enticing. And I did feel something for her. Deep down, I hoped we would get the chance to one day reconnect.

* * *

Upon entering her condo, Dawn panted her way straight to the sound system and blasted a CD of Andrea Bocelli.

Crisis averted.

Plopping herself onto her sofa, she inhaled deeply and wiped her brow. As she let her breathing settle, she lifted her gaze toward the ceiling and sighed. "I kept my promise." Now, she hoped the tenor's soothing tones would calm her state of mind and allow the trepidation that had consumed her since agreeing to meet with Jennifer slowly melt away.

Dawn had been in angst since her call. The timing wasn't coincidental. Couldn't be. Not that soon after she had mailed the confession letter; her idiotic, knee-jerk reaction to Brandon Wong's supposedly thoughtful gesture. She should have declined his desperate invitation to New York. But the temptation to know what George had left her was too great. For days, she imagined his heartfelt apology. Only to be blindsided. What George had confessed hardly mattered anymore. But that he had pined over Connor all that time did. Her fury was instant. She couldn't get rid of the insulting proof fast enough, and should've just thrown them out. But she needed a target for her retribution, so she marched to the nearest store, purchased stamps and an envelope, then addressed it to the Boston police. *Let them see their failure,* she had said to herself when dropping it into a mailbox.

Rushing back to Boston, she had tried putting it all out of her mind, and might have succeeded, if not for an unexpected phone call from Jennifer, followed soon after by an unwelcome visit from two detectives. Never did Dawn consider that Brandon Wong would tell anyone about their exchange; certainly not the police. But he did, so she had to check for herself. That Jennifer was okay, and that she was still oblivious about her past.

The sight of her was reassuring. Surprisingly so. But only at first. Just as Dawn feared, it became impossible to avoid what she wished to unknow, to unsee. And she certainly couldn't trust her mental fortitude when she had the capacity to hurt Jennifer so profoundly. The minute the warning signs of a panic attack began to surface, she had no choice but to leave abruptly.

Dawn let her head fall back against the couch, her hand resting against her belly. Inevitably her mind wandered back to that ill-fated conversation of so long ago. A confrontation with her mother that had gone completely wrong. A disruption of her own doing because she had become emboldened enough to speak her mind. Which would never have occurred had she been more like Connor; able to escape, to rebuild her life. But Dawn was trapped. Always had been. In the lies of her aging, manipulative mother, who had the audacity of becoming incapacitated. In return for offloading her frustrations, she would end up saddled with an even heavier burden.

She reached into the handbag on her lap to pull out the photo she had just been given and stared at the smiling faces, the happy family, her beautiful, grown niece. It seemed like a miracle that hers was a life spared.

Focusing on Jennifer's features, Dawn imagined how her sister might have looked had she survived. Would she have been as happy? She recalled, with shame, how long she had envied Heather's beauty and thin figure. Then she remembered the rage; Dawn's desperate desire to scream for help, to make him stop. But she was silenced. Every time. Lest she endure the same fate, or worse, be responsible for Heather's more violent beatings. The memory of her sister pleading from behind closed doors still sent chills down her spine. The sight of her scrapes and bruises tortured Dawn with helplessness. And the image of their father sauntering into the hallway without a care repulsed her to this day. Never was there a hint of remorse on his face. Only an evil threat that he would kill Heather if Dawn dare say a word. Paralyzed with fear and disgust, Dawn had remained silent. Then, in the blink of an eye, a teenage Heather escaped to marry Connor. Surprised and relieved, Dawn could finally stop worrying about her and start instead to hope for her own fairy-tale ending. That her fantasy of George whisking her away to begin their lives together would come true. But the universe had a different plan for Dawn. One of neglect and solitude, consumed in self-pity, and pathetic envy of her dead, abused sister. Until Eleanor cured her jealously with a lethal injection of the truth. Words that seared her heart like a branding iron, permanently imprinting the gruesome secret she must carry to her grave.

It was 1994, and by then Eleanor had been in the nursing

home for several years. An inexplicable sense of duty had been the sole reason for Dawn's visits, but they were limited to her birthday, Mothers' Day and Christmas. She had been observing, with indifference, as her mother degenerated into a zombie-like frame with zero facial expression or ability to communicate. Eleanor's capacity for movement had been reduced to swallowing and sitting upright, while her sense of awareness appeared nil. Meanwhile, Dawn's life was otherwise solitary. She had found stable employment as a technical writer, enjoying silent comradery among introverts whose predilection for computers left little time nor need for human interaction. By night, she retreated to her condo, silencing her thoughts with loud music and eating her cares away. Artist after artist, snack after snack, she tried her best to quell the pain of her past. But each time she saw her mother, Dawn felt suffocated beneath the weight of that woman's transgressions. The urge to unload her anger grew slowly and steadily, until it finally reached its peak.

Her mind made up, she headed to the nursing home, fueled with determination. Eleanor sat tilted sideways in her wheelchair as Dawn entered her ward. She coaxed her into eating a few mouthfuls by spoon-feeding her some mush. *Enjoy your last meal, Mother,* she thought. *You might not be able to digest after I'm done with you.*

Eleanor's hair hung in a long tangled, grey mess. No makeup or jewelry to distract from the unflattering gown over her frail figure of pale skin and bones. *I should have brought you a mirror,* thought Dawn, who saw past that gaunt, expressionless regard to the core of a woman just as evil as her husband. The socialite who ignored the abuse and showcased her glamorous family across the pages of high society magazines. The hypocrite responsible for Heather's accident. The manipulator who convinced Dawn to lie to the police. Twenty-two years later, here she was, slipping into oblivion, absolved of her sins. And to Dawn, that was unacceptable. She could not let her mother die without knowing she was as much a criminal as the troll she had married.

Dawn wiped Eleanor's chin before wheeling her out of her room, down the elevator and into the garden. A paved walkway circled the building and wound its way through the carefully manicured grounds of vast shrubbery and perennial plants, interspersed with patches of colorful flowers. Several benches were dispersed along the path from which to admire this picturesque setting.

"I think we should look for an especially quiet spot today, Mother," said Dawn with spite, as she wheeled her over grass to cut toward the manmade pond at the far end of the property. Her determined pace caused Eleanor's head to bounce from her limp neck. She stopped at a bench facing the water. "Here. This looks nice and private." She had pivoted the wheelchair to face the side of the bench, then set the lever to lock it in place. Dawn sat at the edge and turned her neck toward Eleanor, resting her opposite arm along the backrest. After taking a moment to catch her breath, she then brought both hands together, rubbing her palms. With a maniacal grin, she said, "Let's have a chat, shall we? Oh and feel free to chime in whenever you like," she added with sarcasm.

Eleanor's eyes were glazed over as she stared blankly in the distance, her head bent slightly to the side. A skeletal blob of passive company upon whom Dawn was about to pounce.

After a few moments to build up her courage, she began, "I have a few things I'd like to get off my chest." Her tone was assertive, harsh. "First, let me state the obvious. You're a witch." There. She got it out. That alone felt liberating. "And might I add, a horrible mother." She looked at Eleanor and waited for the hint of a reaction. Receiving none, she continued. "So I'm just curious. How easy was it for you to pretend we weren't living with a monster? Did you sleep well after hearing Heather scream while she was being bashed around? Or did you think you fooled me, acting like you just realized it the day she was murdered? Oh pardon me, allegedly murdered, since we know that trial was interrupted. The trial that had nothing to do with what actually transpired. You haven't forgotten that I was there, right? That I saw what happened? It's amazing…Heather was killed and no one was ever punished. That's Delano magic at its finest," she proclaimed, arms out wide, palms facing upward.

Eleanor did not so much as blink. But it didn't matter. Dawn was just warming up.

"I bet you knew long before. Maybe from the very first time he started using Heather as a punching bag. And did you know he threatened me too? Yup. He said he would kill her if I said a word. Clever bastard." Dawn paused to take a breath before shouting, "Tell me, damn it! When? When did you know?!"

Still, Eleanor remained motionless.

"And what was with all that criticizing because I was fat?… No, don't answer that. I figured it out all on my own. Took me a while, but I got how it was just a distraction. To make you angry with me so I couldn't be angry with you. How much did it kill you that I was ugly like him? Well here's a newsflash for you, Mother. I'm glad I ruined your precious family image. I was the one flaw you couldn't hide." Dawn was red in the face, speaking rapidly, getting tangled in her own frustration. She rubbed both her palms rapidly against her thighs. "I tried you know. Sticking to a diet. God I tried. It didn't matter. I was graced with the world's worst metabolism, stuck in a home with the stunning Eleanor and Heather Delano."

Dawn could feel herself start to tremble. Her appearance had been a touchy topic her entire life. But that wasn't what she was here to talk about. Her vulnerability had no place in this purge. She needed to refocus.

Squeezing her thighs hard, she forced herself back on track. "Oh and why am I the one stuck with the secret? The one who has to live each day knowing the disgusting truth, the lies I was forced to tell. Do you have any idea how bad my night terrors are? I wake myself up screeching every night." She paused again, as if to catch her breath. "Look at me," she insisted. "Look at me, damn it!"

But Eleanor was still. A lifeless shell of a woman.

So Dawn stood up, held Eleanor's cheeks in her palms and leaned in to face her up close. "You should know. I tried to end it all. Yup. I tried to kill myself. Did you hear me, Mother?" Dawn raised her voice and spoke slowly as though Eleanor, who continued to stare sideways, was hard of hearing. "I tried to take my own life. Had written a note and everything. I wanted to let the whole world know how horrible you both were. What a joke the Delano name is. Share every little detail of what you both did." She let go of Eleanor's cheeks, leaving her head to fall back to the side. Dawn then dropped her gaze to the ground. "But I couldn't do it. Wasn't brave enough. And I hate myself for it." She looked back at Eleanor. "But I can't take it anymore. Waiting on your pathetic self to die, while all this mess eats away at me for who knows how long. So that's it," Dawn said, waving her arms outward. "I'm done. Checked-out. I'm not coming here anymore. You are officially out of my life."

In renouncing her mother, Dawn was ready to put the past behind her once and for all. She had said what she needed to. And though it hadn't been as eloquent as she would have liked, nor as cathartic as expected, it was time for her to let go and move on. Start fresh, Delano-misery free. She inhaled deeply, then leaned over to unlock the wheelchair breaks. But before she stood back up, she heard a sound. A barely audible voice.

"Why do you think I made her swim?" asked Eleanor in a faint, raspy whisper.

Dawn bolted upright in complete shock. Her mother was supposed to be despondent. Had been for years. She couldn't believe she could actually comprehend, let alone speak. Had Eleanor really fooled her all this time? She dropped back down onto the bench, her mouth agape with incredulity, her eyes wide.

Eleanor slowly straightened her neck and feigned a smirk; the first facial expression Dawn had seen from her in years. Slowly, she continued. "A swimsuit doesn't hide bruises."

Nor does it hide fat, thought Dawn, with resentment that

Eleanor's first statement in ages had hit a nerve. But Dawn remained silent, too dumbfounded to reply. Her mother was actually admitting he was violent.

Eleanor huffed in a croaky voice, "Your father couldn't handle anyone seeing the evidence." She took in a labored breath, then added, "And don't think the biggest burden rests with you...I spared you, my dear."

Wow, thought Dawn, who was quickly snapping out of shock. Tempted to react, she chose not to dignify her insolence with a response. Because while Eleanor may appear coherent, Dawn was reminded that her mother's mind was far from intact.

"Your father never laid a hand on you," croaked Eleanor.

At that, Dawn felt defensive, provoked. "And I'm supposed to be grateful?"

"You were fat because I needed you to be."

"My God! Seriously? My obesity?" Dawn threw her arms in the air with frustration. "You just can't leave it alone, can you? Well, guess what, Mother? You look like absolute shit, too. I should send a picture to the tabloids for a shocking *where is she now* piece."

Eleanor turned to look at Dawn, her voice still barely above a whisper. "He preferred them thin and delicate. Large and robust turned him off." Then, turning her gaze toward the pond. "Injecting calories into you is what kept you safe from him. If I had been able to get your sister to eat like you, she would've been fine."

Dawn ran both her hands through her head of curls and squeezed tightly in disbelief. "Oh my God! You're a real piece of work, lady. It didn't occur to you to, oh, I don't know, get us the hell out of there? No, of course not. Let's instead try inflating us outside his preferred proportions." Dawn was fuming. Even in her weakened state, Eleanor still had the ability to infuriate her. "So what then? It was Heather's fault for not eating?" She wanted to slap her, strangle her, throw her to the ground, kick her in the head then walk away. But she felt crippled with anger, and it was draining all the empowerment that had been coursing through her veins just moments ago.

At the mention of Heather, Eleanor dropped her gaze, her eyes swelled, her tone became morose. "I failed my youngest," she admitted. "I failed you both." She paused, then looked back up to Dawn. "There. Is that what you want? To hear me say it?... If that's not enough, then roll me into the pond. Let me drown. Go ahead. Do it if it makes you feel better."

Eleanor's tone now seemed more familiar. This was the manipulative style Dawn recognized. But playing the martyr wasn't going to work, because Dawn had no interest in taking her out of her misery. "Your death won't erase your crimes...or the loss. Also...unlike you, I'm not a murderer."

"So you would have preferred that I let him live?"

Shaking her head in frustration, Dawn questioned, "What? What are you saying? I'm talking about Heather." She had witnessed what happened. It was an image cemented in Dawn's mind.

"It was your father who was supposed to die that day." Eleanor's gaze turned once again to the pond as she remembered the moment. "But Heather wouldn't do as she was told. Neither of you ever did. She insisted she needed to confront him." Her voice sounded tormented, her eyes bloodshot. "Then…"

Dawn waved her off. "Sorry, Mother, but I'm not getting dragged into more of your lies." It was time to end this conversation with her confused, conniving mother. "Time to take you back to your room."

Just as Dawn was about to get up again, Eleanor turned to face her with a stern gaze. "That man was an animal. I loathed him."

At that, Dawn was taken aback. She was convinced Eleanor had actually cared for her husband on some inexplicable level. That she never stopped caring because she refused to ever speak ill of him. Until now.

Eleanor continued. "But he had power…and he always, always got his way." She paused, breathed deeply, her lips pursed. "After his first heart attack, I had hoped he was done. But he pulled through." She paused with a look of disappointment. "Then the doctors said to watch his blood pressure, his diet. As if I was going to help him. Absolutely not. I snuck salt into all his food, urged the cooking staff to prepare artery-clogging meals. All so his next heart attack would come soon…and be fatal."

Oh my God. Her solution to everything is food. She's a complete lunatic, thought Dawn shaking her head.

"When he was honored by the city, I wanted to vomit." Eleanor had rage in her voice. "He boasted of his great success, as he always did. Then insisted on a gala. One that I, of course, would have to organize. His way of reminding me that I owed him for all that he had given me." She paused and stared blankly as if the rest was too painful to express.

"And?" Dawn urged, curious to know if her mother was actually going to admit what she had done.

"I gave him his gala. Even made sure Heather would be there." She paused as a single tear ran down her cheek. "She hated that I asked her. I wanted to tell her why, but I couldn't risk it." She paused, trying to compose herself. "If only my plan had worked. It was so simple. Poison his drink then let him collapse. It would look like a heart attack for all to witness. Then we would be free. For that, I was more than prepared to spend my life in jail." She stared downward, distraught by how her plan had gone awry.

Dawn frowned. "Poison? Really?" Eleanor's flare for the melodramatic made her dubious of this new twist.

"Yes, poison." Eleanor looked back up ready to explain. "I held a glass of champagne in each hand. One was laced with cyanide. I was looking for your father so we could share a toast together. That's when Heather interrupted me…She saw the glasses and insisted she bring them to him. She had something she needed to say. I panicked. I was going to drop them, but she grabbed them so quickly"

Eleanor Delano drop champagne? As if, thought Dawn. But she listened attentively, curious to see if her mother would actually admit to what Dawn had seen happen with her very own eyes.

"I followed Heather into the foyer. Your father was standing at the top of the stairs, smug, like a dictator looking down upon his kingdom. Then she began to walk up the main staircase in her beautiful red gown, so I rushed toward the back stairs. You know, the one used by the staff –"

"No need to remind me of the dungeon's layout," asserted Dawn.

Eleanor ignored her tone. "I was hoping to reach the top before she did. Then, out from a closet came George, embarrassed, his hair all dishevelled, his bowtie undone."

The mere mention of George made Dawn flinch, the context of which only exacerbated her feelings of rejection.

"Rather than scold him, I urged him to run up knowing he could get there faster, and insisted he not let Heather take a sip. He rushed up immediately, arriving behind your father, who he hadn't expected to find standing there."

The scene she was describing aligned with Dawn's first memory. It was the moment she had walked into the foyer. She recalled seeing George up there with her parents and Heather, but only briefly; he had left before the fall. But it was Heather's presence that had stood out most. Dawn hadn't seen her since her wedding day and had no idea she would be in attendance. But a reunion there would never be.

"Once Heather reached the top, your father greeted her with open arms, celebrating her return. George thought quickly, taking both glasses from her so she could hug her father. That's when I arrived, walked straight to George, took them from him and motioned for him to leave. When Heather and your father reached for the champagne in my hands, I pulled the glasses to my chest and told them the maids had chosen the wrong bottle and that I would go get the better one. But your father was perfectly happy to toast his daughter with that one.

They each grabbed a glass. I signaled to Heather not to drink, unsure which one was laced. They each raised them before he took a sip. She didn't. I was so relieved she had understood. But then…" Eleanor paused as tears began to pour down her cheeks. "She looked at me with such sadness, such despair, such contempt. She slowly lifted her glass to her lips. I couldn't let her. I panicked and lunged to grab it from her. But your father berated my awkwardness. I wanted to break a glass and stab him with it. But before I could do anything, your sister…" Eleanor's voice was breaking from grief. "Your sister looked at me and said, *Please stop, Mother. It's over.* She grabbed his glass and gulped both down."

"Oh my God," cried Dawn. "You stupid, stupid woman! Why didn't you just spill them?!"

In agony, Eleanor replied, "I don't know. I froze. Then… then it was too late."

"Except I saw what happened next. So how do you explain that?" inquired Dawn with anger.

"I…I couldn't let it look like she had killed herself. So…I pushed your father onto her." It had sent Heather backwards over the banister. Tears flooded down Eleanor's cheeks. "She was going to die, Dawn. I needed it to look like he killed her."

"But, she…she didn't die!" Dawn screamed.

With barely any strength in her voice, she defended, "I know, I know…some…must have spilled…"

Dawn shook her head trying to process how the entire incident had been orchestrated by her mother. "She should be alive. She was only there because of *you*. She drank poison because of *you*. She fell because of *you*. My God, Mother. She was perfectly fine without us. Why couldn't you just let her be?"

"I...I was trying, Dawn. Trying to make up for all her suffering –"

"Oh my God! Do you even hear yourself?"

Eleanor was now sobbing. She tried to reply, but couldn't.

Dawn, meanwhile, wasn't satisfied. "You never did a damn thing while she lived in our torture chamber. So you waited a decade *after* Heather left, while she was perfectly happy, to finally decide to take action?"

Eleanor's face was flush with tears. "It took time for me to find the courage –"

"Courage? That's what you thought that was? You're truly demented."

"And...I thought," Eleanor hesitated, "that if I got him out of our lives, she would...let me be in Jennifer's."

Dawn was stunned. The real motive behind what she had witnessed all those years ago. Her mother's failed poisoning. Her sister's failed suicide. A fall that was completely avoidable. And her father's incarceration for the one crime he didn't actually commit. All because Eleanor was incapable of letting well enough alone. Pressing into her temples, she exclaimed, "It was entirely your fault. You were deliberate. No part of this was an accident. How dare you make me corroborate your damn story!"

Screeching in shock a few feet from where Heather had landed, Dawn remembered how Eleanor had shoved George away after he had rushed over to her, so she could pull her aside. Not to comfort or express any concern whatsoever. Not even to give her the courtesy of an explanation. No, it was to insist she stop crying so she could listen to her instructions. Upon police arrival, she must come forth to say she had witnessed her father intentionally push Heather over the banister. Too numb to object, Dawn had done as she was told.

"Yes, I did. Because if I was the one to go to prison, how on earth could I protect you?"

Time to take out the violins. "Protect me?" Dawn stood up, flabbergasted by such a statement. "That's what you were doing when you sent me to a mental institution? No offense, Mother, but a glass of poison-infused champagne would have been kinder."

"Or protect Jennifer," added Eleanor.

"Yes, because she was such a huge part of our lives," Dawn replied facetiously, while rolling her eyes. "What, pray tell, does she have anything to do with what happened?"

"Your father's heart attack in prison was not…unexpected."

"Oh, so we're back to him now?" At this point, Dawn had to remind herself her mother's mental state was questionable. She threw her arms in the air, tired of how Eleanor was deflecting.

"It was planned. It had to be. That man was actually going to be set free. I know, because George was keeping me informed of the legal team's progress. So I visited him in jail, but only when it was time to bring his blood pressure medication, which I replaced with placebos. We needed to be rid of him, Dawn."

"I see," replied Dawn with sarcasm.

There was no question her father deserved to die, but as far as Dawn was concerned, Eleanor was bringing him up to skirt the real issue; her sole responsibility for Heather's death. The only appropriate response from here would be a long, emphatic show of remorse. But it would be delusional to expect such humility from Eleanor Delano. So, out of spite, Dawn summoned her inner-Eleanor with the intent to fluster her mother as best she could.

"So…you killed Heather," she began. "And then you killed him. So I guess that means I was next?" Placing her index finger over her lips, she pretended to think. "Did you underestimate the amount of sedatives it would take to bring my fat ass down?"

Eleanor refrained from reacting. She just stared in the distance without flinching.

Redirecting her taunt in a more sensitive direction, Dawn asked, "And what's the deal with protecting Jennifer? Were you going to ruin her life like you did mine?…Did Connor realize it then run away before you could?"

Taking great offence, Eleanor fumed, "I would never hurt my grandchild."

"Oh. Of course not. Because you have such a loving relationship. What does she call you, anyway? Is it Grandmother? Granny? Oh right. She doesn't call you. Because she doesn't even know you exist!"

Without looking at Dawn, Eleanor exclaimed through pursed lips, "Stop."

"Why, Mother? Can't handle it? Maybe we should fatten you up so you can take the hits," laughed Dawn.

"I mean it, Dawn."

"Mean what exactly? Stop reminding you of your evil ways?

CHAPTER TWENTY-THREE

Or just the part about you being a complete stranger to Jennifer?"

Eleanor turned to look her in the eyes. "If your father got out, he would have killed me. Then no one could stop him from getting to Jennifer."

"Connor would never let him near her," stated Dawn.

"Connor was no match for your father."

"So what then, the monster would have used Jennifer as his new punching bag? As if he'd ever get away with that."

The best thing Heather and Connor had done for their daughter was to keep her away from the Delano's. But as evil as Anthony was, Dawn didn't believe it. This was just her mother's attempt at defending her actions.

"It's moot now. I did what needed to be done," said Eleanor, ready to end this conversation.

"It sounds like you're fine with how all this played out. How nice for you." Then, turning to her with scorn. "Seriously Mother,…who the hell do you think you are?"

It was the question that should not have been asked. The one that would push Eleanor too far. Gripping the armrests of her wheelchair so tightly her knuckles went white, she gave Dawn a piercing look. Then, from the rage buried deep within her soul, she declared, "I am the victim of repeated abuse at the hands of Anthony Delano."

Dawn's eye widened. That statement was totally unexpected.

Eleanor began to tremble. She had never told a soul. Never meant to. But there was more. She steadied her gaze on Dawn's eyes. "I am the mother of his most victimized prey, who, yes, I failed to protect." Tears began to flood from her bloodshot eyes, her nostrils dripping just as profusely. Decades of anguish were being released, but none more horrific than the secret she had carried with immeasurable guilt. "And I am the grandmother of his most despicable indiscretion."

Dawn gasped, both hands covering her mouth. Stunned. Horrified. Trying not to gag. Uncertain she heard correctly. Desperately hoping she hadn't. When she could finally bring herself to speak, all that she could utter was, "You mean? No… no. It can't be. No!" She could barely breathe.

Eleanor's tears were flowing, her chin quivering, she whispered, "He did not merely hit your sister."

"Oh my god, no. No! I can't." Dawn bolted upright, pressing her fingers against her temples trying to keep her head from exploding. She bent over ready to purge the contents of her gut. Her face flush, her body feeling faint.

Eleanor observed as Dawn was forced to process what should have been kept secret. Regret consumed her for not having held it in. "He didn't know…that he got her pregnant," she continued, wiping her face with her fingers. "She told me in secret and begged for an abortion. I toiled over it. But if I had agreed, she would be ruined, and he would just persist. Marriage was her only escape. Freedom from his grip. And Connor was such a good boy. He would never hurt her. He could be a good father."

"Connor knew?" Dawn looked up in disbelief. Had he really agreed to marry a pregnant victim of incest? Was it possible for him, or anyone, to love someone that much? Or had Eleanor coerced him?

"He knew he wasn't the father. But he never knew Anthony

was. Heather told him she had been raped by his business associate. I was the only one who knew the truth. I promised to keep her secret. And I vowed that if she got married, we would stay away from Jennifer forever. I just wanted her to be safe, Dawn. And for her baby to know no harm."

To remember that conversation now was no less mortifying for Dawn than it had been in real time. For years, she couldn't rid it from her mind. How Eleanor had used George as an unsuspecting co-conspirator to gather blackmail material so she could threaten Anthony with exposing his financial fraud if he went anywhere near Heather or Jennifer. How Anthony, in turn, had threatened to destroy her reputation if she ever intimated to anyone that he was violent. How he had resumed beating Eleanor after Heather left, but that it was okay because she was so good at covering up the evidence under layers of makeup. The more Eleanor revealed, the more Dawn learned that everything had been so much worse than she ever realized. That her mother was not pure evil, but just a victim in disguise, hiding the scars of her very own abuse.

In the weeks that had followed their surreal confrontation, Dawn had struggled to reconcile their decades of tension, resentment and disfunction. Even with what she knew, forgiveness remained untenable. But Dawn had come to a new decision. She would not abandon her mother. Through pity and music, she had found a tolerable compromise. Equipped with a portable CD player, she paid an unexpected visit to Eleanor's ward. Foregoing all greetings, she stated the rules of engagement: no talking, no tears, no anger. Just music. So they sat, they listened, then she left. After a successful test run, there was another visit, and a fresh set of artists to explore. Before long, it had become a weekly ritual; moments of peaceful companionship, of musical discovery, of silent commiseration between the sworn keepers of the ugly truth. Not a word was ever spoken between them. Except for once. *I love this one,* Eleanor had whispered as they listened to Andrea Bocelli. Those would be the last words Dawn would ever hear her mother speak.

Dawn looked back down at the photo, and this time thought of her mother. She wondered whether there was ever a time when she envisioned her own family could be happy. Or was that notion simply out of reach for the woman betrothed to the heir of the Delano empire twice her age? Dawn had no idea that her mother's suitor had been imposed by her over-bearing father, because the man she actually loved had been disqualified due to his inferior wealth. Nor did Dawn know that the intended groom had been her kind-hearted uncle, Michael, until an unscrupulous and opportunistic, Anthony, used slander to steel both his fiancé and his place within the family's business enterprise. For all the appearances to the contrary, no part of Eleanor's life had ever been unclouded, untarnished, unburdened.

But there was now a silver lining. After all these years of trying to repress the knowledge of Jennifer's very existence, of feeling repulsed by the stain she bore, today, Dawn had seen with her own eyes, that she was completely undamaged. Pleasant, joyful even. Happily married. A caring mother to three beautiful daughters. Spared all the Delano darkness, she shone like a bright star.

"I hate that it happened. And I'll never agree with how you handled it, so don't you dare take this as forgiveness," Dawn said out loud to her mother's spirit. "But your gamble worked. Jennifer knew no harm. Connor was a good father."

CHAPTER TWENTY-FOUR

— 1972 —

The execution of George's plan was a complete success. Except for one not-so-minor detail; he was still alive and moments away from confronting the consequence of that unfortunate reality. But for now, while his brain was still in a dense fog, he lost himself in the outcome that should have been. Hallucinating Satan's evil voice, George imagined his would-be fate. *Jorge Vasquez, please buckle up for your descent into the burning fires of hell.*

"George!" screeched Eleanor with a sharp smack of his cheek. "Wake up!"

The interruption to his state of torpor was met with excruciating pounding in his head. A pain augmented only by an onslaught of persistent face slaps. He tried to open his mouth to plead for a pause, but couldn't dislodge his tongue from what felt like shower tile mold. If only he could raise his arm to shield his face, but his limbs wouldn't respond; they felt paralyzed. Had his soul already separated from its mortal host? Was the light he could sense through closed eyelids emanating from the flames of inferno? He forced himself to open them a thin slit only to recognize a blurred image of Eleanor. But she was the wrong Delano for this place of eternal doom, so it must be a form of torture. Trying to ignore the screaming and slapping, he bemoaned how death felt so awake.

Eleanor was relentless. For weeks, she had been trying to jolt him out of his slumber, unable to accept that he had dared to take his life. She breathed a deep sigh of relief when, finally, George showed a sign of responsiveness. And though it was minimal, it meant he would survive, that her prayers had been answered.

It had taken several journeys in and out of consciousness before George became coherent enough to understand that he had not died. Struck with that disappointing realization, he yearned for Eleanor to just shut up and slip him another bottle of pills so he could do it right this time. Being even slightly awake was torture. He felt nauseous, agitated and gross all over. The more aware he became, the more Eleanor sounded like a party horn in the hands of a festive six-year-old.

He couldn't bring himself to look at her. And he refused to speak. Had she been screaming at him for ten minutes or ten hours? However long, it felt interminable. He drifted in and out of sleep, unable to stay awake. As for his memory, it flashed back in bits and pieces; thoughts that were either too vague or too disjointed, but mostly shocking.

Eventually he remembered writing. And when that thought became clear, he panicked. *Shit. The note. Is it real or is my mind playing tricks on me?* There was no way for him to verify if, in fact, there was a confession letter in his sock drawer. But if it was found, his next bed would surely be in a jail cell.

Time continued to slip by. Whatever day this was, wherever exactly this place was, and however long he had been there, he did eventually become fully alert. Enough to appreciate a moment of silence. Eleanor was away. He was alone with his returning memory; images that seemed so surreal, he wasn't certain whether to applaud or to chastise himself. He had terminated Anthony Delano. Maybe even gotten away with it. Only to be denied the reward of eternal rest.

"Oh good, your eyes are open," Eleanor said upon barging into his room. "Have you found your voice yet?"

George turned his head toward the opposite wall as she approached his bedside.

She grabbed the stubbly chin of his gaunt face firmly. "Don't you dare look away. Not today, George." She then released him and took in a deep breath before sitting in the chair next to him.

Preferring to avert another rant, he decided to finally speak; his first utterance since regaining consciousness. His voice croaked deeply. "Where am I?"

The sound surprised her into a half-smile. "I thought you might recognize the simple decor," she replied with sarcasm, choosing to keep her celebration of his first words to herself. "Perhaps it's missing a record-player."

She's got me in the mental institution. He glanced at the now familiar beige wall color. But George was too shocked, too angry, too depleted to reply.

"Oh don't worry. It's temporary," she said with a wave of her hand. Then, adjusting his sheets. "It was just easier than sending you to a rehab center. There are only so many places I can be at once. And no one knows you're here. Not even Dawn. If that's what you're wondering."

Dawn. How must she be feeling? He tried clearing his throat. "Is she okay?"

Eleanor poured him a glass of water from the pitcher on the bedside table, held it to his mouth then bent the straw between his lips. "Not exactly. She's furious with you, as I'm sure you can imagine. But she's home now. Earlier than she should be. But I had to let her see her sister."

The water helped to bring his mouth back to life. His voice sounded a little closer to normal. "How long have I been here?"

"Over three weeks…You had me scared sick. What were you thinking, George?" She shook her head. "Never mind. Clearly you weren't thinking at all."

George couldn't believe it had been that long. Equally shocking was Eleanor's concern. "So…Mr. Delano?"

"His service was small. Very private." That was all she had to say about him. She then looked George in the eyes with sadness. "Heather's gone."

Devastation overcame him. He squeezed his eyes shut. "Oh, Mrs. Delano. I…I'm so sorry."

She let that reality hang in the air for a while before throwing a dagger. "And because you went and overdosed, I had to rely on a private detective to find a discreet way of getting news to Connor."

Another failure. George should've been the one to inform him. He couldn't begin to imagine Connor's reaction. "Did… he make it back in time?"

"Of course, George. We weren't going to hold her funeral without her husband and daughter present," she replied, flippantly.

"When…was it?"

Her tone was serious and robotic. "I buried my child three days ago. While watching my other daughter practically drown in her tears. But perhaps the most agonizing part was seeing my grandchild. She had no clue who I was." Eleanor's eyes glimmered slightly as she fidgeted with his bedsheets. She cleared her throat, then changed the subject. "But let's focus on getting you out of here so we can get to work on more pleasant projects, shall we?"

She had just buried her daughter, George was barely awake, and already she was thinking about new projects. Whether it was her way of coping, or her attempt at energizing him, George was too lethargic, depressed. He needed more time to resent the fact that he was alive. And before that, a moment to think about Connor. Poor Connor. How must he feel that George didn't even bother to attend his wife's funeral? Had he already planned his next escape? No doubt a permanent one this time. And what about Dawn? She must hate him. Never could he look either of them in the eyes again. He was an even bigger disappointment to them now than he was before his heroics. Defeated, he uttered, "You should've let me die."

"Excuse me?" Eleanor peered. "After saving your life? After telling you my child has died? This?…This is what you have to say to me?" She was not having it.

He stared at her blankly, but couldn't say a word. He had none. His heart may be beating, but George was dead on the inside. And by the way she was looking at him, it seemed as though she could tell. So what would she do now? Provoke him into giving a shit? Threaten or coerce him? And did it even matter? There was nothing he cared about anymore.

"I saved your life, George. The least you can do is give me the courtesy of a response."

"Why did you do it, Mrs. Delano?" he sighed. "How did you even know?"

"Oh please. You think I wasn't on to you?" she frowned in disbelief. "Out of nowhere you come waltzing into the lounge with your big ideas about seeing Anthony and going to Connor. Then two days later, you're telling me you caused his heart attack and your visit with Connor went perfectly fine. Did you think I couldn't put two and two together?"

She was good. In a league of her own. He was certain he had left no clues. But clearly George was no match for her powers. Disappointed in himself, he had to ask, "It was that obvious?"

"Of course it was. You had to know I would see right through that fake self-confidence. You had a death wish and did a poor job of covering it up."

So she knew he intended to end his own life, but had she figured out the rest, he wondered. "Was it you who found me?"

"I sent my driver. It would've been inappropriate for me to leave on the evening of my husband's passing. I told him you were distraught. That you felt culpable and might do something stupid. He found you dangling off your bed with foam at the mouth. By the time he rushed you here, you were already in a coma. Thankfully the doctors were able to save you." She seemed genuinely relieved George was alive.

"I don't know what to say." It wasn't meant as gratitude. All he could think was that if she hadn't sent her driver, this would be over, he would be dead. He should never have gone to her office that night. It was one step too many in his otherwise well-executed scheme. Assuming she wasn't on to the rest of it.

"What's it going to take, George? If you think I'm giving up on you, you're grossly mistaken."

"I want to rest." He turned his head away and closed his eyes. "Please."

"Fine. But I'll be back. We have to discuss an important matter I need your help with. So you need to get better."

It seemed laughable that she would be seeking the help of someone so destitute. But that was Eleanor. The unbreakable. The delusional. And whatever it was she was plotting, George would be ready for one thing only; to turn her down.

The topic had been avoided over her next few visits, either because George was too listless or, he hoped, she had had a change of heart. But as his energy returned, he became motivated to shut her down in the event she might still wish to share her important matter. As soon as he felt strong enough, he would let her know. And today was the day. He even had the nurses raise his bed so he could sit upright; a more assertive posture to better convey his intent.

Upon her arrival, George declared, "Mrs. Delano, whatever it was that you wanted to discuss with me, I just need you to know, I can't be involved. I'm done with life in Boston."

"It's nice to see you getting your strength back, George. How wonderful."

"Please don't change the subject. I mean it. I'm done with this place. It holds nothing but horrible memories for me." If she was hoping that her lifesaving care had somehow compensated for past drama, he needed to clear that up.

"So you need a fresh start. That's fine. Where, George? Where would you like to go?"

Leave it to Eleanor to be unpredictably amenable. He was ready for an objection; at minimum, some confrontation. But by playing along, she threw him a curve-ball he wasn't prepared to catch. Clearly he was unfit to make such a consequential life decision. But he had initiated the idea, so now he was forced to consider some options. Where in this world could George feel at home? His mind went to Southern California where had lived as a child. A familiar place. One that had actually been home once. But he was too different a person now, a criminal who had escaped both death and prosecution. Familiar would feel wrong, backwards. The appeal of somewhere completely new was bigger. A place where he would be a total stranger; free from anyone's expectations and judgement; in hiding where no one was looking. A place that held intrigue; enough of it to possibly awaken his desire to live. "New York," he blurted. "I want to move to New York."

"Oh. Just four hours away. That will do just nicely."

"Do nicely for what?" Her answer might warrant choosing a more remote option. Like Australia.

"There are certain portions of my affairs that I would like

you to handle for me. As my lawyer. I'll pay you handsomely. Including a retainer fee, of course. That should be more than enough to cover your rent and any other expenses. You'll see. You'll be back on your feet in no time."

"I'm not going near anything sketchy. Not even if it smells it."

"George, please. I'm not Anthony, for heaven's sake. This is just something personal that I need taken care of separately from my other affairs. By someone who can appreciate the sensitivity of the matter."

This is where she lost him. George shook his head and raised his palms to face her. "I'm done with sensitive matters. I don't even want to know what it is."

"Yes you do."

"No, I don't."

"It concerns Connor and Jennifer."

"Then I most definitely don't want to be a part of it."

"George, let me make this clear. I'm not asking. You will help me."

"Mrs. Delano, let *me* make this clear. I'm not helping. Period."

"Don't push me, George. I will get my way."

"What are you gonna do? My life is worthless. There's nothing you can take from me."

"Perhaps not. But this is about Connor and Jennifer, remember?"

"So what? You're gonna take something from them?"

"Of course, not. I want to help them."

"Really? Like you helped Dawn when you forced her into this psych ward against her will? I'm not sure you understand the notion of helping."

Eleanor pursed her lips. He had hit a nerve. Which meant he was definitely on the mend. And that was a good sign. "I don't expect you to understand my ways, George. One day, you might –"

"Your ways?" Eleanor Delano's ways were manipulative. And George was done getting sucked in, which he needed to make perfectly clear. "Look, whatever sick pleasure you derive out of controlling – I mean helping – people, knock yourself out. Do whatever the hell you want. Just leave me out of it. I'm done giving a shit about anything." He turned his head away. He had rid the world of Anthony Delano, but it would have to be for someone else to deal with her. He was bowing out.

Silence swept over them as George's words hung in the air.

Eleanor gave him a moment to settle before she eventually spoke again. "Perhaps this might change your mind." She inhaled before sharing what she knew would get his attention. "Connor didn't exercise his power of attorney when it was time for Heather to accept her inheritance."

George turned back to look at her with concern.

She stared in his eyes for the next part. "He said his lawyer was taking care of that for him. So he recused himself from all direct involvement. He doesn't know it, but because of his inaction, the estate has been split between Dawn and me."

George dropped his head forward. "Shit."

"Yes dear. Your drug-induced coma cost him one million dollars. Give or take."

George closed his eyes tightly and cringed. What had he

done? Making Connor sign that reassignment agreement was stupid. A decoy that completely backfired. George was supposed to die quickly so that Connor would know to sign for the inheritance himself. It was only in the event that George would lose his nerve and stay alive, that he would need the alibi. And a purpose; handling matters on Connor's behalf would never raise any questions. Instead, George hung in limbo for weeks, while Connor assumed the paperwork was being addressed. One million dollars had just become the price tag for his unexecuted legal services.

"There's a way to get the money to him."

George looked at her, hopeful, desperate. "How? Tell me. This is my fault. I need to fix it." Of all the mistakes he had made in the past, if this was one he could reverse, he was prepared to make it right.

"I'll need your help transferring money from me to him. The challenge is doing it without Connor objecting. And to make it look perfectly legitimate without requiring any intervention on his part."

Eleanor appeared sincere, despite how suspiciously noble this sounded coming from her. Though George really wanted to believe this could be done, he worried that he wasn't up to the task. "I'm a mess, Mrs. Delano. What if I screw up?"

"I won't let you. I just need you to promise you will not hurt yourself, George. Only you can help me with this."

"But you know far better lawyers than me."

"And they're all consumed with their own self-interests. Not a dime of that money will fill their pockets. This is a matter for you and me. No one else is ever to know Connor and Jennifer have access to these funds."

George paused to absorb her intent. Try as he may, he couldn't help but feel suspicious; a difficult habit to shake when in her presence. "Why is this so important to you?" he finally asked. "I mean, why help them completely behind the scenes? It's not like you're the one who screwed up. You could just blame me and cut them a check."

"Why?" she fixed his eyes. "Because I love my granddaughter and this is the only contribution I will ever get to make to her life. But you know very well that Connor will never accept anything directly from me. It has to look like it's from the estate." She paused before pleading, "Will you help me?"

She was right. Connor would refuse anything from Eleanor and likely question why he would even have to when George was supposedly managing the inheritance on his behalf. "Okay, Mrs. Delano. I get it," he replied. "But you don't ever want Jennifer to know? Even when she's grown?" It seemed more selfless than George imagined she was capable of being.

"What I'd like is to write her a letter, to tell her she mattered to me. Something you can arrange for her to receive. But only after I die. She must never feel any obligation toward me."

Wow, thought George. The expression of her grandmotherly love relegated to a piece of paper shared post-mortem. That was the hefty price of being married to Anthony Delano.

He considered how much had transpired since she and George had first met; all of it bound by a need to keep that man away from Heather, Dawn, then Jennifer. And though Delano was now gone, life wasn't going to necessarily be simple. The spoils of his irreparable damage would always need tending. And it was becoming apparent that it would fall upon the two of them to take on that responsibility.

George's dismal condition aside, he withheld objection in favor of hope that there existed a viable solution to reconcile the wealth he had just cost his very best friend. So while it was far from the outcome he anticipated this day would bring, he confirmed his intentions. "It looks like I need to get healthy." *Healthy enough to make this work, and healthy enough to remain vigilant*, he thought, knowing he would need to watch for any sign of a hidden agenda.

Eleanor grinned with gratitude, then reached into her purse. "I have something that might help…to motivate you." She pulled out an envelope, then handed it to him.

"What is it?" George was skeptical.

"Just open it."

He removed its content; a photo of him and Connor standing outside El Dorado Savings Bank, captured the moment Connor was handing him back the reassignment agreement. Their very last encounter, sealed in time, by the not-so-private photographic skills of the spy she had hired to tail them. The man who, in George's absence, was responsible for making sure Connor and Jennifer came home in time for Heather's funeral. How ironic that the envelope they were exchanging in the picture was responsible for the forthcoming mission to recoup Connor's lost inheritance.

"Thank you, Mrs. Delano." As invasive as it was that she

had Connor and Jennifer followed, at this particular moment, George felt grateful to be holding such a treasure.

It would be another two months before the doctors would clear George for release, though he suspected that the final decision ultimately rested with Eleanor. He had remained in the care of the institution for the duration, more comfortable to rely on their full discretion than risk discovery should they chance moving him elsewhere. It had been a mutual decision that left George rather indifferent; one ward or another was all the same. Besides, he was far more focused on getting out. To that end, he did his best to adhere to medical guidelines, working his way to becoming fully weaned and physically fit. Throughout it all, Eleanor visited daily to check on his progress, gathering newspaper clippings of New York rental apartments for his perusal and inspiration. To her credit, she was arranging necessary furnishings and movers, so that all was lined up for when George was ready. As for Connor and Dawn, she assured him they knew nothing about where he was, only that he had expressed a desire to live in New York.

On the money management front, George was limited in what he could do from the confines of his ward. The material was far too sensitive for the prying eyes of even the most well-meaning staff. It was therefore Eleanor who held onto all documents, which they reviewed during her visits; their business conducted on opposite sides of the small table beside his bed.

His first recommendation had been for her to revert back to her maiden name for this particular documentation. Her mild trepidation around the outward message this might send was easily appeased when he assured her this would only be on paper; she could use whichever she preferred in public.

"If you insist that's best." she resigned. "It's Angelini." A name she hadn't used in over thirty years.

George held back the impulse to laugh. All this time he felt he was in the presence of a demon, only to learn that she had been an angel by birth. The irony to someone who had tried his best to be banished to hell could not be more amusing. "Okay then, Angelini it is."

She must have sensed his reaction. "I suppose that makes me their guardian angel?" she mused.

Though he found the levity refreshing, she was far from reaching that status. "Pretty sure you need to earn your wings first."

As for the inheritance itself, he had proposed setting up a trust from which she could disperse funds to Connor. He drafted a legal notice by hand that he would type-up once in New York. In it, Connor would be advised of a monthly pension to be used strictly for the purpose of Jennifer's care, which extended to housing, schooling, food, clothing, etcetera. Basically every expense possible except for Connor's personal effects. To keep it simple, the account to which it would be deposited would be the same one he had shared with Heather. Eleanor initially pushed back, concerned this approach was too restrictive. But George knew Connor well. He would respect this level of formality and the fact that it was directed specifically to Jennifer's needs. Not to mention that a monthly disbursement would better align with his lifestyle than would a massive lump sum. Connor's sole responsibility would be to advise George in writing of any address change or important status update concerning Jennifer. A New York box office would be set-up to handle that specific correspondence. In return for sharing these updates with Eleanor, George made her promise to never have them followed.

One final account would be set-up specifically for Jennifer, with Eleanor as power of attorney. It was not to be touched while Eleanor was alive.

"We should give it a different name. Any suggestions?" asked George.

"Chastity," replied Eleanor. "That was Heather's favorite. It's Jennifer's middle name."

"Chastity it is."

Finally deemed stable for release, George was at last escaping the drab walls that housed his recovery. He had emphatically refused Eleanor's offer to have his apartment cleaned ahead of his arrival, insisting he was uncomfortable with anyone interfering with his things. Which was especially true in the case of his sock drawer. She didn't press him other than to have cardboard boxes delivered for packing. Whether she was pleased or upset he was leaving for New York, George couldn't tell. A bit of both he suspected. Leaving meant he was better; that he could move forward with finalizing the trust logistics. But whether she was happy to be regaining the extra hours per day, he couldn't gauge. Perhaps she would feel a void.

Upon entering his flat, he was greeted by a wall of empty

boxes, stacked one on top of the other, six feet high, blocking passage beyond his entryway. But the barricade did nothing to quell the nauseating odor of stale vomit that hung in the air. It triggered a gag reflex so fierce, he lunged through the boxes, casting them carelessly aside, then darted toward the nearest window. He lifted the panel with urgency and inhaled the cool October breeze as though just emerging from underwater. He took in a few long breaths then rushed into his bedroom to open that window next.

The site of his bed caused him to gag again. The sheets were in disarray, one draped over the edge well onto the floor. A stain from where he had vomited was encrusted with dried white chunks of undigested food that appeared to be coming back to life. He held his breath and bunched the four extremities toward the middle, then rolled everything tightly before running to pull a garbage bag from beneath the kitchen sink. He let the fumes subside as he caught his breath before heading back into his room for sock drawer inspection. He opened it slowly, praying it was undisturbed. He dug his hand below a few pairs. There was the letter, face down at the bottom, exactly where he had left it. He pulled it out, ready to rip it to shreds, but then stopped.

"I shouldn't leave any traces," he cautioned himself. "I'll burn it." He placed it on top of his dresser for later disposal.

His packing had taken three days, on and off. In addition to the confession letter, he discovered the envelope containing the material photocopied from the war room at Delano Manor. Portions of the many documents he had accumulated during the course of the defense team's strategizing; they, too, needed to be disposed of. He placed that envelope with the confession letter. "My burn pile," he declared.

On day three, the moving van had come and was now on route to Manhattan. All that remained were the boxes packed into George's green Ford Pinto containing his most personal effects. As he turned on the ignition, he took one last glance at his apartment building, wondering if his departure from Boston would bring sadness. "Nope," he said to himself. But before he bid good riddance to the city of his shame, an important pilgrimage to the burial site of the evidence was in order. His dirt road seemed best for the incineration of the letter and the Delano file; their ashes could join those already there.

By the fourth street corner George turned onto, he noticed the black Cadillac in his rear-view mirror. "Damn it," he shouted. "How could I be so stupid? Of course Eleanor would send an escort." He made an abrupt turn to begrudgingly get back on course for New York. His damning material would have to be burned at destination.

It took just shy of four months for all matters relating to the fund to be finalized. In addition to using it for Connor's inheritance, Eleanor was so enamored with this financial mechanism that she augmented the trust to include a monthly allowance for Dawn as well as payments to George. Everything was signed sealed and delivered, with formal confirmation received from Connor to the post office box.

"Finally, I did something right," George said to himself with great relief.

But a celebratory George, in the Big Apple, with a cushy bank account, presented a new kind of challenge. Surrounded by constant temptation, he would struggle to remain substance-free, succumbing repeatedly to its numbing euphoria over the better part of the next decade. And each time he fell off the wagon, in swooped a black Cadillac DeVille to drag him back into rehab. While he was there, Eleanor would call daily, without fail; at times mocking him by saying he did it only because he missed her doting. Then he would promise to get better, that he would stop for good this time. Eventually, he would recover. Be fine for a stretch. Only to fall right back down. By the fourth incident, he pleaded with her to cut him off; he couldn't pay for drugs if he had no money. But she refused. *No George. You're better than that. If you have too much money, give it to charity.* In her tough-love approach, she pushed him to find his strength, his path. And she had no qualms reminding him as many times as necessary.

The pattern repeated itself until, at her urging, he finally joined a support group. There, seated in a circle among recovering addicts, he would meet Brandon Wong, the person with whom he would share the rest of his life. Brandon adored him as George adored Connor, and understood George as no one else did. Together, they commiserated, recovered, dreamed. Both would reach sobriety, regain control of their lives, become active members of society. But throughout their twenty plus years together, there remained a small part of George that Brandon could never access. Within the condo George kept to maintain the appearance of a single straight man, was a drawer containing his deepest secrets. His sanctuary. That sliver of what might have been.

Why it was that George never disposed of the confession letter or the envelope became unclear even to George himself. At first, the excuse was legitimate. Where could he light a fire without raising suspicion or setting off an alarm? Then came the obvious distractions; a new city, an important trust to put together, a sense of freedom. Eventually it was just procrastination; he would get to it later. Only to return from the next stay in rehab in a state of panic, convinced it was discovered, and that he would be heading to jail. The source of relief that came with finding it safely tucked away in his nightstand felt like a reward or warm welcome. Just like the photo of him and Connor, its very existence felt comforting. A badge of honor for his mighty heroics. A testament to the lengths he had gone for those he loved, for what he had overcome. A symbol of his greatest act of bravery and extreme vulnerability, in one single page. He never opened the envelope to reread it. He could barely recall what he had written. But knowing it was there was like holding onto an important piece of himself. A piece he wasn't yet ready to let go of.

* * *

By 1990, Vasquez & Associates was prospering. Before long, George would be recognized as a prominent defense attorney. But it was his status as philanthropist that made him most proud. As his success grew, so too did his donations and the fulfillment he derived from making a difference, from being the one helping others instead of the one in need. He had come full circle, made something meaningful of his life. Surviving had finally proven itself to be valuable. What would Connor think if he could see him now? Did George ever cross his mind? The temptation to reach out to him was constant, but George resisted, knowing he had lost that privilege long ago.

George could not be more excited when informing Eleanor of Jennifer's wedding announcement. Over the past few years, they had spoken only occasionally; George no longer needing her pep talks, and she having no new affairs for him to take care of. So it was a special treat to be sharing her granddaughter's big milestone. But their joy was quickly soured by news of Eleanor's failing health. With a heavy heart, George processed her diagnosis; she had been diagnosed with a neurodegenerative disease. He rushed to her side the very next day.

After years of only speaking over the telephone, he had never envisioned her looking any different. In his mind, she was still the strong, forceful, put-together woman he had always known. But the sight of her was alarming; the decades had not been kind. Overcome, he pulled her close; a very first hug, an overdue demonstration of affection.

"Look at you, George. So handsome and successful." She placed her hands on the lapels of his dark blue suit jacket and examined him from top to bottom as though admiring her little boy, now all grown up.

Meanwhile, to George, her frame felt so thin, almost brittle. And her hair was short and too casually coiffed. Several shades lighter than its former auburn hue, it didn't conceal the gray roots along her hairline. She wore much less makeup than he remembered and its application appeared to be the work of an unsteady hand. It saddened him to view the once glamorous and powerful Eleanor as a weakened elderly woman.

"Thanks to you, Eleanor," he replied with a smile. Addressing her by her first name was a result of the familiarity that had developed between them.

To be sitting once again in the lounge at Delano Manor felt surreal. As was the pot of tea they shared instead of a stiff drink. It was his first return to Boston since he had left almost two decades prior. Like her, the manor looked dated, neglected.

Only her voice seemed unchanged. Perhaps because a slur or stutter seemed natural in that room. "I'm going to donate the manor. Dawn doesn't want it. I'll also need to update my will. Can I count on you to take care of this for me, George?" she asked.

"Of course, Eleanor. Whatever you need."

She went on to insist that she be placed in a nursing home so that Dawn need not be inconvenienced by her care.

"You can afford all the help you need," he urged. "Why not stay here for as long as you can?"

"It's what I want, George. My penance isn't over yet."

"That's absurd. You've paid your dues. Look at me. I am who I am because of you." *And even despite you*, he thought.

As pleased as she was to have done right by him, it still didn't make up for her other failings. "That doesn't change how terrible a mother I was to Dawn. She deserves to be spared having to care for me while I wither away."

"Dawn wouldn't just abandon you."

"Yes she would," Eleanor replied firmly. Then, more calmly. "And I don't blame her."

"How about I talk to her?" George suggested.

"Don't you dare," she peered at him sternly. "You think seeing you after all this time will make things better for her?" She did have a point. "George, I know you mean well, but I need to suffer for my sins while I'm still on this earth. This is my choice."

"You're asking me to abandon you. I can't do that."

"You're not abandoning me. You're respecting my wishes."

"I remember wishing to be abandoned, Eleanor."

"Yes, but you were too young and too broken to think straight. Look at you now, George. You're helping countless lives because you got better. I'm just an old woman with money, whose body is degenerating, and whose soul needs healing. I'm ready for purgatory. I need it, George. I want to earn my place in paradise beside my baby girl."

The discussion went on for a long while, to no avail. Eleanor was decided, unwavering. There was no acceptable argument against her beliefs, and he wasn't willing to overturn her decision by declaring her unfit. Her mind was intact, that much was undeniable. So he would acquiesce and search for a proper nursing home. Before he left that day, they discussed her will, the handling of the trust and then she handed him a letter for Jennifer.

"Keep this safe, George. And promise me you'll wait until

after I'm gone before giving it to her," she reminded him.

"That won't be for a while, Eleanor. But yes. I promise," he replied with a smile of reassurance.

"Thank you, George. I'm counting on you."

That would be one of their very last conversations. Shortly thereafter, she would be transferred to the nursing home, and almost immediately lose her ability to speak and become lethargic, unresponsive. It was as though a switch had been flipped, or the shock of such a lowly environment had destroyed her. But despite the initial speed of her decline, she had held on much longer than doctors anticipated. Eight years, in fact. Which was fortunate, because halfway through, Dawn went from rare visitor to weekly guest. A relief to George, who kept tabs on Eleanor's status through regular contact with staff. Whatever it was that had prompted Dawn's desire to spend time with her mother, he hoped Eleanor was lucid enough to appreciate her company.

When finally learning of Eleanor's death in 1998, George actually shed a tear. It seemed both odd and yet not that he should feel such a sense of loss for a woman he had once abhorred. But she had changed. Become his stalwart supporter since his very first overdose in 1972. The person who refused to ever give up on him, to whom he owed his fate, and with whom he had developed a bond of trust. Days later, at her funeral, he whispered a surprising and heartfelt, "I think you earned your wings."

The settlement of her estate had been quick since the details had been put in order well in advance. Once the four-million dollar Chastity account was closed, all that remained was to deliver Eleanor's letter to Jennifer accompanied by a very generous bank note; a gift so precious, it warranted his personal involvement.

He flew to Boston and took a cab to her office where he would present it to her himself. Just as he reached the entrance of the building, a woman pushed through the glass doors to exit onto the sidewalk. He yielded to let her buy, then froze. Her face was undeniably that of Heather Delano's kin. He turned to catch up to her, but then stopped dead in his tracks. In an instant, feelings of doubt washed over him. *What was I thinking? God only knows what Connor has told her about me. I'm literally the person who failed to protect her mother.* Terrified that Jennifer would never accept anything coming from him, George worried his well-meaning gesture had been misguided. He had to find a better approach, a trusted messenger. Leave no possibility for Jennifer to refuse Eleanor's generosity.

But as George traveled back to New York, so too did his demons. Demons he was convinced had been vanquished long ago. Thoughts of all that had transpired in 1972 plunged him right back to that place of guilt, failure, and anxiety. Fifteen years of wellness suddenly hung in the balance. And to confide in Brandon would only feed into his boyfriend's insecurities. On this, George was alone and vulnerable.

In no more than three days, the urge to get high would spring upon him. And just as quickly, the alarm bells signaled. He couldn't. Not that. He had come too far to go back. Unable to trust himself, he rushed to secure Jennifer's money into a new account, free of tax, to keep it safe until he felt stronger, more grounded. To compensate for the delay, he bumped up the amount with his own portion of her inheritance. It seemed like the least he could do; or so believed his guilty conscience. And why not add Jennifer's daughters as beneficiaries? That would surely make the money too enticing for her to turn down. Then, thinking of the Angelini watching over them, he named it the Angel Fund.

He could do this. He would find a way. He just needed a little more time.

But as the clock kept ticking, George's distress kept growing. Trapped in his past, he felt unable to shake its hold. Meanwhile, every ounce of his resolve was dispensed trying to resist the temptation to do drugs, to function normally without letting on to his entourage that he was struggling.

He continued to let himself believe he would overcome, that it was merely a matter of time before he would complete Eleanor's mission. For her sake. For Jennifer's. But self-loathing was a powerful adversary. And in the case of George Vasquez, it was a paralyzing one. One he would never defeat. Like poison, it slowly destroyed him from within, until pancreatic cancer took care of the rest.

CHAPTER TWENTY-FIVE

— 2004 —

I was sitting at my desk, knee-deep in files, when Perry arrived with a package for me. I hadn't realized how late it was until I heard the knock on my doorframe. The worst part is that I wasn't even doing client work. A new line item was wreaking havoc on the household budget, so I was busy rejigging our finances. Make that *my* finances. Now that Nick was in remission, I needed to prevent him from worrying himself into a relapse. At least he wasn't giving me grief for coming into the office so early. At his insistence, I stopped working in bed, which justified my need for extra morning hours. So far, I had him convinced that everything was under control. But based on Perry's expression, I was probably projecting more of a not-so-on-top-of-things kind of vibe.

It's not that I didn't expect the need for some adjustments. It's that the full magnitude was only revealed after the last of the medical bills came in. The hefty price of cancer treatments was no joke. How anyone without medical insurance could avoid personal bankruptcy was a mystery. Whatever magic they had, I wanted, because even after the insurer outlay, Nick's final deductible tallied too many zeros. And, as he had so kindly reminded me, he wasn't out of the woods. Never would be. Which meant we would always need a cushion to cover not just his ongoing screening, but any future treatment as required. So here I was, trying to find a way to solve our cashflow puzzle.

To simplify the exercise, I had split out the load across three separate spreadsheets, thinking that tackling each on its own would be less overwhelming. Meanwhile, the very fact that I had three separate spreadsheets made it appear even more onerous. If I could, I would throw some of it Perry's way. But even if I swapped out the file names, there was no disguising the personal nature of this covert operation.

For instance, take the first file, entitled Mortgage Mayhem. Like most home-owners, the bulk of our equity was tied to our house. But so much for knocking off our payments before college expenses started kicking in. The wiggle room I had planned now seemed like a drop in the bucket. So something else had to give, and from my perspective, the easiest option was to sell. With the real estate market surging, we could profit from a downsize or even a rental. But the mere thought of suggesting we leave the only home they had ever known, had me imagining my girls' revolt. Not to mention the red flag it would send Nick. I couldn't put them through more distress. Not after all we had been through. So instead, I was trying to calculate the amount we would need to remortgage; something my accountant brain was viciously trying to resist. And it all depended on how much I could trim off of our expenses.

Which brings us to file number two, entitled Disney Depression. Walt's offence aside, that is exactly how it felt to learn that the happiest place on earth was also the priciest. Admittedly, I should have done my research before offering it up to the girls in the first place. But the timing didn't really allow for it. Nick was at his lowest point and my despairing daughters were convinced their father was on his death bed. The wailing was so intense, I had to turn to a glass – make that a bottle – of red wine. And it did the trick. For them, that is. Before I knew it, I was promising a family trip to Disney World upon Nick's recovery. The cheers were so celebratory, they perked him right up. Only now I needed a sprinkle of pixie dust to bring down the not-so-magical price tag so I could make this happen. Postponing Greece wouldn't be enough. Neither would driving to Orlando to save on airfare and car rental. By my latest calculations, a two-day adventure is all we could afford, unless my kids could commit to never outgrowing their current wardrobes, and we collectively agreed on a permanent diet of lentils and grains. Bottom line, we needed more cash.

That quest was covered in file number three entitled, Jerry Maguire; my feeble attempt at cute to detract from my stress. I knew how desperate it was to be manifesting *show me the money* to the universe. As was my impulse purchase of a Mega Millions ticket at the convenience store. I won't even begin to share the harsh judgement accountant brain unleashed on me after that useless expenditure. But no matter how good my Cuba Gooding Jr. impression was, nothing had materialized, so I was left to pursue a more realistic avenue. Pragmatic brain knew that we should cover all our fixed expenses with my income, leaving Nick's for discretionary spending, so that when the next interruption came around, it wouldn't throw everything else off. My options were twofold; same job at a bigger firm, or bigger job at this firm. A prospect that would be so much easier if my ambitions aligned with either. But lo and behold, I was among the privileged few who actually liked my current position, firm and my colleagues.

Speaking of which, Perry's interruption came as I was trying to stay focused on the plus side of this madness; Nick was in remission and nothing mattered more than that.

"This came for you," he said holding a box. "A Max Cisco just dropped it off. Said he would be at the bench if you had any questions." He had one eyebrow raised with intrigue. Then, sensing that I busy, he offered, "Need me to help with anything? I'm almost done the balance sheet review."

"No, I've got this. Thanks Perry," I replied, blindly taking the box from him then checking my watch, surprised at how long I had infringed on work hours. Having just computed what he said, I called to him before he crossed the doorway. "Did you see him?"

"No. He left it with reception. They called me to get it for you. I can take care of it if you like."

"Thanks, but no. I'll get to it later."

The moment Perry turned away, I took the box off my desk and placed it in the trash. Then I closed out my contraband files to resume real work. At about the fifteen minute mark – maybe less – I realized all I had been doing was trying to avoid any thought of Detective Cisco. Why did he have to go and bring me something? And what would make him think I would have any desire to meet with him? So now I was just fixated on that and it was driving me nuts.

"Oh for God's sake," I moaned, while reaching below to pull the package out of my garbage bin. It was the size of a shoebox and wrapped in brown paper, with my name handwritten on the exterior. I detached the tape from the folds to remove the wrapping then opened the lid. A note sat on top of the contents. It, too, was handwritten: *In case you don't have these*. It was signed, *Max C*. The moment I removed it, I gasped. This couldn't be real. Inside was a photograph of Dad and me during the summer of 1972. How was this even possible? I reached in, and pulled out a stack of at least two dozen black and white, five-by-seven prints. I couldn't look through them fast enough. All of them were from our trip.

"Adventuremobile," I cried when seeing it captured at a campsite I had forgotten. As I ran my finger across it, I wished I could wrap my arms around that temporary home and give it a big fat hug. It was like bumping into a long lost friend and feeling instantly transported back in time. I continued to flip through, one by one, until I felt completely overcome with emotion. Really good emotion. "This is an absolute treasure." And I couldn't think of a more perfectly timed reminder that even the most dire situation was surmountable. Because the minute Dad and I had set foot inside that camper, we went from somber and lifeless, to carefree and happy. And our circumstances then were far worse than mine were right now.

Boosted by this positive energy, it was debatable whether I was going to get any work done. And before I bothered to try, there was someone to whom I owed a much deserved thank you. With any luck, the detective who just thrust himself into my good graces was still sitting on that bench. So I closed the box and placed it in my desk drawer, already looking forward to a bedtime perusal, then switched into my runners and grabbed my purse.

Perry seemed even more intrigued as I zoomed by his desk, saying, "I'll be back shortly."

With a spring in my step, I made my way toward The Common. As soon as the treeline came into view after I turned the corner, I smiled with delight. "Oh my God. It's green haze day. Could this morning get any better?"

It was Dad's favorite. That moment when, after months of being completely bare, every branch of the red maples became speckled with tiny bursts of green. *They're taking their first peek at spring*, he would say. Before the week was over, a canopy of dense foliage would reappear for yet another season. I was definitely going to be making a detour after work to take him outside. Maybe Oprah would join us too. I chucked to myself thinking of how there was no going back to ever calling her Debbie.

As I continued to admire the punch of color above me, I did eventually notice the bench in question come into view. Someone was sitting there. Hopefully it was Detective Cisco. If it was, he certainly had more patience than I did or he, too, was marvelling at nature's spectacle.

My life and my spirits seemed so different from the last time we had crossed paths at that exact same spot. Barely six months ago, I was just learning about Nick's diagnosis, was cast aside shortly thereafter by Aunt Dawn, then spiraled all the way into my suspicion of being a love child. There's a thought I could have done without today.

He noticed me approaching and smiled. I sat down beside him.

"Surprised?" he asked.

"I'll say," I nodded, raising my eyebrows.

"I left homicide."

What? I frowned.

"I assume you expected I'd be wearing a suit?"

"Ah." I had to admit, he wore the blue jeans, runners and gray shirt quite well. "So what did you in? Too much death?" If he was trying to cut the awkward tension from our last encounter, I was happy to follow his lead.

"Not enough prevention," he replied, shaking his head. "It would feel like a bigger service to society if I was actually stopping the crime from happening instead of showing up after it's been committed."

He made a valid point. "But you do get to catch the bad guys."

"If they're the ones pulling the trigger. Otherwise, I'm investigating victims who were behaving in self-defense." He paused, then switched gears. "But you didn't come here for my career update. I assume you have a question for me?"

"Um. Yes," I replied emphatically.

"It's Maximilien. With an 'e'. My mother's origins are French Canadian. From Quebec."

Now what's he saying?

"Most people think it's short for Maxwell," he clarified.

Clueing in, I decided I should play along. "I was certain it was Maximus."

"A gladiator. Nice. Way better than a coffee brand," he mused. "So how have you been, Mrs. Vincent?"

I remembered that's what he called me. Yuck. "Please, Maximus, call me Jennifer." That should work. "Things have been...eventful. But good now." I turned to look at him. "My husband had a cancer scare. But he's in remission, so that's a relief."

I could tell that caught him off-guard. "I'm so sorry to hear it." His look of concern was genuine. "That must have been terrible for you."

"It was. But it was detected at stage one and the treatment was a success."

"Well that's very good news."

"Yes it is. What would be even better news is if I could pay the medical bills without having to sell a kidney on the black-market." I then turned to him. "You're not investigating organ trafficking now are you?" I asked sarcastically.

"No, that's the FBI," he smiled. "But for what's it's worth, I have a sneaking suspicion Jennifer Vincent will work things out without need for dismemberment."

"I hope you're right. I mean, I know you are. It's just that you caught me while I've been submerged right in it. Anyway." Time to move on to the actual topic at hand. "Thank you, by the way. Truly. I'm very grateful. And no, I hadn't seen them. Didn't even know they existed. They're priceless."

"Consider it a peace offering for dragging you into the station last year."

"Accepted." In truth, for as annoyed as I had been at the time, these pictures more than made up for it. "So…are you going to tell me where you got them?"

"Jorge Vasquez," he replied. "They were among a bunch of legal files and other effects that were sorted after he passed away. I was involved because of that case. They were going to be discarded. When I recognized your father from that other photo, I knew who they belonged to."

"Well. I can't thank you enough."

"You're very welcome."

"I suppose you're still not gonna tell me what that case was about?"

"Had a feeling you might ask…" he smiled. "It was something Vasquez was involved in a while ago. A new document was revealed after he died. My boss insisted we check for any loose ends."

"And did you find any?"

"None that matter this long after the fact. Case closed, as they say."

It was weird to think that I knew about George, met Dawn, had thoughts about Mom, and now had pictures of the trip, all thanks to that meeting at the police station. Surprisingly, all of it was good. Except for one burning question, of course. The idea of someone else having impregnated Mom was disruptive to my self-identity. It hadn't had time to nag at me while I was singularly focused on Nick's health. But to have the instigator of my concern sitting right in front of me made me wonder if it was just a matter of time before it would. Might I one day start honing in on every strange male who looked at me, wondering if he thought I was his illegitimate daughter? What about how it would make Nick or the girls feel if someone just showed up at our doorstep claiming to be my father? And if I so much as intimated anything about my suspicions to Nick, he'd be on a rampage searching for the mystery sperm donor. Remaining in limbo could end up being a recipe for disaster. But was I brave enough to ask? It might be now or never. So loaded question, here we go. "Detective?" I asked. "You owe me one more thing."

"Oh?"

"I need to know. Why did you ask if he was my biological father?" I then held my breath and tried not to cringe as I awaited his response.

He didn't reply right away. Was he scrambling for an answer? Or was it too many cases ago to even remember? It's not like there was reason to think it had left a big impression. Staring at the ground, he finally said, "Did I?"

"Um yes, you did." There was no way he could interpret my tone as anything other than annoyance.

He then ranted off a lame explanation. "Getting through the paperwork from back then was a challenge. Everything was handwritten and worn. Some of it so illegible, it was hard to decode."

Blah, blah, blah. If he thought I was letting him off the hook, he was sadly mistaken. There was no way he was leaving me hanging. "So you're saying you're not sure?"

He turned to me with a sheepish look. "If I'm being perfectly candid, it was my first time working a case that old."

"That still doesn't answer my question."

"I probably mixed up a few things," he tried to defend. Then, as though magically clearing it up in his head. "There was no adoption record on file, if that's what you're wondering."

I tried to be subtle when exhaling with immeasurable relief, but, "Good to know," was all I replied.

"I should never have asked. That was a mistake. I apologize." He creased his brow with regret.

I didn't respond. I was somewhere between annoyed by the unnecessary angst and relieved there existed no alternate record of my paternity. And here I thought we had made a breakthrough in our relationship. Oh well, case closed on that too, I suppose.

He stood up. "Well, I won't keep you, Jennifer. I know you have to get back to making more of that money," he grinned.

"Thanks for the reminder." As he was about to turn away, I could tell he felt bad about the biological question. Which didn't seem fair after he had gone out of his way to bring me the pictures. If not for him, they would be disintegrating in a landfill instead of being cherished from this day forward. "Oh and Maximus? Thanks again for the surprise." He smiled then turned. I was about to add a goodbye, then realized I didn't know where he was redirecting his career. "By the way, you never did say where you're working now."

He spun around to look at me. "I joined the domestic violence unit."

"Really?"

That was unexpected. I'm not even sure why it surprised me. But it immediately conjured the thought of poor little Noah. It had been a while since I was reminded of Grace's former classmate. When his father was taken into custody for abuse four years ago, it sent shivers across our entire friend circle. Every parent was mortified, fraught with guilt for not having noticed a single thing. Noah was sweet, shy and flinched a lot. But we had no idea he was suffering. None. For weeks, Nick wanted to punch a hole through the wall. As for me, I never realized I had the capacity for so much rage. It must have been buried pretty deep down, because my anger toward the man who had entered my home for our children's playdates was off the charts. I swear, I felt like I could have murdered him with my own bare hands. Six months later, Noah and his mother moved away. We all assumed it was because of fear or the stigma. Then we never heard from them again. As much I hoped they were okay, I had to ask myself if it was even possible for anyone to overcome aggression at the hands of a parent. I know I certainly couldn't.

Thinking back to what Detective Cisco had said earlier about preventing crimes instead of showing up after the fact, there seemed to be no greater mission than that of protecting the innocent in their very own homes.

"Do you have children, Detective?"

He nodded. "A daughter. She turns one in August."

I had no idea how he was going to do it. Get through day after day of heart-wrenching stories, see scrapes and bruises on kids' bodies, then shake it off before going home to his own, and just be her dad. What I felt towards him in this moment was an enormous sense of gratitude on behalf of every parent. "You've embarked on a very noble cause, Detective Cisco."

"We need way more bodies protecting the vulnerable. I'm just one guy, but I'll do what I can."

"You'll make a difference. You're a parent. Your protective instinct is supercharged."

"That it is," he nodded with a grin, raising his hand to wave as he was about to leave.

"Harken you inner gladiator and catch those nasty bastards, Maximus," I shouted. I stopped short of suggesting barbaric punishment. But only because he was law enforcement. And it was 2004; severing appendages was a thing of the past.

Nick couldn't believe his eyes when he saw the photos that night. I had waited till we were in bed and made him pause his book before handing him the box. For a minute I wondered if he thought I had made up the whole trip, he looked so surprised. Maybe he was just too shocked to see Dad and I in action. Outdoorsy orienteers living off the land like true nomads in our swanky motorhome.

"Who took these?" he asked in utter amazement as he leafed through each one.

"Had to be George. He was there. I know from the picture Detective Cisco had shown me at the station. And he wasn't alone because someone else took that one."

"But you never noticed?"

"No. Never. I guess the objective was for them to be as natural as possible. And it worked. Look how nice they turned out without the fake cheese pose."

"They're absolutely fantastic, Jen. It's a shame your Dad never got them."

"They obviously had quite the falling out. But thankfully George kept them. Maybe he hoped they would reconnect one day. I'm just happy they made their way to me. To be honest, it's an even bigger thrill to be seeing them now for the first time."

"You weren't tempted to show your Dad today? They'll blow his mind."

"I considered it, but decided to wait. I knew we'd be spending our time outside embracing green haze. And until I put them in an album, they'll just be too hard for him to handle." I looked at Nick with a selfish grin. "Plus I kinda like having them all to myself for a bit longer."

"I don't blame you," he winked. "So how did the detective find them?"

"They were with George's files. He recognized Dad. Such a weird turn of events." I sighed with amazement.

"You were meant to have them, Jen. There's no other explanation," said Nick as he continued to look at them. "Crap, I almost forgot. You got a letter today. Registered mail. I had to sign for it. I'll go get it. Be right back."

He rushed out toward the desk which, along with cancer, had been vacated from our bedroom. While he did that, I stared at the pictures all over again, letting snippets of memory sneak back in. He re-entered the room and sat himself in bed then handed me the envelope.

As soon as I took it, I couldn't believe the return address.

"You've got to be kidding me." It was Vasquez & Associates.

"Damn, Jen, I didn't even notice. It came while I was prepping dinner. I signed for it and just put it down." Poor Nick felt so terrible. "Leave it for another day. It can wait."

But he knew me better than that. "I may as well just get it over with."

Whatever this was, it would be only a brief interruption to my wonderful mood. I ripped the flap and pulled out two pages that were folded in three. Nick cringed as he watched me open them. The first was handwritten by someone whose dexterity was only a slight notch above Dad's. But it was legible.

I began to read it out loud.

Dearest Jennifer,

This is Eleanor, your grandmother. If you are reading this, it's that I have now passed away.

"Oh my God." I turned to Nick with wide eyes. "I saw this woman once in my entire life. I can't believe she wrote me a note."

Let me start by expressing my deepest regret that we were never close. Alas, some things are not meant to be.

I turned to him again. "Does that sound as cold to you as it does to me?"

"Kind of. But it isn't every day someone says *alas*. She sounds fancy," he cocked his brow.

I continued to read aloud.

I grew up in a family of great wealth and status.

"She left you money!" he exclaimed.

It definitely sounded that way, but I wasn't prepared to celebrate until reading to the end.

But it came at a cost. None greater than never knowing my granddaughter. Your father, on the other hand, understood what it truly meant to be rich. When your mother died, he inherited a portion of my family's wealth. To my surprise, he declined it. He said he already had all that he needed: his Jenny.

"Aw, Daddy," I cried, placing my hand with the note over my heart.

A disappointed Nick asked, with crunched face and pinched fingers, "Are you maybe just a teensy bit upset he didn't take the money?"

I was, but I couldn't dare tell him. He needed to think our finances were under control. Besides I felt too deeply touched by her comments about my extremely biological father.

So I took his portion and invested it to one day give to you.

"Wait what?"

Nick's eyes grew wide, his fists tight, elbows bent, as he waited to hear the rest.

This letter should be accompanied by paperwork for what is now your account. Though I may not have been a part of your life, it is my sincere wish that this money will contribute to making your future as bright as it can be.

Please know that you were loved deeply and always.

Affectionately,

Grandma Eleanor

I thought Nick might grab the pages from me, he was so impatient. But for as shocked as I was, I held my grip and flipped to the next page. It was a bank transfer statement. I raced through it quickly, saw the name, Angel Fund, then noticed that the girls' names were also listed. But it was when seeing the amount, that I let it drop onto my lap, staring forward in astonishment. "Oh my God, Nick. She left us over six-hundred-thousand dollars!"

Nick took the typed page from me and read through it himself. In disbelief he said, "Jen, I'm no accountant, but I'm pretty sure you're wrong."

"What do you mean?" I looked at him with a frown.

"You missed a zero. It's over six-million dollars."

"No way. It can't be." I grabbed it back from him then read the number again. Over and over to be absolutely certain. And every single time, there were seven unbelievable digits. "Oh my God, Nick! Jerry McGuire actually worked!" I exclaimed. "No organ donations...We can eat meat!" Holding my arms out wide. "Grow girls grow!"

"Jen, honestly, you're being super weird. But dammit, we're rich!"

It was a pinch-me moment like no other. We felt teleported to a crazy new reality. All because my birthright was the winning ticket to Grandma Eleanor's lottery.

As I tried to imagine her, a bizarre thought came to mind. "I never even said her name, Nick."

"What?"

"Grandma Eleanor. I have one single memory of her. And you know me, that means it's super vague. She sat beside me at Mom's funeral. Dad held one hand, she held the other. I never said a word to her."

"You're saying her name now, Jen. And as far as I'm concerned, you can say it every God damned day!"

We sat dazed, processing, both of us convinced a camera crew was about to barge in at any moment to tell us we had just been punked. But the longer it took for them to show up, the more I let myself escape from beneath the weight of our expenses. Never would I have to be concerned with them again. And that's when the biggest impact this money could make came to mind.

"Nick," I said with incredible hope. "We can fund cancer research. Help find you a cure."

He grinned in silence knowing, as I did, that neither the amount nor the timeline would be enough to alter the inevitable. But he also knew that doing everything in my power to try was the best use of this generous gift.

Waving his hand as though reading a billboard, he exclaimed, "Jennifer Vincent, millionaire philanthropist. Sounds very sexy." He winked with affection.

"It does, doesn't it?" I whispered with an exaggerated look of seduction.

"You know. I've never slept with a millionaire before."

"Should we maybe change that?" There was nothing like a sudden influx of wealth to spark up the romance.

"Hell ya."

"Get the lights." While he did that, I reset my alarm. No need to wake up at the crack of dawn. *Good riddance three separate spreadsheets.*

CHAPTER TWENTY-SIX

— 2023 —

"You're such a good Brady," I say in fur-baby-speak, while crouching down to his level.

My mutt's sweet spot is right behind the ears. I rub them while leaning my forehead against his. To be this close to his pungent oral cavity takes an extra special kind of love, but I relish these tender moments too much to turn away. His tail wagging suggests he does too; it's so vigorous, it nearly makes us both lose our balance.

Brady is the last holdout of my household, whose days are sadly numbered. Like me, he's watched as the other four members left, one by one, to pursue their adult lives or, in Nick's case, enter the great beyond. He'll be next, but for now he's hanging tight, mustering every ounce of strength to stay by my side for as long as he can.

I stare at his face; the vestiges of his once golden coat now scant, his drooping gray-white jowls tugging his eyelids way down low. I'm the stronger one now. My tear-filled nights, soothed by the warmth and comfort of his loyal companionship, have long since passed. The time has come for me to return the favor. To bring him peace during his final stretch on earth, while I brace for yet another final farewell.

How barren my home will feel after he exhales his last breath. Already it seems much too quiet. But I've pushed through enough loss to know that life goes on. That change is just part of it. That when the present seems too clouded, I need only look to the horizon and trust that the vacancies of my heart will one day be filled with new tenants. Perhaps some little bundles of unequivocal joy upon whom to one day lavish grandmotherly love. It's my secret wish, made with certainty that they will complete me and then some.

Still sporting a t-shirt and sweatpants, I give Brady an extra dose of cuddles to last him till this evening, because once I slip into my dress, the traces of his affection won't be welcome on its surface.

"God you stink." I blow out, while waving my hand in front of my face to disperse the fumes. "Let's get you outside."

I escort him to the back door and usher him out. As I watch him select a target for his markings, I'm reminded of the frenetic bundle of energy that once tore strips across the entire yard, dousing each extremity. Like most pets, his arrival was the result of unrelenting pleas. My girls had pooled their strengths and begun the onslaught with utter determination. The timing had also played a factor. Nick was on his third bout of cancer; each relapse taking its toll, depleting more of his strength and chipping away at his morale. The Angel Fund was buying us more time through access to experimental treatments, but it wasn't enough. Nick needed an injection of joy, something to really cheer him up. And so it was that Brady arrived as the ultimate birthday present, to Nick's priceless look of surprise. Naturally, he was given full authority over name choice. And naturally, Tom Brady would be his inspiration. By then, our superstar quarterback had taken us to four Super Bowls, won three, and looked to still be going strong. Paraded around in his very own Patriots' jersey, our little Brady meshed into the family fabric instantaneously, becoming Nick's shadow from day one.

His bladder now relieved, Brady saunters into the living room where he performs his labored ritual of three full spins before collapsing onto his side. I then walk upstairs to *my* bedroom; that's what I've forced myself to call it from the first anniversary of Nick's passing. Three years later, it's still bathed in his presence. And I'm still standing on my own two feet. Speaking of which, they need to get moving.

I quickly scan my closet for the most suitable funeral attire. A charcoal dress and black blazer will have to do; the last minute notice has left me with no time to shop. But I can't imagine Dawn would care. Not that I would know either way; we never developed a relationship. The only news I've received since last seeing her is that she just died. To say I was surprised when her lawyer informed me I was listed as her next of kin, is an understatement. Now, I have to sign for another inheritance. Another generous afterthought that has me feeling completely indifferent this time around.

Why Mom's family was so unreceptive to establishing a personal connection with me, I'll never understand. I guess I was too much of a reminder of her. Or the opposite: not Delano enough. They're all gone now, so it doesn't matter. The last link was Dawn, whose service I'll attend if for no other reason than to be polite.

It's a shame that our first meeting had been our last. At first, I had been so eager to reconnect. It was Nick who insisted I give Dawn more time. Then, when he finally gave me the okay, I launched my quest with determination. And she didn't make it easy. With no answering machine to leave a message on, I had to let the phone ring. Ring and ring. Sometimes in the evening, different times on weekends, and every time in between. But she never picked up. Still, I kept trying, until for reasons unknown, Nick made an about-face, insisting it was best to let her be, that whatever connection I was hoping for was impossible. It seemed completely unlike him to be defeatist, so I had chalked it up to the side-effects of his medication; mood swings had become par for the course. But his downer attitude had swayed me. I abandoned any effort after that and just resigned myself to Dawn being inhospitable towards me.

But my day isn't going to be all bad. Upon my return back home, I plan to cozy up with a nice glass of wine, while perusing a very special photo album. It was pulled out from hiding on the first anniversary of Dad's passing, and for the last two months, has been sitting on my nightstand, at the ready, for whenever I need a good dose of nostalgia.

To see it's condition, anyone could tell it's had its fair share of handling. The indigo blue hardcover is scratched and worn, it's corners have rounded inward. The hand-written *Adventuremobile* label is faded, and the plastic inserts holding the photos have become loose, most tearing at the edges. I probably should have replaced it ages ago, but like most comfort items, leaving it as is seemed best. The only change there has ever been is the sequence of photos. Dad and I had rearranged them constantly. It was our game. A mental exercise, trying to recall the chronology of our journey. Dad's diction had thankfully improved enough to carry on a very slow but intelligible conversation. It seemed so ironic that the only time in our lives we had ever been chatty was during that adventure. And there we were, decades later, reliving the journey, and resuming that same dialogue. Equally ironic was the fact that the trip we had never spoken of after it ended, had become our single topic of conversation until his death.

I remember how concerned I had felt before showing him, especially knowing George had been the one to have taken the pictures. Would this trip down memory lane set Dad back emotionally? To test the waters, I had broached the topic beforehand. *When did you last see George?* I finally asked him. *California* was his response, *during our trip.* He went on to say that after Dad had signed some legal papers, George brought them back to Boston, then left the city for good. The moment he had shared that with me, Dad burst into tears, repeating how sorry he was. But he never said why, and I chose not to ask.

I let a few weeks go by, bought a photo album, and finally surprised him with this treasure. He had cried and cried, then insisted I bring it back again. Which I did for every single visit thereafter.

It occurred to me much later on, that the very last photo taken might have been the one of Dad and George. Who had taken it, and why it was excluded from the box Detective Cisco had given to me, remains unknown to this day.

For a while, Nick had made it his personal mission to solve that mystery. He had the time. Plus he had a strong penchant for sleuthing. To him, every unanswered question was like a puzzle or, better still, an opportunity to uncover secrets. I always said it was because he read too many crime novels, but it was the internet that took his curiosity to a whole new level. The consummate professor had found infinite avenues for quenching his thirst for knowledge. Which was wonderful. Other than his overwhelming need to impart literally every new discovery on me. I was patient while he was undergoing treatments, but when they were done, I had to put an end to the madness, confess I had reached information overload. I thought he had taken it well, until the day I came into the room and noticed the word *Delano* across the computer screen. The minute he heard me approaching, he powered it down so quickly, as though he had uncovered a horrible scandal. It still makes me giggle when I think of how he walked around the house like the sketchy guy in on a big secret. Meanwhile, I had zero interest in begging him to spill the beans.

* * *

Well, that was a very depressing funeral. I mean, they all are of course; that's their very nature. But Dawn's was pitiful. Only four people, including me, were in attendance, one of whom was her lawyer. A ninety-year-old woman, who lived in her condo building, claimed they had been close for twenty years. By close,

THE BURDEN OF TRUTH

she meant they said hello and talked about the weather when picking-up their mail from the entrance lock-boxes. The other was a scruffy character from her company. He told me how he and Dawn were kindred spirits, both workaholics with no time for frivolous banter. It actually made me feel better about having been ignored. She was just a recluse, who avoided all human interaction, not just mine.

Foregoing the need for a post-service get-together during which to regale in the memories we had all shared with Dawn, her lawyer suggested we meet right away to sort out the paperwork. The funeral home offered us a vacant room for privacy and I was more than happy to get this done quickly.

The condolences now out of the way, Mr. Lynch began by saying, "Mrs. Vincent, this shouldn't take long. Dawn Delano's will is very straight forward."

In his late sixties, his thin stature seemed skeletal beneath his oversized brown suit. He had but few strands of gray hair and a hooked nose that supported his wire-framed glasses. The dossier was open in front of him. He read through the basic language, while tracing the sentences with his finger like my girls did when learning to read.

This wasn't my first rodeo. I had been through this exercise after Nick's passing, then again after Dad's, both within a few years of each other. And because I wasn't fraught with even an ounce of emotion, this time felt purely transactional. No trying to hold back tears or attempting to read and sign documents through blurred vision. I just sat patiently, disinterested and stoic.

Sparing us all the legalese, he cut straight to the chase. "Dawn

Delano bequeathed her entire estate to you."

"She what?"

"Yes, you heard correctly. She did say it would come as a surprise." When he saw that I had nothing else to say, he continued. "But don't expect a Delano fortune. Ms. Delano gave most of her wealth to charity." He went on to list her effects, which included her condo and it's furnishings, a 1999 Honda Accord, a bank account just shy of eight-thousand dollars and a fifty-thousand dollar life insurance policy to cover the cost of her funeral and associated sundries.

"Okay. Did she place any restrictions on the sale of the condo?"

"None. You may do with it as you please. As for her belongings, she specified only her vast music collection. Thousands of albums and CDs. She requested that they not be discarded."

"Oh okay. I didn't think anyone listened to those anymore."

"I do."

Meaning no offence, I explained myself. "I thought digital streaming services – you know, Spotify, Apple Music, – were taking over the market. Endless music in the palm of your hands." I grinned, while raising my iPhone as though I was in a cheesy ad.

"Ah yes. I see. You're a technology person."

My girls would beg to differ. "And did you say thousands?" I couldn't even begin to imagine the storage space that would require.

"Yes. They are in her condo. If you have no use for them,

her request was that they be donated to her charity. If, of course, you were amenable to making the arrangements."

"Yes, that sounds fine." I certainly had no use for them.

"Wonderful. This brings me to her only other request. In the event that you did not have need for any portion of her assets, she wished that it, too, be donated to her charity."

I hadn't realized Dawn was such a philanthropist. It was nice that we had at least that in common. But it made me wish she had simply named her charitable organizations as beneficiaries. "Mr. Lynch," I asked, "Is there a reason she didn't leave her estate to her charities? We really weren't close."

"Obviously, I can't say for certain. I was her lawyer, not her friend. But I would assume, as is customary, she chose you as her closest kin. Without knowing your appetite for acquiring her belongings, she simply wished to provide an alternate destination for them."

Did Dawn really think I would want any part of her estate? That her things held some meaning for me? Or was her offering motivated by guilt for blowing me off all those years ago? Whatever her intent, all I could see was an administrative headache; packing up a condo, putting it and her car up for sale, then transferring her belongings to her charities. Not exactly my idea of a good time. If Nick was around, he would be keen to scour through her things, hoping to find a family heirloom, a piece of history, maybe a collector's item. But he wasn't, so this was all my problem and I was struggling to see an upside.

"Also, you should know, Mrs. Vincent. Your aunt was somewhat of a hoarder."

Oh God. I tried not widening my eyes too much.

"I can sense your trepidation, Mrs. Vincent. It's quite valid."

I now felt conflicted. Dawn was dead to me long before her passing. Like all the Delano's, she had disowned me my entire life. Only in death did she develop a sudden urge to acknowledge me. Grandma Eleanor had done the same. I couldn't wrap my head around it other than to accept that they had their reasons. Which was fine. But for Dawn to expect me to want or need material ties after all this time was foolish. As for undertaking a massive purge of her wall-to-wall junk, I was happy to wash my hands clean of it. So, in the same way she had avoided me, I was prepared to reciprocate.

"Mr. Lynch. I'm afraid I'm going to have to disclaim this inheritance."

He paused uncomfortably. It wasn't every day a beneficiary turned down an estate. For all I knew, this may be a first for him. "Very well, Mrs. Vincent," he replied with mild scorn. "Then I shall bother you only with one last thing." He reached into the briefcase that sat next to him on the table and removed a bulky envelope. "This is for you," he said, handing it me. "You may open it at your leisure."

I could feel something hard inside, which was the only reason I didn't refuse that too. "Do I need to sign for it?"

"No need. Your aunt simply asked that I give it to you in person. But I will, of course, require a written notice of your disclaim within the next thirty days. Otherwise, you are free to go."

"Thank you."

I left quickly as though I was trying to get away with something. But instead of feeling guilty or scared of getting caught, I felt vindicated. Purging all things Delano from my life felt quite liberating.

Brady's snoring woke me up from my snooze on the couch. From the time his hips became too weak to brave the stairs, I've been in the habit of staying in the living room with him until I can tell he's out for the night. The signal usually comes when his sporadic snorts stop interrupting his otherwise consistent rumbling. I'm not sure when exactly that occurred because I didn't mean to fall asleep. Now I'm doomed to be awake for several hours. My fault for letting my arm dangle onto his soft abdomen; the rhythmic rise and fall can be very sedating.

But it's bedtime, so I should at least go upstairs. I sit up, rub my eyes, then stretch before turning off the lamp and standing. My movements are so stealth-like, Brady doesn't notice a thing.

Upon entering my bedroom, I walk straight across to the bathroom, get into pyjamas, do a quick facial cleanse, then floss and brush my teeth. Before climbing into bed, I remember I have not one, but two distractions tonight. Maybe that nap wasn't such a bad thing after all.

I had left the envelope from Mr. Lynch on my bed when I came up to change into sweatpants. I pick it up, prop up my pillows, then lean back against the headboard to make myself comfy.

"Okay, Aunt Dawn. What little gem have you left your favorite niece?" I say sarcastically, intent on not letting any of it get to me.

I insert my finger in the opening of the flap to rip along the top crease, then pour the contents onto my lap. Relief. There's no letter. The backside of a picture frame with it's easel stand folded flat lands on top. I flip it over. "Wow. She actually kept it."

It was our family photo from Grace's birthday. I had given it to her when we had met almost twenty years ago. Perhaps this was her way of showing me that it had meant something to her. "Guess that's better than thinking she just tossed it. Oh wait, she was a hoarder. She didn't toss anything...But she did go to the trouble of framing it, so there's that. Next."

I set the photo down and pick up an off-white trifold brochure, entitled Angel Wings. The front panel features a black and white image of a stately stone building. I unfold it and glance through the description of a women's shelter. "Hmm. This must be her charity."

With regards to how I had gone about directing my own donations after our influx of cash, everything was tied to cancer: researching a cure, the oncology department where Nick had been treated, support groups for families of patients, and academic grants for medical students. It makes me wonder whether Dawn's choice was also motivated by personal interests. Did she know a victim of domestic violence? Could it have been Dawn herself? An abusive boyfriend would turn her off of relationships and explain her preference for remaining single, surrounded by things rather than people. "How horrible."

It makes my mind race back to the one person I knew to have suffered abuse. Noah. He would be a grown man by now. Is he, too, on a path of solitude and self-neglect like Dawn? This all seems so terribly sad. I hated feeling so helpless back then and it's making me feel just as horrible now. Like I should be doing more. Detective Cisco did. Make that, Gladiator Maximus. He hasn't come to mind in ages. I wonder whether he actually lasted in that field, and if so, how many perpetrators he apprehended.

And that's when an idea comes to mind. "There *is* something I can do." I flip to the backside of the brochure to find the contact information for Angel Wings, and resolve to call them on Monday. It seems more than fitting that I should arrange for my own contribution. "At least one good thing came out of this care package."

I close the brochure before setting it down, then glance back at the image of the building on its cover. "It seems so fancy." Though I've never seen one, I always envisioned a shelter as being in a non-descript establishment. This is the opposite. Then I notice the fine print just below. I reach for my glasses on the nightstand and read: *Angel Wings Estate (formerly Delano Manor) bequeathed in 1991 by the late Eleanor Angelini.*

"What? Hold on. This can't be. You're telling me this is where Mom actually grew up? Oh my God, it's palatial." I can't believe Mom had lived in such an opulent home. "Wait. Maybe she didn't." It could have been inhabited by extended members of the family I just disavowed. There was no way Mom could go from there to our very middle-class lifestyle and have been okay with that. Unless... "Mom? Had you renounced them too? Plot twist," I chuckle to myself.

I place the brochure down, thinking of how Nick would

be in his absolute glory with this revelation. Though, for all I know, he would be smirking right now because he had long since discovered Grandma Eleanor's maiden name and even knew about the manor, but wouldn't share it with me until I asked. He must have found my lack of curiosity so infuriating.

There's one last item in Dawn's envelope, which is, believe it or not, a CD.

"You really didn't want me getting away without taking at least one," I grin. It's Andrea Bocelli's Greatest Hits. He isn't an artist I listen to all that much, but I immediately think of the one song he sang with Celine Dion. It was from an animated film the girls watched over and over as kids. "What was it called?" I have zero chance of remembering. This is a matter for the family group chat, so I pick up my phone and type.

Me: *what was the Andrea Bocelli Celine Dion song from that movie?*

I can already hear them laughing. No matter how I craft my text messages, the girls find me amusing. No clue why. Meanwhile, I'm fairly certain it will take no more than a minute before at least one of them responds. And there it is.

Hannah: *The Prayer*

Grace: *Quest for Camelot*

Lisa: *Mom! You loved that song. Play it now!*

Me: *That was fast. Thank you:) Are you girls ever away from your phones?*

To my last question, I expect either a snide remark about how they need to be on alert for my random questions, a hashtag followed by acronyms I can't decipher, or nothing to show that they are away from their phones.

I receive no answer.

I put my phone down and switch to my iPad because it's already paired to the Bluetooth speaker sitting on my dresser beside the framed photo of Nick and me on the beach in Greece; a trip that, I'm pleased to report, was only delayed by one year, and was by far the best honeymoon we could have hoped for. I open Spotify and type Andrea Bocelli in the search line, then scroll down to find his greatest hits. I'm too lazy to venture into the garage in search of our CD player buried somewhere among my daughters' *I don't have space so please store this for me* pile of treasures. Once I find it, I tap *play* to see what I might recognize. Meanwhile, I have no idea why Dawn has included it.

I pick up the jewel case and look at it front and back to see if there's a message to decode, but I notice nothing unusual. *Open it,* I hear Nick say in my head. Which, of course, I obey. "Well I'll be damned." There's a pink post-it attached to the CD with *Mother's favorite* written on it. Why Dawn would want me to have Grandma Eleanor's favorite is a mystery, but the music is quite pleasant. "Who calls their mother *Mother* anyway?" I ask no one. "People who live in a manor. Maybe Mom actually did live there." How nice it feels to not care either way.

Done with Dawn's thoughtful care package, I place the frame on my nightstand beside the family photo that was already there. The one from Disney World; a classic pose, standing at the end of Main Street in front of Cinderella's castle. As I look at both photos side by side, I realize they represent the calm before and after the storm of cash and cancer.

To Nick and the girls, Disney World surpassed all other vacations. No place had been more fun-filled, more joyful, more magical. And while I agree it was an exceptional family trip, I had had another, long before any of them had entered my world, and – beyond exceptional – it was life changing. Still my favorite to this day; my little secret.

"Not gonna lie. I'm not hating this, Andrea." The melodies are soft and soulful, a very suitable soundtrack for my journey back in time.

I reach for the photo album and smile, ready to re-immerse myself, proud to have resumed this retreat into my past without shedding a single tear. I place it on my lap, my palms resting on the cover, then raise my gaze toward the ceiling. After the events of the day, the time has come for me to finally say it out loud. Confess what I know. Or what it is that I've suspected for quite some time.

"So Dad, I think I figured it out. Sort of. And don't worry, it's all good. And yes, Nick, I know you probably did long before me. Oh and Dawn, don't sweat it. I get why you wouldn't want to go there. Same for you, Grandma Eleanor."

The truth of the matter is that I'm not entirely clueless about why that trip had occurred. My suspicions began years ago, when the whole *I'm a love child* debacle was stirring in my brain. Once Detective Cisco dispelled it, I thought I was in the clear. But receiving these pictures changed everything. I went from having forgotten about that trip for three decades to reliving it during every single visit with Dad thereafter. Also, I have *Adventuremobile* quizzes to blame. The day I first told Nick about them, we laughed ourselves silly at how nerdy I used to be. Amused, he began to test my memory every so often by interrupting whatever he was reading in bed to blurt out *Adventuremobile quiz time.* Then he would ask one random question about the trip, while I played along, thinking up absurd answers whenever my lousy memory stumped me. We laughed and laughed, savoring the brief respite from cancer-talk.

Once he had to be hospitalized for the very last time, I tried desperately to distract myself to keep from breaking. Imagining Nick was with me, I decided to attempt a self-quiz. But my flair for humor was nowhere to be found. How could it be while I was waiting for my spouse to take his very last breath? I was in the same position Dad had been decades earlier. And that's when my ultra-depressing quiz question came to mind: would I grab the girls and leave on an adventure? The answer was quick and firm: hell no, never. It was unconscionable to even think it. So then I asked myself, if Nick was brain-dead and had been for months, would I do it then? Again the answer was an emphatic no. I could never leave while he was alive; I wouldn't want to. Then came the real question. What could possibly trigger Dad to just up and escape while Mom was in hospital?

In that moment, it hit me.

I was never supposed to ask that question. Ever.

The plan all along had been for me to forget that trip had even occurred. And it had worked until Detective Cisco's 2003 inquiry. But even then, despite all the pictures and all the memories, Dad still never explained the reason nor timing of our journey. I waited, expecting that he would at some point.

But he never volunteered a thing. Because he never wanted me to know.

My mind went on a rampage trying to reconcile why he had abandoned her, while also trying to defend his actions. Whatever his reasons, whatever he was hiding, it had to be for my sake. And logically, it had to center around Mom's accident. There had to be more to it than I was told. Perhaps my grandparents weren't in the car with her, but instead she was with her lover. And maybe his name was George. And maybe she was carrying his child. That seemed scandalous enough for his and Dad's falling out to have dissolved their friendship permanently.

But did that warrant being kept from me decades later? I didn't think so. Nor did my next suspicion that Mom might have been at fault for the accident. That she had killed passengers in the other vehicle and was heading to prison should she survive her injuries. No, it had to be even more terrible. But what?

And that's when I went into a full-on spiral mode, imagining the unthinkable.

It had to be Dad. He was the culprit. It was his fault. The reason she had been killed. Did she tell him she was leaving him for George? Did she threaten to take me with her? Was he the jilted husband whose anger got out of control, who kicked her out and caused her crash?

And was it even a car accident? I remember Dad rushing out of the house in a state of panic. And he never panicked. Did he find out where they were? Rushed there in a fit of rage, lashed out, then accused George of landing her in hospital? Was that why he was sorry?

And that's when I had to stop speculating. To abort these toxic notions. There was no good reason to poison any of the fond memories that helped me survive the loss of my mother. Nor to diminish the kindness and devotion with which Dad had cared for me throughout my entire life.

So I did what I had to. I chose to revert back to my original understanding of events. Preserving the version wherein her accident was not a criminal act. The version that did not require me to identify as the daughter of a hostile man capable of any aggression toward my mother. Because if, in fact, something different had transpired, clearly I was never meant to know.

And that is fine by me.

To this day, I have no qualms with pleading ignorance. With accepting that my reality might be not be completely accurate. And if that seems selfish, so be it. Because how I truly feel is grateful. Grateful to those who spared me the burden of an uglier truth.

THE END

Made in United States
North Haven, CT
06 September 2024